Matt was struck with how small and childlike Amy was as her eyes filled with tears. "Don't," he murmured in a husky voice.

Slowly he lowered his mouth to her trembling lips and kissed her, then her forehead, her eyelids, and her salty cheeks.

As he left a trail of burning little kisses down her neck, Amy clung to him. Then he reached the neckline of her gown, and the innocent young woman collected her thoughts. *I should stop him, I should push him away,* she thought. Then Matt returned to her lips for a deep, intimate kiss, and time stood still.

Her body began to awaken, and she lost the battle with herself and melted into his arms. She wanted this! She wasn't going to think about right or wrong, what she should and shouldn't allow. No. She would simply enjoy all that he was doing to her . . .

ZEBRA'S GOT THE ROMANCE
TO SET YOUR HEART AFIRE!

RAGING DESIRE   (2242, $3.75)
by Colleen Faulkner

A wealthy gentleman and officer in General Washington's army, Devon Marsh wasn't meant for the likes of Cassie O'Flynn, an immigrant bond servant. But from the moment their lips first met, Cassie knew she could love no other . . . even if it meant marching into the flames of war to make him hers!

TEXAS TWILIGHT   (2241, $3.75)
by Vivian Vaughan

When handsome Trace Garrett stepped onto the porch of the Santa Clara ranch, he wove a rapturous spell around Clara Ehler's heart. Though Clara planned to sell the spread and move back East, Trace was determined to keep her on the wild Western frontier where she belonged—to share with him the glory and the splendor of the passion-filled TEXAS TWILIGHT.

RENEGADE HEART   (2244, $3.75)
by Marjorie Price

Strong-willed Hannah Hatch resented her imprisonment by Captain Jake Farnsworth, even after the daring Yankee had rescued her from bloodthirsty marauders. And though Jake's rock-hard physique made Hannah tremble with desire, the spirited beauty was nevertheless resolved to exploit her feminity to the fullest and gain her independence from the virile bluecoat.

LOVING CHALLENGE   (2243, $3.75)
by Carol King

When the notorious Captain Dominic Warbrooke burst into Laurette Harker's eighteenth birthday ball, the accomplished beauty challenged the arrogant scoundrel to a duel. But when the captain named her innocence as his stakes, Laurette was terrified she'd not only lose the fight, but her heart as well!

Available wherever paperbacks are sold, or order direct from the Publisher. Send cover price plus 50¢ per copy for mailing and handling to Zebra Books, Dept. 2368, 475 Park Avenue South, New York, N.Y. 10016. Residents of New York, New Jersey and Pennsylvania must include sales tax. DO NOT SEND CASH.

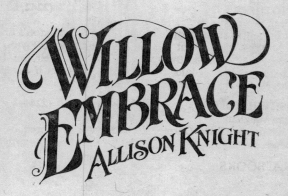

WILLOW EMBRACE

ALLISON KNIGHT

ZEBRA BOOKS

KENSINGTON PUBLISHING CORP.

ZEBRA BOOKS

are published by

Kensington Publishing Corp.
475 Park Avenue South
New York, NY 10016

Copyright © 1988 by Allison Knight

First printing: April, 1988

Printed in the United States of America

To my sons and my daughter, Jennifer, who said I would write a book when the "cows fly!"

Look up, children!

Chapter One

October, 1860

Huddled at the base of a tree, the shadowy shape moved slightly. There was no moon and what little light there was came from the faint stars twinkling overhead in the crisp Allhallows Eve. The damp chill in the air foretold the coming of winter. Mist rising from the river gave an eerie quality to the darkness

It was after midnight, and somewhere in the distance, the barking of a dog shattered the quiet. Amy Sanderson stood up from her crouched position and pulled the old cloak around her slight frame. Adjusting the cap that concealed her long hair, she stretched and twisted, in an effort to relieve the tension. How long should she wait, she wondered. It had been more than an hour, and the old man was not here yet. It was unlike him to be late. Gritting her teeth, she thought, waiting was always the worst part.

She sank back against the rough bark of the tree and thought about the last four weeks. Six times this month she had met the old man. Had he finally been caught? Grateful for the warmth, she tucked the worn length of wool around her and settled back against the tree. An hour, she thought, I'll wait another hour. Frowning, she wondered what her aunt and uncle would say if they knew she was out this late.

Finally the soft call of the old man interrupted her thoughts, and she glanced over toward the river. She could just make out indistinct shapes in the dim light. Behind them was the blurred but familiar outline of the old man. He would be carrying his stick, the stick he used as a walking cane, a prod, or whatever else he needed it for.

Checking her cap again to make sure her hair was covered and the brim pulled low to hide her face, she smiled and thought of her brothers and their solemn admonitions before giving her permission to go on these expeditions. They had warned her many times about the cap, insisting that everyone must think her a clumsy lad of thirteen or fourteen during these late-night flights to freedom. As she smoothed the breeches and flannel shirt under her cloak that were part of her disguise, she suppressed a giggle that threatened to skip over her lips. What brothers were these to insist that their sister dress like a boy?

She waved, and the faint shapes approached and the old man retreated back to the river. When the group was behind her, she whispered gruffly, "Stay close!" Making her way further down the riverbank, she picked her path carefully along the edge of the shallow water. Skirting downed trees and limbs and occasionally glancing back to make sure all seven were moving behind her, she moved along the White River for about two miles. Finally, she left the river and crept through a harvested cornfield to a stand of prickly fir trees that marked the midpoint in her journey.

Indicating with her hand to the group to stop, she sank to the ground for a short rest. No one said a word. They knew how dangerous it was to talk or make any noise, she thought, because sound carried in the still of the night. As if to confirm her thoughts, a distant dog cried his indignities to the moonless sky, and Amy glanced at the somber people sitting near her on the ground. Yes, they knew why, and so did she. She tried to ignore a chill that raced along her spine.

She inhaled the fragrance of the fir trees, but all too soon it was time to move on. She had to get her fugitives to the exchange point. There would be a hot meal and a place for the slaves to rest after the next conductor took them on to the relay station.

Amy stood and motioned to the seven to stand. Pointing at a log fence dividing the Sanderson farm from its neighbors, she moved silently over to the fence as they followed her example. Crouching, she crept along the stacked logs until she reached a stand of maples. She sighed with relief because she knew she could hand over her charges on the other side of those trees. They would be taken on to Westfield where they could sleep the next day before traveling on. Amy grinned. Long before the slaves were hidden, she would be home in her own warm bed.

Leaving the log fence behind, Amy moved into the woods. Suddenly, she felt something was wrong. The small hairs at the nape of her neck bristled. Had she heard a sound? She paused and listened for a voice, a noise, anything that would give credence to her suspicion, but there was nothing. All she heard was the soft stirring of the late autumn wind.

Trying to overcome her fear, she scolded herself about silly women and their intuition. Her passengers were depending on her to stay calm and not panic. Reassured, she moved on, only to suddenly stop again. For no apparent reason that she could fathom she was frightened, terrified even.

She was twenty-one, a woman full grown and a spinster to most of the family friends. She had been the one to insist that she continue her father's work with the underground railroad. Mentally, she scolded herself again. She was letting her imagination run away with her.

She pressed on for another thirty feet, and using exaggerated hand signs, she told the group to squat down and wait. Then, moving ahead another ten feet, she sank to the ground and waited, too. It was nearly black now, the clouds obliterating the sparse light from the stars.

Where was her contact, the tall man who took the slaves on to Westfield? As she waited, she felt something was wrong. She was sure of it. Always before, on this part of the run, the man was there waiting for her. Tonight, he was nowhere in sight.

Slumping against a tree, she watched and waited. The seconds seemed to hang, as if weighted, in the dark night. Panic surged through her body and clawed at her throat. A deep burning began in her chest, and she struggled to breathe naturally.

She tried to blot out from her mind the consequences of her actions but she couldn't. The farm would be confiscated, and she would be fined or, even worse, thrown in prison. Alex and Henry had helped; they could be arrested as well. Concentrating, she tried to remember the tales of escape told and retold in reverent whispers by her brothers and their friends. She recalled the many warnings of her fiancé Adam. He would never know if he had been prophetic, for he had died as had both her parents, during the terrible influenza epidemic of April. They had been engaged only six weeks, and he had been so handsome. . . . Desperately, she tried to block the flood of memories that threatened to engulf her.

She forced herself back to the present. As she tried to decide on her next move, she glanced back at the slaves hidden among the trees. She had two choices, both equally dangerous. She could stay where she was, for the man might yet come, or she could return to her own farm with the fugitives. There was still time to get back, feed, and hide them before daylight.

Finally, with no sign of her contact, she knew she could wait no longer. She had to go back to her farm with the seven. She grimaced at the thought of what Aunt Amelia and Uncle Jeb would say, because she knew they would forbid her to help again. They both had been angry and horrified when they learned the family was involved in the underground railroad.

Out of habit, she adjusted her cap and then crawled back to the group huddled among the trees. Before she reached them, one of the men pointed to the field that Amy had watched so hopefully only minutes before. There! There was the man rushing across the field toward the trees.

Amy moved quickly and motioned for them to follow. As she cleared the woods, she sensed a movement to her left. Had she made a mistake? Close to the trees on her left, she saw a man, a horse, and a wagon. The man coming at them across the field stopped quickly in front of her. He looked around and then slurred, "Change in plans. Bergerman's sick. Agents in Westfield. We're goin' on by wagon."

The wagon rumbled toward her, and Amy pushed the slaves forward, her heart pounding in relief. Retreating, she stepped back toward the trees and watched as they climbed into the wagon. She turned slightly to glance at the man holding the horse. When he seemed to nod his head in her direction, she took several steps backward, to begin her journey home now that her responsibilities were ended.

Springing at her, the man who had spoken grabbed her left shoulder and hissed, "You're goin' too!"

Suddenly it all became clear. These were agents. A shower of white sparks exploded in her head, and her legs turned to mush. She had been caught. They were going to drag her charges south, back to their plantation, and she would be turned over to the authorities. Struggling violently, she tried to free herself. With as much force as she could muster, she brought her clenched fist down on the forearm of the man holding her shoulder. Twisting, she drove her elbow into his stomach. Swiftly, he swung his fist into her chest, and she fell to the ground. Her chest was on fire, and she couldn't breathe. He reached down, and grabbing her under the arms, he lifted her up and threw her into the wagon. The slaves were huddled together in one corner of the wagon bed, and she wondered why until she noticed the second man. He held a rifle, and it was pointed at the frightened group. He didn't even look at her.

In a low voice, one of the men growled, "Let's get the hell out of here!" The other man swung up onto the seat of the wagon, glanced at the occupants, picked up the reins, and shouted at the horse. The wagon jerked and then moved slowly, bumping across the empty field. Amy fought the surge of terror that crept up through her. She had to do something. In desperation, she turned to the two men. While one drove the wagon, the other never took his eyes off the eight people. He kept the rifle pointed in their direction.

Her brain began to function. If she could escape, there were friends along the road who would help hide the escapees and her until these men went south again. Amy shuddered. If the law officers found her before she could get help, the slaves and the agents would be escorted out of the state. The slaves would be returned to their masters, and she would have to await whatever punishment was decided for her. She struggled to swallow the lump in her throat. She simply had to escape.

Once more, she touched the roughness of her old cap and pulled it securely into place. Curling up into a tight ball, she concentrated on ignoring the pounding of her heart and the panic that threatened to overwhelm her. Though her body hurt and she was exhausted, she fought the desire to sleep and ease the pain. She had to stay alert, to search for a way to escape. But was escape possible with a man holding a gun on them? Could she get the group away from these two without injury?

She found no solution, and at length the rocking of the wagon, the strain of the long night, and the knowledge that she had failed finally took their toll. Her senses dulled, and she drifted into a restless sleep.

The sound of voices instantly awoke her. The pain in her chest brought the events of the past night rushing back. It was now dawn, and afraid to move, she lay perfectly still with her eyes closed and listened to the voices arguing in low, husky tones.

"Now, Norman. No one's gonna know. We'll travel at night. Keep offa the main roads. It ain't that far to Kentuck."

"What about her family, Clarence? They gotta know she's missin'."

"Any girl travels like that at night ain't got no family what cares!" Clarence replied.

"I don't like it none. Weren't supposed to be no problems. And Mr. Treadwell, he ain't gonna like it one damn bit. We're already five days late now!"

"I ain't never traveled with a white woman afore. She oughta be better than them darkies. So what if'n we're late. Hell, Norman, it took us four days just to find 'em."

"What happens when we meets up with Mr. Treadwell in Tennessee? What about her then, Clarence? What ya gonna tell him then? How ya gonna stop her from tellin' him about us? He sure won't like

14

it none. Think on it, man! I say it won't work!"

"Afore we get to Knoxville, we can sell her. Come on, Norman. Let's have us some fun. Mr. Treadwell ain't gonna find out."

Amy suddenly realized they were arguing about her. She felt the soft silky strands of her hair lying across her face. Sometime during the night she must have lost her cap, her hair had given her away. Black terror wrapped its talons around her.

"No!" The strangled sound erupted from her mouth, as she scrambled for the side of the wagon and threw herself over the edge. She would not go South, and she would not be sold, either. Falling to the ground, she rolled away from the wagon and tried to stand, but her long black cloak was twisted about her feet, and she was immobilized.

At Amy's hoarse cry, the two men spun around and saw her disappearing over the edge of the wagon. The man with the reins sawed on them desperately. The other man was on Amy before she could free herself from her cloak. He reached down, grabbed both her arms, and jerked her into a standing position. She swayed with pain. His brown eyes flashing, he raised his hand and struck her across the face savagely. Her head snapped to one side, and she fell to the ground. Moisture filled her wide blue-gray eyes.

He sputtered in rage, "Ya don't want to do that, missy, do ya?" Setting her upright again, he dragged her to the open end of the wagon, grasped her waist firmly, and threw her into the wagon.

Stunned, she lay for several minutes, then touched her flaming cheek. It burned as if the devil himself had touched her. Waves of nausea rolled over her

15

from terror. She heard one of the men exclaim, "Now, she knows. Now we gotta keep her." Shaking violently, she felt her control slipping from her. Tears began to flow silently down her dirty face, making little furrows on her cheeks.

When the wagon started moving again, she sat up and stretched her long legs out in front of her. Wiping at her tears, she closed her eyes and tried to silence her fears. Somehow she had to regain possession of herself and escape.

Smoothing down her wisps of soft, chestnut-brown hair, she turned to look at the frightened slaves huddled in a group. Two of them were no more than boys, tall and thin, with clothes that hung from their lean frames. Their bony limbs and gaunt faces spoke of too much work and not enough food. One of the women was plump and much older than the others. She seemed almost sullen and sat apart from the group. When she looked at Amy, there was despair in her dark eyes. Occasionally, she clutched at her chest and moaned softly. The other four, two men and two women, were snuggled together, and Amy wondered how old they were as they gazed at her anxiously. Perhaps they were brothers and sisters, or maybe they were married.

The clothes the women wore were too big and hung loosely. The men appeared to be tall, for both shirt sleeves and pant legs were inches too short. One of the men reached out and patted Amy on the shoulder with his long, thin black hand. The young woman sitting next to him put her head against his shoulder as he wrapped his other arm around her waist. They must be married, Amy thought.

Amy tried to smile, but the shame of what the men called Norman and Clarence had said swept over her, and tears started sliding down her face again. The slaves heard and understood. They know what is going to happen to me, she thought. She tried to speak, but one of the women raised her finger to her lips in a slow deliberate motion. Amy let a sob escape, as she nodded her understanding. They would talk later.

Pulling her knees up under her chin, Amy considered the two men seated above the bed of the wagon. She wished she knew which was one was Norman and which was Clarence. Just then, the man with the gun glanced in her direction, his rifle resting across his legs. His sandy-colored hair was lifeless and dull and spread out in a dirty mass of knots and tangles. Amy shuddered and touched her own chestnut curls that reflected the red and gold of the morning sun.

He gazed at her, a leer on his face. His eyes were shifty and gave the impression of a confirmed liar. She knew no one could trust this man. Though thin and not very tall — only two or three inches taller than she — he was strong. When he slapped her, Amy had known somehow that he had not used his full force, but even so he had knocked her to the ground. His face when he had struck her had caused a chill to run down her spine. This man enjoyed hurting people.

"Clarence! Damn it! Keep your eyes on them slaves!" the other man hissed. Now, Amy sighed, she knew which man was which. She watched as Norman held the reins of the horse. He was much larger and the older of the two. His hair was greasy and black, and he was marked with pox scars. All over his face, there were liver-colored spots that were probably from a lack of soap and water. Amy shuddered. He was filthy. His clothes were spotted with what looked like food stains, and she was certain that he smelled as bad as he looked.

At that instant, he turned to stare at her. His cold gaze traveled over her face and her neck and down her cloak to her waist. She fought the feeling that he was mentally undressing her, and she blushed. Never before in her life had she felt so completely mortified. Somehow, she had to get away from these dregs of humanity.

Turning away from the men, she concentrated on the farm they were passing, trying to remember if she had ever seen it before. If they were still close to Anderson, there were neighbors and friends who would help her even though most of them were not involved in the underground. Although she stared hard at the buildings and the frame house, nothing looked familiar. As they traveled on past another farm, Amy realized that she had no idea where they were or how far they had traveled during the night.

The old wagon bumped and banged along the lonely road, as she watched the two agents. Their heads were together as they talked quietly, glancing at the slaves occasionally. She sobered, remembering that their plans now included her as well. Clarence held the gun across his lap, and as she watched, he lovingly fingered the stock while Norman mumbled something.

Clarence pointed to a large wooded area in the distance, and Norman nodded his head. It seemed that they had been this way before. Clarence turned to the huddled collection in the back of the wagon, and drawled, "We'll be stoppin' awhile. Any trouble and I'll shoot the first nigger to move. That includes ya, missy." He looked at her, a hard glint in his eyes, and Amy jerked her head up. She could almost feel the sting of a bullet.

Minutes later the wagon left the road, and Amy tensed as she watched Norman coax the sweating horse across the uneven ground to the edge of the woods. Clarence jumped down from the wagon and made his way to the rear, still holding the rifle. With the long black barrel of the gun cradled in his left arm, he ordered, "Get down!" He pointed the gun in Amy's direction. "You first." Slowly, she crawled out of the wagon and stood waiting to be told where to go. When they were all on the ground, he pointed to a small path that wound into the woods. "Through there," he growled.

Before she started down the path, she glanced back at Norman, who was busy at the rear of the wagon. When Amy heard the clang of metal she looked again. Norman had lifted rope and some chains from the bed of the wagon and was moving toward them. For some reason her eyes were drawn to the two young boys in back of her. There was sheer terror written in their eyes and on their faces. They both looked as though they wanted to bolt and run, the consequences be damned.

As she started up the path, she heard a rustling sound and a gasp. Whirling around, she saw the gun raised and the slim brown boy leap for freedom. A puff of smoke from the long black barrel preceded the sound of an explosion, and Amy's scream was drowned in the noise. The slaves froze, and Amy tried to still a strangled sob as she wilted to the ground.

Norman rushed to the boy's crumpled form lost in the strawlike grass as Clarence whipped his gun around. He pointed it in the slaves' direction and yelled, "Who wants to be next?" No one moved. Finally, one man, keeping his eyes glued on Clarence and the gun, offered his hand to Amy. As she stood up, she looked at the faces of the captives and she knew instinctively that there would be no further attempts at escape.

Norman knelt beside the dark shape twisted on the ground, and as he lifted the boy and placed him in the wagon bed, Amy wondered if he was still alive. Clarence stood off to one side, his gun pointed in her direction. "Move! That way," he yelled at her and pointed to the path through the trees. As she started toward the trees, she heard Norman scream, "Mr. Treadwell ain't gonna like this."

Amy stumbled into the woods, and when Clarence called a halt, she found herself next to a giant elm tree. She leaned back against the bark and slid down to the ground next to one of the slaves who was already sitting. Exhausted, she watched the two agents talking quietly together. Clutched in Norman's hand were the hated chains and some rope. Bewildered, she asked herself who would be chained and who roped.

Almost as if he read her mind, Norman dropped the chains and came toward her, clutching the several lengths of rope. "Don't want to mess ya up too bad, missy. Them folks what'll buy ya don't like their women marked up bad, leastways not when they first buys 'em." He grinned at her, displaying yellow and brown teeth.

She was filled with too much despair to offer any resistance to the man. In a matter of minutes both her hands and her feet were tied. When Norman seemed satisfied, he returned to the path and retrieved the chains he had dropped. Then he moved from slave to slave, securing a shackle around each right ankle. Amy watched as he picked up a much longer chain and slid a length of it through an eyelet on each shackle in turn, stringing the slaves together. Amy felt sick. If one tried to run, they all would have to run. There wasn't even enough length in the chain to allow a slave some privacy for relieving himself.

Amy could hear the men talking and laughing not far from where she sat, but she didn't bother to see where they were. Her only thought was to try to sleep. Slowly, her eyes flickered closed, and she dozed.

The sun was setting when she was awakened by Norman thrusting a plate of cold beans and bread at her. She waited, expecting that he would untie her hands, but instead one of the dark women was ordered to feed her. When they had finished, Norman yanked the ropes from her ankles and jerking the chains that held the slaves together, he ordered them to their feet. Holding the ends of the chains, Norman barked a command to move. Amy followed behind while Clarence swaggered behind her with his gun.

It was now dark as they stumbled from the woods to the wagon. Norman took the ankle ropes he used on Amy, looped it through the bonds on her wrists,

21

and then tied it to the end slave. The lead slave was tied to the end of the wagon with another rope. The slaves with Amy trailing were forced to plod along behind the wagon. Above the creaking of the wagon and the clank of the chains, Amy could hear the occasional groan of the wounded slave from the bed of the wagon.

All night long, the seven trudged behind the wagon. They were given one short rest of about fifteen minutes, and just before dawn they stopped for the day. Her ankles were tied again, and, exhausted, she dropped off to sleep. Before dusk, they were awakened, and one of the slaves was told to feed the white girl. Then Amy's ankle ropes were removed, she was tied to the other slaves as before, and they again followed the wagon willy-nilly. The wounded slave died that night, and the men waited until they came to a wide stream and dumped the body in it.

The next afternoon, after she had slept, Amy was able to talk to the slaves. The woman who was feeding her, Emma, and the black man who helped her up that first morning, Jacob, were married. The second young couple, Ned and Jenny, were to be married soon, and the old woman, Opal Mae, was the mother of the young black that survived. Opal Mae, Amy learned, had a heart affliction, but she had refused to stay on the plantation when she found out that her son was going to try for freedom.

Amy was surprised to learn that all the slaves were the property of one man. Jimmy and the two couples told her that Phillip Treadwell was bitter and vicious. They would be whipped, and Jimmy was sure that he would be sold. But Opal Mae disagreed, almost violently. She had served in the "big house," she told Amy, and she bragged about how successfully the cotton farm was, and how Massa Phillip had done it all.

She said Mr. Phillip's parents had died when he was only a lad of seventeen, and he had taken over the operation of the plantation and turned it into the profitable enterprise it was now. Amy wondered, as she listened, why Opal Mae's opinion was so different than the other five.

One afternoon, Amy woke before the others and thought of her home with sadness. Opal Mae interrupted her thoughts. "Chile, where do ya come from and why ya do this? Yer're too purdy to be doin' this."

Amy sat up with a start. "Someone has to help," she muttered, knowing she was too tall to be pretty.

"Ya got a man?"

"I had a man." Amy choked on a little sob.

"Ya got other kin?"

"I have two brothers, Alexander and Henry. Also, Aunt Amelia and Uncle Jeb live with us now. There are lots of Sanderson cousins. I don't even known them all."

"Your brothers? They let ya do this?"

"Both my brothers are in school. Alex, the older, is at West Point, and Henry, who's a year younger than me, is studying law. They didn't want me to do this, but years ago, my father started helping, and we kind of followed his lead. Henry was more opposed than Alex, and he's going to be furious."

"Massa Phillip has a little brother. Course, I 'spects he not so little now. Massa Phillip raised him all by hisself, too. Sent him to the best schools, gave dat boy everythin'. Then, one day, Massa Matt became angry at Massa Phillip and up and left for California. That was three years ago. He said he was goin' to look for gold." Opal Mae leaned back and chuckled. " 'Magine! Him findin' gold. Well, Massa Phillip didn't like it much. He's not really mean and vicious like they says. He ain't never had nobody to love him." Opal Mae smiled and closed her eyes to rest. Silently, Amy argued, he certainly has your love, but she said nothing.

Amy let her thoughts drift to her own family. Henry and Alex would have to be told. Notifying Henry would take two days at least. And Alex? That could take weeks.

For three more nights they snaked their way through Indiana, heading south for the rendezvous with Mr. Treadwell. The pattern of their existence was established. During the day they slept or rested until dusk in a woods or deep in a field of drying corn. Then just before the sun set, they were fed the only meal of the day, stale bread and cold beans. Through the long dark hours of the night they stumbled and fell as they were pulled behind the wagon that carried Norman and Clarence.

In the predawn hours of the fifth day, Norman stopped and told them that they would soon be crossing a river. "The river's wide and deep. We'll be ferried across," and then he growled, "Ain't better be no trouble!"

They traveled for another hour, and then they stopped again. Norman dragged Amy to the front of the wagon and pushed her up onto the seat. "You're

24

sitting up here with us." He arranged her cloak so that the ropes on her hands were hidden. The slaves were ordered into the wagon, and when Norman was satisfied with appearances, Clarence crawled up to sit beside her. He placed the gun in his lap so that the barrel pointed in her direction.

Norman hissed in her ear, "Say nothin', or Clarence'll shoot ya." Then he grinned at her. "Maybe he will anyways, owin' as to how ya are more trouble than ya be worth."

She glanced over at Norman and then at Clarence. There was no doubt in her mind that if she made a sound, Clarence would do exactly as Norman had threatened. Norman turned toward the slaves. "If'n any of youse move, she gets it!"

Chapter Two

They reached the river just as the sky to the east was growing light. Norman swung down from the wagon and disappeared. When he came back, "We have to wait," was all he said. Eventually the signal came, and the horse was quickly moved into position on the wooden planks. The wagon was secured, and they started across. Amy tasted desperation, for she felt this was her last chance to escape.

When they reached the other side of the river, they climbed the bank, and were on the move again. Before another hour had passed, Norman halted the horse, and soon the slaves and Amy were once more trudging behind the wagon.

As the morning grew warmer, Amy glanced around at the hills and the many stands of trees that would afford a stopping place to rest for the day, but they didn't stop. She thought back to the plans Norman and Clarence had made that first day, and her heart stopped and she shook with fright. Now, they would sell her.

The day wore on, and by midday Amy was so weary that she felt she couldn't go any further. She didn't even care whether or not Clarence shot her if she lay down in the road. She stumbled along behind the group, and before long, she lost all feeling in her feet. She tripped over a rock and fell flat on the ground.

Jacob saw her fall and shouted an alarm. The company halted, and Clarence jumped down from the wagon, cursing, and yanked her to her feet. They started off again. Twice more she fell, and finally she told Norman angrily, "Have Clarence shoot me! I can't go on anymore."

Norman stopped the wagon and ordered Clarence to put her in the back. He grumbled, "Your damn fool ideas, bringin' her along. We lost two days 'cause we couldn't travel during the day on account of her. We ain't gonna get nothin' for her if'n she be dead." Once in the wagon, her ankles were tied together, and she rode for the rest of the day.

Filled with depression she curled into a tight ball. If she was ever to get home, the underground railroad would have to come to her aid. They would have to carry her description and kidnap her from the agents just as the agents had kidnapped her from her farm.

She rode in the wagon all afternoon, and when the wagon left the road, Amy was startled. They traveled down a hill into a field where only weeds grew. At the edge of the field were a small stream and a stand of trees. Amy glanced around; it seemed so quiet and peaceful.

Hoping for at least a drink of water from the

27

stream, she sat on the edge of the wagon and waited for either Clarence or Norman to come and release her ankle bonds. In the meantime, she tried to smooth her hair, but it was impossible with her hands bound together. She frowned, and looked at the stream with longing. Her long chestnut hair was so matted and dirty. If she could only sneak away and bathe.

Clarence sauntered up and grinned at her, and she turned her face in the other direction. Suddenly, she felt him yank her from the wagon, and losing her balance, she fell to the ground. From the look on his face, she knew that he wasn't going to release her.

Struggling to her feet, she tried to take several tiny steps, but it was so slow and precarious that she gave up and crawled instead to the water's edge. Cupping her hands, she tried to drink, but with her hands tied, it was almost hopeless. She managed to drink only a few mouthfuls of the cool liquid. It was easier to wash her face, she realized, and she splashed water over her clear skin that was still golden from the warm Indiana summer. She spread the water across her high cheekbones and across her short little nose with its hint of a tilt and smiled smugly. She felt better. At least she was cleaner.

Soon, Clarence was behind her, shouting to her to get back to the wagon. She glared at him and pointed at her feet. He lifted his boot as if to kick her, and she crawled back as fast as she could. At the wagon, he jerked her around to one of the rear wheels, and producing another length of rope, secured her to the wheel.

"How am I supposed to sleep like this?" she muttered, but Clarence only laughed and moved away to help Norman set up camp.

They were fed, and then the slaves were led to the opposite side of the wagon from her. After the two men ate their supper and cleaned up, they dragged Emma to Amy's side of the wagon and tied her with ropes.

Amy glanced around her at the small, pleasant valley where they had camped; it was so peaceful there and she was so tired that she refused to think about what the men had planned for any of them. Forcing all thought from her mind, she closed her eyes and sank into deep sleep.

How long she slept she did not know, but it was still dark when she woke. At first, she was groggy and her thoughts were jumbled. Where was she? The hard ground on which she was lying confused her still more. From somewhere, she heard soft moans and hoarse grunts, and she looked in one direction and then another.

At the front of the wagon was a black girl. She was stretched out on the dark ground, and her hands were tied to the wheel of the wagon. Her legs were spread out, and a pair of large hands was holding them in place. Her bodice was torn, and her skirts had been pushed up past her thighs. A man was crouched between her legs.

Amy's eyes flew to the face of the black girl. She grew cold, and sweat broke out all over her as she remembered where she was. Emma! In the soft light of the moon, Amy could see the tears streaming from Emma's eyes. Her face bore a twisted look of resigned anguish.

Something inside Amy snapped. Somewhere in the distance, she heard a deafening shriek of rage coming up from the earth. It completely surrounded her. The din went on and on, piercing the night.

Suddenly, abruptly, her head was snapped back. There was a stab of burning pain on the side of her face. She stared up at two angry faces leaning down to glare at her.

"Why'd ya have to scream like that for? Hell, we wasn't hurtin' ya, not yet anyways," Norman growled. Amy tried to tell them she hadn't screamed, but was unable to. Without another word, they left her. She glanced back at Emma, who was sitting now, leaning against the wheel. In the half-light of night, she looked almost dead.

Without warning, Norman let out a stream of expletives that burned Amy's ears. "Damn it to hell! While she was screeching, one of them niggers got away," he swore. "Damn fool, why didn't ya check them chains like I tol' ya? One of them got away! Damn, damn, damn!"

"It's too dark to look now. We'll have to wait till mornin'," Clarence offered calmly.

"By then, he'll be back over the state line," Norman snapped.

Amy lifted her throbbing head and almost smiled. One of the slaves had gotten away. He would get help, surely. He would bring back someone to free her and the others. She closed her eyes and prayed.

Amy stayed alert as long as Norman and Clarence were awake. Finally they curled up by the fire, and she sighed in relief. The ground was hard, and sleep came slowly. It brought with it visions of terror.

30

First, the two agents were attacking her, then they shot her brother, Henry, then Jacob and Emma. Next, she was wandering in a woods, trying to find Aunt Amelia and Uncle Jeb. When she finally found them, she tried to explain what had happened, but they wouldn't listen. Their faces became blurred and turned into the leering faces of Norman and Clarence.

Morning finally came and with it the angry voices of Norman and Clarence shouting at each other. The day was cold and gray, and the air stung with frost. Amy listened to the men.

"Ya let him go, it's yer fault. Yer're goin' for him," Norman shouted at the shorter man.

"It weren't my fault. It were her screeching that done it," Clarence defended himself just as loudly.

"Don't matter none whose fault it was. I'm boss, an' I say ya go. Ya tied him up, so ya go get him."

"What if'n I can't find him? What do I do?" Clarence asked belligerently.

"Ya stay a-lookin' until ya have him!"

Clarence glared, then finally picked up a length of chain and the rifle, and trudged up the rise, disappearing into the early morning mist.

Amy glanced up to see Norman looking down at her. He leaned down and flicked a long dirty finger under her chin. She jerked her head, trying to get away from him, but he raised her head just enough so that she was forced to gaze into his black eyes.

"Ya, girl, are goin' to cook my breakfast," he purred, his face twisted into a sneer. "Make it good, and I'll let ya have the crumbs." He bent down and Amy cringed, afraid he was going to hit her again. Instead, he untied the ropes that held her to the wheel and then the ones that bound her wrists.

Amy stared down at her bruised wrists and slowly tried to move her hands. This was the first time she had had her hands free for . . . for . . . With a start, she realized that she couldn't remember how long she had been a captive.

Norman reached into his pocket, pulled out a dirty wooden comb, and tossed it into her lap. Then he stepped back and looked her over. She was sure a looker. For one thing, she was tall for a girl, almost as tall as Clarence, and he liked that. Her face was oval, and she had high cheekbones and a cute, little nose. Her dark brows lifted in distinctive curves above her round, expressive eyes. Even when clouded with tears, those blue-gray eyes stood out. They were intense, and when she was angry or afraid, her eyes showed it. There was something about those eyes.

Norman trailed his eyes over her body, imagining what she would look like without clothes. She had a small waist, and he liked that in women. Above her waist, even under the shirt she wore, he could tell she was full-busted, a fully developed woman. The pants she wore accentuated her rounded hips and her long and graceful legs. Damn, he thought to himself, dressed up pretty, she'd look like a queen. Maybe he and Clarence wouldn't sell her. Most of them farmers and trappers never appreciated what they had, anyway.

Meanwhile, Amy had been working at the ropes around her ankles. As soon as she had them untied, Norman grabbed her arm and dragged her to her feet. Without a glance in her direction, he pulled her toward the fire. Pointing out the beans, bacon, corn-

32

meal, and coffee, he hissed, "Call me when it's ready!"

After breakfast, Norman ignored her. She heated a little water for herself and, without the benefit of soap, washed as best as she could. It took time, but she finally got the snarls out of her hair. Then, she plaited it into a long braid that hung down her back.

As the day wore on, there was no sign of Clarence. Amy waited until Norman had left to take a walk, and then she crept around the wagon to talk with the slaves. To her delight, she discovered that Jacob had been the one to escape. Of the men, he seemed the best able to succeed. Surely, he would come back and bring help.

As the evening shadows lengthened across the sky, Norman grew noticeably more irritable. He snapped orders at Amy about the evening meal, feeding the slaves, and even cleaning up the campsite. He swore at the slaves when he checked them after they had eaten.

Amy had just finished cleaning the coffeepot when he grabbed her arm and dragged her toward the wagon. Panicked, she couldn't breathe, and her feet wouldn't move. All she could think was that now she was to be abused as Emma had been the night before. But Norman only tied her hands together and then to the wagon wheel once more. Glaring at her the whole time, he secured her ankles and then stomped off. She breathed a sigh of relief. He was going to leave her alone for a while at least.

She lay there on the cold ground, afraid to move, but she finally drifted off to sleep as darkness settled over the camp. During the night she was abruptly

33

awoken by the sound of the two men shouting at each other. Clarence had returned, and he was swearing a lot. It was clear he hadn't been able to find Jacob. Amy grinned to herself when Clarence stalked off with the comment, "Yah, I know, Mr. Treadwell ain't gonna like it none."

As the dawn spread pink and yellow above the treetops, Norman kicked her feet to wake her. He crouched and untied her hands. He muttered, "Ya fix the breakfast!"

Quickly, she set about freeing her ankles, then made her way to the stream. She prepared the food as quickly as she could and then watched the men. They were in a hurry this morning and ate standing up. The only thing they said to her was to eat what was left and get things cleaned up. In minutes, her wrists were tied together again, and she and the other slaves were walking behind the wagon.

As the day moved on, the small chained party shadowed the wagon and the two men. Amy regretted tidying up earlier because now Clarence was often turning around and leering at her over his shoulder. His eyes were overly bright. Her heart pounded as she shuddered, at times violently, that she could hardly take a step. What would happen that night, she wondered. With each of his glances, she prayed silently for help, any help, any kind at all.

They were hurrying, Amy knew, to make up some of the time lost looking for Jacob. They pushed hard all day, and even after the sun had set, they still pressed on. The night was cold and cloudy, and the road was dark. The slaves helped each other and Amy, but when the horse started to stumble over the rocks, the two men called a halt.

Amy was once again pressed into service as a cook. When she finished preparing the meal for the men, she slipped around the wagon to feed the slaves. She was stunned to find Opal Mae slumped over, clutching her chest and moaning softly. Amy bent over her and tried to find out what was wrong, but the old woman was muttering so softly that Amy couldn't understand a thing. She wondered if she should tell the men, then she remembered the predawn hours their second day, when Clarence and Norman had dumped the boy into the river. The whole day, the men had hurried them along, to make up for lost time. If they thought they would have to slow down for Opal Mae, there was no telling what they might do. Better to wait until morning, she thought. Opal Mae was probably only worn out, and come morning, she would be better.

After she had cleaned up from the evening meal, she glanced at the men. They were deep in conversation. Creeping over to the wagon, deathly afraid that her slightest movement might attract Clarence's attention, she sank down by the wheel, waiting to be retied for the night.

Finally, Norman left his place by the fire and walked around the wagon to check on the slaves. He rushed back to the fire and looked around in aggravation. When he spotted her, he dashed up to her, grabbed her arm, and yanked her to her feet. "The old woman is sick. Ya get back there and see to her." Clarence glanced up from his place by the fire and muttered sounds of disagreement. Norman was not sympathetic in the least. "If that old woman dies, we may not get paid. So, stop yer blubberin'." Amy hurried around the wagon to see Opal Mae, fighting her guilty feelings. When she had prayed for help, she certainly had not meant at the expense of the old woman.

When dawn finally came, it broke bright and clear but very cold. Amy was stiff from the lonely vigil she had kept through the night trying to comfort the suffering Opal Mae. She left the woman long enough to make breakfast for the men, and when they started loading their gear and foodstuffs into the wagon, Amy swallowed her fear and walked up to Norman. Her face grim, she choked out, "Opal Mae is very ill. She must be allowed to ride in the wagon to conserve her strength."

Norman's reply shocked her. "We'll help ya get her settled in the wagon."

Amy smoothed a dirty horse blanket on the bed of the wagon, and Clarence and Norman carried the old woman and eased her down on the blanket. As Norman hoisted Amy into the wagon bed with the sick woman, he said quietly, "Ya stay in the wagon with her!" Then he snarled, "And, she better not die while ya be takin' care of her, either." He turned away, leaving her untied.

Late in the morning, Opal Mae touched Amy's arm and smiled up at her weakly. Softly, she whispered, "I'll try to hang on, chile, till we gets to Massa Phillip. Don't ya fret yerself none. That ol' man'll not get ya, I sees to it." Opal Mae tried to smile, and Amy was so filled with guilt that she turned away. She hadn't meant to pray for help at any cost, certainly not at the expense of the old woman's life.

That was not the help she had wanted.

Throughout the day, Amy wiped the forehead and held the hand of the black woman. Once, early in the afternoon, Norman turned around and asked how Opal Mae was faring. Amy tried to smile, "She's just tired and needs to rest. After she's eaten, she'll be better." Deep in her heart, Amy knew she was lying. Opal Mae was dying, Amy knew it, everyone knew it, even Opal Mae. She had said she would try to hang on until they got to Mr. Treadwell. What would happen to her if the old slave passed on? Amy refused to consider the answer.

When Norman brought the wagon to a halt beside a small creek early in the afternoon, Amy was surprised. Why were they stopping so early? They could still cover several more miles before nightfall, and yet he was ordering Clarence to unload their gear. Amy eavesdropped on their conversation, to discover why they were camping hours ahead of time. Apparently, Norman was sending Clarence for supplies.

"Can I have coin for a brew?" Clarence asked, grinning.

"Nah, there ain't time. Ya get this here list of supplies, and ya get yerself back here. No dallying. We got at least another four, maybe five, days afore we meet up with Mr. Treadwell, and we're so late now, I don't want no more problems. Just get them supplies and get back here."

Amy didn't bother to listen to Clarence's response. Four or five days before they met Mr. Treadwell! Opal Mae would never last that long. She was growing weaker by the hour. She would hold out only a day, or a day and a half at the most. Long before they reached Mr. Treadwell, Amy would be at the mercy of these two men. Tears gathered in her eyes as she grieved for Opal Mae, and for herself as well.

The afternoon gave way to evening, and dusk slowly darkened the surrounding hills and gave the trees a crown of coral. Amy gathered wood for a fire, started the coffee, and even managed, with the help of the other slaves, to get Opal Mae out of the wagon and closer to the fire. She fixed the old woman some coffee and went on preparing the meal. As she cooked, she made her mind a blank.

While she worked, Norman sat with his back toward them, ignoring everything around him. He said nothing when Amy gave him the last of the bacon, cornbread, and beans. After she poured a mug of hot coffee, he looked down at the old woman lying on the ground and mumbled something about Opal Mae nursing Mr. Treadwell. Immediately Amy was curious. Had Opal Mae nursed the master through an illness, or was she in fact his nurse from infancy? Her brow wrinkled into a deep frown. She turned to ask him what he meant, but she never said the words because she saw two men approaching on horseback.

Clarence had left camp as soon as the horse had been unhitched, riding bareback and furious with Norman. That penny-pincher, he had sputtered, had not given him enough money to buy anything to wet his throat in the small village where he was heading. Five miles to cover, and he would be thirsty when he arrived. On top of that, there was barely time to get the supplies and return to camp before dark. Damn that Norman!

As he was jostled back and forth on the draft mare, he thought about the girl he had insisted they bring along. He could hardly wait to get his hands on her. Sick old woman or not, tonight was the night. Grinning, he considered buying her a dress while he was in town. In the heel of his boot, he had stashed a few coins that Norman knew nothing about, and he just might spend them on the girl. Women always liked to get gifts, and a dress was sure to please a girl like her. It might be worth the investment, he smirked, his lips curving into a smile.

Finally, he arrived at the general store, took the crumpled list from his pocket, and swaggered into the building. Norman had written down all the things Clarence was to purchase. As he couldn't read, he handed the paper to the clerk and asked about ready-made clothes for the ladies. The clerk pointed toward a small area in the back, close to the back door. Clarence glanced around. There was the usual collection of bolts of fabric, barrels, and boxes of food. He grunted and made his way back to the section he wanted.

In the corner near the back door was a small pot-bellied stove that stood glowing red against the chill of the November evening. Seated in a chair, warming his hands, was Mr. Phillip Treadwell. Clarence gasped. Phillip Treadwell turned around quickly and, also surprised, recognized Clarence instantly. Leaving his chair with a bound, he stood in front of Clarence, his eyes dark with rage, before Clarence could gather his wits.

Planting his feet apart, Phillip looked down at the

39

man. He was at least a foot taller than his agent, and the fact that he despised the man was in no doubt. "Buying something for the ladies, Clarence?"

Clarence could only stutter, "Why—no—no." He knew Mr. Treadwell would not understand about Amy.

"Where is the rest of your party, Mr. Glanzman?" Phillip asked in a voice as cold as ice. "You should have been in Knoxville a week ago. I don't enjoy waiting for people."

"They—they—they are just outside town. We made camp so's we could get supplies," Clarence stammered trying to explain. "We had us some trouble."

Phillip muttered through his clenched teeth. "I don't pay you to have trouble!" Phillip moved closer and stuck his hand in the shorter man's face. "Get the supplies. I'll ride out with you. I want to see for myself the condition of my property. I want to hear about your trouble from Norman. I had better not have lost a slave, because, if you've mishandled my affairs, I'll . . ." Clarence missed what he would do, for Phillip was already out the door.

Damn, he mumbled to himself. Mr. Treadwell was mad as hell. Why hadn't he listened to Norman? Now there was going to be hell to pay. They might even not get paid. Then Norman would sure be mad, too.

Phillip stood outside waiting for his slave agent. He watched as Clarence carried out two cotton sacks. Phillip mounted his horse as Clarence reached over and swung the two bags, tied together, over the draft horse. As Clarence threw himself up on his animal, Phillip moved north, shouting back, "I take it you are on the north side of town."

Clarence nodded his head. At least he had saved his money, he thought. The dress would have been wasted, because with Phillip at camp, the girl would not be available to him now.

As they rode along in uncomfortable silence, Clarence wondered if he should prepare his boss for the situation at the campsite. The more he thought about it, the more certain he was that he should say nothing. After all, Norman was always telling him he was the boss. Let Norman try to explain what had caused the delay, let him explain about the dead slave, the sick old woman, the missing slave, and, of course, Amy.

They were only a hundred feet or so from the camp, when Clarence spotted Amy looking in their direction. He glanced over at Phillip Treadwell to see if he had noticed the white girl. "Here comes the fireworks!" Clarence mumbled.

Amy had been about to ask Norman to explain what he meant about Opal Mae, when out of the gathering dusk she caught sight of two riders. One she recognized instantly as Clarence, but the other man looked like someone from the military, with a rigid poised cavalry bearing. "Oh, no!" Amy cried, as she started to tremble, thinking Clarence had already sold her. As the men approached, Amy fought for breath, her heart was in her throat, and she couldn't swallow. In despair, she turned back to the fire. All was lost.

Out of the corner of her eye, Amy saw Norman

stagger to his feet, and suddenly she could sense the
tension that weighted down the very air. As she
looked back at the stranger, Opal Mae also turned
her black head.

Opal Mae made the first noise. She sighed loudly.
"Oh, Massa Phillip, I knowed you'd come, I knowed
it."

Chapter Three

Amy stared at the man she had not expected to meet for at least four more days. How did he get here, when Norman and Clarence had thought he would be waiting in Knoxville? Amy studied him carefully. He was tall, over six feet, and fashionably trim. His large shoulders made his waist look slim. He had a long face and straight sandy-colored hair, which was thin at the temples, and a trim mustache accentuated thin straight lips. His sandy eyebrows curved above dark eyes, and Amy wondered what color they were. The firelight gave his hair a golden halo, and she decided then and there that she had nothing to fear from such a handsome man. He would save her just as Opal Mae had said.

Opal Mae struggled to sit up, and her effort was causing her to breathe in loud gasps. With one fluid movement, Phillip knelt down beside the figure on the ground, looking concerned. Amy glanced at her charge and at her flushed face. Opal Mae was trying to smile. Amy moved as quickly as she could to help

43

the old woman into a sitting position, but strong arms brushed hers away. Phillip, himself, helped Opal Mae sit up.

"Opal Mae, why did you run away? I thought you liked my home. You've never tried to leave Willows before," he murmured softly. "I didn't expect it from you."

Amy interrupted him. "She shouldn't try to talk. And she should be lying down."

Phillip glanced from Opal Mae to Amy, startled. "And who are you?" he demanded.

For a second, there was a hushed silence. Then, everyone started to talk. Norman was the loudest, but Amy, and even Opal Mae, were trying to shout him down. "Quiet!" came Phillip's booming voice. "I can't make any sense out of this noise. You! You go first," he shouted at Amy. Everyone stopped talking, everyone but Opal Mae.

She tugged on Amy's cloak. "Tell 'im chile."

So, Amy recounted her days since she had been dragged along with the slaves. Before she had finished telling about her capture, the tears started falling, and she couldn't see the grim expression on Phillip's face. When she got to the part about the shooting, Norman tried to interrupt her, but Phillip glared at him and ordered him to keep quiet. Amy wiped her tears away and continued. When she had finished her tale, she looked at the two men responsible, standing together by the fire. She drew a ragged breath. By the look they were both giving her, she knew that if they ever got their hands on her, they would injure her badly.

"Massa Phillip," Opal Mae demanded his attention. "Dat's the way it be."

Phillip turned back to Amy, and in a brittle voice, he asked, "You helped my slaves escape? You knew they were the property of someone from the South? Did you know the punishment you would receive if you were caught?"

Amy dropped her eyes. Slowly, she nodded her head.

"Well, young lady," Phillip said matter-of-factly, "you broke the law. You are nothing but a common thief."

Amy felt as though she had been struck in her middle, and her breath came out in a gasp as she stared at the man. Why hadn't she noticed the cruel twist to his lips and the coldness in his eyes, she wondered. He was not going to help her. No, he would probably turn her over to the first authority he found. She would be in jail as soon as they reached a town large enough to have a jail.

Amy was afraid, more afraid even than she had been with Norman and Clarence. This man was cruel, she thought, and she remembered what the other slaves had said. She heard Opal Mae struggling to defend her. "Massa Phillip, please. She's a good girl. She was a-tryin' to help me."

Phillip ignored what Opal Mae had said and instead turned his attention to her needs. "We're going to have to make you more comfortable, and perhaps some warm food might help." He stood up from his crouched position beside her, made his way to the fire, and looked at the skillet Amy had used for the evening meal. "Has she been fed?" He pointed to Opal Mae.

Amy tried to say something over the lump in her throat, but she couldn't get the words out. Instead she nodded.

Phillip turned to the two men still standing by the fire. Norman's face was tense, and Clarence wore a belligerent grimace. "We'll talk now," Phillip said unceremoniously and walked away from the fire, as if he was accustomed to having his every word obeyed.

Both Norman and Clarence stumbled after him. They moved far enough from the camp so that Amy could hear none of what was said—at least at first. As she watched them, she thought they were laughing, but as the conversation continued, she decided that they were arguing. Norman's voice grew louder, and she heard some of his words and a lot of swearing. At one point Clarence swung away from the group and came stomping in her direction. Amy shuddered when he looked at her as if he could personally cut her into small pieces with pleasure. He grabbed his bedroll and a knapsack, slung both over his shoulder and slammed out of camp.

Amy glanced back in the direction of Norman and Phillip. They were heading toward the fire, and Norman was trying to walk in front of Phillip and talk to him as they walked. Phillip seemed to be ignoring Norman, as if everything had already been decided. Norman's voice was almost a scream now, and Amy heard every word he shouted.

"Mr. Treadwell, I've been with ya fer four years now. Ya can't do this to me. So we shouldn't a took the girl, but she seen us. What was we supposed to do? She ain't nothin' but white trash, anyway. And, that boy Mark, he was a mean one. Always trouble,

46

fightin', runnin' away. Ya are better of without 'im. Mr. Treadwell, ya ain't gonna do this, is ya? We ain't got no food or nothin'."

Phillip waved his hand in dismissal and sauntered up to the fire. She saw the hard glint in his eyes, and she guessed that he had fired the men on the spot. To judge from Norman's words, they must have been let go without food or pay. And, Amy could tell, Phillip Treadwell didn't care.

Norman gathered his things and stalked away from the camp. When he got about fifty feet up the hill, he turned around, and in a raspy voice full of hate and rage, he shouted, "Ya ain't seen the last of us. Ya can't treat us like this! Ya sure will be sorry, just ya wait. Ya ain't done with us, not by a long shot!" He shook his fist in Phillip's direction and then moved off into the dark night after Clarence. Amy felt a chill run down her back. Somehow, she knew she had not seen the last of those two. The threat Norman had yelled would affect her too. She knew it.

The threat still hung in the cold night air as Amy stood trembling by the heat of the fire. Phillip didn't seem disturbed by the words the agent had flung at him at all. Then he glanced at her and barked, "Have the other slaves been fed?"

Amy gulped. "No, sir!" Did he never speak in a normal tone of voice?

"Then feed them and get this mess cleaned up." He kicked at the empty coffeepot.

Amy prepared the food, fed the slaves and herself. Putting another pot of coffee over the coals, she cleaned up the cooking utensils. When everything had been put in place, she poured herself a cup of coffee and asked Phillip if he would care for a cup. He declined, speaking politely for the first time. This encouraged her to ask him to help her get back home. After all, he had probably been upset over Opal Mae's condition and hadn't been himself, she reasoned.

"Mr. Treadwell, I'd like to go home."

The man didn't even look at her or even seem to hear as he continued to stare at the fire. Amy tried once more. "Mr. Treadwell, sir, could I please go home?"

Amy was rewarded with a startled glance as he asked quietly, "What's your name, girl?"

"Amy."

"Well, Amy whatever, how do you propose to get home? Do you have money, relatives in this area, people you could ask?"

Sinking down before the fire, she lowered her head and shook it solemnly. No, she had no money, no relatives in the area, and she knew no one in Kentucky—if they were in Kentucky. She glanced up. He knew all this. What was he trying to prove? She fell silent.

"I have to get these slaves back to Willows," he said. "It'll be getting colder each day, and they are no good to me sick or dead. I must get Opal Mae home before she dies. I certainly am not going to turn around and take you back to Indiana and run the risk of losing my property. And I'm certainly not going to provide funds for you. You have already cost me a great deal of money. What I should do is turn you over to the authorities, but I'll never get my money that way. I have decided that you will accompany me to Willows. Then, when you've worked off your debt to me, your family, if you do have a family, can send for you or come and get you. I won't care which."

"My debt? I don't owe you any money!"

"Oh, yes, you do! You are going to pay me back in full for all the money I have spent to recover my slaves, slaves that would have stayed put if it hadn't been for your kind! You will work until you have paid me back."

Amy colored a bright pink. "I am not a servant and have never been one. I am not working for you. I—I—don't owe you a thing!" She was so angry her words faltered.

"Oh, come now!" Phillip snapped. "You have already been working as a servant. You served Norman Barber and Clarence Glanzman. You will do the same for me."

Amy shot to her feet. "I was forced to do what they said. I only started cooking for them a day or two ago, and I was forced to do that."

Phillip laughed, a dark, menacing laugh. "Well, then, consider yourself forced. You *will* work off your debt, and you *will* begin tomorrow." With that he turned his back on her and walked to his horse. He untied his bedroll, spread it out next to the fire, removed his boots, and lay down.

Amy sat fuming before the fire. How dare he speak to her like that! She was not a common servant to be ordered about. Her mother had seen to her education, she could read and write, and she was not going to pay off a debt that existed in his mind only. There was no way she would be treated like one of his slaves. But when she stopped her mental rantings, she realized that he could do all the things he had said he would. She had broken the law. He could turn her over to the authorities, and she could go to prison. And when she thought about it, she knew she would be better off as his servant than in a Southern jail. At least, then, she might be able to get word to Henry.

Henry! She sighed deeply. He knew enough about the law to be able to tell her what do do. Would Phillip punish her family for the crimes he thought she had committed? She trembled. It would not do for the man to learn her last name or the name of her hometown. Somehow, she would have to get word to Henry without Phillip Treadwell finding out.

Amy shook herself from the depression that had suddenly closed in on her. She had Opal Mae to care for, and perhaps she could help the others. At least Opal Mae had been glad to see her Massa Phillip, she thought as she went over and settled down beside the sleeping woman.

During the night, Opal Mae's groans awakened Amy, and when she raised herself up on her elbow to check on the old woman, she was surprised to see Phillip leaning over the slave. Well, Amy thought, if I have to start as a servant, I might as well get my sleep tonight. Phillip could take care of Opal Mae. She curled up in her cloak and went back to sleep.

Just as the morning sun was coming through the trees, Phillip shook Amy awake. She stood straight and erect as he ordered her to make coffee and prepare breakfast while he harnessed the horse and loaded the wagon. After a quick meal of corn cakes,

Amy and the two other men put Opal Mae in the wagon on the blanket and Phillip's bedroll, which he insisted they use. As Amy cleaned up the camp, she glanced over at Phillip, who was sipping the last of the coffee and watching her every move. By this time, Amy was bristling with resentment. She fought the temptation to turn around and march off to Indiana, Phillip Treadwell or no Phillip Treadwell.

Finally, Phillip growled in her direction, "Get in the wagon!" She glared at him, then scrambled into the back as he slid onto the driver's seat and urged the horse back to the road. Once more they were moving south.

They were now heading toward South Carolina, and Phillip established a routine. Each day progressed just as the previous one had. They would wake at sunrise, have a quick breakfast, pile into the wagon, and move on. Then, as the long shadows of twilight began to lengthen in the west, they would stop for the night. Amy, now with Emma's help, prepared the evening meal. Sometimes, Jenny helped. If Phillip took the time to shoot birds or rabbits, they ate fresh meat.

Even Opal Mae improved, and although Amy was told that Opal Mae was her sole responsibility, Opal Mae ate, slept, and rode in the wagon the whole time, leaving Amy free to work and walk with the other slaves.

Along the way, Phillip stopped and purchased supplies, the most important of which, Amy decided, was soap. She bathed Opal Mae and then herself. Even though she spent a long time scrubbing herself by the stream, she still didn't feel clean. She had been

51

tempted to follow the stream a distance, disrobe, and wash properly, even in the November chill. But she had decided that Phillip Treadwell wouldn't like that, so she made do with a sponge bath.

Everything moved along smoothly with Phillip in command, and he was always in command, barking orders to first one and then another about the work that needed to be done around the camp. True to his word, he treated Amy exactly as he treated the others.

Phillip angered her but also intrigued her. He rarely looked at her, and he never spoke to her except to give an order. It seemed to Amy that she, too, had become a possession, just like the slaves.

On the road as she walked, she tried to devise a plan to let Henry know where she was and what had happened to her. Perhaps she could write him a letter as soon as they arrived at their destination. Somehow, through one of the slaves, she would get the letter posted, and Henry would come to get her. He must! True, she still had no idea just where the plantation was, but she would know by the time they arrived.

Amy considered asking Phillip to let her send a message to her brother, if only to let him know that she was alive and well, but she quickly discarded the idea. Phillip would probably turn Henry's name over to the authorities, and Henry might land in prison himself. She couldn't jeopardize his career. In any case, Phillip would probably destroy any messages to her family until he felt that she had paid her so-called debt. No, she had to make her plans without Phillip.

The days wore on, and the hills turned into mountains. As the tenth day dawned, Amy noticed a slight change in Opal Mae. She seemed weaker, and by the end of the day, Amy became aware that the older woman had quit fighting. By the morning of the twelfth day, Opal Mae wanted nothing to eat, and Amy watched her closely all day. She saw no further deterioration in the slave's physical state, but emotionally Opal Mae seemed drained, too tired to go on. The next day, she slept until long after they were traveling. By noon, she was gasping for breath, moaning, and occasionally clutching her chest. By late afternoon, she was rocking back and forth on her wagon bed, tears in her eyes, mumbling that her chest hurt so bad. Amy hovered over the woman through the long afternoon and during the preparations for supper.

Even after the sun set and the camp was cleaned up, Amy refused to leave Opal Mae's side. Jenny and Emma both offered to sit with the old woman, but Amy insisted. Amy had said nothing to Phillip, but he stayed up through the whole night also. Once, hours after the others were asleep, he brought Amy a cup of hot coffee and spoke softly. "She was my nurse. She nursed both Matt and me from the time we were born. She was like a mother to us." He fell silent and then moved back to the fire and gazed at the flames. Amy watched him as he sat there motionless.

At last, dawn came. With the first light in the east, Phillip roused the sleeping slaves. As if driven, he urged them all to make haste. He swore at Emma as she tried to hurry with breakfast, he cursed the other slaves when they failed to move fast enough to suit him, and he swore at the horse as he harnessed the poor beast to the wagon.

Amy moved around him as quickly as she could, but she didn't escape his wrath either. He shouted obscenities at her when she didn't return to Opal Mae's side as quickly as he thought she should. No one, Amy decided, could move fast enough for him. Disgusted, she shouted at him. "Quiet down! Opal Mae seems unconscious, but if she does regain her senses, you'll scare her to death!" Phillip grumbled, but he did stop his yelling, and they were back on the road in record time.

After only four hours, Phillip turned the wagon from the main road onto a wide private drive. Amy looked at the others, and she knew from their tense expressions that they were close to their destination.

She didn't see the beautiful house at the end of the curved drive, nor did she see the long double row of weeping willows that shadowed the entrance and for which the plantation had been named, because just at that moment, Opal Mae breathed her last. Amy held the old woman tight to her young heart. Opal Mae would never see the willow trees again, and Amy saw nothing through her tears.

As Phillip guided the horse and wagon around to the back of the large house and between the neat white barns and tiny dilapidated shacks that lined the back roads to the cotton fields, Amy wiped her tears and gazed through clouded eyes at the contrast with the main house.

When the wagon stopped Amy sobbed out loud and her tears fell freely. She shook her head and said, "She didn't get here in time. She passed on when we turned off the main road." For one second Amy thought she saw grief in Phillip's eyes, but then, as if the old woman's death had been wiped from his mind, his eyes turned icy and dark.

He yelled for the overseer who came up to the wagon. Grabbing both Ned and Jimmy, who were still chained together, he handed the chains to the overseer and barked, "First give them each ten lashes, and then sell them." Jenny started to sob, and Emma put her arms around her to try to comfort her. As the order was given, Amy stopped crying and stared at Phillip in horror. She hung onto the still body of Opal Mae.

The overseer leered at her. "What about the white girl, boss?"

"Send her to the kitchen. She can start earning what she owes me right away!" Without a glance, Phillip strode off toward the big house.

The overseer waited until Amy had gently laid the old slave back down on the bedroll. Then, he pulled her from the wagon. Several black women were standing around the sobbing Jenny. "They'll care for her," Emma whispered as she reached for Amy's hand and led her toward a back door. When Amy turned to look back at the wagon, Emma mumbled softly, "She'll git a proper burial. Don't ya worry none." And she ushered Amy into the main house.

Amy found herself in a large kitchen with an enormous table in the middle of the floor and a big stove against one wall. Cabinets covered another wall, and from hooks in the center crossbeams hung pots and pans of every size and description. A large fireplace occupied most of another wall. Several large, uncurtained windows let in the bright late morning sun, making it a cheerful and pleasant place.

It seemed much later when Emma took her to a small room off the kitchen. A large copper tub, filled with steaming hot water, stood in the center and Amy breathed a sigh of relief. At last, a bath! Emma helped her peel off the grimy and tattered breeches and shirt. Even her pantalettes and chemise were gray and crusty, and Emma mumbled something about burning them. A large piece of cotton toweling was folded on a small stool next to the tub along with a sliver of soap and a sponge. As Amy sank down into the tub, the hot water covered her tired and bruised body, and some of her shock dissolved as well.

After several minutes of soaking up the relaxing warmth, Amy looked around her. The tiny room was probably one of the household slaves' bedrooms because there was a single cot along one wall with a chair and small wardrobe on another wall. Amy picked up the sponge, lathered it with soap, and scrubbed and scrubbed. When she felt reasonably clean, she turned to the task of washing her hair.

By the time she was finished, the water in the tub had cooled considerably, and she stepped out. Grabbing the toweling, she rubbed her hair and wrapped it around her body. Though she felt much better, she was exhausted, having stayed awake with Opal Mae for almost forty-eight hours. The little bed in the corner of the room looked inviting and Amy stretched out on the clean mattress and drifted off to sleep.

Hours later, she awoke with a start. What time was it? How long had she slept? There were no windows in the small room, but she could tell it was still daylight because sunlight was coming into the room from the wide crack under the door.

The copper tub was gone, and the small stool now stood at the edge of the narrow bed. Folded on the stool was a fresh calico dress of simple lines in a dark brown print. A clean pair of pantalettes, and a plain muslin chemise were folded on top. She smiled because Emma had brought them. Removing the toweling, she donned the clothes and looked around for a comb or brush. She was puzzled that her hair was completely dry, for it usually took a long time to dry. There was no comb or brush evident, so she ran her fingers through her tresses and then tied it back with a bit of the thread she pulled from the muslin chemise.

Amy opened the door and looked into the kitchen. Jenny was there, and she raised her head when Amy entered and closed the door. Jenny smiled faintly, and Amy noticed that her eyes were red from crying. She said quietly, "Good mornin'."

Amy was stunned. Morning? It had been afternoon when she finished her bath and lay down to rest. Had she slept the night through?

Jenny handed her a cup of chocolate. "Emma be servin' breakfast. She be here in a short while."

Amy sat down at the large table in a daze. As she tried to figure out how long she had slept, she sipped her chocolate. It must have been fifteen or sixteen hours! Why had they allowed her to sleep so long, she wondered.

Before she finished her chocolate, Emma came through the door, breaking out in a big grin when she saw Amy. "So ya finally decided to wake up," she purred.

Amy glanced around the room, then she muttered softly, "Emma, you've got to help me. I need paper and something to write with, a pen and ink. I have to write to my brother and tell him where I am, that I'm all right." Amy's anxiety showed in her voice. "He has to know where I am. He'll come and take me home." Tears filled her eyes, and she looked down at her chocolate cup. "I must go home!"

"And where is home?" a deep, resonant voice asked. Amy whirled around to face a younger version of Phillip. His eyes were the same intense dark blue, but there was no coldness in them. His face was perhaps a little broader, and his lips were full. But his chin was square like Phillip's, and his hair was the same sandy color, except it was thick and lay in soft waves. His shoulders were wide, and he had the same narrow waist. He was so handsome, and he was smiling at her. Her heart missed a beat as she stared at the man, and she couldn't find her voice as he stood looking down at her.

"Say something!" she chided herself, but no words came.

Emma came to her rescue and introduced the man. "This here is Massa Matt, Massa Phillip's little brother." She chuckled at the word "little."

"I thought you went to California," Amy blurted.

Matt laughed. "I see you have been talking to Opal Mae. I haven't seen her yet. Where is that ol' woman?" Matt looked around and then started for the door of the room where Amy had bathed and slept. Amy stood very still. He didn't know. Phillip hadn't told him anything. She suddenly realized she spent the night in Opal Mae's bed. It was more than Amy could bear and the bright light shining through the windows started to spin around her.

"I think I'm going to faint," she murmured. "And I've never fainted before." She slipped slowly into a long corridor of total blackness.

Chapter Four

When Amy opened her eyes, she found Emma, her black face wreathed with concern, staring down at her. Raising herself up on her elbow, Amy glanced around at the pretty feminine bedroom she was in. In wonderment, she asked softly, "Where am I?"

"Ya's in Miss Anna's room," Emma told her. "Massa Matt brought ya up here hisself."

Angry muffled voices sounded in the distance. Even with the bedroom door closed, Amy could tell that it was men shouting angrily at each other. She wondered who were arguing, and looked at Emma questioningly.

Emma shrugged and confirmed Amy's suspicions. "Oh, them brothers, they's a-fightin' again."

Amy dropped back onto the pillows and closed her eyes. Emma made it sound as though the brothers fought all of the time.

A thought struck Amy, and she sat up again. This time she studied her surroundings carefully. Who was Miss Anna? Opal Mae had said nothing about a sister. Somehow, she was sure that Phillip was not married. Could Matt be married? But, no, he had been in California prospecting for gold, and she doubted that a wife would roam around California with a man looking for gold. The shouting continued, and she worried it was about her. She had to get word to Henry; she had to get home.

Rolling to the edge of the bed, Amy tried to get up, but Emma's long brown arm shot out and held her shoulder to the bed.

"Ya wait here for Massa Matt," Emma ordered sharply.

Something in Amy snapped. She had been kidnapped and forced to travel hundreds of miles, act like a servant, and endure the nasty temper of a Southern gentleman, who was, in truth, no gentleman. She had had enough.

"This is it!" she announced. She sat up again and yelled, "I'm leaving this place now." Then she added more quietly, "If I have to walk all the way, I'm going home!"

She knocked Emma's arm away, heaved herself from the bed, and marched to the door. Determination written on her face, she yanked the door open so hard that it banged into the wall. In the hall, she saw a curving staircase leading to the first floor. As she made her way down the steps, she realized that she had no shoes.

"Well," she muttered to herself, "I'll just have to go home barefoot." At the bottom of the stairs she saw the large double front doors and dashed across the elegant foyer to go outside.

Her hand closed around the knob of one door,

when a voice behind her boomed, "Stop!"

Glancing over her shoulder, she saw Matt Treadwell standing behind her. He looked furious. "I'm going home," she said flatly.

Matt looked down at her, and the anger left his face. Then he grinned at her. "Like that?" he said, pointing to her bare feet.

"Yes!" Amy muttered. Then, in a firm loud voice, she stated, "And you can't stop me." She turned back to the door, twisted the knob, and opened the door.

Matt's hand shot out and slammed it shut. "Let's talk first, and then you can go home. May I ask you again, where is home?"

Amy turned to face the tall man standing so close to her, and once more, her heart missed a beat. "My home is in—" She stopped in horror, she had almost told him where she lived. "I have no intention of telling you where I live. If I may have paper, pen, and ink, I'll write to my brother. Then, when he receives my letter, he'll come for me or send me the funds to go home. He'll be most happy to come and take me away from this place." Her voice rose in frustration.

"You can write?" Matt asked, his voice sounded astonished. He turned to his older brother, who was leaning against the staircase. "White trash?" Matt directed his question to an expressionless Phillip.

Amy drew herself up to her full five feet seven inches and snapped, "I am not white trash! I'm the daughter of a lawyer, now deceased, and I can read and write. I have a brother in West Point and another brother studying law. I have enough knowledge of the law myself to know that you cannot hold me here against my will—" Amy shut her mouth quickly; she had said too much, much too much.

Matt looked amused and grinned at her, his blue eyes twinkling. "Proud little minx, aren't you?" he murmured. The smile left his lips, but not his eyes, as he gravely offered her his arm, which she took. He led her to a door on the right of the stairway and escorted her into a room that was obviously the library.

Three leather armchairs, dark with age, and a heavy oak desk that gleamed from polish stood in the room lined with shelves and books. Matt seated her formally in one of the leather chairs and asked if she cared for a glass of wine. Without waiting for a response, Matt turned, took a bottle, and poured amber liquid into a glass. Smiling, he handed the wine to her.

She took the glass he offered, waited until he poured himself a drink, and then raised the glass to her lips. Before the glass touched her mouth, she gasped and set the wine down on the table next to her chair. "I don't drink this early in the morning," she said in amazement.

Matt took a deep swallow and grinned. "I think we both need it!"

As Matt stood sipping his wine, he considered the girl before him, which made her blush. When his glass was empty, he walked to the door and closed it firmly. Turning back to Amy, he questioned her softly. "Now, where did you come from? How did you get here? Phillip refuses to explain anything to me except that he feels you owe him a great deal of money. He is insisting that you work it off."

Amy took a deep breath, folded her hands in her

lap, and frowned. "I don't owe him any money." She wondered what he would think if she told him about the trip south. Would he help her go home? He might be her only chance. Starting slowly she stuttered, "My—fam—I—we help take the slaves north to freedom." She told him about the agents, the shooting, and Jacob's escape, and she cried as she told about Opal Mae. For some reason, she couldn't bring herself to tell him about Emma's rape. When she had finished her tale, tears were streaming down her face. She noticed that he looked grim and tense as well.

He asked quietly, "Where is your home?"

Amy hesitated. Could she trust him? Would he tell Phillip where she lived and what her surname was? Raising her chin and cocking it slightly, she mumbled, "I can't tell you where I live. I might place my family, what's left of it, in jeopardy. Phillip might try to punish them too." As an afterthought, she added, "Nor am I going to tell you my family name."

Amy gazed up into Matt's intensely blue eyes. They were staring at her so sadly. She wondered why he was not pressing her for more information. A warmth flooded through her body, her hands began to shake. Whatever is wrong with me, she questioned silently. Even her breath seemed to catch in her throat. What was there about this man that caused such a reaction in her? Softly, she ventured, "If someone will supply writing materials and take me to the nearest town, I'll send word to my brother immediately."

Some of the tension seemed to leave Matt's body. "I would like nothing better than to take you into town this afternoon, but I don't think you want to go looking like that, do you?"

Amy sat very still. She smoothed the calico dress with her hands. Did she look that bad? She glanced down at her bare feet. He was right, of course. She couldn't go dressed as she was.

"First, we'll see about getting you something to wear. In the meantime, I want you to make yourself at home. You are a guest at the Treadwell estate of Willows, and you'll be treated accordingly," Matt said firmly.

Amy started to argue. "But Phillip said I had to work in the kitchen—"

"Phillip go hang," Matt roared. "This is my home too!" His response startled Amy, and she said nothing more. Phillip, she was certain, was not going to approve. Would they argue again as they had only an hour ago?

Matt walked to the door, threw it open, and bellowed for Emma. In seconds she was there, and Matt guided her down the hall, talking softly to the black woman as he went.

Amy rushed after him and called, "When can I write my letter? You didn't say when I can post it."

"Will tomorrow be soon enough?" Matt asked over his shoulder as he started toward the large double doors. Amy stood and watched as he went out with Emma following at a run, trying to keep up with his long strides.

Amy spent the rest of the morning wandering through the house. There were eight rooms downstairs, all elegant and beautifully appointed. Off the foyer and to the left was a drawing room, and next to the drawing room was a small study. In back of the study was a large and richly decorated ballroom. To the right of the foyer was the library and in back of that room was a formal dining room. The spacious kitchen opened into the dining room as well as to the outside. There were two small bedrooms, one off the foyer, in back of the curved stairs, and Opal Mae's room off the kitchen.

Upstairs were five doors, but Amy couldn't bring herself to open any of them. She went downstairs to the kitchen and found Jenny preparing the evening meal. She asked the slave about the doors upstairs.

Jenny smiled, "There is four bedrooms and a sitting room. It used to be the nursery."

Amy's curiosity was piqued. "Jenny, who is Miss Anna? Matt Treadwell took me to her room when I fainted this morning."

Jenny frowned. "Miss Anna was Phillip's and Matt's mama, and she passed on long afore I comes here. Emma say that's your room now."

Amy grimaced, that certainly sounded permanent. She wondered if Jenny would answer some more questions. "Are either Phillip or Matt married? Opal Mae never said."

Jenny threw her head back and laughed loudly. "Honey, no one will have Massa Phillip, and as far as I knows Massa Matt just ain't interested."

Amy couldn't stop the smile that curled on her lips. That only meant he hadn't found the right woman yet, but she kept her thoughts to herself. She was delighted with the news, but why was she so pleased? Could Jenny tell how happy she was?

After a light lunch, Amy went back upstairs to the

room to which Matt had carried her that morning. It was a beautiful room with lace-curtained windows looking out over the plantation in back. The walls were covered in pink-and-yellow-flowered paper. A large four-poster bed was covered with a ruffled quilt with the same pink and yellow flowers. Against one wall stood a wardrobe, and on the opposite wall was a dressing table with a mirror and a chair next to a door, probably to the sitting room. On the other side of the door was a washstand with a bowl and pitcher, again with pink and yellow flowers.

Amy walked over to a window and glanced out. A large white barn and two smaller ones framed the eastern sky. The small unpainted clapboard shacks of the slaves lined the roads leading to the cotton fields. The contrast she had noticed the day before brought tears to her eyes. Phillip might be a successful farmer, she thought, but he wasn't much of a human being.

Moving back to the bed, she stretched out on the soft feather mattress and closed her eyes. If she had to face either man again this day, she needed to be rested and alert. But she was unable to sleep. Her mind remained active. Why had she not seen Phillip since her conversation with Matt? Where had Phillip gone? Had Matt sought him out and told him her new status? What had Phillip said to that?

On the surface, it appeared that the two brothers were at odds. If Phillip, who was the older, had the final authority, she would probably be back in the kitchen tomorrow. Where would she sleep then? Would she have to return to Opal Mae's small room? She shuddered at the thought. She must write to

Henry as soon as she could, but if Phillip insisted she return to the kitchen, would he even allow her to send a note?

Tossing and turning, she thought perhaps some tea might help her relax. She went to the kitchen where Jenny was busy with dinner, and fixed herself a small pot of tea, her mind still in a turmoil. Where was everyone? Emma had never come back to the house after Matt left, and Matt had yet to return. Phillip seemed to have disappeared.

She finished her tea and gave up the idea of a nap. She wasn't sleepy, and she was too concerned about the future to be able to relax.

She considered going into the library to find a book to read when she heard voices coming from the front of the house—a woman's voice along with Matt's deep masculine tones. Since Matt had hinted that she did not look presentable and since she had no desire to meet anyone, she decided not to go to the library and continued sitting right where she was.

At least twenty minutes passed when Emma stuck her head through the kitchen doorway and saw Amy. Her black face broke into a grin. "So this is where ya is. Ya best get up them stairs, young 'un." Amy smiled in spite of herself. Young one indeed! She was almost as old as Emma.

Amy hurried upstairs to the bedroom and found boxes littering the floor at the foot of the bed. Tissue paper had been thrown in careless abandon. On the bed lay a cotton dress of soft apple green, and several chemises and lace-trimmed pantalettes and a pair of silk stockings were stacked beside it. Several nightgowns and petticoats were displayed next to the dress, as if to await her inspection. She walked over to the dress and fingered the crisp cotton. It was as nice as any of her own dresses at home.

A tapping on the bedroom door startled her, and she spun around to see Matt in the open doorway. A wide grin was spreading across his face, and the corners of his bright blue eyes were crinkled with tiny lines. He looked pleased with himself. "Tomorrow, when we go into town to post your letter, we'll stop at the dressmaker's and see about something a little more formal. She can also alter any of these things, if needed."

Amy looked at the tall form leaning against the doorjamb. "Mr. Treadwell, I can't accept any of these things," she said, gesturing toward the bed.

Matt frowned and asked with noticeable displeasure, "Don't you like them? This is a small town, and ready-made clothing is hard to find. Aunt Elizabeth thought this would do for now. As I said, the dressmaker can alter the fit. If you don't like the color, we can find something else."

She sighed. It would be difficult to explain, especially since he appeared to be so pleased with himself. She tried again. "Mr. Treadwell—"

"Oh, just call me Matt. Everyone does."

"All right, Matt. The color is beautiful, the dress is beautiful, but I can't let you provide clothes for me. It isn't proper."

Matt's grin started to fade. "Why?"

"It just isn't done." Amy's voice belied her aggravation.

He no longer looked pleased. "Look! You must have something to wear. If it would make you feel more proper," Matt replied, placing a great deal of stress on the word "proper," "let's just say that it is a loan until you get home. Or, better still, you can pay me when your brother comes for you." He stood erect now and did not give Amy a chance to reply.

"Get dressed," he snapped. "I'm sure Aunt Elizabeth would like to see how you look in her contribution. She has come to stay until your brother arrives to take you home. She is a lady and accustomed to a formal dinner. We will dine in one hour!" He turned on his heel and strode down the hall.

Amy closed the bedroom door and leaned against it. She had very little money of her own and might have to borrow money from Henry to pay for all these lovely things and "something a little more formal."

Frowning, she looked down at the brown calico dress that Emma had given her. Already she was wearing borrowed clothes, and Matt was right, of course. She did indeed need something to wear. Struggling with her conscience, she went to the bed to touch the lace things spread out for her. A rap on the door interrupted her train of thought, and, turning back, she opened the door and saw Emma there, holding a can of fresh hot water.

"I been told to help ya dress for dinner," she muttered.

"By whom?" Amy made no attempt to cover the surprise in her voice.

"Why, by Massa Matt," the slave said quietly.

Amy followed Emma to the washstand and took the wet soapy rag Emma handed her without another word. She was to have no choice in wearing apparel it

70

seemed. Emma had been sent to make sure she dressed in the green gown and lacy undergarments.

With Emma's help she donned the undergarments and the silk stockings and then tried on the slippers. Astonished, she looked at Emma. The slippers were a perfect fit. Matt Treadwell must be quite a lady's man if all he had to do to outfit a lady was look at her, she thought. Emma looked at her frown and said matter-of-factly, "I gave 'em yer old ones." Amy blushed as she realized that Emma had correctly read her mind.

Next, she put on the three petticoats that gave the full skirt the correct shape and then the dress. Amy touched the lace collar and straightened the lace-edged cuffs of the full sleeves while Emma fastened the buttons at the back. It was much more fashionable than any of the gowns she had at home. She whirled around in delight as the skirt billowed out around her. The dress fit very well even if it was a bit too short.

Searching for something, Emma rummaged among the things on the bed and smiled at Amy triumphantly when she pulled a comb and brush out from under the nightgowns. Amy suddenly suspected that Emma had somehow been involved in collecting these garments. As the black woman pushed Amy to the dressing table and told her to sit, Amy wondered if Matt had taken Emma shopping. That didn't seem likely. And who was Aunt Elizabeth?

Emma brushed the chestnut-brown tresses until they gleamed. Frowning, she stood back and looked at Amy's hair spilling every which way. Amy glanced up at her. "I don't have any pins."

Emma smiled. "I knowed he'd forget somethin'."
Deciding that braids were the only solution, Emma
quickly plaited the silky strands and tied them
around Amy's head with a piece of green cotton from
the dress. Standing back, she stared at Amy and then
grinned, obviously pleased with what she had done.

Amy looked in the mirror and approved. She stood
up and patted her full skirt with pleasure. "Do you
think I'll do?" she asked, but she felt absolutely elegant. Emma nodded and led the way out of the bedroom.

Coming down the stairs, she saw Matt and Phillip
waiting in the doorway of the formal dining room.
As she approached, she glanced up at Phillip. His
face was devoid of expression, but his cold eyes
glared at her in the flickering candlelight from the
sconces that ringed the foyer.

She turned her gaze to Matt. His eyes bright and
warm, he looked down at her with appreciation. Her
heart did a funny little flip-flop, and she lowered her
eyes, murmuring softly, "Good evening, gentlemen. I
hope you're not waiting dinner for me."

"We are!" Phillip replied curtly.

Matt offered his arm to her and as she placed her
fingers on his hard muscles, a tingling sensation shot
through her, followed by a warmth that started at her
fingers and ran to her toes. She sneaked a glance at
Matt, and he looked as surprised as she felt. He must
have felt something too, she thought.

As they walked into the dining room, a slim silver-
haired woman stood beside the table waiting for
them. Her blue eyes were similar in intensity to both
Phillip's and Matt's eyes. She was attractive, well

dressed, and about fifty years old, Amy guessed. Matt introduced her as Aunt Elizabeth Elton.

Smiling at Amy, Aunt Elizabeth graciously nodded her thanks to Phillip as he stepped behind her chair to seat her at the table. She looked at Amy in a friendly manner after she had been settled. "We will have to get acquainted in the next few weeks before your brother arrives. I hope that we become friends," she purred in a soft melodic voice.

Amy lowered her eyes, suddenly embarrassed. Elizabeth Elton knew about Henry. Had Matt told her how she got to Willows? Had Phillip repeated his charges of "white trash" to this elegant woman? Matt must have told her some of the story for her to agree to come to Willows to stay. If the men had their customary brandy and cigars after dinner, as they did at home, Amy decided she would ask this woman some direct questions, whatever her opinion was of Amy.

For a few minutes, the table was uncomfortably silent until Matt asked Aunt Elizabeth what she thought of the fit of Amy's dress, and then it was even more awkward. Amy squirmed in her chair and blushed crimson. The older woman scolded him. "Matt, you've embarrassed the girl. No woman likes to be reminded that her own clothing is not available to her at the moment, no matter what the reason." Amy wanted to crawl under the table, she was so embarrassed.

Dinner proceeded tensely, even though Matt and his aunt tried to keep the conversation general, with a discussion about the weather and the usual round of parties at holiday time. Phillip sat at one end of the long table, scowling and saying nothing. Amy tried to answer the few questions directed her way without giving either Matt or Phillip any more information about herself than she had already told them. When the gentlemen rose to hold the chairs for the women, Amy breathed a sigh of relief. Dinner was finally over.

"While the men have their brandy and cigars," Aunt Elizabeth said, taking Amy's arm, "let's, you and I, have our coffee in the parlor."

Once in the formal room, Aunt Elizabeth turned to Emma, who had been hovering behind, and said, "Coffee, Emma." She sat down in one of the small couches that lined the wall and gestured to Amy to sit next to her.

"Now, let's get acquainted. You must call me Aunt Elizabeth. Mrs. Elton sounds too formal between friends." She paused and folded her hands in her lap. "I'll tell you a little bit about me. I don't imagine Matt or Phillip has said much." She smiled at Amy, trying to put her at her ease. "I'm the youngest sister of the boys' mother. I've been widowed for several years now. I live about two hours from here on a much smaller plantation. We never had any children of our own, and John, my husband, and I tried to help here as much as we could, especially after the boys' parents died. I was so surprised when Matt came today. He hasn't changed a great deal in the last three years."

Her last remark startled Amy. Matt must have just come home, she thought. As if she could read Amy's mind, Aunt Elizabeth added, "He has been out West seeking his fortune, and he only returned the day before yesterday." The older woman glanced over at

Amy, and Amy could almost see the pity in her dark-blue eyes. "Matt told me that Phillip dragged you here because of a misunderstanding about his slaves. I know how possessive Phillip is about his property. Would you like to tell me the whole of it?"

Amy hesitated. She wanted to share the story of her abduction and the long frightening journey to South Carolina with someone who would understand her fears. Could she trust this woman? True, Matt had offered to help, but the sympathetic ear of another woman would be comforting.

Slowly, she told Aunt Elizabeth about the nightmarish beginning in the field at home. She tried to explain why Phillip had insisted that she return with him without mentioning her personal impressions of the man. Aunt Elizabeth asked several questions, and Amy decided that before she asked about the location of her home, she had better make her feelings known. Thrusting out her chin, she said stubbornly, "I'll not tell anyone here where I live or what my family name is. I am afraid Phillip or Matt might feel obligated to turn that information over to the authorities."

Aunt Elizabeth smiled. "Amy, I respect your position." Then she frowned, adding, "Sometimes Phillip can be very cruel."

The burden of the past weeks swamped Amy, and she turned to the woman, tears blurring her vision. "Oh! I'm so glad you're here."

"So am I!" She patted Amy's arm. "When Matt came this morning, asking for help with the clothes, I insisted that he tell me what was going on. I'm afraid that I demanded that he bring me here. I don't think a young girl of breeding should be in this house with two grown men without a chaperone. Anyway, with Matt home for the holidays, I would probably have spent more time here than at my own home. I needed a change of scenery, too. You know, at my age, it's always so much nicer to be with friends for the Christmas season. This will work out well for both of us."

Amy glanced up in surprise. Was Christmas that close? She was afraid to ask as she watched Aunt Elizabeth add cream and sugar to the coffee Emma served on a silver tray and take a small sip.

"Amy? May I call you Amy? We must find a suitable surname for you and agree on a plausible story that will explain your presence here. We must protect your reputation. This is a small community and gossip spreads quickly. We certainly don't want tales spread about you over something that isn't even your fault."

Amy interrupted her. "My reputation won't be harmed, there won't be time. My brother will come for me just as soon as he knows where to find me."

"Amy, it may take weeks to get a letter to your brother. Communications take time. It's winter now, and travel through the mountains is difficult. You'll have to be patient. While you're waiting, Matt has suggested that he escort you to the holiday parties that we have here."

Amy's heart started to pound. She glanced over at the woman sitting beside her and wondered if she could hear the beating in her chest. So Matt wanted to take her to his parties. She drew a ragged breath and sat frozen, a stricken expression on her face. Per-

76

haps he only wanted to display her. After all, she was a slave conductor from the North, and she had been caught.

Aunt Elizabeth ignored Amy's strained look. "Matt is intrigued with you, I think. Now, to come up with an acceptable last name for you." She paused. "Amy Smith? No . . . that's too common. Amy Schultz? No . . . you don't look German. Dutton? No, we have too many Duttons here." She frowned in deep thought. "I have it! Amy Stuart!"

She took Amy's chin in her hand and turning her head from right to left. "With your high cheekbones, you could pass for a Scot." She chuckled. "The local citizenry will speculate about that name, but we won't tell them a thing." She seemed delighted with the game she was playing.

"Now, why are you here?" She looked at Amy for several minutes and then took another sip of her coffee. "I know! You are a distant cousin from the North, who has come for the season to meet your relatives. You have heard about them, but you have never met them. Before the situation between the North and the South makes travel impossible, you have come to visit." She continued to stare at Amy. "And you have been in a Northern convent school for the last six . . . no, eight years." She sipped her coffee, then laughed out loud. "You'll be related on the Bishop side, my side. Phil Treadwell could never have been related to royalty."

Amy looked at the woman in wonder. Aunt Elizabeth had just made up a name and background for her as if it was an everyday occurrence.

"Well, Amy Stuart," Aunt Elizabeth said, putting

her cup and saucer on the tray, "tomorrow, the three of us, you, Matt, and I, will go into town to see the dressmaker about several more dresses. I'll tell my nephews what we've decided." She winked. "Now off to bed with you. Tomorrow will be a busy day." She led Amy to the stairs and gave her a hug. "I'll send Emma up to help you get ready for bed. Pleasant dreams," she said.

Chapter Five

Amy's mind whirled as she climbed the stairs. Matt was going to escort her to the local parties. What had Aunt Elizabeth said? Because he was intrigued with her? Goose bumps rose up on her arms as she thought of the jolt she had received earlier that evening when she put her hand on his arm. A sigh slipped past her lips as she remembered her position. She couldn't work in the kitchen all day as Phillip had ordered and attend holiday parties with Matt at night. She stopped at the head of the stairs. How long before Christmas, she wondered.

The incredible story Aunt Elizabeth had dreamed up, almost out of the blue, still had her stunned. Clothes were her biggest problem. She would have to be most selective and pick out inexpensive things. It just wouldn't do to be indebted to either Aunt Elizabeth or Matt, but what else could she do? So much was happening and so fast that she wondered if she would be able to sleep at all.

* * *

Aunt Elizabeth watched as Amy climbed the stairs, then she went in search of Emma, and sent her to help Amy prepare for bed. Setting out to find her nephews, she chuckled at her own imagination. Matt was alone in the library, sipping a brandy, smoking a cigar, and frowning at nothing. She interrupted his thoughts. "I've sent the girl to bed. I think Phillip has made a grave mistake. She is well bred and obviously suffering in her present position." Chuckling, she explained the story she had concocted and the name she had given Amy.

Matt grinned. "What will Phillip say to all this? We'll have to make sure he agrees not to contradict us. One of his caustic remarks could ruin the girl."

Aunt Elizabeth nodded in agreement. Phillip could indeed ruin everything. She wished Matt a good night and pleasant dreams, then went in search of Phillip, who was in the study, busy with paperwork. He finally agreed, reluctantly, not to comment about Amy's surname or the contrived story. Wishing him pleasant dreams as well, Elizabeth Elton finally sought her own bed.

Long after the other occupants of the house retired, Matt sat in the library, thinking of the girl who had swooned in his arms only that morning. She was educated and intelligent, and she had a temper. Aunt Elizabeth had confirmed that she was very frightened. He considered whether Phillip had abused her and then dismissed the idea. His brother used people, but Phillip had always been too disciplined to take advantage of innocents. Where did she come from? Phillip either didn't know, or he wasn't saying.

She was certainly a beautiful creature with her large expressive eyes. There was no denying his interest in her. At dinner, she had looked at him, and her eyes had spoken volumes—that she was tense, alarmed, and finally, very relieved that the meal had ended. It was clear she came from good family and had breeding. Aunt Elizabeth had insisted upon a formal dinner to determine just that point. The girl had not faltered once, and she had seemed at ease with the formal table service. Yes, she had breeding. So why had her family allowed her to lead a group of slaves north across her land in the middle of the night? Could she have taken on that responsibility without her own family knowing about it? That hardly seemed likely.

He let his thoughts drift back over the past months and his own activities. The ranch was waiting, flat lands of Texas waiting to be shaped into a cattle ranch with the special animals he had made arrangements to purchase when he stopped in St. Louis. He had the gold mine and his part interest in the Colorado Territory. As long as the gold vein held out, he would have all of the funds he needed to build his dream.

He grimaced as he remembered why he had come East. There would be war, he was sure of it, and knowing how Phillip felt about the plantation, he knew his brother would join the army of the South. Matt, if forced to serve, would side with the North. Before it came to that, Matt wanted to make peace with Phillip. He had to settle their differences before they took sides on the war issue.

The girl complicated things. She had been at Willows for only thirty-six hours, and already she had caused two bitter arguments between them. Matt wondered if he would leave Willows with his brother a friend or if Phillip would send him away, cursing and yelling obscenities as he had done three years before. He loved Phillip in spite of all his older brother had done to him, but he didn't like Phillip, not at all. Angrily, he ground out his cigar and stalked out of the library to seek his own bed.

Amy slept soundly the whole night through and was amazed, when Emma tapped her on the shoulder, to see sunlight streaming through the bedroom window.

Emma smiled down at her. "Ya don't want to keep Massa Matt awaitin' too long, young 'un."

Amy stretched, raised her arms high above her head, and glanced at Emma, who was holding a tray. "I've never had breakfast in bed before." Amy chuckled.

" 'Bout time!" Placing the tray on a table, Emma fluffed up the pillows and then handed Amy the tray.

While Amy munched on a hot sugar roll and sipped hot chocolate, Emma fetched a can of hot water for Amy to wash her face and hands. Then Emma shook out the green dress and brushed Amy's hair.

Amy slipped on the silk hose. "These have been washed," she said with some surprise.

"I laundered them last night," Emma answered softly.

"I'm capable of taking care of my own clothes, Emma." Amy's voice was a bit sharp.

"No need," Emma stated flatly. "Aunt 'Lizabeth thought you might need this." Emma handed her a soft, white wool stole.

Dressed, Amy followed the slave downstairs, and Emma pointed to the library. "Massa Matt says to write yer letter." Then the thin black girl disappeared through the dining room.

In the library, Amy found pen, ink, and paper laid out neatly on the desk, obviously for her. She looked around and listened intently to make sure she wasn't going to be disturbed. Why, she questioned, did she feel a need for complete privacy just to write a letter? She grimaced and answered her own thoughts. "I don't trust Phillip one little bit!"

Seating herself at the desk, she smiled and thought about her brother. When he had failed to find her, he would have gone back to school. Aunt Amelia and Uncle Jeb would have insisted. A frown wrinkled her brow. Of course, he might still be looking for her.

She stared at the white paper spread out before her. Where should she send her letter? If she addressed it to Henry's school and he wasn't there . . . The school would send the letter on, but that would take too much time. Aunt Elizabeth might be right. Last night Emma had told her Christmas was in three weeks. This letter would probably not reach him until after Christmas. Choking on a sob, she blinked the tears from her eyes. By then he would be back at school.

Dipping the pen in the ink, she started to write. Before she had completed the first sentence, she realized that she didn't have the faintest idea of the name

83

of the nearest city. Well, Henry would have to find her from the mark on the envelope. Quickly, she scribbled where she thought she was located and that she was unharmed. She added that she would be anxiously waiting to hear from him. Then she sealed her note in the envelope and addressed it. She sat staring at the envelope for several minutes, then folded it in half with the address on the inside.

With no bag in which to carry the note, she wondered if she could ask that their first stop be the local post office. In dismay, she realized that she would even have to ask for the few coins needed to post the letter—this on top of her borrowed dress and the loaned stole. Well, Henry would come, but until that time, she would just have to make the best of a bad situation.

Amy had no trouble convincing Matt to make their first stop the post office, and soon they were on their way. The ride into town was pleasant, with Matt pointing out places of interest as they traveled. Near the town, Amy asked quietly, "What is the name of your town?"

Matt answered just as softly, "This is Anderson, South Carolina."

Amy gasped. Anderson! No, it couldn't be! She glanced over at Aunt Elizabeth, and the woman's concern was written in her eyes. Amy wondered if she had given herself away.

In minutes Matt stopped the carriage in front of a small, drab, unpainted building and swung down from the carriage. He helped her down and pressed several coins into her hand. Taking her arm, he led her toward the door. As she hesitated, he offered,

"I'll wait outside."

She posted her letter quickly and made her way back to the carriage. As she arranged her skirts, she smiled at her companions. It was a great relief to have finally sent the letter. Soon Henry would receive it, and she would be on her way home. But as the carriage moved down the street, a sinking feeling suddenly engulfed Amy. How could she have been so stupid? Surely, the Treadwells knew the postmaster, and probably Phillip knew the man very well. If Phillip wanted to know where and to whom the letter went, he had only to ask the man who had taken her letter.

For a moment, Amy felt sick. Matt must have noticed, for he asked with concern in his voice, "Is everything all right?"

Amy hesitated and then mumbled quietly, "I hope so."

Matt, noticing the sheer terror that glittered in her eyes, sought to distract her by describing the stores lining the street. When he guided the carriage to a stop before a trim white one-storied cottage, he glanced at Amy once more. Aunt Elizabeth, however, seemed unconcerned and said, "Here we are!"

After Matt had helped both ladies down from the carriage, he jumped up into the seat and promised, "I'll be back in an hour or two," and drove off.

As Aunt Elizabeth moved to the gate in the front of the small house, Amy clutched at her arm. "I'm paying Matt back every penny we spend. Everything we order I will pay for. My funds are a little — limited . . ." She paused in embarrassment.

"Mrs. Wilson is very reasonable." Aunt Elizabeth

85

smiled reassuringly. "But you have to work out the financial arrangements with Matt. Matt told me what he wanted ordered, and if you disagree with him, you'll have to take it up with him when we get back to Willows." Taking Amy's elbow, she ushered her through the door. Amy was sure the subject was closed as far as Aunt Elizabeth was concerned.

Mrs. Wilson turned out to be a chunky, cherub-faced woman in her middle years with curly graying hair. When she saw Elizabeth Elton, her broad face lit up in pleasure. Elizabeth greeted her like a long-lost friend and, introducing Amy with the same enthusiasm, immediately launched into the explanation as to why they were there. "Something appropriate," she commented, smiling. Amy had little to say, it seemed.

The dressmaker scurried off to another room and within minutes returned loaded down with plates and sketches of the latest fashions. The two women discussed the styles and colors of a dozen outfits before Aunt Elizabeth decided on two dresses, one a dark-green velvet with full sleeves and a sweetheart neckline and the other a simple dark-blue silk, which made Amy's eyes look very blue, with a small collar as the only trim. While Mrs. Wilson took Amy's measurements, Aunt Elizabeth talked about the current fashion and the accessories they would need for the two dresses. Aunt Elizabeth asked if Mrs. Wilson had a dark day dress almost finished that might fit Amy.

Once more, the dressmaker hurried from the room. Before Amy had a chance to object, she was back with a dark chocolate-brown day dress of corded silk. Aunt Elizabeth insisted that Amy try it on, and when Amy stood before the two women, Aunt Elizabeth smiled and pronounced it perfect. "We'll need it before Sunday," she said quietly.

Amy stared at her in confusion. Why did she need the dress before Sunday? And how on earth was she ever going to pay for everything Aunt Elizabeth had ordered? Her panic started to build.

As Mrs. Wilson helped Amy change, she commented to Elizabeth, "I don't understand why Amy has nothing acceptable to wear. I'm not sure that I can finish these dresses in the time you've given me."

All the color left Amy's face, and she felt her knees sag, but Aunt Elizabeth merely grinned. "Amy's just finished her education in a convent school and has nothing I find acceptable," she explained easily. The dressmaker nodded in understanding, but she was so astonished at Aunt Elizabeth that Amy was speechless.

After Aunt Elizabeth and Mrs. Wilson had discussed the necessary fittings and arrangements, Elizabeth said quietly, "Come, Amy. Your cousin, Matt, is waiting. We must take our leave." Although Amy was unable to speak, she was befuddled by Aunt Elizabeth. It was as if the charade had come true, and she was indeed the distant relative visiting for the season.

Matt was waiting in the carriage and jumped down to assist the women into their seats. Aunt Elizabeth asked that they stop at the milliner's shop before they started home.

Amy shook her head to regain her sanity and then turned to Matt. "Please retain all the bills for my expenses. I'll repay you when Henry arrives," she said with quiet dignity.

At the small shop tucked between the inn and a bakery, Aunt Elizabeth made a small purchase and pressed it into Amy's hands. "You'll have need of these," she said. It was a flat tin of hairpins.

At last they were on their way back to Willows. Amy was trying to calculate just how much money she now owed and heard little of what Aunt Elizabeth and Matt were saying. But when Aunt Elizabeth said, "The brown dress will be just perfect for the tea," Amy jolted back to the present.

Amy cringed inwardly. "What tea?"

Matt grinned at her. "Oh, so you are going to pay attention now? Didn't she tell you?" He inclined his head toward his aunt. "She's going to see that you are properly introduced to our Southern society. After all, you are a distant cousin with an illustrious name. It wouldn't do at all to keep you hidden away. People would only gossip then. No, my dear Aunty is going to present you formally at a proper Sunday tea."

Amy gasped. Was he making fun of her? As he watched her, an easy smile spreading across his face, Amy was sure her heart missed a beat. Scolding herself, she attributed the palpitation to the excitement of the shopping trip and she managed to smile back at Matt.

The conversation turned to the parties people gave during the holidays. Amy wondered as they talked if she and Matt would attend every one. The pleasantness continued through the dinner hour that evening. Amy had now found her tongue and joined in the talk, joking about some of the things they had seen in town and discussing the tea planned for Sunday.

The only unpleasant person at the table that evening was Phillip. He sat at the head of the table and glared at the three of them throughout the meal, refusing to even answer a simple question. He clamped his mouth shut and stared straight ahead. He made Amy feel uneasy.

After dinner, Aunt Elizabeth demanded that Phillip join her in the library. Amy knew something was about to happen, especially since Aunt Elizabeth then snapped at Matt with an authority Amy had never heard before, "Take Amy for a walk in the garden!" Aunt Elizabeth marched past Phillip toward the library.

While Emma was fetching Amy's shawl, she could hear raised voices coming from the library. Matt grinned. "I think Aunt Elizabeth is giving him a piece of her mind."

Outdoors, Matt pointed out different areas of the vast gardens behind the house. Even though most of the blooms were gone, there was still the fall color of the shrubs and trees. The grounds were soothing and restful, and Amy breathed deeply in an effort to let the calmness of the clear moonlit night ease her tension.

Suddenly, Matt turned, slid his arm around her narrow waist, and bent his head to brush her lips. "I've wanted to do that ever since I saw you in the kitchen yesterday," he whispered in a husky voice.

Amy's breath was taken away, and for some reason her lips felt as if they had been burned. "You shouldn't do that," she whispered.

Matt tightened his hold ever so gently, "There is

something about you . . ." His voice trailed off. Bending down, he pressed his warm lips against hers in a tender kiss that deepened quickly. Amy's knees turned to butter, and her hands slipped up around his neck without her willing them to do so. He pressed her slight frame to his, crushing her breasts against his chest. She felt as though she were being drawn into his strong body, and her heart started to pound.

Gradually, she came to her senses. What was happening? What was he doing, and why was she allowing it? As she struggled to free herself from his embrace, she was breathing heavily and shaking.

"I should apologize for that, but I won't. I enjoyed it, and I think you did also." Matt dropped his hand from her waist, took her arm, and without another word led her back into the house.

In a daze, Amy mumbled a good night and ran up the stairs to her bedroom. She closed the door and leaned against it, trembling with emotion. When she had been engaged to Adam, he had kissed her, but only short, pleasant kisses. They had not left her breathless the way Matt's kiss did. Why did Matt Treadwell affect her so?

For the next two days she tried to amuse herself. Except for dinner each evening, she was left to her own devices and spent most of the time in her room, reading books from the library. On the morning of the third day, Amy sought out Aunt Elizabeth and explained that she was bored, almost to the point of tears. "I'm not used to such inactivity. At home, I baked bread, helped my father with the farm accounts, helped with the meals and the housework. I even led a church youth group once a week. Isn't

90

there something I can do?" Tears of frustration formed in her blue-gray eyes.

Aunt Elizabeth smiled. "Most of the house is run by the slaves, but if you must have something to do, then I see no reason why you can't plan the meals. I don't enjoy doing that. And you can bake the bread. Emma's bread is not the best."

With Aunt Elizabeth's encouragement, Amy went to the kitchen to start right away. She was happily making bread, her hands floured, when Matt came in and looked at her with concern. Then his face twisted in anger. "Did Phillip tell you to do this? I told you that you're a guest here. Guests do not need to make bread!"

Amy's smile faded, and she muttered feebly, "I needed something to do." Matt didn't seem to hear because he turned on his heel and stormed out of the kitchen.

Aunt Elizabeth came just after Matt had left and, glancing over her shoulder, said, "Whatever did you say to upset Matt?"

Amy bristled. "He didn't approve of my activity." She continued to knead the dough. Aunt Elizabeth smiled wryly and reminded Amy that she had a fitting that afternoon. Amy set the bread to rise and went to change into her green dress.

That afternoon she went downstairs to wait for Aunt Elizabeth. As she approached the drawing room, she heard Phillip's angry voice from the library. "I don't care. I want her out of here. You will pass that Northern white trash off on our friends over my dead body!"

She heard Matt's caustic reply. "Over your dead

body? You threatened that once before, brother dear. Don't tempt me!" The viciousness of Matt's response alarmed her almost as much as Phillip's rage.

And Phillip's words stung. She was not white trash, and she had not asked to meet their friends. It wasn't even her fault that she was here. It was all Phillip's doing. And besides, all she wanted was to go home, and Phillip was the one who prevented her.

She stood shaking her head. Phillip and Matt hadn't seen each other for three years, and yet they were screaming at each other. They seemed to hate each other. But what could she do? "Oh, Henry!" she murmured to herself. "Come quickly."

Eventually Aunt Elizabeth, followed by Matt, joined Amy and they started off, but the trip into town was strained. Matt sat quietly, his eyebrows drawn into a deep furrow above his cold eyes. His face was grim, and his mouth was a tight, straight line. Amy looked from him to Aunt Elizabeth, who also sat quietly staring ahead. Matt must have told her about his argument with Phillip, Amy told herself. She wanted to scream. As soon as she had the opportunity, she would ask Aunt Elizabeth if she was the reason why the brothers quarreled.

Matt dropped them off at the dressmaker's and sulked away, growling that something required his attention. In the shop, Amy tried on the brown day dress and the soft kid slippers that Aunt Elizabeth had ordered. The dress fit beautifully, and the slippers were a perfect match. Amy was delighted, but suddenly she felt very guilty. She would never be able to pay for all this from her own money. What would Henry say when she gave him the bill?

After the fittings, Amy was still feeling miserable as they walked to the milliner's to pick up the bonnet Aunt Elizabeth had ordered. Matt met them there, and his mood seemed much improved. By the time Amy, Aunt Elizabeth, and their collection of boxes were in the carriage, Amy was the only one who was glum.

Chapter Six

Sunday dawned crisp and bright, and Amy was downstairs just as the sun edged its way over the horizon. She would show Phillip Treadwell! Entertaining was not new to her; the tea trays would tell him in no uncertain terms that she was his social equal. She smiled as she arranged the tea cakes on the brightly polished silver trays. It hadn't been difficult to convince Aunt Elizabeth to let her do the trays.

Amy was putting the final touches on the last tray of sandwiches when Emma came looking for her. "Yer bath's ready. Yer gonna be late for yer own party. Now go!" she ordered softly.

Amy gave a last glance at the trays, then fled up the stairs to her room. Throwing off her clothes, she eased herself into the scented bath, the delicate fragrance of oil of roses drifting up from the steaming water. She had not allowed enough time for her bath. She would have to hurry.

She patted herself dry with the fluffy cotton that Emma had waiting and dressed quickly. Emma stood at the dressing table, comb and brush in her hands, repeating over and over, "Yer hair's gonna take time, lots of time."

Finally, Emma was brushing and combing and pinning her hair into curls, and all the while mumbling about the lack of time. When Emma was done, Amy glanced in the mirror. Her hair hung in a cascade of curls that trailed down her left shoulder. Amy's breath caught in her throat. She looked beautiful.

Standing up, Amy turned around so that Emma could make any needed last-minute alterations. Then Emma stood back and gave Amy a critical look, and her face broke out in a wide grin.

"Oh, my, young 'un, you do look mighty lovely, just purfect," she purred.

Amy smoothed the rich brown silk of the skirt and smiled. The silk bolero jacket opened down the front to reveal her soft cream lawn blouse. Little tucks on each side of the placket emphasized the small pearl buttons that closed the blouse, and the full gathered sleeves peeked out from under the wide jacket cuffs. She felt absolutely elegant.

Emma opened the bedroom door and stepped back so that Amy could leave the room, but Matt's wide shoulders barred the way. As he stepped into the bedroom, he indicated with a nod of his head that Emma could go. She slipped out as Matt turned to Amy. Solemnly, he handed her a small jewelry box. When she opened it, she stared in amazement at a pair of small pearl earrings and a string of matched pearls.

Amy opened her mouth to refuse the gift, but Matt

reached out and laid his finger over her lips as if he had read her mind.

"Its a coming-out present. I thought you might need a little gift to help you through this afternoon and the people you'll have to face." He grinned as he added, "Especially with the name Aunt Elizabeth's given you."

Amy's stomach twisted into a knot as she remembered the reason behind all the preparations. She had been so intent on making a point with Phillip that she hadn't once thought about the masquerade in which she was involved. Amy glanced up at Matt as he watched her with concerned eyes.

"I didn't mean to upset you," he said softly. "I came to give you these and ask you not to discuss your views on slavery with any of the guests. I suspect they wouldn't understand."

For a second her anger at this statement overrode her fear. "I hadn't planned to discuss my views on anything, especially slavery," she muttered.

He changed the subject, and reached for the string of pearls. "Here, let me fasten these. Then I'll escort you downstairs. It's time to meet the neighbors."

She placed the pearls on her earlobes and turned so that Matt could fasten the clasp of the necklace. Fingering the string of pearls, Amy turned again to face him.

"Thank you. This was very thoughtful of you. I feel elegant now."

Matt's dark eyes gleamed as he looked at her. He whispered, "Elegant, and very beautiful as well."

As he took her by the elbow to lead her from the room, a warm tingling sensation spread through her, and she felt as though her legs had melted. "I must be more nervous than I thought," she mumbled.

Matt sensed the change and tightened his hold, patting her arm. He said, chuckling, "You'll be fine." They descended the winding staircase where Aunt Elizabeth was waiting with outstretched arms.

"Well?" Matt asked.

Aunt Elizabeth looked at Amy carefully. "Pinch your cheeks, dear. You look a little pale." Then taking Amy's arm, she led her into the nearly filled drawing room. As they moved from one group to another, Aunt Elizabeth repeated her fabricated story until Amy felt like screaming.

As the afternoon wore on, Amy watched Matt entertain the gentlemen, by taking them into the library for brandy and cigars and then returning to the drawing room to stand beside Aunt Elizabeth. Amy suddenly realized that Phillip was not there. He was nowhere to be seen. At first she was angry, and then, for some reason, she began to relax.

Late in the afternoon, as Amy was talking to a family friend, she overheard Aunt Elizabeth speaking about the convent school she was supposed to have attended and her desire to meet the family. As she nodded her head to the woman who was speaking to her, she tried to hear what Aunt Elizabeth was saying. In that instant it dawned on her. She *was* Amy Stuart! She was whatever and whomever Aunt Elizabeth said. The tale about being cousin to Aunt Elizabeth and the Treadwell brothers could not be disputed. She would never see these people again. Smiling, she turned her attention back to the guest.

Now she could enjoy herself. It was a grand party,

and everyone was pleasant. She did her best to be charming and to visit with as many of the invited guests as she could. There were many questions about the North, and she tried to answer them as honestly as she could. As the tea drew to a close, she heard Matt telling an old friend of Aunt Elizabeth's that Amy could read and write and had studied law. She chuckled. Even Matt was getting carried away with the charade.

After all the guests had departed, Aunt Elizabeth collapsed on a drawing room chair and sighed in satisfaction. "You were superb, my dear." She smiled at Amy. "I have three invitations for you for next week alone."

"And several of the ladies I talked to insisted that I promise to escort you to their balls." Matt grinned affectionately.

Amy tried to thank them both, but the words stuck in her throat. Aunt Elizabeth beamed in delight. "I don't remember when I've had such fun. That stuffy Mrs. Pendergras was beside herself because she couldn't politely ask if Amy was a royal Stuart." Aunt Elizabeth laughed out loud. "And I refused to give her a chance to more than speculate. She'll have tongues wagging over your name, or I'll miss my guess. Amy, you were splendid." She got up from the chair and gave the girl a hug.

"I think you'll have to forgo making bread," Matt muttered as he grinned in satisfaction. "You'll be much too busy accepting social invitations."

That night, as she sat brushing her hair, Amy thought about the afternoon. She had enjoyed it. Most of the people had been so nice, and Matt and

Aunt Elizabeth had demonstrated such a natural affection for her that she felt warm and safe. For the first time since that awful night in October, she relaxed. Hugging herself, she smiled and thought about Henry. Even if it did take eight or nine weeks for him to come, it would be all right. She was on a holiday, and she was going to have a good time, a very good time.

Four days after the tea, Matt informed them at dinner that he would be traveling to town on business in the morning and would be gone for the day. He added, "I'll pick up the gowns that Mrs. Wilson has finished and check at the post office. I'm sure it's much too early for a reply, but I'll check just in case."

"Will you be home in time for the evening meal?" Aunt Elizabeth asked.

As Matt shook his head, Phillip's harsh voice broke the quiet. "I'll be gone as well. Don't wait dinner on my account."

Shortly after breakfast the next morning, Amy heard the carriage wheels crunch on the gravel, and slamming doors echoed through the house. Minutes later she heard the sound of a horse being brought to the front of the house. She breathed a sigh of relief. This was the moment she had been waiting for. Now she could seek Aunt Elizabeth and find out why Phillip and Matt were at each other's throats.

When she found the slim, silver-haired woman in the study answering the invitations that had accumulated since the tea, Amy asked if she could join her. Encouraged by her welcoming smile, Amy plunged in with her questions.

"Aunt Elizabeth, would you be offended if I asked why Matt and Phillip argue so much. They act as if they despise each other. Have they always felt this way, or did something happen to make them enemies?" Her voice faltered. "Or is it me?"

Twirling her quill pen, Aunt Elizabeth studied the girl before her. She had a right to know.

"I'm sorry, but I think you're bringing their true feelings to the surface, but the mistrust and dislike have been there for some time now." She rose from the desk, called Emma, and ordered tea for the two of them.

Amy waited impatiently for more information as the woman moved toward one of the chairs.

"Perhaps you should know what happened. Then you might understand why you're affecting them the way you are."

Just then, Emma arrived with the teapot and two cups. Amy settled back in the chair she had chosen while Aunt Elizabeth sat down herself and poured tea.

"It started after Anna and Phillip senior died in 1845 during the typhoid epidemic that took so many lives," she began. "Phillip was just seventeen, away at school, and he had always felt a great responsibility for his nine-year-old brother. Anyway, after his parents died, he left school and returned home to run the plantation and take care of Matt. He saw to Matt's education while he himself was trying to learn the cotton business.

"He did a superb job with the farm, but Matt resented an older brother who told him when to sit or stand, or even blow his nose. By the time Matt was twelve, he and Phillip spent more time yelling at each other than they did talking."

She paused to take a sip of tea. She stared across the room, her eyes sparkling with unshed tears as she remembered. Slowly, she turned back to Amy.

"When Matt was twenty, he started courting one of the young belles in the next county. He was infatuated with her and even brought her home to meet me. She was a lovely young thing. They decided to marry just as soon as her father gave his permission."

Amy sat very quietly. Matt was married? Was that possible? Her heart gave a lurch. Aunt Elizabeth continued.

"When Matt told Phillip about his plans, Phillip was furious. He laid down the law: Matt was too young, he didn't have any income, he could not support the girl, and he didn't know enough to help in the business of running the plantation. I think Phillip's words to Matt were 'Over my dead body!' Matt was devastated. He talked to his young lady, and they decided to elope.

"Somehow, Phillip found out and went straight to the girl's father. Oh, my! What a scandal! Phillip packed Matt off to England to make trade arrangements for Treadwell cotton, or so he said.

"Matt was gone for over a year, and when he finally came home, the girl in question had married a gentleman from Georgia. Phillip and Matt had a terrible row. Matt packed up and left for California to find his own fortune." She paused for another sip of tea.

"That was over three years ago. Matt told me he came back last week to make peace with his brother.

He no longer needs Phillip's support or his money. He is part owner in a gold mine in the Colorado Territory and has even acquired 640 acres of land in Texas. He plans to homestead, then buy more land. He has his own plans for some kind of special farm in Texas where he can raise cattle.

"He was terribly upset when Phillip dragged you here without a thought to what he was doing with your life. Matt feels that Phillip is still trying to control the lives of others with no thought to the consequences. I think that's why Matt has gone out of his way to be so sweet to you. I am sure you can understand why Phillip is being so nasty." She finished her tea in silence.

Amy was stunned. That Matt had once been in love with another woman, perhaps loved her still, upset her for some reason. It hurt even more to consider that Matt was treating her so pleasantly only because Phillip had forced his will on her. Her expression grim, Amy thanked Aunt Elizabeth and made her way from the study. "Henry, come quickly!" she muttered.

That night Amy couldn't go to sleep. Long after dark she heard a carriage arrive, followed by voices in the foyer. Matt had returned, she reasoned, or perhaps Phillip was arriving. After a time, the house returned to quiet, and Amy could hear the wind rustling through the willow trees. When she finally drifted off to sleep, the sky had begun to lighten as pale streams from the rising sun played over the roofs of the barns.

Emma roused Amy late in the morning and looked at her critically. Amy's eyes were dull and ringed with dark shadows, her face pale. Clearly Amy was ill, and Emma hurried off to find Aunt Elizabeth. Both women soon returned, and the older woman rested her cool hand on the girl's warm forehead. She announced that Amy was to stay in bed for the day. When Amy protested that she was only tired, her pleas were ignored. Emma scoffed and Aunt Elizabeth said, laughing, "No, my girl! It's bed for you, and for all day."

A healthy portion of chicken soup appeared for Amy's lunch. After she had managed to eat a good part of the soup, she felt so drowsy that she snuggled down into a feather mattress and drifted off to sleep. For some time, she thought she was floating between reality and sleep. All the events of the last two months crowded into her mind. Matt's long face and expressive blue eyes appeared time and again. When she came awake with a start, Matt was leaning over her, concern written in his dark eyes.

"I didn't mean to startle you, but I brought us some tea." He straightened and pointed to Emma standing behind him, tray in hand. "How are you?" he asked. "Aunt Elizabeth thinks that you might be ill, and Emma says you're worn out." He didn't give her a chance to respond but reached instead for the tray Emma held.

Amy looked around the room in panic. She was not dressed to receive visitors, especially not male ones. Matt, seeing the distress in her eyes, guessed the cause. "Emma will help you freshen up, although you look mighty good to me right now. I'll be back in a few minutes." He grinned at the two women as he sauntered from the room.

Hurriedly Emma handed Amy a moist cloth and brushed her hair. Then she helped Amy into a robe that Aunt Elizabeth had generously given her only the day before. Amy crawled back into bed as Matt, with muffled curses, and carrying a stack of large dress boxes, attempted to get through the door. The boxes he dumped on the bed, explaining, "I picked these up when I was in town. I believe they're m'lady's wardrobe."

Eagerly, Amy attacked the boxes, throwing tissue paper in all directions as she removed the finished finery. The gowns were beautiful, and Amy ran her hands over the luscious fabric of each in turn, her blue-gray eyes gleaming with pleasure. She had never had anything to compare with these at home.

Blushing, she extracted lacy petticoats and several pair of silk hose from one box. On the bed lay the two gowns that she and Aunt Elizabeth had ordered, but there were two boxes yet to be opened. They were a mystery.

Amy opened the first box gingerly and gasped. A day dress of blue-gray cotton twill, just the color of her eyes, lay nestled in its bed of paper. She lifted it from the box and shook it out. The simple lines of the bodice were accented with a small corded collar, and tiny mother-of-pearl buttons closed the front. The full skirt was trimmed with the same delicate cording in bands above the hem. She laid it aside and opened the second box.

As she gazed at the creation in the second box, she couldn't believe her eyes. Emma stepped forward to lift the gown and display it. Amy was speechless as she stared at a ball gown of fine tulle silk, the color of freshly churned cream. Lace balloon trimmed the deep neckline, and the same lace trimmed the edges of the full puffed sleeves. The skirt, fashioned from yards and yards of the same fine tulle, was gathered at the waist. The hem was scalloped with matching lace peeking from under the silk. Carefully sewn into the lace of the neckline were hundreds of tiny, creamy-white seed pearls. Barely able to speak, Amy gasped, "I—I—I can't possibly accept this—this—"

Matt grinned and interrupted her. "Merry Christmas."

Emma poured tea and then put all the new garments into the armoire. Amy's eyes glistened with tears of happiness. "Matt, I've never seen anything like the ball gown in my life. I can't afford it and I certainly can't wear it. Please accept my gratitude, but it's much too costly." Amy sat, still fingering the cream-colored ball gown that Emma had yet to put away.

Matt brushed aside her objections and her thanks as he handed the gown to Emma. "We have been invited to the mayor's New Year's Eve ball." He grinned affectionately. "Wait until you see what I got for Aunt Elizabeth. This ball is the social event of the season, and I like my women to be well dressed."

Her heart jumped into her throat, and she fought for control. She wanted to laugh out loud or sing. He had casually said, "My women!" Suddenly, she remembered what Aunt Elizabeth had said. Was he only using her to get even with Phillip? Her eyes clouded, and a frown crossed her expressive face. Of course. He was trying to anger his older brother.

Matt watched her change her expression and

sensed her tension. Misreading the reason, he said quietly, "There was no letter. It could take a month for your note to reach your brother, and it will take that much time or more for you to receive a response. You probably won't hear anything until the end of January."

Amy looked at him in confusion. What letter? What note was he talking about? Suddenly, she remembered her position and her note to Henry. Fighting her frustration and disappointment, she wanted to tell him that was certainly not what was bothering her. She had already decided that it would take at least that long to hear from Henry if he was in school, and perhaps a week longer if he was at home. Squaring her shoulders, she wondered if she should confront Matt with what she knew. She could tell him that she was onto his game with his brother. But what good would that do? Then, she would be in the kitchen, working as a servant for sure. Instead, she tried to smile, but tears glistened in her eyes.

Matt quickly changed the subject to avoid upsetting her further. He asked about the tea and dinner they were to attend that weekend. "Aunt Elizabeth has really gotten into the spirit of the thing. She's already accepting invitations for January. She mentioned that you're going to be calling on several of her old friends who live nearby. You're going to be busy, very busy." He chuckled.

He talked about the approaching Christmas and reminisced about those of his past. He laughed as he told her about his last Christmas. "My mine in the Colorado Territory had started paying off right before Christmas, and my partner and I spent Christmas buying the biggest steaks we could find and getting very drunk."

Amy looked puzzled and asked, "I thought you went to California to make your fortune?"

"I did," he answered. "I spent six months standing in a cold mountain stream two feet deep, with a little pan in my hands, and getting wet and cold. I made a total of twenty dollars. I figured it wasn't worth it. Word was spreading that they were taking chunks of gold out of the mountains outside a mining camp called Denver. So, I went to Denver." He smiled as he remembered.

"When I got to the territory, I met an old-timer who was down on his luck. We joined forces, my money, what was left of it, and his knowledge. We sank a lot of shafts, and the last one paid off. In fact, I went to Texas last spring and picked out 640 acres. I intend to buy more. I plan to live there and raise cattle. Don't worry about the clothes, Amy. I'm a wealthy man."

The excitement had tired Amy, and she tried to stifle a yawn. Matt stood up to leave. "You rest for the day, and I'll see you in the morning." As he left, Amy couldn't help thinking about the beautiful new gowns. She tried to banish her feelings of guilt and snuggled under the quilt to sleep.

To everyone's relief, Amy was up and about the next morning. She grinned. She had been overtired, nothing more. The teas and the dinners now began in earnest. Nearly every day, she was dressing for one affair or another. Somehow, two more gowns appeared without any explanation. Matt was taking care of her no matter what Phillip thought.

Amy thought it strange that Phillip was never invited to any of the affairs. When Aunt Elizabeth announced a week before Christmas that the whole family, Phillip also, was invited to the adjoining plantation for dinner, Amy was shocked. The Parsons, who owned the plantation to the south of Willows, were old and close friends of the Treadwells. Matt had told her that they had known both boys since they were infants. When Phillip and Anna Treadwell died, the Parsons had tried to help, even though they had three children of their own. Matt had said, "If I hadn't been able to escape Phillip by going to the Parsons, I don't know if I'd have survived."

Phillip, however, refused to go. Aunt Elizabeth demanded that he attend the dinner whether he wanted to or not, and they argued noisily about it. Amy could hear them from the parlor, which she was decorating for the holidays.

When it was time to go to the Parsons, the tension and strain had grown. Aunt Elizabeth had given both men a severe lecture to behave before they dressed for the dinner, and the glare she gave them as they climbed into the carriage was a stern reminder. In stoic silence they traveled to the neighboring estate. Phillip was so sullen and unpleasant that Amy was afraid to speak. By the time they finally arrived, she was thinking of pleading a sick headache and asking to be returned to Willows.

Instead, she let Matt lead her into the parlor to meet her host and hostess. Phillip did not behave and became even nastier, and the more offensive he became the more charming Matt tried to be. Amy wanted to run from the parlor, but Matt hung onto her and led her from one group to another. She tried to pull free to join Aunt Elizabeth, but he looked down at her with a hurt expression on his face and muttered, "Don't you want my company?"

Amy felt herself blush, but she couldn't think of a response and saw no way to rid herself of his unwanted attention. She tried to hint that Aunt Elizabeth might appreciate their company, but Matt discounted that. "She's busy visiting with old friends." Amy finally gave up and let Matt guide her around the room.

As they went in to dinner, Amy was eternally grateful that the Parsons knew the boys well and were aware of the difficulties between them. She was relieved when she saw the place cards at the dinner table. Matt was at one end with some of the younger men and Phillip was close to his host. She and Aunt Elizabeth sat across from each other, and on either side were other neighbors and friends of the family. She was uneasy though; somehow she knew this would be a meal she would never forget.

Chapter Seven

At first dinner was tolerable, but a chance remark by the one of the men next to Aunt Elizabeth drew Amy's attention. "What did you say?" she asked, her voice little more than a whisper.

The man looked uncomfortable. "Why, I said that I was pleased that South Carolina has shown Washington just how her citizens feel."

"And . . ." Amy waited.

The man was clearly embarrassed. "I forgot that you are from the North. I suppose you'll be going home now that South Carolina has seceded from the Union."

The words thundered through Amy's head. South Carolina . . . seceded from the Union? Then the trouble had started! A deadly calm descended around the center of the table, but Amy didn't notice. Nor did she see Aunt Elizabeth's attempts to fill the silence. Amy wanted to scream and run from the room, but to where? Struggling to regain control, she sat as still as she could. What would happen to her now?

Further down the table, Matt looked anxious. Damn, he thought to himself. From Amy's expression, he could guess what she had just heard. He should have realized this would happen. Everyone was discussing little else tonight, and he should have warned her himself. Why hadn't he? Because, you fool, he answered himself, you're afraid now she'll go home. He watched her carefully, aware that she was trying to act unaffected by the conversation whirling around her, but something about her eyes told him that she was badly frightened.

When it was time for the gentlemen to have their brandy and cigars, the women moved into the drawing room for coffee and feminine conversation. Amy took the opportunity to pull Aunt Elizabeth into a corner. She whispered, "Please, could we go back to Willows? I didn't know about South Carolina. I can't stand around and talk as if nothing has happened." Her voice shook. "Please, Aunt Elizabeth, please could we leave?"

Aunt Elizabeth patted her arm. "Amy, I'm so sorry. I should have told you. As soon as the men are finished with their brandy and cigars, I'll find Matt. Then, in a few minutes, I'll say something to the Parsons, and we'll leave. Keep smiling."

It was not long before the men rejoined the women, and Aunt Elizabeth did what she had promised. She then informed Phillip that she would like to leave. Amy was amazed to see the relieved look on Phillip's face.

The short trip back to Willows was more strained than the ride to dinner had been, and Amy was glad when they finally got home. She thanked Aunt Elizabeth for the evening and fled to her room. She got herself ready for bed without waiting for Emma's help. The comments from the dinner guests came back in full force in the quiet room. Would the North and the South go to war? Of course they would. She remembered the talk she had heard at home. The Union could not, would not, allow a state to leave the fold. Now she had to go home, but how? Phillip would not let her leave. No, she had to wait in South Carolina until Henry or Alex came for her. There was nothing she could do.

The dark train of her thoughts continued as she wondered if Phillip had discovered the name and location of her brother, Henry. Was he already in prison? If the farm had been confiscated, she had no home in Indiana. She would be forced to live with relatives, that is, if they would have her. Maybe Phillip didn't intend to let her ever leave Willows. She might never see her brothers again.

Gone was all the excitement of the social whirl she had enjoyed, and even the anticipation of Christmas had disappeared. In their place was a feeling of total despair. Tears welled in her eyes and slid down her cheeks as she sat on the soft feather mattress. Her burden overwhelmed her. She had no home, no money, no way to leave, and not even her own name for fear of harming her brothers. Phillip thought of her as a slave, and Matt saw her as a means of retaliating against his brother. Aunt Elizabeth had said so. She was lost! Her soft sobs turned to heart-wrenching anguish.

Amy was crying so hard she didn't hear the sharp banging on her door. Nor did she hear the door open and close. She barely knew that Matt was sitting on her bed, reaching for her shaking form with his strong arms. He cradled her and stroked her head gently, letting his fingers trail through her chestnut curls. Stopping briefly, he dug into his pocket for a handkerchief, and, without a word, pressed it into her hand. Her misery was so great she was unaware of burying her head in his broad chest, and of weeping salty tears onto his waistcoat. He rocked her tenderly, in his arms to soothe her.

Gradually, she calmed down as her sobs lessened and finally stopped. Lifting her chin, Matt stared into her wet, sad blue-gray eyes as the soft candlelight played across her tear-streaked face. He was struck by how small and childlike she was. As her eyes once more filled with tears, the depths of her despair touched him, and he murmured in a husky voice, "Don't." He lowered his mouth and kissed her trembling lips, then her forehead, her eyelids, her salty cheeks, and then back to her soft quivering lips.

Amy let him enfold her in her arms. She needed comforting, and his arms offered her the sense of security she so desperately craved. Neither one of them thought about what was happening; they only responded to need. But as Matt's lips touched Amy's once more, her heart fluttered dangerously and began to beat wildly.

His chaste tender kiss started to deepen, and his arms gathered her to him, pressing her breasts against his chest. Without thinking, she slipped her arms up around his neck. He embraced her more tightly, and, responding, she pressed against him. Vaguely aware of a sense of anticipation, she returned his kiss without hesitation. She wanted him to kiss her, but she wanted something more—what she didn't know. Molding her slender body to his, she instinctively tightened her hold, wanting to stay where she was, wrapped in his arms and caressed by his lips, forever. When he finally raised his head, a soft sigh escaped her.

Matt left a trail of burning little kisses down her neck, from her ear to the edge of her gown. As she clung to him, a bit of sanity returned. She should push him away, she should stop him. He shouldn't be doing this. But then Matt raised his mouth to hers for another deeply sensual kiss, and time stood still. As Amy's body started to awaken, she lost the battle with herself completely and melted into his arms. She wanted this! She wasn't going to think about right or wrong, what she should and should not allow. No, she would simply enjoy what he was doing.

He traced her lips with the tip of his tongue, then moved to the soft corner of her mouth. He claimed her again, and then hesitantly, he probed gently with his tongue. She parted her lips shyly to allow him access. Her slender body stiffened in shock, and tiny flames of desire crawled over her body. She felt as though she was floating in a sea of pleasure. Surely, if she moved, she would be lost forever.

She was totally unprepared for the feelings that surged through her as he explored her sweetness, gently tasting the inside of her cheeks, stroking the softness of her inner lips, and touching her tongue. Glorying in the warmth that spread through her, she lost any touch with reality.

He held her tightly and felt the firmness of her breasts burning into his chest. She was so close to him that he could feel the beat of her heart as it echoed his own. As he continued to kiss her, he moved her away ever so slightly. His left arm encircled her shoulders, and his right hand began a deliberate exploration above her waist. He reached the softness of her breast, and his fingers located the small peak for which he was searching.

Little sparks of sweet pleasure raced from his fingertips through her whole body as he teased the small tip into hardness. She drew in a ragged breath and clung to him. Don't stop, don't let the pleasure stop, she silently pleaded as her whole body leaned toward him. Suddenly, she started to tremble and shake.

Matt stopped his caressing strokes and lifted his mouth from hers. For a second, he sat there, stunned. Cruel reality forced him to consider what he was about. He pushed her away abruptly and peered into her passion-glazed eyes.

"Oh, my God! Amy, I'm sorry. I didn't intend to do that." His voice broke. He was shaking himself. It had been a long time since he had been so affected by a kiss. He tried to smile, but it was lopsided.

Amy was dazed. What happened? Why had he stopped? Her pleasure had been so intense that she felt robbed. As she stared into his guarded eyes, reality started to surface. She took a deep breath, and it was like a bucket of cold water. She had almost been seduced! And she had wanted it. In fact, she wanted him to continue. Shame caused her to choke.

"I think you had better leave," she finally managed to say.

"Amy, please forgive me. I heard you crying. I felt so . . ." His voice trailed off. He looked away. "I didn't mean . . ." Placing his hands on her shoulders, he looked at her, and his eyes were pleading, "Please, forgive me!"

"It's all right. Please, go. Please, go now!" Her voice was still shaking. She pushed at him, and Matt stood up. He looked down at her and opened his mouth to speak. But he couldn't find the words, so he turned and left her room.

As the door closed softly, regret and relief poured over her. Staring at the candles throwing their thin rays of pallid light, she admitted she felt something special for Matt. Something that had caused her to set her standards aside. It was more than physical attraction. There had to be more to cause her to lose control so completely. When he merely spoke, the muscles of her stomach tightened. Even when he glanced at her from across a room, her heart fluttered. She was confused.

Tonight, she had made no attempt to stop him; she hadn't wanted him to stop. She tried to tell herself that she was tense from the upsetting evening and felt despair at the news about South Carolina. Could her loss of restraint have anything to do with the strain she was under? But why had she responded so eagerly to him? Finally exhausted by her soul searching, she blew out the candles and crawled under the comforter to drop off into a troubled sleep.

Meanwhile, Matt, thoroughly ashamed of himself, had gone to the library and poured himself a large brandy. He sat in the dark room, trying to figure out what had happened. When he had heard the heartbreaking sobs coming from her room, he had only wanted to comfort her. He had intended to do no more than wipe her eyes, yet her tears had shaken him so deeply that he had felt a tenderness he had never experienced before. He had seen many beautiful women, but they had never affected him as she had done. It was not only her beauty that had caused him to lose control. No woman before Amy had ever had that effect on him, and he didn't like it.

He had his land in Texas, he had come home only to make peace with Phillip, he was not ready for any permanent relationship, not yet. A permanent relationship? He sat stunned. Where were his thoughts leading him? Amy had an effect on him, one that he wasn't ready to explore. Until he had his emotions under control and had analyzed her effect on him, he had to stay away from her, far, far away. He needed to discover, by himself, just how important she had become to him. Avoiding her was absolutely necessary, especially when she was alone. He could possibly lose control again, and the next time it might go too far.

Frowning, he considered insisting that Phillip send her home, before anything happened, but so far Phillip had refused to agree to any of Matt's suggestions. Phillip wanted to take her to the main road, dump her there, and let her find her own way home. Matt slammed his hand down on the table beside him. He had come home to make peace, and here he was, starting his own war and over another woman.

And the woman? He wondered how he would ever be able to face her. He had almost seduced her. With her chaperone, his own aunt, only two doors away. And in his own home. He needed time to think; then he would apologize. Sipping his drink, he made plans to leave the plantation early the next morning, long before Amy awoke. He was, he admitted to himself, no better than a coward.

The next morning Amy wasn't interested in seeing Matt either and was relieved when Aunt Elizabeth assured her that Matt was gone for the day. Aunt Elizabeth wanted to go to Anderson, and Amy saw the opportunity to stop at the post office to check the incoming mail and to post another letter to Henry, this time addressed to him at home. So off they went, and when they returned to Willows, it was time to see to the evening meal. They both went upstairs, Aunt Elizabeth to rest and Amy to freshen up.

As Amy came back down to the foyer, Phillip appeared from the library with a half-smile flitting across his face. "Is Aunt Elizabeth resting? She usually does too much when she goes into town," he commented.

Amy nodded. "Yes, she's resting," she said as she moved toward the kitchen.

Phillip stopped her and said quietly, "Amy, I want to talk to you." He stepped aside and waited for her to enter the library. She hesitated, wondering what he could have to say to her. He was almost pleasant. Perhaps he had changed his mind and had decided that she was not white trash. For a fraction of a second, she entertained the thought that he might even want to apologize.

Phillip closed the door and turned around to look at her with grim eyes. His face was twisted in a black expression. Her heart stopped, and she lowered her eyes. "I must not let him know how frightened I am," she told herself.

Phillip glared at her. "You think I don't know what

you're trying to do. Well, it won't work. Matt is here for Christmas, and then he'll be going back to Texas. You still owe me for the trouble you caused me, the food you've eaten, and your care while you've been socializing. I intend to see that you pay me back. I brought you here to work, and work you will. You are not going any place until your debt to me is paid."

She felt as though she had been struck with a whip. "If my family comes for me—"

"What family? Your family is not coming," Phillip hissed. "And if you attempt to leave before *I* say you can go"—Phillip made the "I" sound like a death knell—"I'll follow through with my legal rights. You know what that means. Never fear, my beauty. I'll see you rot in prison before I let you escape." He smiled at her cruelly and then walked to the door. Once more, he turned back to look at the girl. "Don't think Matt will help you either. He'll be gone." With that Phillip left the library.

Amy fled from the room and ran for the stairs, all plans for dinner forgotten. Reaching her room, she collapsed on her bed, too stunned to cry. Matt was going back to Texas. He had told her that, but she had forgotten. And did Phillip know her family weren't coming, or was he just trying to frighten her?

She tried to remember exactly what he had said. All she could recall were the words that Matt was leaving. She sat up suddenly. Why did that fill her with such dread? Why did the thought of Matt's return to Texas bother her more than Phillip's cruel words. What was the matter with her? Instead of worrying about going home, she was pining away because Matt was leaving. Nothing made any sense.

Her soul searching found her no closer to understanding what was happening to her, and Amy sighed.

The sun was setting when Emma came through Amy's door. "Why ya not downstairs, seeing to dinner? Ya sick again?" "I forgot about dinner." She told Emma about her confrontation with Phillip and added softly, "I have to go home — and soon."

For several days, Amy stayed out of everyone's way but the day before Christmas, Matt caught her in the kitchen.

"I need to talk to you for a few minutes," he said and gave her no chance to respond as he led her to the drawing room. The festive decorations belied the tension that strained the household.

He guided her to a couch, and when she was seated, he sat down himself and took her hand in his, "Amy, I want to apologize for the other night. My behavior was unforgivable. I'm sorry."

Amy glanced at him shyly. "Matt, I told you then that I accepted your apology. I was beside myself and was upset. The fault was as much mine as yours. I realized that, even before you left. Please, let's not talk about it any more." Her face was bright red.

He frowned at her blush, still feeling guilty, but he squeezed her hand. "I'm sorry I let my emotions get out of control." His face was a study in seriousness. "It won't happen again."

Amy gazed at him. His eyes sparkled, and she could read the concern there. But there was something else in his eyes. Then it hit her. He cared for her, he really cared. Excusing herself, she got up from the couch and floated back to the kitchen. Matt Treadwell cared for her. Phillip would not be able to hurt her now, not if Matt cared.

Christmas came and went, and as each day passed, Amy grew more concerned. She had really expected some word, at least from her aunt and uncle, before the first of the year. Tuesday night was the mayor's ball, the last day of 1860, and she had not heard anything. She was depressed, but more than that, she was frightened. Home, she sighed, please, just let me get home. To make matters worse, she was having a terrible time going to sleep. She would toss and turn in her bed for hours before finally drifting off.

The more she thought about it, and she thought about little else, the more convinced she was that somehow Matt and Phillip had joined in a conspiracy against her family. Whatever she thought she saw in Matt eyes, was nothing more than pity perhaps. Matt didn't care for her, he was never around. She stayed in the kitchen or in her room, and the only time she spent with the family was the evening meal. It was usually a strained affair and as a result she ate little. Matt always tried to be charming, and Amy tried, she really tried, but the tension was always there. Phillip continued to sit at the table and glare at everyone. Aunt Elizabeth was unusually quiet and pensive. The situation was growing unbearable.

The day before the ball, Amy drew Aunt Elizabeth into the library. "Please, Aunt Elizabeth, can we not go to the mayor's ball? I'm so tired, and you know as well as I that Matt doesn't truly want me to accompany

121

him."

"I don't know that at all. Now, child, Matt purchased our ball gowns, and we are not going to disappoint him. Tomorrow, you'll just relax. I insist that you spend the whole day resting. Amy, it's too splendid an affair to miss." With that Aunt Elizabeth closed the subject.

Chapter Eight

Early the next day, Aunt Elizabeth peeked into Amy's room. "We'll leave about seven this evening. Matt will see you then. And, Amy, Matt is looking forward to this evening and escorting you to the ball."

Amy cringed. "You didn't ask him, did you?"

Aunt Elizabeth smiled. "No, but I hinted a bit, and your fears are totally unfounded. Now you rest. After lunch you can have a nice, long soak and a nap, and then Emma will help you dress."

True to her word, after lunch Aunt Elizabeth insisted that the copper tub be prepared for Amy. After her bath, Emma came to her room with orders that she take a nap. For a change, she was relaxed and did sleep. Emma had to wake her for supper. Amy ate a light meal before dressing. Then Emma fashioned Amy's brown locks into a coronet of curls piled high on Amy's head. With Emma's help, Amy put on the many petticoats and finally the exquisite ball gown.

Amy didn't even glance into her mirror above the dressing table. If she had, she would have been startled by the dark shadows under her eyes, caused by her restless nights. Her skin no longer held any trace of summer tan, but was instead pale and delicate. She looked like a fragile porcelain doll, a regal doll.

As she donned the kid slippers Matt had purchased to match the gown and hung the small pearl earrings on her ears, she wondered if she would survive this evening. Emma fastened the pearl necklace around her throat and handed her her gloves, bag, and shawl, given by Aunt Elizabeth. Amy was now dressed and ready, and she sighed; her first formal ball and she would give almost anything not to be going.

It was just after seven when she made her way down to the foyer where Matt and Aunt Elizabeth were waiting. As she glanced at Aunt Elizabeth, she remembered Matt's pleasure over Aunt Elizabeth's gown. For a second, Amy smiled. It was a creation of dark teal blue satin covered with cascades of matching lace.

Matt must have heard the rustle of the soft silk of Amy's gown because he turned toward the stairs and stood there with his mouth open, his sentence unfinished. Amy managed a faint smile for Aunt Elizabeth, but the stunned expression on Matt's face confused her.

"Do I look all right?" she asked hesitantly, looking from Matt to Aunt Elizabeth.

Matt tried to answer three times, but he only succeeded in clearing his throat. Aunt Elizabeth stepped forward, took Amy's arm, and gave it a little squeeze.

"My dear," came the older woman's soft reply, "you look absolutely stunning." She smiled up at Amy and gave Matt a gentle nudge with her elbow.

With difficulty, Matt recovered enough to murmur,

"Your highness . . . you are breathtaking." He bowed low before her and muttered to himself. "Every man there will want an introduction. I won't be able to let you out of my sight." He was still muttering as he turned to retrieve Aunt Elizabeth's cloak from a small chair in the foyer.

Just then, Phillip appeared at the study door and looked from Matt to Aunt Elizabeth. Amy shrank behind the two so that she would be hidden from his view. But as Matt moved back to help his aunt with her cloak, Phillip caught a glimpse of Amy. He stared at her, his mouth open with astonishment. Finally, he regained control and closed his mouth, his lips forming a contemptuous smirk. "Going partying again, I see. That gown does not change the fact that she's white trash," he snarled and then slammed the door as he retreated into the study.

Matt glanced from Amy to the closed door, and his face lit up in an engaging grin. "See, even Phillip was at a loss for words, for a while anyway." With that, he laughingly took Aunt Elizabeth's arm, offered his other arm to Amy, and led them from the house to the waiting carriage.

The mayor's house was a large and imposing two-story structure. Many lanterns had been placed to aid the arriving carriages and gave the house an almost dreamlike quality. Amy drew a ragged breath. The house looked to her like one of the great houses of Europe in some of the drawings she had seen. She was awed.

They alighted, and with Aunt Elizabeth on Matt's left and Amy hanging on lightly on his right, they started up the steps to the entrance. At the doorway,

125

Matt glanced down at Amy and said gently, "Smile, Amy. This is supposed to be fun." But Amy was overwhelmed as a servant opened the door, and she gazed into a large foyer filled with a thousand candles and a hundred gaily dressed people.

After greeting their host and hostess, they moved on to the parlor where Matt immediately found almost every man in the room was clamoring to be introduced to Amy. Matt was forced to escort a beaming Aunt Elizabeth to a couch at the edge of the ballroom. Before he could return to Amy's side, her dance card was filled, and he had to watch as she was waltzed and whirled around the ballroom floor. He was disgusted that most of the so-called gentlemen cut in on her partners, dance after dance.

Matt even berated himself for having selected her gown, for it emphasized her tiny waist and her soft young breasts, and the soft clinging fabric dramatized her height. The color of the silk made her pale skin look even softer and her coronet of chestnut hair shimmered in the candlelight as though made of woven gold sprinkled with rubies. "God, she's beautiful," Matt muttered above a thick lump in his throat. She did indeed look like a princess.

Amy was having the time of her life. Her partners proclaimed again and again that she was beautiful and elegant. They complimented her loveliness, her charm, and her gracefulness. Although she blushed, she enjoyed the attention she was receiving.

While Amy waltzed around the room, Matt stood next to Aunt Elizabeth and glared, one by one, at each of Amy's partners as he came to claim his dance. Why hadn't he been quick enough to sign her dance card?

He hadn't danced with her yet. The scowl on Matt's face grew deeper and deeper and he even neglected to offer to dance with Aunt Elizabeth.

Amy was very much aware of Matt's displeasure as she glanced at him over her partner's shoulder. She suddenly realized that he was jealous. Matt Treadwell was jealous! If that was the case, she told herself, then he must care for me a great deal, much more than I thought. She had no time to analyze this startling idea, for suddenly she was whisked back to the center of the floor for a Virginia reel.

Temporarily tired, Amy convinced her next partner, one of the older gentlemen, that she needed to rest. He grudgingly returned her to Aunt Elizabeth, who sent Matt for a glass of punch for Amy. When Matt finally returned, he was still glaring. Amy chuckled and couldn't help teasing him. "Matt, smile! This is supposed to be fun." Matt, however, didn't think it one bit funny and continued to stare belligerently at the other men.

He exercised his escort's privilege and cut in on that dance and on each dance thereafter but Matt had had enough. He complained that Amy wasn't paying any attention to Aunt Elizabeth or to him, and she was there, after all, because they had brought her. He muttered in a husky voice, "You are being entirely too charming to some of these men, especially the married ones."

As she whirled about in his arms, she smiled up at him, her heart singing. He's jealous, she kept repeating over and over. She tried to explain to herself why that discovery made her so happy, but she had no answer.

The last dance, a waltz, was planned to end at exactly midnight. Matt claimed the dance as his own. Another young man came forward, saying that Amy was his partner, but the dance card somehow had disappeared from Amy's wrist. Matt sent the young man off to look for another partner. Amy was beaming.

Matt spoke not a word to her that last dance, but his eyes never left her face. He was a superb dancer, and they moved smoothly and effortlessly around the floor. As he held her firmly and a little too tightly, Amy felt wonderful and secure once again. Forgotten were her suspicions.

As the last chords of the music died away, Amy turned her sparkling blue-gray eyes up to his face. He was still holding her tightly and looking at her with such a tender expression that Amy wanted to shout with joy. That she was falling in love with this man hit her like a thunderbolt.

Glancing around the room, Amy sighed. "Matt, the music has stopped." He dropped his arms but kept his eyes on her face. Warmth spread through her. Like it or not, she admitted to herself, her feeling for this man made him very, very special.

In a trance she allowed Matt to lead her from the dance floor, but when she realized that he was heading for the dining room, she stopped. "Matt, what about Aunt Elizabeth?"

Matt grinned. "My memory seems to have suffered from the dance." He strode over to where Aunt Elizabeth sat, beaming. He offered his arm, and they made their way to the elaborate buffet in the dining room. The repast did not take long, and in a short time they were thanking their host and hostess for the enjoyable evening and making their way back to their waiting carriage.

The ride back to the plantation took the better part of the hour, and Aunt Elizabeth chatted on about this person and that, continually mentioning the effect she thought Amy had had on the assembled citizens of Anderson. She was pleased with the evening, more than pleased and she said so frequently. She didn't even seem to notice that neither Matt nor Amy bothered to answer when she directed a comment or, occasionally, a question at them. Matt only grunted, and Amy muttered unintelligibly, as if she were asleep.

But Amy was not asleep. Instead, her mind was spinning in a thousand different directions all at once. That Matt was fond of her, very fond, she was sure. So, if he cared for her, then he could not possibly be involved in anything that would hurt her family, could he? Maybe he helped Phillip at first and was now regretting his actions. Was he trying to stop Phillip from sending her to a Southern prison for her part in the slave escape? She was simply too tired to put all the pieces together tonight. She sighed happily. It had been a marvelous evening.

Back at the house Matt helped Aunt Elizabeth from the carriage and then returned to help Amy down. As he lifted her, his arm tightened around her and his lips grazed her temple. Against her ear, he whispered, "We've got to talk."

Her feet touched the ground and Amy whispered back, "Tomorrow! I'm too tired tonight."

Inside the door, Emma was waiting, and she followed Amy up to her room. Gratefully, Amy let her undress her, help her into her nightgown, and even tuck her into bed. Amy vaguely remembered Emma wishing her pleasant dreams before the black girl blew out the candles. Amy never heard her leave. Her triumph at the ball had dissolved all of her tension, and she fell fast asleep.

Amy slept very late the next day. As she stretched on waking, she thought of the night before and suddenly remembered that Matt had wanted to talk to her. Curious, she dressed quickly and slipped downstairs. As she made her way to the kitchen, she noticed that the library door was closed and heard angry voices filtering through the heavy door. Matt and Phillip were fighting again. She understood only a few of the muffled words, but they were enough to tell her that Matt and Phillip were arguing about her again.

Suddenly, the door was jerked open, and Matt stormed from the room, his face red and enraged. He marched through the foyer, his body rigid and his eyes straight ahead, and slammed out the double doors to a waiting horse.

Amy heard the horse tear over the gravel drive. Glancing back toward the library, she saw Phillip standing in the doorway. He spotted her and glared angrily in her direction, then opened his mouth as if to speak. For some reason, he said nothing, but instead spun around and went back into the library and slammed the door closed with great force.

Amy ran up the stairs as fast as she could in search of Aunt Elizabeth. She had to talk to her and get her Aunt Elizabeth to help her leave before one man killed the other. No longer could she stay in this house of hate, brother against brother, and all because of her.

No, she couldn't live with that.

To her dismay, Aunt Elizabeth was still asleep. Amy wandered back downstairs and tried to hide in the kitchen. Was there no one to whom she could turn? Matt had left, driven off by Phillip, and Aunt Elizabeth was asleep, and even Emma was gone, probably helping one of the field hands.

For the next six weeks, Amy didn't see Matt Treadwell at all. He left the estate early, usually before dawn and when and if he returned, it was late at night. He left no messages for her and made no attempt to see her.

Amy was confused and a few days after the ball cornered Aunt Elizabeth to speak of her fears. The older woman told her that she was making too much of the boys' arguments.

"Amy, you can't go home without an escort. I will gladly pay for a carriage or train or however it can be arranged, but you can't travel without a companion. You're a lady. Phillip would never allow any of his slaves to travel with you, and I don't dare leave with Matt and Phillip so angry. Don't worry, dear. We'll hear from your brother soon, and then you can go home properly."

As each day dragged by, Amy spent more and more time in her room. She convinced herself that the fight she had overheard had been caused by Phillip telling Matt that he was forbidden to give her any assistance. She even imagined that after the ball Matt had decided to help her. "But he really doesn't care enough," she told herself.

131

Amy couldn't have been farther from the truth. Matt still went into town to check on the mail each day that he was home. He couldn't understand why Amy's relatives seemed to have deserted her, and then Phillip was so intent on characterizing her as white trash that Matt felt a growing certainty that something had happened between them on their trip to South Carolina. Had his older brother tried to seduce the girl, and she had rejected him? Phillip was now insisting that Amy be sent home in any way possible and had suggested putting her on the train north and be done with it. Anything, he said, to get her out of the house. In turn, Matt maintained that she could not travel alone, that she must remain at Willows until her family sent word and she could be escorted properly.

The ugly doubts about Amy's trip with Phillip swirled around in Matt's head until he knew he had to find out what had happened on the way to South Carolina. He traveled to several of the plantations close to Willows, looking for the two slaves Phillip had sold.

Then he talked to Phillip's overseer, who told him that the older of the two men had been sold to a farmer in central South Carolina. Matt left immediately for that plantation, and when he arrived, he succeeded in talking to Ned. Ned described the trip south, but the facts, as Ned presented them, couldn't explain Phillip's attitude toward Amy. Ned was sure that nothing had happened between the two.

On the long ride back to Willows, Matt made up his mind. There was only one thing to be done. He would have to take Amy home himself. He would arrange for one of Aunt Elizabeth's slaves to accompany them so it would be proper. But first, he would have to take Amy and Aunt Elizabeth to Elton Estate, and then he would have to convince Amy to trust him enough to tell him where she lived.

Smiling to himself, he wondered just how Phillip would react when Matt explained that he was very fond of a feminine slave conductor, fond enough of her to want to meet her whole family. He laughed out loud. Phillip would bust a blood vessel.

While Matt was busy away from the plantation, Amy was trying to stave off Phillip's vicious verbal attacks. Whenever their paths crossed, he glared at her and mumbled disparaging remarks. "White trash!" and "Thief!" seemed to be his favorites. Her need to escape grew stronger each day, but she fought the desire to run. Phillip would follow her and would drag her back. Of that she had no doubt.

Besides, she couldn't count on help from Matt or Aunt Elizabeth. Matt was in his brother's power, and Aunt Elizabeth refused to consider that she travel north by herself. Aunt Elizabeth had said, very clearly, that she must wait for her family to see her safely home. That knowledge did not make Amy feel any better. And she hadn't seen Matt for six weeks.

Suddenly, late one morning in February, Matt came home. He stormed into the kitchen, demanding to know where Phillip was. Amy caught a glimpse of his scowling face. His eyes were cold and dark, and his voice cut like a knife as he ordered Emma, "Find my brother! Tell him we're going to talk—now!"

Matt stood in the kitchen, glaring, until Phillip also came storming in just as angrily. He yelled, "What's so damn important that I have to be dragged away from my work? I have a plantation to run!"

"We're going into the library, and we're going to settle this thing right now!" Matt yelled back.

Matt and Phillip stomped off to the library, and Emma grabbed at Amy as she tried to slip out of the kitchen. "Yer're going to help here. Ya best keep busy. And I don't want to have to go a-lookin' for ya, too." As Emma pushed Amy toward the dining room, Amy couldn't keep her eyes from the massive door of the library. Even through the thick wood Amy could hear loud voices, and once more the argument was about her.

Emma whispered, "Ignore it!" as she handed Amy the table covering and left to get the rest of the table service. Phillip's angry voice was louder, and Amy could hear most of what he said. Matt's voice was more restrained so she could make little out of his comments. She heard Phillip screech, "common thief . . . no family . . . white trash . . . taking us for all we're worth." She set about her task trying desperately to ignore the comments Phillip was heaping on her. She had heard them all before.

Once when Phillip made a loud comment about the cost of room and board, she heard Matt's response as he thundered, "I bought all the damn clothes." As the argument grew louder, Amy tried to still her shaking hands. Emma handed her the dinner plates just as Phillip started to shriek again, and Amy wondered if she would have to add broken dishes to her list of crimes.

Suddenly the sounds from the library died down. At first, she expected to see either Phillip or Matt slam from the room, but after a few minutes, Amy decided that the men had come to some decision. She tried to calm herself enough to begin placing the plates on the table. The quiet was broken by Phillip's swearing. Then he yelled something about throwing her out and being done with it.

There was a pause, and then Matt added something she did not understand, but his next words were clearly spoken. They stabbed at her breaking heart. He shouted, "Stay right here until . . ." There was another pause. Then, "And go to prison." Amy could not move. Tears streamed down her face, and she was afraid that her legs would not bear her weight as she leaned against the edge of the table.

From out of nowhere, Emma appeared and took the plates that Amy had forgotten and set them aside. Emma dragged her through the door to the kitchen and into the small pantry off the main room.

As Emma closed the door, Amy looked at her and whispered in a breaking voice, "Emma, hel—help me!"

Emma patted her hand. In a soft voice, she breathed, "Jacob, he come back for me. In three weeks, we're goin'."

Amy stared at her, trying to understand through her fog. Emma gave her a reassuring hug. "You come too."

Amy shook her head, trying to clear the mist before her eyes. "But Matt and Phillip will know. They'll stop you."

Emma smiled, and her voice was sarcastic. "They may come after us, but they'll not be here to stop us. Massa Phillip's leavin' in three weeks. He's goin' to

Charlotte for business, and he tol' ol' Jed he'd be gone for four or maybe five days. Jacob's been awaitin' for this. He knows the way. They'll not find us." She lifted a finger to her lips. "I'll tell ya mo' later." Then she turned and left the pantry.

Relief flooded through Amy. She was going home — if there is a home, she thought. As she started through the door of the pantry, she felt a sharp pang; she would never see Matt Treadwell again. Shaking, she berated herself. How could she even think of him? He thought she was a thief, and he meant to see her punished. No, she had no choice. When Emma and Jacob left, she would leave too, or face prison. Matt had said so.

Chapter Nine

Amy fled up the stairs to her room. A thousand questions whirled around in her head. What if Phillip decided not to go to Charlotte? What if Matt stayed at home? What if someone discovered Jacob? What if . . . What if . . . She gritted her teeth and tried to calm down. Emma was a cautious person, and Jacob had avoided capture for months. If Emma and Jacob planned to escape, then they must have considered all the problems. If they were going, then it must be all right for her to go also, she tried to convince herself.

During the next week, Amy died a slow death. She managed to avoid Matt, but she never found a chance to talk to Emma alone. One afternoon, with Aunt Elizabeth visiting friends, Matt in Anderson, and Phillip gone, who knew where, Amy finally could speak to Emma.

She whispered her concerns. "Emma, what if Phillip does leave? What if Matt stays here? Maybe Phillip has asked Matt to guard me while he's in Charlotte. Are you sure no one has seen Jacob? Who else knows about this plan?" Amy fired off her questions in rapid order, giving the slave no chance to answer.

Emma tried to calm the excited girl. "Amy, Phillip's plans is all made. He done made all the arrangments. Massa Matt's leavin' in the mornin'. He says he got business that he must sees to. I heard him tellin' Missus Elizabeth. He'll be gone for a week. And, Jacob"—she chuckled and her dark brown eyes twinkled—"my man knows how to hide. We be goin'. Now ya rest, 'cause it will be a hard trip."

As the week wore on, the tension in Amy built unbearably. Whenever a door slammed or the heavy boots of the overseer broke the quiet of the house, she jumped. She was sure that Matt would return at any moment, but apparently he was gone for good. Had he gone back to Texas? Emma assured her that Matt would be back, but then it would be too late. Amy rested as much as she could. Since she already kept to herself much of the time, no one thought anything about that.

By the day before the escape Amy was a bundle of nerves. In the mid-afternoon, Emma ordered her to stay in her room. "To look at ya, everyone in the house will know that somethin' is up. Ya stay upstairs!"

At last Phillip's trunk was carried down to the first floor, and Amy told herself the waiting would soon be over. Going to the kitchen, she passed the study and overheard Phillip giving instructions to Aunt Elizabeth. "I'll be gone for four or five days. If you need me or have a problem, you know where I can be reached."

Early the next morning, Phillip left, and Amy drew her first real breath in several days. She retreated to her room to write a thank you note to Aunt Elizabeth to tell her how much she appreciated everything Aunt Elizabeth had done for her. For over an hour she labored, trying to find the right words. She also wrote that as soon as she reached home, she would send money to pay for everything. Wrapping the note in the white woolen shawl, Amy put the shawl where it would be easily found.

Next she wrote to Matt. It was even harder to find the words. She had to fight her anger and a strange longing with each line, and her debt to Matt, for the beautiful clothes, was very large indeed. Folding the note, she couldn't decide where to leave it.

The notes finished, she stretched out on the bed and was just dozing off when Aunt Elizabeth knocked on her door.

"Amy, I'm going to spend the afternoon with Mrs. Parsons. I think the outing would be good for you. Will you come with me?"

Amy panicked. Did Aunt Elizabeth know something? Was she trying to get her away from the house?

"I was going to take a nap," Amy mumbled through the door. "I really am a little tired."

"All right! You rest. I'll be back by dinnertime."

Amy listened to the sound of Aunt Elizabeth's small heels tapping across the hall floor and fading down the steps. Amy breathed a sigh of relief, but now she could not nap, for she was too frightened and apprehensive to sleep. In a few minutes Emma came into the room.

"Are you still awantin' to go?"

"The sooner the better," Amy stated firmly.

Emma sat down on the bed beside Amy. "Aunt Elizabeth left instructions for a supper tray. Tell her, ya's still a mite tired and want to eat in your room. Ya come to the kitchen for a glass of milk just after dark. Come down in yer robe and nightgown. No." Emma shook her head as Amy tried to disagree. "I wants nobody to know what's goin' on. I got yer clothes and things. I'll send Jenny to help Aunt Elizabeth. I done tol' Jenny that one of the farm hands is sick and I'se got to go help the family. As soon as Jenny leaves the kitchen, I'll gives ya the clothes, and ya can change in Opal Mae's ol' room. Then we go."

"Emma, Jenny will know I'm not there, when she goes back to the kitchen."

Emma laughed. "Jenny will think that ya had your milk and went back to bed. Then when Massa Matt comes in the morning, Jenny'll say you had a bad night. They let ya sleep until real late. Only, ya won't be there."

Amy paled. "I forgot about Matt coming back tomorrow. When there's no one to fix his breakfast or fetch his bath, he'll know something is up."

Emma patted Amy's arm. "Chile, I done tol' Jenny to do all that. It ain't that unusual for me to help some of the field hands. I done it all afore." Emma let herself out the door with a stern message, "Ya rest, and don't worry."

Aunt Elizabeth returned early in the evening and stopped by to see how Amy was feeling. "Amy, child, you seem tense. Is everything all right?"

Once more, Amy panicked. Did she suspect something? "It's waiting for word from my brother, Aunt Elizabeth. He should have sent word weeks ago. I know Phillip doesn't want me here, but I can't go

140

home until Henry writes."

Aunt Elizabeth nodded her head; she seemed satisfied with Amy's explanation. "I'm having Emma fix me a supper tray. Why don't I have her fix you one as well? What you need is rest, I imagine. Matt will be back tomorrow and I want you alert and fresh when he comes to talk to you. In fact, why don't you sleep late? Matt won't get here until late morning, and you can stay abed until he's had his breakfast."

Smiling encouragingly, she walked to the door, turned, and added softly, "If you need anything, Jenny will fetch me. Emma is going to help one of the field hands for the next day or two."

Minutes later Emma arrived with Amy's tray. "Don't take nothing with ya. I got everything ready. Just come downstairs after dark," she cautioned softly.

Amy pushed the tidbits around on her plate for several minutes and then gave up trying to eat. Her stomach was in knots. Finally the sun started to set, and it was time to slip into her nightgown. She checked Aunt Elizabeth's shawl and the note wrapped in it, then decided to place Matt's note in the box that held the pearls he had given her. She removed the pearls and fastened them around her neck and tucked them under her gown. They had been a gift, she thought. Perhaps she could trade or sell them on the road for needed supplies or medicine during the trip north. They would need money, and after all, the pearls were hers.

Amy sank down on her bed and waited, her heart beating loudly in the quiet house. Leaning toward the door, she listened for footsteps that would warn of the approach of Aunt Elizabeth. She strained to catch the arrival of a horse or carriage that would sound the return of Matt or Phillip and the end of her flight to freedom before it ever started. She heard only the early spring winds rustling through the willow trees. Amy imagined that they sounded sad and were crying for her. Pulling herself together, she whispered, "Nonsense, you're getting morbid." Jacob had chosen the night well, she realized, as the shadows lengthened and melted together. There was no moon tonight, and it was dark. If their absence was discovered, the pursuers would have to wait until morning to search for their trail.

At length Amy rose from her bed. With shaking fingers she secured the buttons of her robe. It was time. Jacob and Emma were risking much to take her along. By themselves they would not be found out until late the next day, but with her, their escape would be discovered much earlier. She looked at her bed. If it looked as though she were still asleep, she might buy them more time. Arranging the pillows to look as if she were curled up in the big bed, she covered them with her quilt. Then she took a deep breath and walked to the door.

She glanced back at the bed and giggled nervously. It did look as though someone was sleeping in the bed. She squared her shoulders and cautiously made her way down to the kitchen. There, Emma, a cloak wrapped around her, was preparing a basket. Jenny was sitting at the end of the table and sipping a cup of tea.

"I can't sleep. I came for a cup of warm milk," Amy muttered.

"I'll fix it." Emma sighed and removed her cloak. She grabbed for a pot from the beams overhead. "You go see to Messa Elton," she ordered Jenny. Jenny shrugged her shoulders and left the room. Quickly, Emma put the pot back where it belonged. She pushed Amy toward the small bedroom door as she whispered, "Hurry."

Once in Opal Mae's old room, Emma closed the door and then reached under the bed. She handed Amy a dress and laid a pair of boots and a cloak on the bed. "Give me yer gown and robe," she muttered softly. Amy quickly removed the gown and robe and with shaking hands, she gave them to Emma. As Amy slipped on the dress, Emma rolled the nightwear into a small ball and pushed it into a corner under the bed. She handed Amy the boots. Amy struggled with the heavy shoes, but her fingers shook so badly that she looked at Emma with tears of frustration and breathed, "I can't seem to lace them." Emma knelt down and quickly laced the boots; then she shoved the cloak at Amy and pushed her out the door and into the blackness of the night.

They moved along the edge of the house, and Emma, in the lead, pulled a terrified Amy behind her. They crept between the willows and the road toward the houses of the slaves. As they reached the last shack, a tall thin form sneaked out from behind the small house. The dark man hugged Emma quietly and then turned to whisper a quiet greeting to Amy. "Hello, Miss Amy."

Amy threw her arms around his thin shoulders and whispered in return. "I'm so glad to see you, Jacob."

"We go," he whispered and started toward the woods that lay to the west of the house. Amy was still shaking so badly that Jacob leaned toward her and placing an arm around her waist, he supported and propelled her for several yards until her feet began to move under their own power. He moved ahead and then stopped and listened. Amy listened, too, but all she heard was the braying of a donkey in the distance. They moved forward again, and the cracking of twigs underfoot sounded like small explosions to Amy.

They traveled as rapidly as they could throughout the murky night. Jacob seemed to be able to see in the dark, and Amy was certain he had a definite destination in mind as he pushed both women forward. At length the eastern sky began to lighten, and Amy wondered if they would stop for the day as the slave agents had on the trip south. But no, Jacob pressed on through the pine forests and crawled through the edges of harvested cotton fields. By mid-morning Amy was so tired that she thought she would drop. Jacob had allowed them only a short rest the few times they stopped, but that had not been often enough, Amy thought.

When she felt she could go no further, she told Jacob, "Go. Go on without me. I can't make it."

In answer he pointed through the trees up ahead, to what looked like a clearing. "There. We stop there."

Somehow, Amy managed to cover that last stretch under her own power, and finally, she stood before a small, deserted cabin.

Jacob smiled down at the two exhausted women. "Now — we sleep."

Inside the little shack were several ragged straw pallets and a crude table. There were no chairs or stove. Amy guessed that its sole function was to serve as a resting place for slaves on the road to freedom. If she hadn't been too tired to talk, she would have asked Jacob why the shack had not been discovered and destroyed by the plantation owners. As it was, she sank down on one of the straw mats and fell instantly asleep.

They must have slept all day, for it was dark when they woke. Amy watched by the light of a small candle as Emma pulled bread and sausage, dried fruit and nuts from the basket she had brought. Amy felt reassured. Emma and Jacob had planned well, and their escape from Willows would succeed. As she thought about Willows, she wondered how Matt had taken the discovery that she was gone. Would he blame Aunt Elizabeth? She could almost hear his furious words. Had the search for them begun? She had no doubt that Matt would spend any amount of time and money to find her and put her in prison. Only when she reached Indiana would she be safe. But would Henry be in jail? At least she had relatives who would help her—if she could get to them.

Emma shook Amy out of her reverie. "Time to leave," she said, and the three fugitives set off into the dark night once again.

It was still early when Matt halted his tired horse before the stables of Willows. He had left before dawn to get back to the plantation. "Where's Emma?" he asked as he spotted Jenny starting the preparations for breakfast.

"She go to help Maude's man. He been hurt two

145

days ago. She say she be gone at least one whole day and maybe longer."

"When did she leave?" Matt poured himself a cup of hot black coffee.

"She go last night, just afore Missus Elizabeth and Miss Amy go to bed." She started for the door. "She tell me what I'se got to do. If'n ya want, ya can have your breakfast."

Matt stood up and brushed the travel dust from his jacket. A change of clothes would be welcome, he thought, as he followed Jenny from the room. After breakfast, he would talk to Amy.

On his way back downstairs for the breakfast Jenny had waiting, Matt paused at Amy's door. He listened and then shook his head. He would just have to wait until she was awake to talk to her. Anyway, he needed to discuss his plans with his aunt before he made his plans known to Amy.

He was on his fourth cup of coffee when Aunt Elizabeth stepped into the dining room.

"Why, Matt, I didn't expect you for several hours yet. Not out pounding the local countryside, I see." She laughed. "Tell me, are you going to stay here and keep an old lady company for a change?"

Matt looked up at her pensively; then he rose and helped her into her chair, "Now, Aunt Elizabeth, you know I had to leave while Phillip was here. And I couldn't return until I was sure he was gone." He paused and took his seat once more. "I have a favor to ask though. How would you like a house guest for several days, perhaps a week or two? I could move both you and Amy to your estate today, if you agree." Matt glanced out the doorway, then muttered almost to himself, "Phillip wants her gone from Willows."

Aunt Elizabeth nodded vigorously. "You know I would love to have her."

"I've decided to take her to her home, too. Of course, she can't travel by herself, not with all the trouble brewing, but until she learns to trust me and tells me where she lives, she can stay with you. It may take some time before I can convince her she has nothing to fear from me." Matt grinned sheepishly at his aunt. "And I really don't know yet whether I want her to go home."

"Why, Matt," she asked, smiling broadly, "are you falling for the little Northern flower?"

"Just might be, Aunt Elizabeth, just might be," Matt replied softly, his dark eyes warm.

In a more serious tone, Aunt Elizabeth leaned toward him. "I do agree that we have to get her out of this house, and as soon as possible. She has been so depressed lately that I'm afraid she'll become truly ill. Phillip is a bad influence on us all. However, young man," she said, grinning at him, "I will gladly take Amy into my home, but you will have to find another place to stay. Imagine what my friends would say if I let you move in, too?"

"Would you care?" he asked as he rose from the table, grinning in return. "I'll have Jenny take breakfast up to her, and then you can invite her. In the meantime, I'll see if I can find a wagon big enough to cart all your belongings home," he said teasingly.

After going to the kitchen to instruct Jenny, he returned to the dining room and began discussing their immediate plans as Jenny went up the stairs, loaded with a breakfast tray. In a few minutes she came run-

147

ning down, dashed for the dining room, and stopped at the doorway. Wringing her hands, she sobbed, "Oh . . . Massa Matt, oh . . ."

Matt stared at the weeping girl for several seconds, then jumped to his feet. In three strides he stood before her. "What is it, Jenny? What's wrong? Is she ill?"

"Oh . . . Massa Matt, oh . . ."

The color faded from Matt's face. He pushed the girl out of his way. Taking the steps three at a time, he tore up the staircase. Without hesitation, he burst through the door. The carefully laid pillows were lying in the middle of the bed, and the quilt and coverlet were pulled aside. He scanned the bed, then glanced around the room. He stood there shaking, the evidence before him having not yet registered.

Aunt Elizabeth followed him into the room. "Oh, no!" she gasped. "I should have seen this coming."

Matt wheeled around and yelled for the slave, who had also followed them up the stairs. "Jenny, go find Emma," he barked.

"Emma won't be there, Matt. Amy would never have tried this alone." Aunt Elizabeth sank down into the chair by the dressing table and stared at the bed. Jenny had already flown at Matt's command.

Pale and shaken, Matt turned back to look at his aunt, "Two women, one white and one black, traveling alone . . ." His voice trailed off. "Why couldn't she have waited—waited one more day? You told her that we would talk today, didn't you?"

"Yes, I told her." Aunt Elizabeth smoothed her skirt nervously. "But something has been bothering her for quite a while. She seemed overly disturbed about something for the last two weeks. Did you say anything to upset her?"

Matt slurred his response. "I haven't said a thing to her for weeks, not a word."

"Well, that just might be part of the problem," she ventured softly, apparently in deep thought.

Matt stared at his aunt. He didn't understand her words at all. How could his not saying anything to the girl cause her to run off? He snapped, "Check and see what she took, and I'll get a horse ready. I'll have to go after her."

Matt left the room, and Aunt Elizabeth searched the wardrobe. She soon found the shawl and Amy's carefully worded thank-you. As she read it, she brushed the tears from her eyes. Truly she had failed the girl if Amy felt escape from Willows was her only course of action. As she continued searching, she rummaged through the dressing table and found the sealed note addressed to Matt in the empty pearl box. She made her way down to the library, wondering as she went, why the pearls, why did Amy take the pearls.

Matt was waiting for her when she got to the library. Handing him the two notes, she said sadly, "She didn't take any of her dresses. The only things missing are the robe I gave her and one of her nightgowns. She did take the pearls you gave her."

Matt stood staring at both pieces of paper for several minutes before he broke open his note. He sank into a chair and read the carefully penned words.

Thank you for treating me with such courtesy. After the New Year's Eve ball, I had hoped that we might become better friends, but I realize that that is not possible now. I can't thank you enough for intervening for me with your brother when I first arrived. I also want you to know that although it may take some time, I will pay you back for everything you provided.

He folded the note several times before he mumbled, "She says that she'll pay me back."

He was visibly shaken, but he read the second note and then gazed up at his aunt, his eyes suspiciously wet.

"I don't even know her name. I don't know where her home is, I can't even write to her damn brother!" Matt collapsed back into the leather chair, the note clutched in his hand. His face was grim and ashen from shock. Gradually he managed to collect his thoughts and leaned forward.

"Jenny was on that first run for freedom, wasn't she? Maybe Jenny knows where Amy came from. At least she should be able to tell where the agents caught them."

"I doubt that she knows, Matt," Aunt Elizabeth replied softly. "Jenny is not the brightest of Phillip's girls."

"I'll talk to Jenny, as soon as she gets back," he continued as if Aunt Elizabeth had said nothing.

They waited together until Jenny returned with the news that they both half-expected. Emma had never arrived at the cabin of the injured slave. In fact, no one had seen or heard from her all day. Matt interrogated Jenny for a half-hour, but she had no information other than about the supper trays and Amy's milk.

Matt paced the library as he thought out loud. "They can't be more than twenty to twenty-five miles from Willows, not if they left at dark." Matt's excitement cooled. "Unless they took one of the mules or the horses." He paused for a moment; he had no idea whether Amy could ride or not. He sent one of the younger slaves scurrying out to the stable to bring the overseer to the house. The man arrived quickly, for word had already spread that the white girl and one female slave had disappeared.

The frown on Matt's face deepened as he listened to the news; not one animal from either of the barns was missing. If they left the estate, they had gone on foot. Matt sent the overseer out to look for a trail.

He grimly commented to Aunt Elizabeth, "Well, at least Phillip can't accuse her of horse stealing," and headed for the stairs.

Gathering several changes of clothing, he went down to the kitchen for some food. Aunt Elizabeth helped him pack his supplies in his saddlebags, and by the time Matt was ready to leave, the overseer had returned and his report was gloomy.

"That black girl knowed what she was doing, Mister Treadwell. There ain't no sign of which way they went. They could have gone south, for all I know."

Aunt Elizabeth joined Matt on the porch to wait for his horse. Jenny also joined the group, and by this time, she was weeping in earnest. When the horse arrived, Matt took the reins and mounted his stallion. Jenny pushed forward, around Aunt Elizabeth and approached Matt.

"Massa Matt, I is not supposed to know, I should not tell ya, and ya must not tell Massa Phillip . . ." The black girl stopped sobbing long enough to explain as she leaned toward Matt. She whispered so softly

151

that Matt had to lean down from his horse to hear her.

"Jacob, he come back. He come get Emma, I seen 'im. Jacob is with 'em, Massa Matt. Jacob, he's with 'em."

Matt looked down into her frightened face. He breathed a sigh of relief. At least they weren't traveling alone. "I won't tell, Jenny. Just pray that I find them."

He turned back to Aunt Elizabeth, who now stood with tears rolling down her cheeks. "I'll get word back to you," Matt promised, his voice husky with emotion.

"Matt." Her voice broke. "Send word no matter what. Even if you have nothing to tell me, send a note that you've found nothing. I must know."

Chapter Ten

Matt glanced back at Willows and the small congregation gathered on the porch, then headed west, his spare mount trotting behind. By traveling northwest, he was able to stop at three plantations before darkness called a halt to his search. The owners of the farms, though sympathetic, had no information for him. Matt talked to their slaves, but they all responded, "No, suh, no, suh," to all of his questions.

As he traveled, he stopped at several small towns along his route, but no one had seen the trio. He also stopped at small farms that had no slaves. The responses were always the same. No one had seen the chestnut-haired beauty or her black traveling companions. He sent two messages back to Aunt Elizabeth, as he had promised. His first note offered little hope, and his second note was filled with despair.

At the end of the second week, he admitted he was getting nowhere and was only wasting his time. Amy and Emma—and Jacob, if Jenny was correct—had either taken an indirect route, or they had been captured by someone who knew nothing of the Treadwells. He turned his horses around and headed back to Willows.

On the ride back, Matt tried to reconstruct every conversation he had had with Phillip. Nothing his brother had said indicated that he knew where Amy was from. The one slave Matt had traveled to see had told him they were captured by two men who worked for Phillip. Ned had explained that Phillip had fired the two when they arrived in Kentucky. Suddenly, Matt had a solution. If Phillip didn't know where Amy was from, the two men he had hired should know where they found the slaves and Amy. His heart beat rapidly. He had to get back to Willows, and Phillip had to help him find those slave agents.

Pushing his horses as rapidly as he dared, he raced back to the plantation. He was certain he could find Amy's brother, or at least the family, even if it turned out that she lived in the most populous area of the state. Such a beautiful woman would surely have been noticed by the male population. Finding her home should not be too difficult, once he knew in what area she lived.

As he rode, he thought about Amy's brother. Would Henry help? There had been no message for Amy. He had checked with the clerk himself. Her letter had been sent the day she posted it. "Damn," he muttered. He should have asked to see where the letter was addressed.

Late in the afternoon in mid-March, Matt returned, tired and disgusted. He hadn't found a trace of the three escapees. Aunt Elizabeth was waiting for him, and he shook his head to say there was nothing. He sat and told her of his trip and all the stops he had made. Several times he had to pause to clear his husky voice and wipe the wetness from his eyes. "They seemed to have disappeared," he added, his head lowered in dejection.

"I have to talk to Phillip," he commented gruffly. He told her of his plans to follow Amy north and enlist the aid of her brother when he found him. "If she's back with her family"—his voice grew firmer, and his eyes brightened—"Then I'll stay and court her properly. If she isn't there, I'll have to convince her brother to help me trace her. You see," he tried to explain, a tired little smile on his lips, "I think I've fallen for that girl. I have to find out, and to find out, I'll have to find her!"

Aunt Elizabeth gazed at him with tears in her eyes. "You'll be gone for some time then?"

"I'm afraid I may be gone for several months, maybe even longer." Matt stretched and rubbed his hand over his week-old beard. "I haven't bathed or shaved for several days. I was pushing to get back here as soon as I could. Now I must talk to Phillip." His face turned grim. He glanced around the parlor. "Where is he anyway?"

"He went to town to check the mail. He's been going almost every day. He should be returning soon."

"Checking the mail?" Matt couldn't keep the astonishment from his voice. Slaves usually brought the mail to the plantation.

"I'm sure that he feels responsible for Amy's disappearance. He's afraid, I think, that her relatives will send word before they arrive. He wants to be prepared."

Matt tried to digest that piece of information as he

excused himself and made his way to his room. He shrugged. Dealing with his brother was difficult enough without a crisis, but now he would need to have himself in control. And confidence, he needed his confidence to demand that Phillip tell him what he wanted to know. The bath and shave should help restore his sagging spirits, he thought to himself. At least, they would give him time to pull himself together before facing his older brother.

Phillip arrived just minutes after Matt had disappeared upstairs, but he knew his brother had already arrived, having spotted Matt's horses in the stable. As he made his way to the kitchen, he decided to meet the matter head on and ordered Jenny to tell Matt that he would be waiting for him in the library. Then he looked for Aunt Elizabeth. Matt was younger and stronger than he was, and he tended to become violent when he lost his temper. With Aunt Elizabeth in attendance, Matt might exercise some control.

Aunt Elizabeth was in the drawing room, and Phillip asked her to join him in the library. "I would really like you present when I talk to Matt."

She followed him into the comfortable room and accepted his offer of a glass of sherry. Tight-lipped, she said softly, "I have no intention of acting as a referee between the two of you."

She watched with reservations as Phillip's lips thinned and whitened, and she added for good measure, "There will be no shouting!" She gazed at her older nephew as she settled back into the leather chair to wait for Matt.

As Matt headed for the library, his blond hair still wet from his bath, he promised himself he wouldn't lose his temper and would stay calm until he had the information he wanted.

Unexpectedly, Phillip greeted him cordially as he came through the door, "Would you like a brandy? Aunt Elizabeth is having sherry."

Matt accepted the liquor, a frown playing across his face. Phillip was being very pleasant, much too pleasant. Obviously, he was delighted that Amy had run away. Phillip's voice forced Matt to attention.

"There was nothing at the post office again." He continued in a sermonizing voice. "I think you both should realize that the girl was not who or what she said she was."

Aunt Elizabeth opened her mouth to object, but Phillip went on.

"Now, I don't want to belabor the point, but four months ago, she wrote a letter to her home, supposedly. We haven't heard a word. Not a word. If she had any relatives, which I doubt, they care nothing for the girl. If they ever show up, we'll just have to tell them that we sent her home weeks ago. There's no way they can blame us if the girl decided to go another route after we started her on her way."

Aunt Elizabeth gasped and sagged further into her chair. "Phillip, that poor girl may never get home, and whether you like it or not, it's our fault."

"Nonsense! It is not our fault. I saved her from God knows what when I fired those agents. I brought her here, fed, and clothed her, and in gratitude she took off the first chance she got. No, I've decided that if her relatives ever do show up, we'll say we sent her home."

Matt raised his head in a daze. "What do you mean, you clothed her? *I* clothed her. You should have sent

157

her home when you found her, but no! You had to drag her here on a phony excuse that she pay you back for the money you spent looking for the slaves. What did you think you would do with her when you got her here, brother? Did you plan to make her your mistress? Did she refuse you?"

"Matt!" Aunt Elizabeth said with a gasp.

Matt took a deep breath. He glanced at his aunt and then back at Phillip. "Right now, *brother*, I would like nothing better than to beat you to a pulp! I'm not going to do that." Matt straightened in his chair. "What I am going to do is take Aunt Elizabeth home. Then I'm going north. And you're going to tell me where to go. Then I'm going to find her brother. Together, we'll find her, if she's alive. And Phillip, she had better be." Matt was shaking. "Phillip, where did she come from?"

Phillip shifted uncomfortably in his chair, "Now, Matt, let's be reasonable. You really don't know anything about her. She could be after your money or even this plantation—"

Matt was out of his chair and on top of him before Phillip could finish his sentence. "Where did she come from, damn you? Where is her home? What have you done to her relatives, you bastard?" Matt shook Phillip by the neck.

Aunt Elizabeth was out of her chair. "Matt—Matthew! Stop this at once!"

Matt released his hold, and Phillip slumped back into the chair, his face pale. He put his hand up to his throat. "You could have killed me!"

"Don't you think I won't. Now, tell me what I want to know."

Phillip continued to stare at Matt as he rubbed his

158

throat.

"Phillip, where did she come from?"

Phillip glanced at Aunt Elizabeth and then at his younger brother's angry red face towering over him. "All right! The agents told me they caught the slaves before they reached Westfield. They figured she had to live around Anderson."

"Anderson?" Matt said in disbelief.

"Anderson, Indiana," Phillip repeated. "Westfield is just a little northwest of Anderson. Ironic, isn't it."

"You son of a b— You've known all along, haven't you? What have you done to her family? Is that why she's heard nothing? Did you set the law on her relatives?"

"I've done nothing to her family. Nothing! I don't even know her family name."

Matt rushed out of the room, heading for the stairs. Phillip jumped up out of his chair and charged to the door, yelling as Matt took the stairs two at a time, "You fool! You don't know anything about her."

Matt turned. "It doesn't matter," he said with finality. He started up the steps once more, shouting to his aunt, "Come on, Aunt Elizabeth. Let's get your things together. If we leave now, we can get to Elton Estate before dark."

Aunt Elizabeth glanced back at Phillip as she started for the guest room she had occupied for the past months. She sighed. They couldn't be friends, not now, perhaps never.

Within the hour, everything Matt had given Amy was gathered, and the boxes and trunks were loaded into the waiting carriage. Aunt Elizabeth packed her own things while Matt gathered most of his personal

159

items. His horses were saddled, and he ordered one of the older slaves to accompany them so that the carriage could be returned the next day. Matt refused to say good-bye to Phillip even though Aunt Elizabeth pleaded with him.

As they traveled back to Aunt Elizabeth's farm, they both rode in silence. Aunt Elizabeth sat alone in the carriage, and Matt rode one of his horses. Both were completely engrossed in their own thoughts.

Shortly after dusk, they pulled up in front of Elton Estate. Matt looked out over the farm, a smaller version of Willows, for Elton Estate stood on the banks of the Savannah River. It was built on a rise, high above the water so that the spring floods would not ruin the house. The long, sloping lawns were beautifully manicured, and a warmth radiated about the place. The personality of the woman who called it home was everywhere. Matt leaned back in his saddle and relaxed as he watched the smiling faces of her slaves rush out to greet their returning mistress.

Matt saw to the unloading of the carriage while Aunt Elizabeth discussed the property with her servants. She ordered a light supper for the two of them, and in soft tones, she directed the preparation of a guest room for Matt. Her servants quickly carried Amy's things up to another guest room, next to Matt's. Long after the sun set, Matt came in from the stable and joined his aunt for a late supper. They ate in comfortable silence.

After supper, Matt raised his head and looked over at his aunt. "I hope you don't mind, but I seem to have invited myself into your home."

"I would have insisted that you come here after I saw

you almost strangle Phillip. Whatever possessed you?"

Matt lowered his eyes and answered in a shaky voice. "I don't know. All of a sudden, I realized what a scoundrel he was, and I was certain at the time that he had done something to her family. I just wanted to stop his lying mouth permanently."

"Promise me," she begged, "that you'll make no attempt to see him again, for a while at least."

"Oh, I won't see him, at least not until after I've found Amy. Then . . ." His voice trailed off. Matt gave himself a shake as if trying to remove Phillip from his mind. He continued. "I won't have time to talk to him anyway. I have to get instructions to my foreman in Texas. Then I'll need to talk to the postmaster. I want you to get any mail directed to Amy. I also think I better find out something about Anderson, Indiana. I'll have to get clothes and supplies together for an extended trip. I want to be ready to leave in a day or two."

"You're going then?" she questioned, already knowing the answer.

Matt only nodded his head as he unwound his tall frame from the dining room chair. He leaned over and pecked his aunt on the cheek. "I'll see you in the morning. I want to get an early start, so I'll say good night." He left the room as she gazed, unseeing, into the cup of tea on the table in front of her.

It took all of four days for Matt to accomplish everything to his satisfaction before he left for Indiana. He made no attempt to see or talk to Phillip, and his brother made no attempt contact him. Smiling grimly, Matt thought that it was a good thing that he had his own source of income now. Phillip had no hold over him this time. Matt even gave serious thought to seeing his lawyer and disavowing any claim to the estate of Willows.

The night before he left, Matt and Aunt Elizabeth retired to the spacious study after dinner for a long talk. For a few minutes, Aunt Elizabeth sat quietly, trying to put her thoughts in order. When she spoke, she voiced her fears.

"I'm afraid of what you might find when you arrive in Indiana. Amy's brother may decide to shoot you without giving you a chance to explain, especially if she's not there. Then, again, if she is there and she has described her treatment at Phillip's hand, he may fire on you at the mention of your name."

Matt grinned at her sheepishly and shrugged his shoulders. She continued as if she was thinking out loud."

"You are a Southerner. They are going to be hostile. I doubt that they'll even discuss the underground railway system with you. Remember, your brother owns slaves, and he was responsible for Amy's kidnapping. If she's not there, however, the underground system may be the only way you'll find her. If her brother refuses to give you information, what will you do?" She paused in her speculation. "Are you sure she's worth all of this?"

Matt only nodded his head. As they sat quietly, Matt, digesting the words Aunt Elizabeth had spoken, realized that neither one of them could mention his or her fears. They were both assuming that Amy could not have arrived at her home yet, or that she would not have arrived by the time Matt got there.

For another hour, Matt described his plans, the route he would take, the arrangements he had made, and what he wanted of his aunt while he was gone. "My greatest fear is that Phillip will hire more agents and send them after the runaways. If they should find Amy, Jacob, and Emma before I do . . ." He could not go on.

Aunt Elizabeth offered what comfort she could. "I'm sure that Phillip will think twice about trying that this time. He nows you're going after the girl." She sat quietly thinking before she asked, "Is there something you want me to do?"

Matt shook his head. With everything in readiness, they ascended the stairs together and said good night.

Shortly after dawn the next day, Aunt Elizabeth, still in her nightcap and wrapped in a warm woolen robe, saw Matt off. "I'll be waiting for you both." She kissed him on the cheek and hugged him tightly, "Go with God!"

Matt rode off into the gray dawn with promises of frequent letters hanging in the still, cold morning air.

Amy, Emma, and Jacob slowly made their way through the forests and into the mountains, moving toward the northwest. The basket of food Emma had brought with them lasted for almost a week. With that source depleted, Jacob delved into the sack he carried over his shoulder. Amy was delighted to see the assortment of knives, fishhooks, and other necessary items.

For the first week, they had avoided building a fire for their evening meal. They added what fruits and nuts they could find to the contents of Emma's basket. On several of the larger plantations they passed, the slaves fed them.

163

As the items in the basket dwindled, Amy offered to slip into a nearby town and exchange her pearls for food. Jacob was almost severe in his condemnation. "You does that, and we'll have all of Willows down on us. We is too close. Somebody might get mighty curious. And no lady travels alone. It just ain't done. No, them pearls ain't to be used for a long time, maybe never."

Once they got to the mountains, they built a fire and Jacob started fishing. Except in the worst weather, the slave was able to provide enough to keep them going. Once he stole a chicken and some eggs as they passed a small farm.

The days dissolved into weeks. They were making progress. At first they had traveled only at night, but as they reached the mountains, Jacob assured them they could travel during the day. It was much colder in the mountains, and travel became more than difficult. Often, Amy found herself wondering why she had agreed to this dangerous scheme. Then she would remind herself of the prison term that awaited her in South Carolina, and she would forge ahead, certain that this was her only course of action.

On the days when cold spring rains threatened, they stopped in one of the many caves that crisscrossed the mountains. Jacob would scrounge around until he found enough dry sticks and bark to build a fire. Then they huddled close together, trying to absorb the warmth from the tiny flames.

As they traveled, Jacob kept assuring the two women that many of the common folk of Tennessee did not tolerate slavery. And some of those would be more than happy to provide shelter, food, and trans-

164

portation to any slaves who passed on their way north. Once they got to the center of Tennessee, their walking journey would be at an end. Jacob knew of a brother and sister . . . Slowly, they made their way through the mountains.

As Amy and her companions began their trek into the mountains, Henry, full of despair, returned to the Indiana farm. For four months, he had traveled back and forth across the routes taken by the underground railroad, looking for the tiniest piece of information that might lead him to his sister but found nothing. All the days, all the hours, all the minutes, and there was nothing. She seemed to have disappeared from the face of the earth. He had even gone north into Michigan to talk to the last group that Amy led successfully across the farm, but no one knew a thing.

He visited his older brother. Poor Alex was forced to stay in school while their sister wandered about. Even the news of South Carolina's defection from the Union didn't dissipate the gloom that hung over the two brothers.

Henry clearly remembered the day, months before, when a tragic figure had stood outside the dean's office. Uncle Jeb, his shoulders hunched forward, his face drawn, had waited to tell him about Amy's disappearance. Henry had left school that day, and he had met with the members of the underground that he knew. The word had gone out. Amy Sanderson had been kidnapped. Henry left Indiana in less than a week to begin his own search. But there had been no word, none at all, and while he traveled, the family waited, praying.

The minute he walked into the farmhouse, he knew there had been word, and from the smiles spreading across Uncle Jeb and Aunt Amelia's faces, it was good news.

Henry grabbed at the letter Aunt Amelia waved in his face. Amy was in South Carolina. She was safe, and she wanted to come home. Henry felt like falling to his knees to give thanks. He had a thousand questions, but he grinned as he hugged first his aunt and then his uncle. Amy could explain everything when they were reunited.

Quickly, he composed a short note, addressing it as she had requested, and then packed his saddlebags once more. Kissing his aunt good-bye, he assured his uncle that he would have Amy home in a short time, two months at the most.

Henry had trouble containing his exuberance. His sister was all right. She was safe, and he knew where she was. The horse couldn't travel fast enough to suit him, there weren't enough hours in the day, and the weather could have been better, but he was on his way to fetch Amy.

Delighted with the time he was making, Henry congratulated himself. He reached Kentucky in four days.

He traveled through Kentucky and into Tennessee with an anxious eye on the sky. The cold, wet, blustery weather now slowed him down. He left Nashville and started east in mid-April. The day dawned cold and gray, and as the minutes became hours, the blowing wind started to howl. Great gray clouds boiled across the sky. Keeping an eye on the weather, he made slow progress.

By midday, there was very little light, and the wind, blowing out of the northeast, heralded a fierce storm. He had no choice, he told himself in disgust, he had to stop until the storm had passed.

At Tucker's Crossroads, he inquired about an inn. The two people he asked assured him that there was an inn bearing the same name as the town and he was in luck, for the inn was famous across the state. He would find an excellent meal, a clean room, and a worthy host and hostess to see to his every need. After receiving directions, he plodded on, continually repeating to himself, he had to stop, he had no choice. Even his horse couldn't travel through a nor'easter.

Chapter Eleven

For four weeks Amy, Emma, and Jacob struggled across the mountains and through the Cumberland Gap toward Nashville. Twice they were forced to stop and wait out a savage spring storm. Both Emma and Amy were much thinner, and by the end of the third week they were exhausted. Amy began to doubt seriously that she would survive.

Jacob tried to encourage them by telling about the place they were headed for, Tucker's Inn outside of Nashville. There would be food, Jacob said, and clothes and a wagon for the trip north. All they had to do was get to Tucker's Inn. Once there, Benjamin Tucker, the proprietor, would take over. He had been helping slaves on their way north for years. He would take care of them.

To keep their spirits up, Jacob told them about Molly Tucker, younger sister of Benjamin. She was a bit of a rebel, Jacob explained, and not the Southern kind. Molly Tucker took any kind of risk to help slaves. As Amy listened, she echoed his words, just get to Tucker's Inn.

The only life they saw was on the small farms set deep in the hills and far apart. There were no slaves on the small farms, no help for the fugitives as they struggled on. Jacob wouldn't let them approach the farms in case the tenants might turn them over to the authorities for the rewards posted for runaway slaves.

Amy thought of the pearls tucked in Emma's basket. Even if Jacob let her trade them for food, there was no place she could find a buyer. So she trudged after Jacob, hour after hour, day after day, wondering how much longer she could go on.

The last week of their flight was unbearable. It turned very cold, and they had to travel through a violent spring snowstorm. Game was scarce, and they could hardly see the ground in front of them. Amy pulled her cloak around her and shuddered. Would they ever make it to Tucker's Inn? Her face was gaunt, and her blue-gray eyes carried an expression akin to deep despair. Her hair was matted and dirty, and her arms and legs bore countless cuts and scrapes. There were bruises all over her body. Trying to ignore her pain, she pushed onward. When she got home, she told herself, she could rest. She would rest for as long as she wanted.

She watched Jacob and Emma carefully. Despite the fact that they had led a much harder existence as slaves, they were in no better condition than she was. They needed to rest also.

Finally, five weeks and three days after they had stolen away from Willows in the dark of the night, they crept toward Tucker's Inn under a moonless sky. They had managed the first and most difficult part of the

169

journey. Soon, Amy whimpered, they would be home.

It was long after dark when Jacob led the weary women to the back door of the inn. The innkeeper and his sister greeted them and led the way to one of the barns where a room was hidden behind the horse stalls. There were no windows in the large room to let in the light from the stars or the sun of the day. But in spite of the cold night, it was warm, and Amy looked longingly at six pallets lined against the wall. A square oak table with four mismatched chairs stood in the center of the room, and Amy sank into the one closest to the doorway, wondering what would happen next.

Molly and Benjamin Tucker were everywhere that Jacob had said and more. Amy stared at the attractive redhead. She was almost as tall as Amy, and slender with a narrow waist and a full bosom. Her soft almond-shaped eyes were the color of a deep green lake. She is probably several years older than I, Amy thought, but Molly had an almost childlike face with a voice to match, and Amy could only guess at her age. Amy immediately discovered that Molly, with her happy giggle, laughed at everything.

Ben — he preferred that to Benjamin — was older than his sister by at least ten years. He was as broad as Molly was thin and tall. His long arms ended in large clublike hands that were covered with thick calluses from years of strenuous work. Massive muscles rippled as he moved. His round face sported a bulbous nose that seemed suspended between his full, ruddy cheeks. His thick lips curled up in frequent smiles, and dark curly hair hung over his black eyes in a haphazard manner. Amy thought he was like a friendly, dark lion.

Molly followed Ben to the barn with a tray of

chicken and dumplings, apple pie, and a pitcher of cold, creamy milk. Amy thought she had never eaten anything so good. After they had eaten, Amy and Emma sank into the pallets. Ben conferred with Jacob, saying that it would take two or three days to arrange their transportation north, but they would be safe in the barn as long as they did not venture outside. They could rest and eat and prepare for the last leg of their journey.

"In the morning," he assured Jacob, "Molly will bring breakfast and clothes for all of you." He left, taking the lantern and plunging the room into darkness. Amy was already fast asleep.

Morning came, but the three exhausted travelers slept long into the day. Molly checked twice before there was any recognizable stirrings from any of them. Then she brought a huge breakfast of ham and potatoes, biscuits, and an enormous pot of fresh coffee.

After breakfast she suggested, "I can sneak the ladies into the inn for a bath if they want. It'll take some soaking to get all that dirt off," she said as she eyed Amy with a critical look.

Jacob shook his head. "Not fer Emma, no bath. She can't go into the inn. She'd best stay with me."

Amy couldn't resist the offer. "Oh, how I would love a nice hot bath. Can you get me into the inn without anyone seeing?"

Molly giggled and nodded her head. "After lunch," she said and was gone.

As she had promised, after lunch Molly came for Amy. She led the way to the back of the inn and into a small room no larger than the Willows pantry. In the center was a brass tub filled with the most heavenly

171

thing Amy had seen for weeks. "Hot water," she said with a sigh.

Molly handed Amy soap, a rag with which to wash, and a large square of cotton. "I'll be back with some clean clothes." Once more she giggled and rushed from the room.

Amy pulled off the rags she was wearing and stepped into the tub. As she sank down into the steaming liquid, her cuts and bruises stung, but when the glorious wet warmth had covered her, the stinging disappeared. Amy could feel the strain and tension slipping from her. She closed her eyes, ready to enjoy an hour in paradise.

Molly's giggle alerted Amy that she had company. "Ben says you're a conductor, just like us." Molly moved to the stool in one corner of the room. As she flopped onto the stool, she watched Amy with curiosity. "How on earth did you end up with Jacob and Emma? And what were you doing in South Carolina?"

Amy grimaced. So much for a quiet soaking, she thought. But she smiled at the childlike creature on the stool. "Well, it started one night in October." Amy wrinkled her forehead for a second. "You know, I don't even know what day this is."

Molly smiled gently. "Today is Friday, April twelfth, 1861." Amy shuddered. She had been gone from her home for a long time.

Molly urged her to continue. "Go on, tell me how you came to be in South Carolina."

And Amy explained about the agents, about Phillip, and even a little about Matt. Her eyes filled with tears as she whispered, "I had to run away with Emma and Jacob. Phillip and Matt wanted to send me to

172

prison."

Molly reached out, and with an awkward gesture, she patted Amy's arm. "Don't you worry none. We'll have you home in two or three weeks."

She slid from the stool on which she had perched, exclaiming, "Lordy me, the water's cold, and I've stayed too long. You dress, and I'll sneak you back." Molly danced from the room. Even before Amy had put on the clothing Molly had left, the girl was back with a heavy dark cloak. "We've a real nor'easter coming in. The fog's already so thick you can't see ten feet in front, and the wind is really howling," she whispered as she handed Amy the cloak. Almost to herself, she added, "We'll be busy tonight."

Clean and relaxed for the first time in weeks, Amy hurried back to the barn. She had been gone a long time, and she knew that Emma would be worried sick. Jacob will scold me, she thought.

Emma did not look worried, and Jacob was sitting quietly at the table, holding his wife's hand. Amy felt embarrassed. The three of them had eaten together and slept together for weeks. In all that time, Emma and Jacob had never had a moment alone.

Amy sank down on her pallet, deeply engrossed in thought. Occasionally, she glanced up, blushed, and then stared off into space. Her mind was busy with what Molly had said about the weather, and with Emma and Jacob. They needed to have at least one night without her. She owed them that much at least.

She smiled up at Jacob, sure she had the answer to the difficult situation. "After sleeping under the stars," she began, "this room seems awfully closed in, don't you think? I don't know about you, but after it

173

gets dark enough, I'm going out to the stables and sleep in the hay. It won't seem so confined."

Even to herself, Amy thought the reason she had just given to leave them alone sounded contrived, and she giggled to herself. She was sure that both of the slaves saw right through her, but the look in Jacob's eyes confirmed her suspicions. They did need some time alone.

Heavy fog blanketed the mountains, and cold spring rains fell as Matt traveled north. Tracking through the mountains was slower than he had expected and several times he had had to stop because of foul weather. This trip north, he thought, was taking too long. Once more he was forced to stop for the night. He looked at the calendar in the inn. April twelfth! Amy had been gone for almost six weeks.

The next morning, he was back on the road. It was a dark, dreary dawn, and it had rained the night before, but Matt pushed on. "I'll travel straight through and stop late tomorrow," he mumbled as he pulled his cloak together against the chill wind.

Even as Matt pleaded to the heavens, "Not now!" the gathering darkness and the whining winds from the northeast heralded yet another storm. With the heavens conspiring against him, too, Matt silently cursed his luck. He had no choice but to stop for the night. His horses could not travel through the darkness with nature fighting him at every step. He resolved to stop at the first inn he found in the next town, Tucker's Crossing.

* * *

Henry stopped his horse in front of Tucker's Inn and made his way into the brightly lit main room. Pleased with what he saw, he made arrangements for a room for the night and a hot bath. He reflected that both he and his horse needed a good night's rest. After he bathed, he put on fresh clothes and went to the main room of the inn for ale and a quiet dinner.

The serving room was already filled with guests, and Henry watched a man talking with the buxom hostess, who saw that several pitchers of heady stout found their way to the man's place.

Henry sat at one end of a long table and enjoyed his excellent meal while he amused himself with watching the seduction scene at the other end of the room. The red-headed girl was trying hard to persuade a tall, muscular man with light curly hair to join her. Henry chuckled, for it was usually the other way around. Fascinated, Henry watched as pitcher after pitcher of stout disappeared. The man seemed so disinterested and the maid was trying so hard, Henry wondered if her intent was to get the man drunk.

Molly was indeed trying to get the handsome stranger drunk. She judged him a man who would make an excellent bed partner for the night. Sighing, she watched as he lifted the glass to his mouth. It was enough to make a girl wonder. Letting her eyes travel over Matt — for it was he — she giggled softly to herself. This man was indeed handsome, and he definitely needed her company, even if he didn't know it. She offered quietly, "After the dinner guests have eaten, I'll meet you in the barn. You should check on your horses. As soon as I finish here, I'll join you."

Once more Matt spoke in protest, slurring his words, decidedly. "No, ma'am, I'll just go to bed. I've got to sleep."

Molly smiled down at him sweetly. "Check on your horses. I'll be waiting."

Matt finished his drink and started up to his door. He told himself, as he moved up the stairs, that the stout had had little effect and smiled grimly as he tried to put the key into the lock of his room. Well, almost no effect. Perhaps now he could sleep.

He finally succeeded in unlocking the door and stumbled toward the bed. Without removing his clothes, he sank into the softness as images of a tall, slim chestnut-haired creature danced across his mind. Banishing her face, he willed himself to sleep. As he drifted into a restless dream, the girl disappeared.

Suddenly, she returned. He saw her first struggling through the fog, and then she was alone and asleep on a pile of pine boughs, her glorious hair spread out around her. In the craggy slopes above her, with bared fangs and saliva dripping from their open mouths, two mountain cats crouched. They were quickly replaced by men announcing that they were agents. All of the perils that he had tried so hard to ignore consciously surfaced in his dream. Dangers that he had refused to acknowledge during his waking hours now paraded across his fevered brain.

Abruptly, he awoke. He sprang from the bed, sweat pouring down his cheeks. His back and arms were wet. He could not allow himself to sleep again; his dreams would destroy his sanity.

As he stood beside his bed, he remembered his horses. The maid had insisted that he check on them. She had told him something else, but his tired brain couldn't remember what. Something about meeting him, he thought. He rubbed his hand across his brow, trying to clear away the cotton in his brain. Did she have some special power to see how tortured he was? Was she offering herself for the moment, so that he could forget. He should never have consumed as much liquor as he had, he berated himself.

His thinking wasn't too clear, but he knew that he had to get out of the room. He had to get away from the bed and the vivid dreams his sleep conjured up. Perhaps the serving wench was the answer. As he washed his face and hands and smoothed his clothes, he rationalized by thinking he must care for his horses. Both animals would be necessary if he was to get to Amy's brother in Anderson. Yes, he would check on his horses. Perhaps the spring wind would clear his head. He made his way out the room and down the stairs.

Matt went directly into the main room of the inn to find the proprietor, and he looked around to see if the attractive redhead was at hand. Neither Mr. Tucker nor the redhead were there, and Matt made his way past the kitchen, scanning the halls and the kitchen itself.

Ben Tucker was just returning from the barn when Matt caught him at the back entryway. "I'll need a lantern," Matt mumbled. "I want to check on my horses before I retire."

Without a word, Ben handed him the lantern, and as Matt wrapped his great coat around his shoulders, Ben pointed to the barn. "Yer horses is in the first two stalls to yer left."

Matt stumbled out the back door of the inn, missing the confusion of a half-dozen late arrivals.

It had been dark for over an hour before Molly got a chance to serve supper to the hideaways in back of the stable. Molly set the supper tray on the table. "We've a full house tonight."

Amy pulled her aside and whispered, "Jacob and Emma need some time alone tonight. I'll be safe, won't I, if I sneak out into the stable and sleep in one of the empty stalls?"

Molly studied the girl for a full minute. " 'Tis a nasty night and won't many be wandering around on a night like this. If you take a stall toward the back of the barn, away from the horses, I don't think you'll be found," she whispered back in a conspiratorial tone. She scooted out the door, winking at Amy as she went.

Amy waited for what seemed like hours and then wrapped her woolen cloak around her shoulders to ward off the chill of the cooler stable. She grabbed the lantern Ben left for their meals and worked her way out into the main section of the barn. In full view of the door, she settled herself in the hay of an empty stall far from the numerous horses that were resting from the stormy night like the weary travelers inside the inn. She pulled the cloak tightly about her shoulders and gratefully slipped the hood around her face to keep the chill from her neck and blew out the lantern. As she lay back in the sweet hay and waited for her senses to dull and drift into peaceful slumber, she listened to the winds whistling through the hayloft. At least, she thought, I'm safe and dry.

For a long time, she lay in the hay, trying to relax enough to sleep. She had just started to drift off when she heard the creak of the barn door. Driven by a gust of wind, it crashed against the wall. Amy sat up startled, grabbing at her hood for protection. The horses stirred, and several began to whinny as the sharp wind brushed through their resting place. She watched a man with a sheltered lantern make his way into the barn. With his back to her, he reached for the door to secure it against the wind. Then holding the lamp high above his head, he turned around. The noises from the excited horses covered the gasp that escaped Amy's lips. The face of the man holding the lantern and searching for something intently was a face she would never forget. Matt Treadwell had come for them!

179

Chapter Twelve

Desperately trying to force herself down into the hay without alerting him, Amy drew her hood tighter about her face. Had Ben and Molly given them away? No, that was not possible. And after six weeks, surely he wasn't still pursuing her? But of course he would follow, she told herself. He had said prison, and he was a determined man. Maybe he hadn't noticed her in the woolen cloak, as it was dark in the barn.

He moved away from her hiding place to a stall that had horses in it. Her heart was thumping so loudly she was sure he could hear it. Perhaps he would go away. She wondered if she should stay still or try to sneak back to the room behind the stalls. Could she move without drawing his attention? He moved again toward her hiding place, and she stopped breathing.

Matt, for his part, had chuckled as he glanced around the barn on entering. She was a little flirt, that redhead, planting herself in the back of the stable in clear view of the door. He couldn't miss her. He walked over to his horses and was pleased with what he saw. They were fed and watered, and Ben had seen to their brushing. He started for the stall where the girl was and wondered why she held her hood so tightly about her face. Was she afraid that someone else might come to the stable and recognize her? "Damn," he muttered, moving toward her. Why had he drunk so much tonight?

Without warning, the door flew open and slammed against the side of the barn. A bitter wind whirled through the barn and the lamp in Matt's hand fluttered. Another sudden gust, extinguished the lantern and the barn was plunged into darkness. With only the pale light from the distant inn to guide him, and with his gait unsteady, Matt struggled toward the barn door. He carefully calculated the distance to the stall where the woman waited and then, with exaggerated concern, fastened the door securely.

Amy's heart had leaped into her dry mouth at the bang of the door and the ensuing darkness. Now she couldn't make her way back to Emma and Jacob without alerting the one person in the whole world who could destroy her. She was shaking so badly she feared she would give herself away. Tense, she sat motionless and prayed, go away, oh, please, go away.

But Matt, groping his way to the stall, the dark lantern still hanging from his hand, stumbled toward Amy. Pausing next to the stall, he dropped the lantern on the floor and cursed himself for drinking so much. At the lantern's bang, Amy's heart stopped. He was coming for her. He had seen her. It was too late to run.

He lunged toward the mound of hay, slurring softly in the direction of the dark form before him, "Bet you thought I wasn't comin'."

Stunned, she moved back. She didn't expect that kind of greeting. Did he think she was someone else? The smell of stale brew was heavy in the darkness, and when he then slipped down into the hay, she realized he was drunk.

Matt grabbed for her, and Amy stiffened. She knew, from comments made by her brothers, that some women made themselves available for a price. Could Matt have made an arrangement with one of those women to meet him in the barn? Did he think he had that kind of woman in the hay? For an instant, she remembered Clarence and Norman. If that were Matt's intent and she let him have his way, perhaps he would never know that he had his prey so close at hand. It was her only hope. In the dark, Amy knew he couldn't tell whom he had in his arms, and, she reminded herself, he was drunk.

For a fraction of a second, she remembered his kisses that night at Willows when he had attempted to comfort her. She could almost feel the tingling she had felt in his arms. Her inability to stop him then made her face grow warm in the cold barn. Instinctively, she knew she could not allow him to kiss her, but if she offered no other resistance, it would be over quickly and he would be gone.

Matt broke into her confused thoughts. "Here, take this off," he mumbled as he slipped her cloak with its protective hood from her shoulders. Silently, she pleaded, don't let anyone else come, don't let anyone open the barn door.

He took her face between his hands and leaned forward. Amy was sure that he was going to kiss her, and she put her hand over her mouth, shaking her head.

"Don't like to be kissed, eh?" he muttered. "We'll see about that." He dropped his hand to the soft roundness of her breast as he let his other hand roam up and down her back. The fingers of his hand cupped her breast, then ran across the soft crest, teasing it into a tight rigid mass of fire.

Amy forced herself to submit to his pawing, at the same time, asking herself why it felt so good. A soft sigh slipped past her lips. Suddenly she sensed his other hand working at the buttons of her bodice. Her bodice was loosened, and then she felt it pulled free of her arms, to drape around her waist. He whispered instructions to her, and she raised her arms. As suddenly as he freed her bodice, she knew her chemise was gone. She was sitting in the hay, next to the man she feared most, and she was naked from the waist up.

Matt grabbed off his boots and then his pants and lay down next to her. Amy glanced over at him. Her eyes had grown accustomed to the darkness, and she could make out his large frame. He still wore his shirt and vest, which made the whole thing seem sordid and ugly. Could she go through with it, she wondered.

Matt turned toward her and pulled her down to lie in the hay with him. Taking his time, he let his hands travel up to her breast, again and again, teasing the small bud between his fingers. At it grew hard, pleasurable sensations began to surge through her slight body and she started to tremble.

For a second, his hands were gone, but just as quickly she saw his shadowed form rise above her. He pulled her skirt and petticoat up to her waist, exposing her legs and pantalettes. Instinctively, she fought the urge to shove him away and run. Even before she had quelled her impulse, his hands were running over her legs, up to her hips, and over her underwear. As her shock retreated, she felt him brush her breasts, first one and then the other.

Matt continued his explorations more gently now. Raising himself up on his elbow and bending his head, he trailed soft kisses from her chin to her shoulders and further down still to the valley between her breasts.

Amy lost herself to the feeling that he evoked. Every place his lips touched felt like little pinpoints of fire, and those points soon joined into a flaming torch ready to consume her. As his mouth moved across her breast to the hard peak, he gently teased, first with his lips, then his teeth.

When his moist tongue twirled around her nipple in a tingling caress, she sighed and unconsciously lifted her arms up to his neck and held his head to her breast. An explosion of sensations surged through her. She didn't want him to stop. She had lost touch with reality.

Lifting his head and moving to the other nipple, Matt muttered, "You like that, don't you?" She gave no answer but her breathing became ragged, and Matt chuckled. Her whole body was responding. She was very sensual. No wonder she approached him in the inn.

While he played at the tips of her breasts with his mouth, his hand drifted up to her tiny waist to untie the strings that held her pantalettes in place. He worked the rough fabric and pushed it down her hips.

He coaxed her into raising her hips ever so slightly and he pulled and pushed until he had access to the soft flesh of her thighs. Starting at her knees, he let his fingertips wander up to the tuft of hair that curled at the triangle of her legs. She tensed slightly, but Matt only increased the motion of his warm tongue on her throbbing breast. Gently, his fingers brushed through the soft fuzz between her thighs and crept into the moist flesh below the curls.

Amy jerked and gasped. The impact of his touch was like a hot torch consuming every fiber of her young body. The sensations started at the point where his fingers moved against her and went to the very roots of the hair on her head. She was so stunned she released her hold, and every nerve tingled. She tried to move away from the touch of his fiery fingers.

Matt lifted his head. She was ready for him. Even as dazed as he was, he knew. He rolled up over her, nudged her knees apart, and positioned himself between her thighs.

She felt the hardness pressed against the warm skin of her leg, and for a second she was filled with anxiety. For the first time in her life, she was sensually aroused, fully awakened, and she forced back the feelings of concern as she wondered at the strange sensations racing through her. Anticipation clawed at her taut stomach muscles. With her heart pounding frantically, she barely heard his breath coming heavy and hard. Her own breathing was fast and shallow. She knew she wanted whatever it was that came next.

Matt strained toward her, knowing that the long-needed release was only a minute away. Panting with desire, the tension in his maleness was nearly unbearable. Now. He had to have her now. As he surged forward, so great was his need the momentary barrier did not register.

As he plunged into her, white-hot pain screamed through Amy's body, and she went rigid. She struggled, attempting to push him away, but he moved with her and plunged deeper again and yet again. She felt herself being torn apart. Tears streamed down her cheeks, and she bit her lips to keep from screaming. She had to make him stop. Somehow she had to get out from under.

Suddenly, he shuddered and then relaxed against her. Amy took a deep breath, and she sensed that he was moving toward her lips. No, he must not kiss her. She turned her head aside.

As Matt's lips grazed her damp face and tasted the salty tears, he began to take note of his companion. By slow degrees, he became aware that she was shaking with sobs and not with passion.

"What the hell!" he roared, rolling away into the hay. Instantly sober, he lay still for a minute or two. Was she a virgin? It made no sense at all. Molly was certainly no virgin, so the girl lying beside him could not be Molly. But then who was she? He stumbled from the stall and felt along the floor until he found the lantern. Reaching into his pocket, he retrieved a matchbox and carefully struck a small splint. He lit the wick, adjusted the globe, and swung around toward the enclosure, holding the lantern high.

Amy was too distraught to realize that Matt had moved away from her until she heard the scrape of glass against metal as Matt was lighting the lantern. She grabbed at her bodice and tried to locate the arm-

186

holes just as the soft gleam of lantern light illuminated the stall. Her rumpled skirt and petticoat, around her waist, bore the stains of her lost virginity, and Matt saw that her thighs were streaked with traces of red.

The light fell on Amy's tear-stained face, and she jerked her head around to hide it, but Matt's befuddled brain had seen whom he had taken without a thought.

"Oh, my God!" Matt gasped.

Violent sobs racked Amy's thin frame as she realized that Matt had recognized her.

Galvanized into action, Matt set the lantern down outside the stall, knelt before her, and gathered her into his arms. He held her tightly against his pounding heart for several long moments, as tears streamed down his face.

In mumbled tones, he kept repeating, "What have I done?" Struggling against a hard lump in his throat, he tried to speak, but what words of comfort and love could he, should he, offer to the sobbing woman in his arms. He rained gentle kisses that were the essence of tenderness over her cheeks, across her forehead, on her eyelids. Finally, he reached down and tilted her chin up so that his lips could touch her mouth.

When Amy felt his lips brush hers, she began to struggle. She clenched her fists and tried to beat him away, but he grabbed her wrists and held them against his chest, then bent his head and kissed her again, tenderly, without passion. Her traitorous body responded to the comfort of his arms, and the very center of her body was warmed by his kiss. She went limp in his arms.

He pulled away from her and gazed down into her face. Tears were still sliding down her cheeks. As his eyes met hers, he drowned in a sea of fear, pain, and shock, and a flood of questions surfaced in his brain.

In a voice that shook noticeably, he asked, "Amy, what are you doing here? Why are you sitting in the hay, and why, dear God, didn't you stop me?"

Amy only stared at him, unable to respond. He knew who she was. He had taken her body, and now he would take her back to South Carolina. Sitting very still, she tried to make her mind a blank.

After he had straightened her clothing back, Matt struggled into his own pants and boots. He wrapped her cloak around her, swung his own coat across his shoulders, and lifted her gently into his arms. Stooping down, he grabbed the lantern and started for the door.

Suddenly, Amy realized that he intended to take her from the barn. Her shock disappeared, and she started to struggle, pushing against his chest with all her might. "No!" she sobbed. "No, I don't want to go to prison. *Nooo!*"

Matt froze. Prison? Where had she gotten that idea? "Amy, I'm taking you up to my room. You'll be warmer, and we can talk. I am not taking you to prison, but I have a lot of questions I want answered."

Matt paused for a moment, still stunned. Had her mind snapped? No, he couldn't believe that. Still, she continued to resist him. He tightened his hold.

"If you keep fighting me, I'll drop this lantern, and there'll be a fire."

She stopped struggling immediately and glared up at him. Jacob and Emma could not reveal themselves as they would have to if there were a fire. She would have to bide her time.

Matt was confused. She was so thin, and she acted like a small cornered cat. What on earth had happened to her? At the door, he managed to set the lantern down and pull the door open enough so that the glow from the inn would light their way. The storm, which had been just a promise earlier, had arrived. Sheets of cold rain lashed into the barn. Matt swore softly. He had to get her to his room quickly.

He started for the inn. He could get her up to his room using the back stairway to the second floor and avoid any unwelcome questions. Then he could find out what had happened to her and calm her down. He pulled her cloak tightly about her, slipped the hood up over her head, and forced his way through the drenching downpour toward the glowing light of the main building.

As each step brought them closer to the inn, Amy struggled against panic. She must keep a clear head if she was going to escape him. There was no choice; she had to get away from him. Surely Ben and Molly would help her. If she pretended to relax, would Matt release his hold? She could get free of him then. Willing herself to relax for a second or two, she prepared mentally to run.

Matt sensed the change in her, and he even guessed the reason for it. He pulled her to him more tightly, and she went rigid.

Angry that her plan hadn't worked, Amy tried to think of another way to escape. As they slipped into the back area of the inn, she could hear noises from the kitchen and the murmuring of many voices from

189

the main room. Perhaps she could call for help.

But Matt foiled her again. He set the lantern down and read the rebellion in her eyes, and planted his free hand over her mouth as firmly as he could without hurting her. "Not until we've had a chance to talk," he whispered.

He started up the dark stairwell, as Amy clawed and scratched in a frantic effort to break his hold. Slowly, she realized that escape was not possible for the moment, and she would have to go along with him for the present. Perhaps there would be another opportunity. Confidence built in her slightly, and she relaxed.

What was it that he wanted? Did he expect her to give the details of their escape? Was he after the names of the people who had helped them on their way north? Were Ben and Molly, even now, being held for their part in the plan? No, he hadn't known it was she in the barn, so Ben and Molly weren't in danger yet? Well, she wasn't going to tell him a thing. She wondered how he planned to take her back to Anderson and to prison. He might fabricate a story about Henry finally coming to fetch her. She would see right through that scheme. No; she would tell him nothing.

Chapter Thirteen

Matt was more than thankful that his room was at the end of the hall by the stairway. Amy was thin and light, but if she continued to struggle, he had visions of actually hurting her. It was hard enough to hold her with one hand over her mouth. He sighed as he reached his door. For a second, he withdrew his hand and as softly as he could, he said, "Don't."

Pulling a key from his pocket, he opened the door and carried her into the large room. Amy tensed and looked around. There was no one else in the room. Against one wall was a bed covered with a bright and colorful quilt. Across from the bed was a small fireplace where wood was laid for a fire. A set of large windows framed a small couch and table. Next to the door stood a small wardrobe and a washstand on which sat a plain white pitcher and bowl.

Matt also looked around the room and, after eyeing first the bed and then the couch, decided on the couch. He strode over and set her down carefully. Retracing his steps, he closed the door, locked it, tried the door, and dropped the key back into his pocket. Amy watched his every move, then sighed and frowned; there would be no escape for a time.

Next Matt threw off his cloak and pitched it on the

bed. Then he lit the firewood and several candles before finally facing her. As he looked at her, his heart felt as though it had been wrenched out of his chest. She was so thin, and she looked so frightened.

"Have you had anything to eat this evening?" he asked. She nodded her head.

Pulling a small flask from his saddlebags lying by the couch, he poured some amber liquid into a glass, from the washstand, added water, and walked back to the couch.

"Give me your cloak," he said. He placed her cloak with his on the bed and then handed her the glass. "Here, I think you need a little of this."

She took a taste. It was bitter and burned her throat. She attempted to give it back to him, but he pushed it toward her. "Take another swallow," he suggested. She did as he asked. It was still bitter, but it didn't burn quite as badly this time.

Matt took the glass she held up to him and lifted it to his own lips for a long drink himself. Setting the glass on the table in front of them, he sat down on the couch beside her. Gazing at his hands, he hesitated.

"Amy, what happened — back in the barn — I'm s-sorry. I had no way of knowing . . . I wouldn't hurt you for the world." His chest ached as he glanced over at her. "You believe me, don't you? What I did was inexcusable. I thought you were . . ." Matt stopped; he couldn't tell her he had planned to make love to someone else, he just couldn't.

Her own heart was beating frantically, and she sat staring into the fire. His mention of the barn brought back a flood of hurtful memories. She refused to deal with any of them until she had somehow managed her escape. The muscles of her throat seemed frozen; she couldn't say a word.

Gently, Matt grasped her chin, turned her face toward him, and studied her in the soft candle glow. God, she was thin, and her eyes seemed to look straight through him. Was she still in shock?

"Amy?" he questioned softly. "Are you all right?"

She finally glanced at his face and then looked away. "Yes," she whispered in a shaky voice.

"What did you mean when you said you didn't want to go to prison?"

She stared at him. Would he deny it? "I overheard you talking with Phillip. Don't try to deny it. Yes, I helped the slaves escape, but I'm not going to prison for that." The words hissed past her lips. "I'll get away from you. I'll escape. You are not sending me to a Southern prison!" Her voice cracked, and she started sobbing again.

Matt panicked. Now that he had found her she mustn't run away from him again. She wouldn't be safe on her own. And what had she overheard? He was certain he had never mentioned sending anyone to prison. Matt slid his arm around her shaking shoulders, and while he patted her, he tried to remember saying anything about prison. Suddenly, the spiteful words that had passed between Phillip and himself thundered in his head. She must have overheard part of that.

He tried to draw her closer. "You heard a part of an argument I had with Phillip. I told Phillip I'd like to kill him, but *I* didn't want to go to prison." He stressed the word "I."

Amy's sobs stopped as she stared up at him. She

stiffened and tried to move out of his arms.

"Amy." Matt reached for her again. "You'll have to marry me, now," he said quietly.

Her head shot up, and she glared at him. "No, no, no!" she shouted.

"Shhh," Matt whispered. "We'll go back to Anderson, to Aunt Elizabeth, until you have your strength back, and then I'll take you to your home. You don't have to decide anything until you get home." Matt did not mention the fact that he had already decided to talk to Henry if she refused him.

Amy's less than enthusiastic response made Matt look at her carefully. She was glaring at him almost as if she expected him to tell her that Henry was on his way. Her whole demeanor was one of distrust, and Matt suddenly realized that she did not believe him.

Amy stood and went to the fireplace. Even if Matt was lying, she could tell from the set of his jaw that he wasn't going to let her get away from him again. She had no choice; she had to go back with him. Her eyes filled with tears.

Matt moved to her side and placed his large hands on her shoulders. He turned her enough so that he could search her moist eyes. "Amy, where are Emma and Jacob?"

She stiffened. Now the villain was showing his true colors. "I'm alone," she said, her voice a husky growl.

"Didn't they make it?" Matt's voice crackled with concern. "Were you traveling alone?" That might account for her obvious fear, he thought.

"They're gone," Amy lied.

Matt shook her gently. "I'm not going to take them back, Amy. I want them to come to my Texas ranch as

194

a free man and woman. They can have a whole new start there." He paused and added softly, "Just like us."

Amy did not miss the poignant last phrase, and although her traitorous heart skipped a beat, she scoffed at him. "I'm going home to Henry."

"That's all right. I'll go with you, and then we'll go to Texas." He lifted her chin and stared down into her frightened eyes. He kissed her gently on the lips and stepped away from her. "You need sleep and should get into bed."

"I'm not sleeping with you!" she screeched.

Matt chuckled. At least she still had some pride. "No, I'm sleeping on the couch or on the floor. You're sleeping in the bed. We'll have to leave early tomorrow morning, and I need to do several things before I can sleep. But before I leave, I want you ready for bed."

Amy gasped. She wanted to tell him just what she thought of his idea but decided that the best course of action at the moment was to wait. Perhaps she would be able to talk to Ben or Molly in the morning. They would help her. She watched as Matt hung their cloaks on pegs by the door and turned back the bedcovers. His eyes swept the room as he considered what to do next. Then he strode over to his bags and pulled a clean shirt from the confused contents.

"Here. Put this on. You can sleep in it." He laid the shirt on the bed. Taking the key from his pocket, he unlocked the door and stepped from the room.

Amy watched the door swing closed and heard the key turn in the lock. Something snapped within her. He had locked her in and she was his prisoner. In spite of all he had said, she was headed for a Southern prison or worse. She stared at the locked door. He did not plan to take her home. Well, she may be his prisoner for now, but not for long.

Exhausted both physically and emotionally, she decided there was nothing else to do but go to bed. Right now, she was simply too tired to deal with the situation. Sleep was an immediate need. When dawn came, she would be rested and could think with a clear head.

She glared at the shirt Matt had laid out. "I'll not undress," she muttered. She didn't believe his words of remorse. If she wore only his shirt, it would be too easy for him to bed her in the middle of the night. No, she would stay dressed, and if he attempted another rape, he would have a real battle on his hands.

She needed a weapon. Her eyes inventoried the objects in the room for something suitable. Her glance fell on the fireplace poker. That would indeed serve as a formidable weapon. She grabbed the poker and laid it down in the bed. She lay next to it, her fingers closing around the handle. No, he would not touch her tonight, she thought grimly. Just let him try.

Matt walked down the hall, feeling very guilty. He had reservations about locking her in the room, but he was afraid she would bolt and run. He sensed that the misunderstanding about the conversation she overheard at Willows had left her with a deep mistrust, and he knew he hurt her badly when he took her in the barn. He shuddered. Had he destroyed what few pleasant feelings she associated with him? And why hadn't she tried to get away from him in the barn? She hadn't even tried to stop him. "Damn!" he muttered. Somehow he had to convince her that she could trust him and that he was worthy of that trust. Somehow he had to tell her that he loved her.

Stunned, he stopped on the stairs and ran his fingers through his hair. He did indeed love her. "This is a poor time to figure that out," he mumbled as he started back down the steps. First, he had to teach her to trust him, and that would take time. Did he have the time? With his luck, her brother would probably be waiting for them at Elton Estate when they got home. Of course, he could talk to Henry, but then the man really had a reason to shoot him, as Aunt Elizabeth had once suggested. The sooner they started south, the better, just in case. And he still needed to know where Emma and Jacob were.

Matt found Ben in the spacious kitchen and quickly told the innkeeper about his original plans. He tried to explain why he was turning back. "When I went out to check on the horses, I found Amy sleeping in the hay. For six weeks I've been following her, praying she was all right. I know she was traveling with two escaped slaves, and if they're still here, I'd like you to deliver a message for me."

Matt paused, watching Ben for some sign that would tell him his suspicions were correct. "All I want you to do is deliver my message. I have no intention of taking them back with me. If they want to continue on to the north, then nothing more need be said. I'll leave in the morning with Amy, and they can go on as they planned. However, if they would like to come to Texas with Amy and me, then I'll have work for them both, as a free man and woman. Unfortunately, if they want to go to Texas, I'll have to know tonight."

Ben wondered if he should deny any knowledge of the two slaves. He wasn't sure how much, if anything, Amy had already confided to the man, so he sat and listened intently, trying to keep his expression blank. Was the young man interested only in having his message delivered, he wondered.

Matt added quietly, "If they decide to go to Texas, will they be safe here with you, until I can arrange things at my end? It may take a couple of months before we're ready to leave for Texas. I'll be happy to pay for their room and board if they can remain here. They'll not be safe if they come back to South Carolina with me."

Ben frowned; the comment about South Carolina just about decided it for him. It appeared the man was not going to take them back to the slavery they had known. "I'll be back in a bit," he said quietly as he rose from the table.

Matt grinned a little sheepishly; it was obvious that Emma and Jacob were still at the inn. He sat back in his chair to wait for Molly to appear. There were several things that he needed from her as well.

Before long Molly burst into the kitchen, looking harried. Seeing Matt startled her, so Matt quickly asked if she had some clothing that he could purchase from her. In the next breath, he found himself explaining about Amy and why they must leave at dawn the next day.

"I'll need several changes of clothing for our trip, and I'll be happy to pay for them." He took out a roll of bills and smiled up at the surprised girl.

Molly stared at first Matt and then the roll of bills

he held in his hand. "You're serious," she said, her surprise ringing through her words. Matt nodded his head.

She left him for a few minutes and returned with several dresses that she offered for his inspection. He picked out three he thought appropriate. With embarrassment, he asked if she would add several changes of underwear as well. Molly grinned, thinking to herself, that was why he was so indifferent during dinner. Amy, she decided, must occupy a special place in his heart.

"I'll have everything ready before sunup, and I'll even throw in a valise." She folded the dresses carefully. "Can I get you an ale?"

Matt grimaced. He had had enough spirits for one night. "I'll take a cup of coffee, if there's any of that."

Molly laughed. She had really thought he could hold his liquor better than that, but she fixed him coffee without comment and set about packing the things for Amy.

Before Matt finished his coffee, Ben came back, followed by a frightened Jacob who was visibly relieved when he saw Matt seated at the large table. Matt repeated what he had told Ben but in more detail. Jacob asked many questions about the accommodations at the ranch, what his duties and Emma's position would be, and what the future prospects were. Matt tried to explain his plans and answered as many of Jacob's questions as he could.

"There are some things that will have to wait until after we arrive. As far as I'm concerned, if you travel with me, you and Emma are free. And when the time comes, I'll deed you your own land, so you can remain free."

Jacob seemed satisfied and commented, "Texas sounds like a surer way to freedom than dat long trip north."

"Phillip may have hired agents to look for Emma up north, and you might just run into them if you head toward Canada. I would be happier if you went west with me, instead of north with the railroad."

Jacob got up from the table and started for the door. "You don't trust dat brother of yers either, does ya?" he said as he left.

Matt grinned after the slave. No, he didn't trust Phillip, and he was glad Jacob didn't either. He took the valise Molly had packed and a complete change for Amy for the morning. He thanked Molly and left the kitchen.

Ben followed him from the room. "I think they'll stay." He pointed toward the barn.

"I think you're right. I'll settle up with you in the morning. You can figure out what three months of care will cost and ask Molly how much for the clothes." Matt left Ben scratching his head and retraced his steps to his room.

He unlocked the door and quietly entered the cozy chamber. The fire had burned down, and only glowing embers remained. When he reached for the poker, to stir up the fire, he was startled. The poker had been there when he fixed the fire before. He distinctly remembered standing it up in the toolbox next to the fireplace. Glancing around the room, he saw that it was nowhere to be seen. He tiptoed over to the bed and gazed at his sleeping beauty. Her hand was gripping something, and in the soft light, it looked like metal. He was not too surprised, when he raised the blankets cautiously, to see the poker clutched tightly in her hand.

He replaced the covers and picked up his bedroll. Shaking it out, he laid it before the fire. Adding wood to the embers, he finally stretched out before the catching logs, laid his head on his arm, and stared into the flames.

An incredible task faced him. Amy was frightened, and he had just abused her. It was no wonder that she didn't trust him. He would need time to change her opinion of him. If she insisted on going home to Henry when they arrived at Elton Estate, he would have to take her. He frowned. If all else failed, when they arrived in Anderson, Indiana, he would tell Henry what had happened in the barn. Surely, then Henry would want them to marry right away.

He lay back on his bedroll. Would Amy agree to marriage? She might resent being forced, and that just might make matters worse. But then, she had originally been attracted to him. He was certain of that. If he was on his best behavior, perhaps he could respark that attraction. He smiled as he thought of the coming morning. The first thing he would do was begin to convince her that she was the most important person in his life and that her own life with him would be special, very special. Smiling, he drifted off to sleep.

Chapter Fourteen

Dawn filtered through the windows, and Amy stirred, rolling over on the poker that had remained with her through the night. She bolted into an upright position, memories of the night before vivid in her mind. Glancing around the room, she saw Matt stretched out in his bedroll on the floor. Amazed, she realized that he kept his word, at least about that.

For a second she wondered if this would be a chance to escape and looked at the door. Carefully she swung her legs out of the bed and stood. She hadn't taken a step before Matt rolled over and looked up at her.

"Good morning." Grinning, he stretched. He pointed to the clothes that he brought up the night before. "I bought some clean things for you to wear."

Amy immediately objected. "I didn't ask you to get me anything. I can't afford to owe you any more money. Take them back!"

Matt ignored her comments. "I talked to Jacob last night." He chuckled at her gasp, remarking softly,

"He and Emma are going to Texas with us. Would you like to have breakfast with them? We can eat in the barn," he said pleasantly.

Amy bristled. She had not agreed to go to Texas with him; she didn't want to go anywhere with him. She did want to talk to Jacob and Emma, but not with Matt listening to every word they said.

"I'll see them later," she said.

"I think you should spend a little time with them, but it must be soon. We have to start south this morning and travel hard and fast. Amy, we have to leave in an hour or two."

Amy glared at him. "I'm not going anywhere with you."

"You have no choice. I've moved all your things to Aunt Elizabeth's estate, and unless you want to stay with Phillip, you better plan on traveling back to South Carolina with me." He gazed at her intently, a frightening thought surfacing. "Amy," he questioned, "you can ride a horse, can't you? A carriage will be much too slow."

She gave him a disgusted look. "Of course I can ride. I was raised on a farm, and I worked that farm. I'm not one of your pampered Southern belles with slaves to do everything for me."

Matt chuckled and let the remark pass. Climbing out of his bedroll, he started for the door. "You dress. I've several things I must do before breakfast."

Left alone, Amy glared at the closed door. She sank down on the bed. What was she to do? She had to go back with him, just in case Henry came. It would not do, not at all, for Henry to meet Phillip, not if it could be avoided. And what about Emma

203

and Jacob? How on earth had Matt talked them into going to Texas? Were they coming back to South Carolina with Matt? That would end any bid for freedom they made. Matt had said nothing about Emma and Jacob traveling with them to Anderson. She shook her head. What was going on?

As Amy sat on the bed trying to sort through her confusion, Matt started for the kitchen of the inn. "She's certainly in a hostile mood," he muttered. He met Molly in the sunny main room and ordered a lunch packed for their trip. Requesting a substantial breakfast for them both, Matt went to find Ben. There was still the matter of the bill, and he wanted to see Emma and Jacob.

With everything in order, he made his way back up the stairs. "I'll be so pleasant, she can't find fault," he told himself as he knocked on the door. As the door swung open, he bowed low, announcing "Breakfast awaits, m'lady." He swept the floor with his open hand, banging it resoundingly against the wood. "Damn!" he snarled.

Amy laughed for the first time in days. He deserved that and more, she thought to herself, as she watched him massage his red knuckles. Still giggling, she accepted his extended arm. At that moment, the door directly across from them swung open, and there stood Henry.

Henry turned to face his missing sister on the arm of the man he had watched at dinner the night before. Henry took a step forward and grabbed for Amy as her mouth dropped open.

She lunged toward him, forgetting about Matt completely, and her tears started to flow. Clinging to him, she sobbed and touched his face, ran her hands through his hair and kissed his cheek.

Henry's eyes glistened with his own unshed tears, and he held her tightly for several minutes before kissing her forehead. Gently, he pulled her arms away from his neck and looked at her closely. "Sister," he said, gazing at her tenderly, "you look a little underfed." He glanced over at the man standing just behind his sister in the hall. He and the man were the same height, but the man was much broader, much more masculine than Henry. For the moment, Henry turned his attention back to his weeping sister.

Matt stood very still. This could only be Henry, Amy's brother. He was thin, with dark hair, much darker than Amy's brown hair, but he had the same expressive blue-gray eyes, and at the moment, those eyes were staring at him, cold and questioning. Matt stepped forward, extending his hand. "Matt Treadwell. You must be Henry."

Henry looked from Amy to Matt to the door of the room they had just vacated and then back to Amy. "Didn't you get my letters?" Henry searched her face, and Amy dissolved into tears again.

Matt thought of his carefully laid plans for their future, and as the hurt expression spread over Henry's face, he saw them ebbing away. He would have to act quickly. Opening the door of his room, he grabbed Amy's arm and suggested as gently as he could, "Wash your face and then come downstairs and join us for breakfast." He grabbed Henry by the arm and started for the stairs.

Henry, shaking his arm free, followed Matt down the steps, demanding in a loud voice, "What the hell have you done to my sister?"

Amy didn't hear Matt's answer, if he gave one. Well, Henry was here now. He could take her home. Why, she asked herself, wasn't she overjoyed? It was what she wanted, what she had wanted for a long time. And Henry would not hesitate. They would be on their way in a day or two, perhaps they could leave today. So why didn't she feel happy? Was it possible that a part of her wanted the plans Matt had outlined for their future? No, there were no plans. Matt had locked her in his room and told her all those things just to get her back to South Carolina. She stood in the doorway, the tears still streaming down her face. Was it possible that she still cared for the man in spite of her suspicions and what he had done to her?

Amy moved into the room and went to the wash-stand. Until she knew what Matt wanted from her, she couldn't leave Henry and Matt together for long. This was certainly not the time to sort through her feelings. She had to get downstairs and quickly. Drying her tears, she sponged off her face and ran for the stairs.

When she entered the main room, neither her brother nor Matt were in sight. Where had they gone? Fear forced her heart into her throat. She looked around the room a second time. Men fought duels over things like kidnapping and rape, and Henry was not a particularly good shot. Was Matt? Standing very still, she remembered Henry's angry voice as the two men had started for the stairs. Was Henry angry enough to demand satisfaction? Would Matt encourage such a show of strength? No. She could not allow that. Frantic, she made a dash for the back door of the inn.

Molly had been watching her from the corner of her eye as she prepared to serve the early risers. She intercepted Amy as she bolted toward the door.

"Amy, it's all right. They're in the barn." In whispered tones, she added, "They're talking to Emma and Jacob. Here, sit here, and I'll bring you a cup of coffee. Wait until they return." She pushed Amy into a chair at a corner table away from the main serving area of the room. "You sit here. See, you can see the door from here. They'll be right back." Molly brought the coffee and went back to serving her customers, watching Amy as she worked.

After what seemed like an eternity to Amy, the two men, both looking solemn, returned to the dining area. Matt offered Amy his arm, and Henry stood off to one side. Amy looked from Matt's grim face to Henry's equally dark frown. She felt a shiver of apprehension. What had transpired? Why was Henry allowing Matt to take her arm? Panic started to rise. What had Matt told her brother?

"Amy," Matt began quietly, "Henry will accompany us back to South Carolina. He'll stay for the wedding."

"What wedding?" she demanded.

"Ours."

"No!" Amy whispered, then screamed, *"No!"*

"Yes, Amy, it must be so," Henry said firmly.

Amy was stunned. She let Matt lead her to a larger table, with Henry following. Matt seated her, and Molly brought out breakfast. Amy could only sit and stare. Her brother was not going to take her home.

Matt must have told him exactly what had happened in the barn the night before, and her gallant brother had agreed to a marriage as an honorable solution. No, no, her mind rebelled. This could not be happening. Henry didn't understand that Matt was not an honorable man. Somehow, she had to make him see Matt for what he was. If they were going to travel back to South Carolina together, she would have the time to talk to her brother. She had to convince Henry that she could not marry the man.

After breakfast, Amy said good-bye to Emma and Jacob, relieved to learn that they were staying on at the inn. Matt didn't allow her much time for questions before they were on their way.

Both men were afraid to push Amy, so they agreed there was no hurry to reach South Carolina now. Each day they traveled twenty-five or thirty miles and then stopped for the night at the nearest lodging. Each night, after Amy retired, Matt and Henry discussed her physical and mental condition at great length. Ever since they had left Tucker's Inn, Amy had been withdrawn, and she ate almost nothing, usually pushing her food around her plate. She was visibly exhausted and thin to a fault.

As they traveled, she remained cool and uncommunicative. Both men tried to draw a response from her. When Henry told her about the happenings at home, she seemed uninterested, and when he told her about the time he had spent with Alex, she didn't ask any questions. Matt told her about Elton Estate and how he and Aunt Elizabeth had moved her things to a room there. She looked right through him.

Both men were startled to learn that a small fort in

the bay of Charleston had been attacked and that open hostilities were beginning in the East. When they described the conflict to Amy, she merely shrugged her shoulders. She had her own war to worry about. She refused to open her mouth unless they asked her a direct question that required a response.

As Amy withdrew more and more, Matt and Henry worked together to bring her out of her depression. Henry often sat up with Matt late into the night, listening to him berate himself for Amy's condition. Henry was concerned, but he spent no time blaming himself for the girl's malaise, although he respected Matt's genuine anxiety over his sister. Matt, he thought, would make an excellent husband for his little sister. Once she regained her health, she would see for herself that he had much to offer.

As the days moved slowly along, the two young men found that they had a great deal in common besides a concern over Amy. They both were enthusiastic about the expansion of the West. They discussed slavery and found they agreed on that as well. Henry was delighted to learn that Matt shared his feelings on the necessity of maintaining a strong central government and one union.

When Matt disclosed his plans for his cattle ranch and the home he planned for Amy, Henry relaxed with him completely. Matt was going to provide well for his sister. Henry, in turn, told Matt about his own dream of going into the gold areas of the Colorado Territory and starting a law practice. Matt was able to share with him some the common mining problems, from the miners' point of view. They laughed together about the money that Henry would make settling disputed gold claims. "Probably more than the miners make themselves," Matt told him good-naturedly. By the time they arrived in Anderson, Matt and Henry were good and true friends.

As the men grew closer, Amy became more distant. She watched as Matt charmed her brother, and she assumed the guilt for what she considered a traitorous situation. It was her fault, for she made the seduction of her brother possible when she had not run from Matt that night in the barn. Over and over she played that scene in her mind, and she knew she should have fought him, or at least cried out for help. She hadn't been struggled.

She was certain that Henry was trapped in Matt's web of intrigue and deceit. If Matt wanted information about the underground railroad, he would find out from Henry whatever it was that he wanted to know. She had delivered her own brother up to the enemy, and he was so enthralled with the foe that he didn't see the danger. As her horse carried her closer to South Carolina, she was convinced that as soon as Matt had the information he wanted, he would disclaim the engagement. And although she couldn't explain it, that thought, above all else, hurt the most.

After nearly four weeks on the road, they finally arrived at Elton Estate. Matt had sent several frantic messages to Aunt Elizabeth, trying to prepare her for Amy's physical and emotional condition and the need for their slow travel. He tried to explain about Henry and ended up asking her if Henry could stay with them for several weeks. When they finally reached their destination, everything was ready and had been for quite a while.

Aunt Elizabeth met the weary travelers on the broad porch of her home. Even with the terse and pointed remarks that Matt had included about Amy in his notes, it did little to prepare her for the stark, pale girl Matt presented. Aunt Elizabeth led the way back into the house and before she realized what effect her words might have on Amy, she glared at Matt. "What did you do to her?"

Amy looked around the hall at the black slaves waiting to assist with the baggage, at Henry standing solemnly behind Matt, at Aunt Elizabeth frowning at Matt, and reality seemed to fade. She took a step toward the older woman, swaying slightly. Suddenly she collapsed.

Matt was closer to Amy than Henry, and as she sank toward the floor, he scooped her up into his strong arms. Without a word he started up the stairs, leaving Aunt Elizabeth to send for the doctor and to calm Henry. He laid Amy down on the bed in the room he was sure would be hers, and before he had time to check her, Aunt Elizabeth was at his side.

"I've sent one of the slaves after the doctor. Now, I want you to go downstairs and take Henry out to the kitchen for something to eat. I'll take charge here."

Within minutes, a can of hot water appeared, and Aunt Elizabeth gently removed Amy's travel-stained clothes. She bathed the thin little body, stunned at the yellowing bruises inflicted during the long struggle to Tennessee. Amy's whole body was covered with healing cuts and scrapes, and there was no spare flesh on the child's bones, Aunt Elizabeth thought. She was battered beyond description, and the woman marveled that she was alive.

Amy stirred slightly and then tried to raise herself from the soft bed. Aunt Elizabeth held her thin shoulders and gently pushed her down into the feather mattress.

"It's all right, Amy. You're safe now. You're going to rest and gain . . ." There was no need to continue, for Amy was fast asleep. She wrapped the girl in a simple nightgown and supervised the straightening of the room. She left one of the older slaves with the girl, giving instructions that she be called if Amy awakened. Then, satisfied with what had been done so far, she went in search of Matt and Henry. She was going to get some answers.

She found them talking quietly over coffee at the kitchen table. When they became aware of the silver-haired woman in the doorway, they both stood and asked in unison, "How is she?"

Aunt Elizabeth gazed at the concerned faces looking at her. "She is exhausted, she is hungry, and she is probably very sick," she stated. She didn't mean to sound so harsh, but she was horrified at what she had seen. "Now, gentlemen, you will come with me to the study, and you can tell me what has been going on."

Matt gasped and glanced over at Henry sheepishly. Henry put his arm around Matt in a consoling gesture. Aunt Elizabeth noticed the look that passed between them and Henry's gesture. She said loudly, "Now!" and led the way to the study as the two men lagged behind. She had a sinking feeling that Amy's condition might be as much emotional as physical. And she knew, somehow, that Matt Treadwell was responsible.

She motioned the two hesitant men to the two large leather chairs and then closed the door. Gathering her skirts, she sat opposite them on a smaller desk chair.

"Now, let's start at the beginning," she said quietly.

Matt actually blushed. She frowned. There was something very wrong here. She sat waiting until Matt regained some of his composure.

He gazed at a spot far above her head and stuttered, "I-I-I ra-ra . . . oh, hell! I thought she was someone else. It was dark; I didn't know it was Amy. I didn't know . . ." His voice faded to a whisper.

Aunt Elizabeth sat stunned, motionless, and Henry wriggled uncomfortably in his chair. He cleared his throat. Aunt Elizabeth recovered and looked at Matt, who sat hunched over, holding his head in his large hands.

Henry ventured softly, "Do you suppose she's . . . pregnant? That might explain her being so withdrawn."

Matt's head shot up. Aunt Elizabeth and Matt disclaimed that in one voice. "No!"

Henry, confused, looked over at Matt, "You said —"

Matt interrupted him, his voice shaking. "She couldn't be, she couldn't be."

Aunt Elizabeth glanced at her nephew in disgust. He hadn't even considered that a possibility. She said, "No, she is not carrying a child."

Matt sagged back in the chair in relief. "Henry and I have talked about this all the way from Tennessee. We both agree that Amy and I should be married

213

right away." Then he added as an afterthought, "Pregnant or not!"

Henry added, "And the sooner, the better."

"No!" Aunt Elizabeth spoke sharply. When both men looked up in surprise, she continued. "Yes, you should be married, if—" she paused; Matt would not like the conditions that she was going to propose. "If after you've courted her properly, she wants to marry you."

Matt and Henry fought for the right to speak, both talking at the same time. Henry's stronger voice won for the moment. "Mrs. Elton, Matt really cares for Amy, and I think she had strong feelings for him." Matt winced at Henry's choice of words, but Henry continued. "I mean, she may love him, too, and I think she should marry him."

Matt tried to speak. "Aunt Elizabeth, please—"

"Matt," she said quietly, rising from her chair. "It will be up to Amy." She moved to open the door. "And that is final."

Aunt Elizabeth left the two men in the study. While she waited for the doctor, she ordered a pot of tea. She made two quiet trips up to Amy's bedroom to check on the sleeping girl. Standing beside Amy's bed, she watched as the girl tossed and turned. Such a frail thing, she thought, and to be abused by the very man that had declared himself to be her savior. She clucked her tongue as she made her way back to the parlor to wait for the doctor.

Two hours dragged by before the doctor finally was ushered into the parlor. While Aunt Elizabeth accompanied him up the stairs, she tried to explain what little she knew. As she struggled with a few words and phrases, the doctor guessed at her meaning. He had known Elizabeth Elton for years and he smiled at her.

"Elizabeth, I'll take care of the girl." More to himself than to her, he mumbled, "I had best do an internal exam."

Aunt Elizabeth waited at Amy's bedside as the girl roused herself and then introduced her to the doctor. When she started to leave, Amy whispered, "Please, don't go!"

Aunt Elizabeth turned and searched the face of the doctor. When he smiled back at her and patted the edge of the bed, she went back and sat where he indicated. She gazed at Amy's blank stare.

"Amy, Matt told me what happened, and I've told the doctor. Are you sure you want me to stay?"

"He told you?" Amy gasped.

"I'm afraid I forced him to. Shall I go?"

"No," Amy whispered, her voice breaking. "Please stay."

Aunt Elizabeth smiled sympathetically and sat holding Amy's hand while the doctor examined her. After her gown was back in place and the bed linens arranged, Amy stared at the wall opposite the bed. The doctor smiled tentatively at Amy and then turned to Aunt Elizabeth.

"There's no damage done that I can tell." Aunt Elizabeth sagged with relief. "She's tired and suffering from exhaustion, but with plenty of good hearty food and lots of sleep"—he patted the quilt covering Amy's legs—"you'll be fine in a couple of weeks." He went to the door with Aunt Elizabeth following him. "And no visitors for several days," he said sternly.

Amy closed her eyes and sank back into the mattress. Henry was on his own, she thought as she drifted off to sleep.

Quietly, Aunt Elizabeth told the slave in the room to remain and followed the doctor to the ground floor. Her brow was creased with worry.

"She's a strong girl, Elizabeth. What she needs is rest and food. She's had a shock, but in a couple of weeks, under your fine care" — he grinned at her — "she'll be good as new." She returned his smile and nodded. "Call me if you think I'm needed," he offered as she saw him to the door.

Aunt Elizabeth closed the front door and turned to face two pairs of questioning eyes. "She's tired and needs rest and good food. Other than that, the doctor thinks she'll be fine."

Matt and Henry clasped each other on the shoulders and together they headed for the stairs. "No visitors for several days, and that means both of you!" she shot back at them over her shoulder as she headed for the kitchen to give instructions to the cook. The doctor had said food, and she was going to see that Amy got exactly what she needed to get well.

Chapter Fifteen

As the household settled into a strained routine, Amy remained at the center of everyone's thoughts, but she was unaware of the tension she had created. She slept most of the time and ate little, only nibbling at the delicacies Aunt Elizabeth urged upon her.

At the end of two weeks, Amy was still in bed and showed no interest in anything or anyone. When Aunt Elizabeth sat with her, Amy asked almost nothing about the household and not once, Aunt Elizabeth realized with concern, about Henry or even Matt. The girl was content to just lie in bed and hold Aunt Elizabeth's hand.

Henry spent the days trying to keep Matt from forcing his way to Amy's side. At first, they prowled the grounds of the estate, but they quickly became bored with the lack of activity. One morning, as the sun was spreading ribbons of gold across the lawn, the men left for Anderson and were gone most of the day.

During dinner that evening, Matt drew a small white box from his jacket pocket. "Aunt Elizabeth, would you take this up to Amy after dinner?" Grinning, he pulled an envelope from another pocket. "This goes with it."

Later, in Amy's room, Aunt Elizabeth silently handed the box and envelope to Amy. Amy held the box for several minutes without asking who had sent the gift or why. Finally, with a little prodding from Aunt Elizabeth, she opened the box. There on a bed of cream-white satin was a small, brilliant blue-green emerald pendant. It was square cut and surrounded with icy white diamonds. She took a quick breath and stared at the exquisite jewel. Was it from Henry? She thought not. He could never afford anything like that.

"I can't accept this," she declared in a flat unemotional voice.

"Why ever not?" The older woman laughed softly. "It is a beautiful gift, and there are no strings attached."

Amy glanced at the unopened envelope and back at Aunt Elizabeth.

"If you need anything, let me know," Aunt Elizabeth said quietly, sensing the girl wanted to be alone. Closing the door softly behind her, she shook her head. Amy seemed better physically, but she had not regained her spirit. Perhaps the doctor could help. She made her decision quickly. If there wasn't some obvious improvement within two days, she would send for him again.

Meanwhile, Amy lay in her bed, turning the white note over and over for several minutes. She finally opened it, telling herself it could be from Henry.

She read the carefully penned message, "I'm sorry, Matt," and bolted upright, staring at the card. How dare he. Did he think he could buy her forgiveness? Gift or not, she would throw the jewelry in his face. He couldn't buy her; she was not for sale.

Galvanized, she struggled from under the covers and stood beside the bed. The room reeled, and she felt dizzy. How can I be so terribly weak, she wondered as she sat down on the mattress. She tried again with no better result and sank back into bed. Tomorrow, she would get up. She had a thing or two to show Matthew Treadwell. She was not going to be paid off with a trinket like some lady of the streets, no matter how costly the gem.

The next morning, she consumed more than her usual quantity of food. Aunt Elizabeth, seeing her tray in the kitchen, rushed up to see what had brought about such a change. She noticed the color in Amy's cheeks, but that wasn't what caused Aunt Elizabeth to almost dance with joy. It was the fact that Amy wanted to get up.

"I've been in bed long enough. I want a nice hot bath," Amy said quietly. Though Aunt Elizabeth urged a compromise sponge bath, Amy would not be swayed. "I want to get up, and I'm going to have a bath."

Aunt Elizabeth, seeing the snapping blue-gray eyes and determined chin, sighed in pleasure. She hadn't seen this much spirit in the girl since Christmas.

"I think Henry and Matt will have something to say about that." She left the room with her arms crossed and a mock scowl on her face, but much to her disgust, both men had already left for town.

Amy had her way and enjoyed a luxurious bath before returning to bed to rest.

Later that evening, Amy joined the others for dinner. She smiled to herself when she saw the shocked expressions on Henry's and Matt's faces as she took her seat at the table. Although visibly tired by the end of the meal, she had enjoyed herself and her eyes were still bright and clear.

After dinner, Matt swung her into his arms and, despite her angry protests, carried her up to her room. He set her gently on her feet before her door and gazed down into her upturned face. Raising her hand to his lips, he placed soft kisses on her outstretched fingers.

Amy felt the tingle travel along her fingers, up her arm, and through her body. Jerking her hand away, she tried to intimidate him with a scowl, but he only smiled back.

"I'll see you in the morning," he whispered in a husky voice. Then he opened the door, and she entered her room.

Leaning against the closed door, Amy wondered how he could still affect her so when he was such a cad. Unconsciously, she rubbed her tingling fingers.

For the next several days, Amy napped both morning and afternoon and ate more and more each day. It was not long before she was eating a full dinner. Her strength returned, and she gained weight. By the end of July she could wear some of the dresses Matt had purchased for her in November, although several

220

still hung from her shoulders. She vehemently refused to let Matt buy anything new for her.

Every two or three days Amy would find a small box or package by her plate at dinner. On one occasion Aunt Elizabeth gave her a gaily wrapped package before dinner. Each token was accompanied by a note, expressing some general sentiment — "Glad you're better," "Nice to have you at dinner," "You look well" — and they were always signed, simply, "Matt." The gifts were tasteful and usually expensive — emerald earrings to match the pendant, white kid gloves, a lace scarf, and a bracelet of tiny rubies held in place by a delicate gold wire.

Amy accepted the gifts without comment. She never wore them unless Matt asked if perhaps she didn't like the color or the design. Then she put it on for the next meal. Back in her room, she tucked the gift in its box and put it with the other gifts at the bottom of her armoire. If he said nothing about a particular item, she put it away immediately.

As her health improved, Matt attempted to be alone with her in the drawing room, the kitchen, or wherever he could, but she was successful in avoiding him. Once he even came to her bedroom, but she stood on propriety and ordered him out of the room.

By mid-August, Amy started to receive visitors, and many of the women she had met during the Christmas season came to call. At first, she was upset. "Aunt Elizabeth, what will they think? Do they know that I ran away?"

"Amy." The older woman patted her hand. "They think that you started for home and were taken seriously ill before you got to Indiana. We've hinted that

221

it was easier for Henry to bring you back than to attempt the trip to Indiana."

For his part, Matt hinted broadly that Henry had returned with Amy because she and Matt wanted more time together.

Henry was an instant success. He played court to the older women with such charm that many of the visitors were heard to remark that Henry had surely been educated in the South, he was such a gentleman.

As the visitors increased, so did Matt's frustration. He could not seem to find Amy by herself. The few times he succeeded, she feigned exhaustion or a headache, and on one occasion she turned on her heel and left him standing in the drawing room.

In desperation, Matt sought out Henry. He needed advice badly. Henry, in turn, approached Amy on Matt's behalf, but she told him to mind his own business and laughed when he said, "But, Amy, he's trying to court you. At least grant him some of your time."

When nothing worked, the two men cornered Aunt Elizabeth. She was sympathetic as she listened to Matt's tale of frustration. After a few minutes, she announced, "I have a plan." She explained that it was time that Amy began to travel abroad. A trip to town would be the perfect excuse they needed.

"You both can drive to town in the carriage. The weather is beautiful this time of year, and the outing will do her much good. All you have to do is have a horse waiting at the stable in town for Henry. Matt, I'm sure you can think of some excuse to leave Henry at the stable. Then drive over to the lake. You'll be alone for several hours."

Matt frowned, "She won't go any place with me."

"No, but I'm sure she'll accept the invitation from Henry."

Delighted, the two men threw themselves into planning the elaborate charade. Henry approached Amy and suggested a trip into town. Surprisingly, she agreed. Matt ordered a large picnic basket packed and secretly stored it in the carriage the morning of the proposed outing. The horse had already been ridden to the stable the day before.

Amy was excited about the trip to town in spite of the simple nature of the jaunt. It would be her first excursion from the plantation since her return to South Carolina. She dressed carefully, and she excused her care by telling herself that she certainly wanted to look her best if she met any of Aunt Elizabeth's many friends in town.

When she finished dressing, she inspected herself in the mirror. The gray suit that Matt had purchased for her at Christmas fit reasonably well, though still a little loosely. She thought she looked well and felt good about that.

What she didn't see were the subtle changes that had resulted from her travels. Though her hair once again shone with amber highlights, her eyes had taken on an intensity that made them appear larger than before. Her clear pale skin, now devoid of any tan, made her look more delicate, and there was still a trace of hollows in her cheeks. What she didn't see was that where before she had been beautiful, now she was ravishing.

Amy came down the stairs warily. She had decided

that if Henry wasn't waiting for her at the bottom of the stairs, she would turn around and run back to her room. But Henry was there, and she sighed her relief.

He offered her his arm, and they went out the front door to find Matt waiting at the carriage. It was Henry who helped her into the carriage, made her comfortable, and sat next to her.

Waved on by Aunt Elizabeth, sporting a happy smile, the three of them drove off. For an hour they traveled under the warmth of a bright September sun. Matt and Henry talked about the plantations they passed, the glorious weather, the profusion of summer blooms that waved gaily in the soft breezes. The time passed swiftly, and Amy relaxed. It was a beautiful day, and she intended to enjoy it to the fullest.

Even before they reached Anderson, Matt and Henry were exchanging glances, but Amy was so busy looking at the sights that she completely missed the exchanges. Matt stopped the carriage in front of the local carriage shop, and both men jumped down. They talked for a minute, and then Henry walked into the shop. Matt climbed back into the carriage, picked up the reins and urged the horses to move.

Confused, Amy started to tell him to stop when she saw Matt's lips drawn into a tight line. She suddenly realized he had no intention of waiting for Henry. Angrily, she gritted her teeth.

"I demand that you stop. I don't want to go any place with you. Wait for Henry." But Matt continued on without a word. Desperate, she turned around in hopes of signaling her brother to help her. She saw Henry leading a horse from around the shop, but he

224

mounted and raced off in the opposite direction. She turned back to Matt, her eyes flashing.

"This is your idea, isn't it?"

Matt's lips curled into a boyish grin. "Back at the house, you could get away from me much too easily." He sobered and stared ahead. Soon, he turned to her and said, "Amy, we have to talk."

She felt betrayed. Henry certainly and perhaps Aunt Elizabeth also had done this to her. They both knew she didn't want to be alone with Matt. He had nearly destroyed her once, and they were giving him the opportunity to do it again.

"I have nothing whatever to say to you." Her voice was caustic.

"Well," Matt growled, "I have things to say to you."

For half an hour, they rode in silence. This was not the way he had planned it, Matt admitted to himself. Somehow, using all his charm and reason, he would have to ignore her anger and say his piece. Aunt Elizabeth still insisted that Amy be given a choice about marriage, that she had to give her consent freely. Matt frowned. That might take some doing.

Every so often, Matt sneaked a glance at the young woman sitting so rigidly next to him. Her luscious lips were drawn in an angry line, and her nose was held high, but more than once, he detected a slight quiver to her chin. For the first time since he had met Henry, Matt began to seriously wonder if she would accept his proposal.

A fleeting thought crossed his mind. Did she hate him? He hunched over in the seat, stunned. That idea had never occurred to him. He tried to dismiss it. She was just angry. She had responded to him on a number of occasions and had to feel some kind of attraction for him to have responded as she had.

Amy sat on the carriage seat, rocking with the motion of the vehicle, her back straight and stiff. She held her hands tightly together in her lap and debated whether he would take her back if she demanded it. Not a chance, she decided. He wanted to get her alone, had been trying for weeks to do just that, and—thanks to her traitorous relative, and perhaps his as well—he had her just where he wanted her. Her chin quivered as she blinked away her tears. She looked out over the passing landscape, and in the distance, Amy noticed what looked like a large lake.

Matt traveled on until he came to a grove of trees, and he pulled the carriage to a stop. From the position of the sun, Matt judged that it was about noon. He swung down from the carriage and stood at the door for several minutes before Amy even looked his way.

"Please, can we at least have lunch?" he asked softly.

She allowed him to help her down from the carriage and watched as he dug under the carriage robe. He lifted out a large hamper, grabbed the robe, and took her arm. Going toward the woods, he found a suitable spot and spread the woolen square under a large maple tree.

"Lunch is served," he said quietly. Taking her arm, he guided her to the blanket and helped her to sit on it.

Amy steeled herself for whatever Matt had planned. Resolving that she would not say a word to him, no matter what, she looked out through the trees to the edge of the lake a short distance away. She glanced around. They were in a small clearing in what seemed to be an isolated stand of maples and fir. She permitted herself to glance at him for a fraction of a second. He planned all of this, she thought angrily.

Matt smiled in her direction, then pulled two glasses and a bottle of wine from the hamper. "Amy," he said softly as he held the glass out to her. He poured her wine, wondering if she would say anything at all. If he could see her eyes, he thought, that might give a clue to her thoughts.

In that instant, it became very important to him to know if she hated him. He reached out and grabbed her chin. With a shaking voice he whispered, "Amy, do you hate me? Is that why you won't talk to me?"

Amy jerked and tried to pull away. She didn't want to look at his anxious face. What a peculiar question, she thought. When he released her, she gazed at the lake and shrugged her shoulders. "No. I don't hate you." She glanced back at him and then looked away once more.

Matt had read the surprise in her eyes, and he sighed in relief. At least that was in his favor. But there was an emotion in her eyes he had never seen before. Suddenly, he realized that it was apprehension. She was afraid of him. And it was no wonder, he admitted. He had been less than gentlemanly. "Amy," he whispered, "you don't need to be afraid of me."

Holding tightly to the glass in her hand and trying not to tremble, she stared down at the wine. She was

227

certainly not ready for this kind of introspection. How she felt about him really had no bearing on what she thought he wanted from her. And, yes, she admitted to herself, she was afraid of him, a little. In truth, she was really more afraid of what her own traitorous body would allow him to do to her than she was of him. However, she wasn't going to let him hear that from her lips.

Matt saw the fear in her eyes and misread its meaning. He was filled with self-disgust. Frowning, he considered what he had done to her. A small corner of his brain cried loudly, but she responded to you. And in the barn, she knew who you were, even if you didn't know who she was. He took a long, ragged breath. None of that mattered now. She was afraid of him, and he had to teach her to trust him somehow. He would simply have to start all over again.

The temptation to pull her into his arms was great. He wondered if he reached for her now, would she bolt and run. Deciding not to push her, he clenched his fists and stayed where he was. But he wanted her so badly that he suddenly blurted out, "Marry me!"

There, he had said it. Although it wasn't quite the way he had wanted to propose, it was a proposal nonetheless. Hesitating, he continued. "I . . . I want you to come to Texas with me. I want to build a home for you, for both of us. Don't answer me yet. Think about it for a day or two." He watched her carefully. There was no anger in her eyes that he could detect. Shock, yes, and confusion but no anger.

Afraid to look at her again, and petrified that she would reject him, Matt put his glass down and began attacking the picnic basket. As he pulled each carefully wrapped item from the straw hamper, he asked, "Would you like a piece of chicken, a biscuit, some fruit?" Quickly he filled her plate and one for himself and then refilled their wineglasses.

Amy stared at him in confusion. She had never expected a proposal. She had decided on the way to South Carolina that his insistence that they marry would be withdrawn after he and Henry became acquainted. This proposal was almost as if it had been dragged out of him. He said nothing about how he felt or even why he was proposing. As she ate the food and drank the wine, she sorted through a dozen questions she was afraid to ask.

As they ate, Matt told her about the lake and the river that flowed from it. "In the summer, the lake is filled with a flood of barges full of cotton bales as they float toward the sea. The cotton comes from all the plantations around here." He moved his arm in a wide arc. He told her about the Texas ranch he owned and about the house he wanted to build. When they had finished eating, he took her wineglass and plate and repacked the basket.

"Amy, why don't you stretch out for a nap? After I check the horses, that's what I'm going to do."

Amy listened and watched him. The idea of stretching out for a nap was a delightful surprise. At least, if she lay down and closed her eyes, she wouldn't have to answer his questions or listen to his plans.

Matt walked to where he had tied the horses at some distance from their picnic site. He strolled to the edge of the soft sand beach that ringed the picturesque lake, and for a long time, he stared out over

229

the expanse of rippling water. Finally, he strolled through the woods, back to the blanket, and his heart was pierced with such a tender ache, his breath caught in his tightening chest.

How he loved that gentle vision slumbering peacefully on the carriage blanket. When had she become such a necessary part of himself that he would never be complete without her? Somehow he had to convince her to go with him into a future full of promise in his bright new land.

Carefully, he stretched out next to her, wondering if he might be able to put his arm around her. He chuckled as she snuggled up next to him in her sleep. Whether she wanted to admit it or not, she did feel some attraction for him. It would take time and patience on his part, but he would make her recognize what they shared. He put his arm around her, the need to protect her welling up in his chest. She felt so warm, so fragile. He hurt from the pure pleasure of being so close to her. Somehow, he finally drifted off to sleep.

Chapter Sixteen

When Amy stirred, she felt the warm arm resting across her narrow waist and turned her head slightly to stare into Matt's sleeping face. More than anything, she was bewildered. He hadn't asked her about her past; instead he had talked about the lake and about Texas. She watched as he slept, his sandy brown hair curling over his head, and small bumps formed all over her skin. What was there about him that defied any experience she had had before? Just his nearness took her breath away. She frowned. He had made no declaration of love for her, and he had said nothing about how he felt. Did he feel strongly about her?

She paused. Henry. Her brother was determined to see her married. Through some mistaken desire for revenge, had Henry threatened the man lying at her side with harm if he did not propose marriage to her? But surely, Henry wouldn't force the issue without considering her feelings. Was Matt asking to marry her out of a sense of obligation? Her cheeks grew warm with embarrassment.

She felt his arm tighten around her waist ever so

gently, and her heart fluttered. Facing her own emotion with great alarm, she admitted he affected her strangely. In spite of what she thought he was, regardless of what he did to her, she felt a strong, irrational pull toward Matt Treadwell. Oh, no, she tensed, had she fallen in love with him? Yes, she was sure that she had. How could it have happened? And when?

His eyes fluttered open when she stiffened, and gazing into her solemn face, he grinned engagingly.

"Good morning. No, I guess it's good afternoon."

Suddenly filled with the desire to claim the slightly parted lips, he said quietly, "I'm going to kiss you." As he touched his lips to hers, time stopped.

In her fingers, a tingling started and then spiraled like wildfire through her body. She grew very warm. Deep in her subconscious, a small voice screamed, push him away, but her body refused to listen. She found herself succumbing to the sweet sensations surrounding her. Her arms slipped up to his neck and she embraced him.

Matt pulled away from her and gazed into her passion-dazed eyes. His voice, husky with emotion, was but a whisper. "If you keep kissing me like that . . ." His voice trailed off as he bent to once more drink from the sweetness of her lips. When his tongue pressed against her soft lips, they parted hesitantly. He tasted the sweetness of her mouth and probed deeply in a gentle invasion.

She thrilled at the intense pleasure that built within her as his tongue wandered within the dark recesses of her mouth. A warm pressure grew in her very center, and she felt an intense desire for more.

Her heart was pounding rapidly. Never before had she experienced such overpowering sensations.

Matt released her gradually. Holding her tenderly, he pleaded with her.

"Amy, will you marry me? Please say you will. Please say yes."

Amy looked into his eyes and was immediately drawn into his intense blue gaze. She could not deny her feelings to herself or to him, for he stirred something in her that she had not known existed. Whatever his reasons for proposing, she knew she would marry him. Perhaps later she could win his love. He felt something for her, even if only sensually. She was sure of that. For now, it seemed enough.

She murmured, "Yes, Matt. I will marry you."

When Amy agreed to his proposal, Matt tightened his embrace and covered her lips with his in another soul-shattering caress. After he kissed her mouth, he brushed his lips against her eyelids, across her cheeks, her temples, and finally, he rested his head on top of her gleaming brown curls, trying hard to regain a steady breath. A surge of joy brought tears to his eyes. His happiness was so intense he wanted to shout to the whole world. He wondered if he should reveal his feelings to her. This afternoon, he had gained more than he had dreamed possible. If he confessed the depths of his emotions now, would he frighten her more? Instinctively, he shook his head, no, he needed to show her by his actions how he truly felt. He must wait to say the words. But he had to tell her what was rolling through his soul. "Amy, I want you, I want you so much."

Immediately, he captured her lips, and she thrilled

to the exploration he made of her lips, her teeth, her tongue. Something was happening, and she was losing what little control she had. Desire curled its enticing fingers around her body, and somewhere in the distance she heard a soft sound like the purr of a contented cat. Had she made the sound, she wondered. The kiss went on and on until she knew that if she could breathe, her lungs would not function. Her heart was trying hard to escape its confines.

Instinctively, she knew that he was releasing the tiny buttons of her gray suit, but she couldn't protest. She didn't have the strength. She felt his warm breath tickling her neck before she melted under the touch of his lips, nibbling down her neck, over her shoulders, down, down, to the throbbing mound of flesh that begged to be touched, caressed, teased by him. As if he could read her mind, his tongue trailed over her breasts, first one and then the other, avoiding the peak.

She wiggled, arching herself up, hoping, praying that he would know what she wanted. When she felt his tongue brush across the nipple, she sighed in pleasure. The words spilled over her lips. "Oh, yes, yes."

Suddenly her bodice was gone and so was his shirt, and he pulled her next to him, his ragged breath echoing through her head. "Amy, somehow I'll stop if you want me to."

She shook her head. No, she didn't want him to stop. It was unthinkable. Her whole body was crying for his touch. He couldn't stop now. She pulled at him, trying to tell him without words, that she didn't want to leave his side. In the back of her mind, a tiny voice cried out to be heard, but she wanted no part of the questions, not now, and she pushed the voice back, away from the world of pleasure that surrounded her.

She reached up to run her fingers across his broad chest. There was a smattering of blond fuzz, and she pushed her fingers through it, touching, stroking, kneading until she reached the tiny pap over his heart. She felt the quick intake of breath, and she wound her hands through his hair, easing his head up toward her lips.

As his lips pressed into hers, his fingers took up the play where his lips had been, and Amy wondered if she would explode from the growing sensations that traveled through her. This time, when his tongue made bold play, she met him in a game of her own.

She wasn't really surprised when she felt the waistband of her skirt and then the drawstring of her petticoats loosen. She sensed that he was pulling them from her, and she didn't care. Arching up against him, she held her arms around his neck. As long as he kissed her the way he was kissing her now, he could do anything.

Matt pulled away from her, and she whimpered. He whispered against her ear, "I have to remove my shoes and my pants." Reality tried to force its way through her mind, and for an instant she tensed, but just as quickly he was back, drawing her into his arms and holding her tightly. She felt the coarse texture of his bare legs, the skin of his belly, the evidence of his desire hard and throbbing against her stomach. Some fuzzy memory was trying hard to

235

surface, but she fought to ignore it. He was kissing her again, and that was all she could recognize now.

He moved up over her, and the memory surged to the fore. The pain, that awful pain in the barn. It would happen again; she must not let it happen again.

Matt seemed to sense what was in her mind, and he pleaded in a husky whisper, "Amy, please! I won't hurt you. It won't hurt again, I promise." He kissed her hard, and as he pushed his tongue into the sweet cavern, he eased his manhood into another sweet cavern. She sighed. No, it wasn't pain she felt, but something else. A need, a want, a desire that twisted and curled around the place of their joining.

She relaxed against him, and he savored the moment. He had waited so long. He continued to kiss her and, pressed against her, fought for control. Gradually, he withdrew, then he thrust forward again, and she cried out in surprise. Alarmed, he froze. Had he hurt her? He jerked his head up and stared down at her. She sensed his gaze and lifted up her lids above her blue-gray eyes clouded with desire. She smiled at him. He pulled away and once more sank deep into her warmth. Her eyes drifted shut, and she sighed in pleasure.

Matt was lost. He struggled to bring her up the stairway of ecstasy without losing himself to the realm of pleasure before she had touched the heavens. He felt her tense, heard the tiny gasp, and knew that she was floating above him, waiting for him to join her in that perfect moment. He gave himself up to pleasure.

Amy drifted back down to reality, aware that

something very unusual had occurred. Warm lips nuzzled her throat, her earlobes, her eyes, and she sighed in contentment. Somehow, she didn't feel guilty about what she had just done, and she opened her eyes to stare up into the somber gaze of her husband-to-be.

"Amy, I didn't — I wasn't going to —" he stuttered, wondering if he had lost everything."

She smiled up at him. "It's all right, Matt. I'll marry you."

He kissed her once more, and then he slid to her side. Silently, he handed her her clothing and turned to pick up his own. When they were once again dressed, he pulled her into his arms and stared down into her face. He said nothing, but before he lowered his lips to kiss her once again, he smiled. That smile warmed the center of her heart, and she kissed him back shyly.

The ride back to Elton Estate was a much different trip from the one to the lake. They traveled at a slow and leisurely pace, and Matt held her close to him on the carriage seat. He told her all about the old prospector and his hunt for gold in the mountains of the Colorado Territory. Frequently, he reached out to hold her hands, glancing at her often.

Amy was amazed that he appeared as happy as he did. As the miles slipped past, her suspicion that Henry might have forced the issue grew slimmer and slimmer. Dusk had turned the sky into a sea of crimson splotches when they pulled up at the gates of Elton Estate.

Henry greeted them at the front door and he breathed a sigh of relief. Neither one looked angry or upset. Since Aunt Elizabeth had been so determined that Amy be allowed to make her own decision concerning Matt, Henry was more than a little apprehensive. Amy was a stubborn girl, Henry knew from past experience. She was also independent. She could easily have bolted and run for home. Henry scowled. It wasn't that he was selfish, but after her lengthy absence from home and the kidnapping, finding a suitable husband for her would be nearly impossible. And, damn it, he liked Matt. The man seemed personable, and he cared deeply for Amy, Henry was sure. As far as he was concerned, she couldn't do much better. But if she truly disliked Matt or felt that he was unsuitable, she would be very difficult indeed.

The smiling couple were barely through the door when Matt pulled Henry to the side. "Amy needs to change for dinner, and you and I need to talk."

Henry raised his eyebrows. "The study?" Matt nodded his head, and the two men moved toward the study.

As they left, Amy rushed upstairs to change for dinner. She dressed hurriedly so that she could go talk to Aunt Elizabeth before the men came out.

She found Aunt Elizabeth in the kitchen, giving instructions for the evening meal. Amy looked self-conscious, but she dragged her to the parlor. "I need to talk to you."

When they were seated, Amy said softly, "Matt has asked me to marry him."

"Yes, dear. I know."

"How did you know?" Amy's voice echoed her surprise.

"Matt told me months ago he wanted to marry you. I told him he had to wait and court you properly, before he asked. You did say yes." It was more a statement than a question.

Amy wasn't ready to answer that question yet. "Did Henry have anything to do with it?"

"I don't think so." Aunt Elizabeth frowned. Matt had sounded much too happy for the girl to have turned him down. "What did you tell him, dear?"

"I said yes."

Aunt Elizabeth hugged her tightly. "I know you'll be happy. Matt is a good boy, and he'll be a good husband."

Aunt Elizabeth missed her softly muttered response, "I hope so."

The two women waited for over a half an hour before Matt and Henry left the privacy of the study. Both men were smiling broadly, and Henry looked very relieved.

When they were settled at the table for dinner, Matt, with great solemnity, rose from the table, his wineglass in his hand. In a grave voice he said, "It gives me great pleasure to announce that Amy Sanderson has agreed to become my wife." He sat down and grinned like a small boy with his first puppy. Aunt Elizabeth, Henry, and even Amy laughed.

Aunt Elizabeth was wiping tears from her eyes as Henry, still chuckling, turned to Matt. "That was totally unnecessary."

Matt grinned back. "I was just practicing." That brought more peals of laughter from everyone at the table.

The evening was as glorious as the day had been,

239

and after dinner, Matt took Amy out into the soft September evening. They sat on a stone bench in the garden, which was fragrant with late summer blooms. He held both her hands in his large ones.

"You don't mind if we don't wait too long before we marry, will you? I'm afraid there's no getting out of an announcement party. Aunt Elizabeth already mentioned something to me before dinner. And the banns have to be published. Could we set a date, say, three or four months from now?"

Amy watched him carefully, still not quite sure of him despite what they had shared. "Four months will be fine," she said quietly. She counted on her fingers. "The end of January?"

Matt sat still for a minute and then pulled her into his arms. "I think I can wait that long." He grinned down at her, then brushed her lips with a light kiss, and held her as gently as he could, denying his need to hold her closer. Suddenly, his whole demeanor changed. He was rigid.

Amy looked at him in concern. What had caused the change? She fought her panic. Something was wrong.

"Amy," he said quietly, "maybe we better not wait. What if we have a baby."

She stared at him. A baby? No, it wasn't possible. She shook her head. No, it couldn't have happened. She forced the words over the lump in her throat. "Can't we wait? I don't think . . ." She turned a bright pink and tried to pull herself from his arms.

He held her tight. "We'll wait and see. Lots of little ones arrive before their parents have been married for nine months. If we've started a child, he'll be in good company." He chuckled softly. "It just means that the parents were so attracted to each other that they couldn't wait." He brushed her lips tenderly and held her gently against him. Gradually, she relaxed and finally snuggled up to him. He whispered, "I'll tell Aunt Elizabeth the wedding will be the end of January."

Kissing her once more, he gazed at her intently. "Do you want a wedding trip?"

Amy glanced up at him with a weary expression. "I don't know."

"With all your traveling recently, I hesitate planning any kind of trip. We could always send Aunt Elizabeth away and stay here ourselves."

Amy smiled at him gratefully. "Could we do that?"

Matt looked at her thoughtfully. "You know, that's not such a poor plan." He glanced at her seriously. It was a great idea, and it would solve many problems. He wondered how Aunt Elizabeth would react to enforced travel herself. "I'll talk to Aunt Elizabeth." He murmured into her hair, "There's one other thing we have to do."

Amy pulled away from him and looked at his face. His eyes were cold, and there was a scowl on his face. Whatever else they had to do was something that Matt didn't like at all.

"We have to tell Phillip." His tone was grim.

"Can't you tell him? I really don't have to go with you, do I? He doesn't like me."

"I think you should go," Matt said softly, and to himself he added, "I won't do something to him that I'll regret if you're along." Aloud, he said, "but, we

241

won't stay long, just long enough to issue an invitation to him. It will be the last time you have to go to Willows. After we've faced Phillip, we can go into Anderson and see about a new wardrobe for you, something for the announcement ball and your wedding gown." Matt grinned at her, looking quite pleased with himself.

Amy giggled. "Matt, you can't go with me to see about my wedding dress. It isn't done."

"Well, we'll see. And now I think it's time for you to retire. You still need rest, and there are a hundred things to do and not much time in which to do them."

He stood up and drew her into his arms. He kissed her hard and felt the shiver pass through her slender body. When her arms slid up to encircle his neck and she pressed her body next to his, he pushed her away gently, but deliberately. "We're not married yet," he mumbled, more to himself than to her.

After he had escorted her up to her room, he went in search of Aunt Elizabeth to cajole her into an unplanned January trip to visit her family in Georgia.

Alone in her room, Amy stood in front of the dressing table. Automatically, she picked up her hairbrush and began to brush her long tresses. She stood deep in thought, a frown playing across her face. What had she done, and why, oh why had she agreed to marry him? When she was close to him, she couldn't think straight.

She was sure that she was deeply in love with him,

242

but he had never once indicated feeling anything more than an attraction for her. There was no question he was attracted to her, just as she was to him, but without love . . . Could she make him love her? Should she back out and go home, even though she had given her word? Did she really want to marry him? Yes, she did want that, she was sure of that. She was terribly confused, and there was no one she could talk to. Even Aunt Amelia would have been welcome this night.

A light rap on the door interrupted her thoughts. Henry stood at the door, smiling at her. He took her face in his hands. "Sister, I wish you all happiness. I know Matt will make a good husband for you. I feel certain that Matt will shower you with affection." Henry chuckled, then added, "It seems you've stolen his heart." He kissed her on the forehead and left her standing in the doorway. Well, she admitted grimly, at least Henry was happy, but she couldn't believe that Matt had surrendered his heart. Henry was mistaken about that.

The next month flew by in a flurry of preparations for the ball and the wedding to come. Amy told Matt with much embarrassment that they had not started a child, and she threw herself into the plans for the wedding. Aunt Elizabeth spent her time making lists of things that everyone had to do and all the people that had to be invited. She decided on a November date for the ball, and she and Amy went into town to select a gown for the ball and one for the wedding.

243

One Sunday evening, Matt gathered his weary Amy in his arms and announced that before the week was over, they had to go to Willows to see Phillip. But the next day Matt and Henry went to town to take care of the bans and the church and send all the messages Matt had written. He sent a letter to the Georgia relatives to arrange for Aunt Elizabeth's trip of six months. She, herself, insisted that if she was going to visit, two or three weeks wouldn't justify the time. And she pointed out that he and Amy needed at least that amount of time together before they left for Texas.

Amy had forgotten about Phillip herself, for one of the tasks Aunt Elizabeth had assigned her was writing the invitations to the ball and the wedding. She also wrote her own relatives, telling them of their plans. The South had been isolated from the North back in June when the Postmaster ordered that no Southern mail could travel through the federal system, but Matt and Henry devised a method to smuggle the notices home.

Amy had demonstrated her ability at Willows, and Aunt Elizabeth insisted that she plan the menu for the dinner for the ball and the wedding as well.

Even Henry was told tersely by Aunt Elizabeth that he had to oversee the cleaning of the plantation grounds and the rearranging of the stables to accommodate all the carriages and horses that would arrive carrying the visitors who would stay for several days.

Three days before the ball, Matt took Amy out to the garden, and together they sat next to an old rosebush. Amy brushed against the dead blooms and frowned. Surely this was not a symbol of her future. She tried to discount the brooding feeling as Matt held her hand, and she waited expectantly for him to broach whatever subject he had brought her out into the chilly evening breezes to discuss.

Her heart sank when she looked up at his anguished face. Had she trusted too soon? Was he about to call off the wedding? She waited, afraid to breathe.

"Amy, we have to go see Phillip."

"Is that why you look so upset?"

"That, and we've not discussed our future beyond the coming few months," he muttered softly.

Amy took a deep breath and glanced at the rose-bush. What kind of a future did he mean?

"We need to make plans for our trip to Texas," he began. "We can't leave until May, and I think we should wait until September at least. There are no inns along the way, so we'll have to travel in the wagon, and it's just too hot to travel all that distance in a wagon in the summer heat. Also, I'm not sure how the cattle will handle the trip, so we have to wait for nearly a year. I'm afraid it will be a rough trip for you. With the war on, there's no way to tell what we may run into."

Amy began to breathe naturally, his concern was for her. "Matt, I've never traveled much. I think I'll enjoy the trip. It will be like an adventure."

"You're sure?"

Amy nodded, a small smile playing across her lips.

Matt pulled her into his arms and, succumbing to the powerful natural urges he had been fighting for days, kissed her hard. When he pulled away from her, they were both visibly shaken.

"Lady, you do something to me," he muttered.

He rose from the bench and took Amy by the arm. "We'll leave for Willows right after breakfast tomorrow. Let's get it over with. Now, I think you ought to get some sleep." Once more, he pulled her into his arms and kissed her like a man dying of thirst facing a cool mountain stream.

Amy smiled up at him. Sleep was going to be very difficult this night, especially when he kept kissing her like that.

The next day dawned gray wet, and Amy shivered against the chill in the air. It almost seemed that the weather was a herald of a battle yet to come. She dressed carefully, telling herself that she didn't want Phillip to find more fault with her than he did already. Matt also appeared to have spent more than his usual time dressing when he joined her for breakfast.

Breakfast was a somber meal, and Amy could think of nothing to say. Matt looked equally grim. His only comment came when he handed her into the carriage. "I don't want to do this," he mumbled as he took his place beside her. They traveled for almost an hour before anything more was said. Amy watched him carefully. Phillip, it seemed, affected Matt even more than she had thought.

When they finally arrived at Willows, one of the slaves opened the door and left them standing in the foyer, while he sought the master of the house. Matt frowned. It was clear that Phillip had already issued orders that they were not even to be shown common courtesy.

Phillip came from the dining room and greeted them with indifference. He listened to Matt's announcement without comment.

Finally, he glanced at Amy and said smugly, "Well, I suppose I am to blame. I did bring you here, didn't I?" He turned to Matt and snapped, "If you think that I'm going to offer congratulations, you're wrong." Suddenly Phillip's face reddened, and he glared at Matt. "I sent you to the best schools, even sent you to England, and you end up marrying Northern trash. I saved you from one disastrous marriage. You'll have to get yourself out of this one."

Matt bristled and he clenched his fists at his side. In a voice that thundered through the hall, he hurled, "I feel Amy will make an admirable wife. I don't think I could have chosen a better mate, and, brother, if I were you, I'd watch what I call your future sister-in-law. Aunt Elizabeth isn't here to stop me from strangling you this time." Matt turned on his heel and rushed for the door.

Phillip shouted after him. "Don't think I'll grace your little party, or your wedding either."

Amy gathered her courage and smiled sweetly at him. "We didn't think you'd come, but my upbringing has taught me not to exclude anyone from family functions." She turned to follow Matt to the door.

Phillip shot past her and grabbed Matt's arm as he reached for the doorknob. "I told you more than once that you don't know anything about her. You don't know if she's a tramp or whether she's been tried before. You don't—"

Matt gave him a murderous glance, and before Phillip had finished speaking, Matt swung. He caught Phillip on the chin and sent him sprawling. Then Matt grabbed Amy's arm and pulled her from the house. He helped her into the carriage and followed her into the seat. He was shaking with anger.

He looked back at the house, his eyes snapping, his lips a thin white line. Jumping from the carriage, he ran back toward the house "I'll be right back," he called as he went through the double doors.

Amy frowned. They shouldn't have come. She had no idea what Matt meant about strangling Phillip and the punch Matt delivered could have been serious. They seemed to hate each other. In fact, Matt was probably fighting with Phillip now. She debated whether she should climb down and go to Matt's aid, but before she could decide, Matt came swinging out through the massive portal.

Amy was close to tears as Matt bounded into the carriage. He grinned down at her. "I went back to get something that belongs to me." Matt patted her hand. "I demanded an apology from him, but I didn't get it. I'll apologize for him. I should never have put you through that. The only good thing to come from all of this is that he told me he has joined the Confederate Army. His commission came last week. He'll be leaving in a day or two. Phillip won't be here to dampen any of our celebration." She felt as relieved as Matt looked.

Chapter Seventeen

Each absorbed in thought, Amy and Matt were silent as they traveled through the gray day into Anderson. It was clear that Phillip hated her and everything she stood for. It was for the best, Amy decided, that she and Matt would live in Texas. They would probably never see Phillip again.

After they lunched at the local inn, Matt took her to the dressmaker where she picked up her ball gown. She had ordered a dark-blue watered silk that matched Matt's eyes. The deep sweetheart neckline had a draped collar of the same shimmering fabric, and the full puffed sleeves ended above her elbows. The full skirt cascaded in layers of ruffles. Petticoats, silk hose, and shoes to match were ready for her, and Matt teased her about all the many packages as he led her back to the carriage.

By now the gray clouds had begun to puff and boil across the sky. They were in for a storm, and

Matt hurried her along. Once they were well on their way back to Elton Estate, Matt relaxed. He commented about Aunt Elizabeth's pleasure in planning the party and the wedding. They both chuckled about her enthusiasm for the visit to her family in Georgia and at the way she was working poor Henry to death with her countless little projects.

They still had several miles to go when Matt stopped the carriage by the river and jumped down from his seat. He swung Amy down in one easy motion, then walked the horse to a nearby bush, and loosely tied the reins to a branch. They stood for several minutes as they watched the swirl of the river made full by the fall rains of the preceding weeks. Then Matt led her along a narrow path by the edge of the river. Years before it had been constructed to allow the mules to pull the cotton barges back up the river to their point of origin.

They had walked only a few feet when Matt placed an arm around Amy's shoulders and pulled her to a stop. Taking a small velvet box from his vest pocket, he handed it to her. "I went back to the house this morning to get this. It isn't expensive, and it's not all that elegant, but I wanted you to have it."

Amy gazed up at his solemn face before she opened the worn little box. Inside, lying on a bed of aged yellowing satin was a gleaming golden pendant and a matching gold chain. Amy lifted the unusual charm out of the box and turned it around in her fingers. It was an ornate letter *A* laid against an intricately cut gold rose.

"It belonged to my mother. My father had it

250

made for her when they were betrothed. Her name was Anna." Matt sighed softly.

"Oh, Matt, it's lovely."

"Will you wear it with your dress Saturday? Diamonds or sapphires would be more elegant and probably more proper, but I would like you to wear this. It would mean a lot to me."

"I'll wear it always," she promised softly. Her eyes were shining with her unspoken love. Holding the pendant against her throat, she turned her back to him so that he could fasten the chain. Matt turned her around and stepped back a full arm's length to view his gift around her neck. Pulling her into his arms, he kissed her so softly her knees melted and she swayed against him.

Matt held her tightly, and his voice, little more than a hoarse whisper, murmured against her small pink earlobe. "I can't live without you. I couldn't survive."

Amy felt her heart float up and lodge in her throat. He wasn't marrying her because he felt it was his duty. Although he probably wouldn't admit it yet, he did love her. In time, he would say the words. Suddenly, she was deliciously happy, and she felt more secure than she had in months.

Feeling guilty about doubting his intentions, she did something she had never done before. She lifted her arms up to his neck, pulled his head down gently, and touched his lips with her own. Gingerly, she traced his lips with her tongue. She guided the tip of her tongue between his parted lips and hesitantly touched his tongue with her own. Her sensual nature was expressing itself, and to her pleasant surprise she was drowning in warm sensations. She trembled from pure pleasure.

Matt stood shaking as he sensed her surfacing emotions. He could read them in her expressive eyes. She was giving herself to him completely. He staggered under the sweet responsibility of her trust. And he was fast losing control. He broke off the kiss, and his voice sounded distant and strained even to him.

"We better go back now, or I'll take you over to those woods, and I won't care about the wedding at all." He gestured to a small stand of trees several yards from the road.

She looked at him and smiled. "Yes, let's go back." Fingering the golden rose that hung about her neck, she wondered if she should tell him how she felt about him or wait for his declaration that she was certain would come in time. Smiling easily now, she gazed up at him. Soon she would tell him how much she loved him. She could wait.

Matt led her back to the carriage and hoisted her up to the seat. She smiled over at him when he took his place beside her. Fingering the small letter, she glanced up at the sky. "It looks like rain at any moment," she said as he chucked the horses into movement.

"We'll be back at Elton Estate soon," Matt assured her. She looked a little doubtful, but she said nothing.

They had been back on the road for only ten minutes when Amy felt the first cold drops of rain. "Matt, we're not going to make it."

Matt gazed at the sky and then turned to her.

"There used to be several old cabins around here. The men that handled the barges used them. We better try and find one." He started the horse down a path away from the river, his face drawn in concern. Amy had only just recovered and she mustn't get wet and cold, or she would be back in bed again. He coaxed the horse on at a faster clip.

The rain was gathering speed, and Matt said a quick prayer that he remembered correctly. During the time that he had worked with Phillip on the plantation he had been forced to rout their bargemen out of the shacks once or twice. The cabins were nothing fancy, but they would provide shelter.

The wet drops were coming down in a steady stream when Matt finally found what he was looking for. Set off to one side of the old path was a dilapidated frame structure. He stopped the horse and rushed Amy into the empty building. She stood shivering in the cold, damp room while Matt went back out to secure the horse and bring in the boxes that contained her apparel for the ball.

While Matt was gathering the boxes, Amy looked around. The cabin was about the same size as the one she, Emma, and Jacob had stopped in the first night away from Willows. It was just as empty, except this structure boasted a fireplace and a huge stack of cut logs. She stared at the empty hearth. A warm log fire would be delicious, she thought. She was cold and wet.

The door slammed shut, and she turned to her soon-to-be husband. Suddenly, the intimacy of the moment struck her, and she wondered if this was a good idea. The air crackled with expectation, and she lowered her eyes. Matt's husky voice broke the silence.

"I think a roaring fire is in order."

She glanced up at him, and one look told her that his thoughts were the same as her own. In that instant, she knew. He was going to make love to her again, and despite the wet, cold clothes that clung to her, she felt a warmth stir through her. She was stunned when she realized that she wanted him to love her, right here and now.

Matt tackled the job of laying a fire. As he worked, he commented, "You better get out of those wet clothes. Once the fire is started, they'll dry out quickly. There'll be plenty of time. We'll have to stay here until the rain stops."

She raised stiff fingers to the buttons of her bodice and tried to force the small bone balls through the slits in the fabric, but she succeeded in freeing only a few before Matt's warm fingers covered hers.

"I'll do it," he whispered softly.

Amy stared into his face and watched as his eyes followed the line of her bodice. She felt the brush of cold air as he eased the wet fabric from her shoulders. Seconds later, she felt the heavy, damp material of her skirt drift down her legs. She glanced down and stared at the chemise that covered her. Even it was damp and cold. She stepped closer to the fire, trying to absorb some of the heat. The rustle in back of her could only be Matt loosening his own garments, and she stared into the fire. Was this truly what she wanted? She forced her cold hand out to welcome the building heat of the fire. She wouldn't think. There were no answers

254

anyway. She turned around.

Matt stood before her. Gone were his jacket, his shirt, his shoes, but he was still wearing his pants. She sighed in relief. Her imagination was running away with her, she told herself, yet she couldn't explain why she was disappointed. And she was.

Matt moved away from her, to the woodpile, and then he stepped in front of the fire, flipping the blanket in front of the fire. He added another and then held out his hand to her. She took his hand, stepped to the blanket, and sank down before the fire. He followed her down, and together they sat staring into the fire and listening to the droplets of water strike the fire and hiss. Amy was never sure when he put his arm around her, but when he drew her up next to him, she sighed in anticipation. He was going to make love to her.

He turned her head toward his and probed her eyes, as if the look there would give him the answer he needed. His husky voice rose above the crackling of the fire.

"I ache with wanting you. I don't think I can leave you alone."

She brought her arms up around his neck and stared into the dark pools of midnight blue. She was certain that what she saw in those eyes was love, a quiet, reassuring love. She smiled at him and gently pulled his head toward hers.

Matt lowered his lips to cover hers. He probed with his tongue, and she opened to him without hesitation, her tongue meeting his. He spread his hands behind her back and traced the ribs around to the front. Through the clinging damp fabric of her chemise, he sought the firm flesh of her breast. He could feel the tightening of the tiny bud, and he flicked his thumb across it. She stiffened for a fraction of a second and then melted against him. He worked his fingers up to the neckline of the chemise and pulled at its ties. He broke his kiss and gently laid her back on the blanket. Stretching over her, he rested his weight on his hands and kissed her eyelids, her cheeks, her chin. He nibbled at her throat, over her collarbone, and across the firm flesh of the swells partially hidden by her chemise.

Amy opened her eyes and glanced at the dark head just below her chin. Amazing, she thought. Only minutes before she had been so cold, and now she was warmer than she had ever been in her life, warm from the heat that stirred her soul. A sigh left her lips, and Matt lifted his head to stare into her eyes. He grabbed at the ties of her chemise with his teeth and tugged it down over her breasts. The damp fabric grazed her breasts and her nipples, and tiny waves of pleasure shot through her. She sighed once more and lifted heavy arms to drape them over his shoulders. Running her hands over his muscles, she marveled at his strength.

He trailed his teeth over her taut skin, settled against her breast. As she fought to control her ragged breath, he sucked the nub into his mouth, and she arched up against him. Pleasure wound through her, and she gasped. Suddenly her chemise was gone, and she sensed that he was working to free himself of his breeches. She felt him kick the garment free, and then his mouth was over hers again. She strained against him, holding him close.

256

How she would love to run her hands over his body as he had hers. Perhaps someday she would gather enough courage.

At that instant, she felt the touch of his manhood against her thigh, and she lifted her hips to meet him and welcome him home. All thought deserted her as she thrust against him, waiting for the building pleasure that now she knew would come. And it did. Pressing against him, she climbed higher and higher yet until she was floating above herself. There was a pause, and then she flew out against the heavens, small parts of her shooting out and then returning to once more form a whole. She glided back down, aware of his body, so different from her own, aware of the warmth from the fire and the warmth within her.

She turned to look at him. At some point he had rolled her over so that she was on her side, and he was beside her. She gazed into his eyes, no words necessary. Her eyes drifted shut, and she floated into a peaceful sleep.

How long she slept she didn't know, but Matt was tugging on her shoulder. "Come on, sleepyhead. The rain has stopped. We better go before it starts again."

She rolled over to look at him. He was standing over her, struggling into his clothes. She sat up and began to put on her own things. In short order, the blankets were folded, the fire was doused with wet sand, and the carriage loaded. Matt led Amy out to the carriage, but before he hoisted her into the seat, he wrapped his arms around her waist and drew her close. Once more he kissed her; then he swung her up and placed her on the carriage seat.

Amy looked around her. The day was still wet and gray, but the contentment that wafted around her made the day seem bright and happy. Her fingers drifted up to the pendant Matt had given her. They would have a good life. She snuggled up next to him as he climbed in beside her. A happy smile tugged at her lips. It had been a glorious day, and there would be many others.

Phillip was in a rage. He was more furious than he had ever been in his life. Matt had had the audacity to demand an apology from him. An apology. Matt should have been apologizing to him. Phillip smirked when he remembered yelling that he was going to fight for what was his. Matt had asked quietly if he had joined the army. In spite of all of the education Matt had received, he wasn't the brightest boy around. No, he wasn't talking about the Confederate Army when he said he was going to fight. He was thinking of the Northern trollop Matt said he was going to marry.

Where had he gone wrong? He shook his head. Perhaps he should have told Matt what he had planned. For years now, he knew that the plantation would go to Matt. The land he loved, had denied himself everything for, would go to Matt and his heirs. He would never marry, for he had been less than a man ever since an hunting accident when he was twenty-three. And he would not allow what was his whole life to fall into the hands of Northerners. He would not, could not let that happen. Matt had to marry a good Southern girl from a decent background.

There must be something he could do. Somehow, he had to force Amy to desert Matt and run for home, back to Indiana. He cursed himself for not sending her back when he had first found her with the slaves.

He sat and stared at the empty hearth. He didn't have the time to figure out how to stop the wedding. There just wasn't time. But he had to devise a plan that would keep Matt from taking the girl to Texas. He had two weeks before he had to report to his regiment. He had to think of something in two weeks.

Phillip paced the floor of his study. Could he separate the couple? Could he get Amy alone and destroy her feelings for Matt? He could make her suspicious, he was certain of that. It had worked once before when Matt was too young to marry. He could make it work again. It mattered little that they would have already spoken their vows. As far as he was concerned, marrying a girl from the North was no marriage at all.

If he kept Matt away from Amy long enough, could he convince her that Matt was . . . Stroking his chin, he sank into his chair. What could he force Matt to do that would turn Amy against him? Probably nothing. He had trouble forcing Matt to answer his questions. Could he trick Matt into doing something? No, he couldn't make Matt do much of anything. Could he make it appear that Matt had done something, something that Amy would hate?

He reviewed all the conversations he had had with Amy, with Matt, with Aunt Elizabeth. Suddenly, an idea started to surface. He grinned. There was something he could do. It would take careful planning, but it just might work. No. It had to work. He would make it work. He jumped up from his chair and hurried out of the study. He had work to do.

He packed quickly and left for Charlotte that afternoon. A Mr. Paxton had been recommended by a good friend, and Phillip knew he was the man for the job. He found him easily. When Mr. Paxton informed Phillip that he was available, Phillip outlined the job, and they agreed on a price. For two days, Phillip and Harvey Paxton went over details. By the time Phillip was ready to leave for his regiment in Atlanta, the plans had been fine-tuned and Phillip was satisfied. The wedding would proceed, but before six months had passed, Amy Sanderson would be back in Indiana, hating the South and Matthew Treadwell with her heart and soul.

He arrived in Atlanta and reported to his commanding officer with two days to spare. Even though he had no intention of attending his brother's wedding, he needed the time to finish his plans. When he met his commanding officer, he told him about Matt's wedding, explaining that this was his only blood relative, his younger brother. He requested a short leave of absence, from the middle of January to the first week of February, so that he could attend this one-time family occasion.

Phillip was delighted with the way everything was proceeding. By the end of December, Harvey sent the information Phillip had requested and informed him that everything was ready for the last step. He would be at the designated place the eighteenth day of January. Phillip laughed with satisfaction. "You're going home, you little Northern bitch," he muttered.

Chapter Eighteen

The day of the ball came quickly, and Amy tried to relax. She assured herself that everything that could be done ahead of time was done, and there was nothing to worry about. All she had to do was rest, bathe, and dress. She spent the morning helping Aunt Elizabeth arrange bouquets of strawflowers for the house. After lunch, she crawled into her bed for the nap Aunt Elizabeth insisted she take.

When she awoke, a bath scented with roses waited for her, and Aunt Elizabeth sent one of her own servants to arrange her hair. She dressed carefully, and after the servant left, she fastened the delicate letter pendant around her throat. She sat before the mirror for a long time. She was scared to death, and she didn't know why. When Matt and Aunt Elizabeth had squired her to all of the parties before and after Christmas, Amy had been playing a role. She had been someone else.

But she was not playacting now. She was Amy Sanderson of Indiana. Tonight, Matt would officially announce to his Southern relatives and friends that he was marrying her. What would they say, how would they feel when they learned the truth? She had to look her best for Matt. Staring in the mirror, she tried to view herself objectively. The new hairstyle Aunt Elizabeth had insisted upon was becoming, and the dress was such a brilliant color that it made her eyes more blue than gray. She was pleased with what she saw. At least, Matt would not be ashamed of her.

At last the time for the ball arrived. For most of the evening, she stood by Matt's side, greeting their guests and, when there were no guests at hand, listening to Matt's whispered terms of endearment. Once or twice, when he thought no one was looking, he kissed her temple, her cheek, and all evening long, he held her hand. Amy glanced around in embarrassment, but Matt didn't seem to mind in the least what people might think.

Shortly before midnight, with Aunt Elizabeth and Henry joining them, Matt took her hand and led her before the crowd of their friends. In solemn tones, he declared that Amy Sanderson had agreed to become his wife. There were congratulations and toasts, and to the few questions that were raised about her name, Matt just beamed. He explained quietly that Amy Stuart Sanderson used both names, and no, to their knowledge, she was not related to the Scottish Stuarts.

Amy retired that night exhausted but deliriously happy. No one had seemed the least upset that she was not what they had hinted at before Christmas. All the friends had seemed genuinely happy that she and Matt had found each other. It had been a wonderful party. Matt had been a perfect host and had been so concerned with her happiness and so attentive that any tiny doubts she had floated away to oblivion. Matt loved her; he just didn't know it yet. Snuggling into her soft bed, safe and secure, she closed her eyes and drifted into a deep and peaceful sleep.

Two months remained before the wedding, and the time was speeding by at an alarming rate. Henry's plans were made. He would start home the day after the wedding. Aunt Elizabeth packed her trunks for her six months' stay in Atlanta. Matt and Amy attended several prenuptial parties given for them by Matt's relatives and family friends. Christmas came and went in the flurry of wedding preparations.

Several times, Amy traveled into Anderson for fittings for the wardrobe Matt insisted upon for their trip to Texas. As Matt pointed out when they argued about the clothes, out in the wilds of the West there were few dressmakers and less cloth. Amy would have to take her clothes with her or make whatever she needed until the area developed enough to have a town with a dressmaker. Amy quit arguing and agreed to the fittings.

Her last trip into Anderson was to pick up her wedding dress. In November Aunt Elizabeth had helped her choose the style and fabric. It was a pale, soft pink satin. It had a high neckline and tiny satin buttons closing the plain bodice. A long narrow point at the front of the waist emphasized the full, flowing skirt that trailed into a short train. The puffed sleeves were elbow length and gathered about the cuffs with a cluster of silk daisies nestled in the gathers. Small clusters of daisies covered the hem of the dress and were sprinkled across the train. Aunt Elizabeth insisted that she carry a bunch of silk daisies for the wedding.

Amy couldn't figure out how Aunt Amelia managed to send a veil of lace so sheer that it appeared to float above her like a soft mist following a summer storm. When Matt saw the veil, he went to Anderson and returned with two small golden pins made of tiny rosebuds to hold the veil in place.

The day before the wedding the house was cluttered with boxes, gifts, trunks, and people arriving for the celebration. Amy hadn't realized that Matt had such a large family of aunts, uncles, and cousins until she met them all as they arrived for the nuptials. None of Amy's family was able to make the long trip, so Henry was her only representative.

Matt made a point of wondering why Alex couldn't come. Alex had sent word that he had left school and was heading for a small regiment of Indiana volunteers in southern Ohio, but there was no military action where Alex was located. Angrily, Matt told Henry, "He's the oldest, he should give the bride away. You can't be best man and give the bride away, too."

Amy couldn't understand why Matt seemed so disappointed about Alex. Henry was there and could give her away. Any one of Matt's cousins could act as best man. She wiped at the tears that glistened when she thought about Henry's departure the day after the wedding. She wondered how long it would be before she saw her brother again. Texas was a long way from Indiana.

The evening before the wedding, when Matt commented on how pale she was and how nervous she seemed, she was sent to bed early. Even Aunt Elizabeth expressed a fear that she might have overdone, that perhaps she was becoming ill again. Amy couldn't tell anyone, not even Aunt Elizabeth, that the whole day, all she could think about was her growing doubts about the future.

Matt had spent the week before the wedding completing his plans for Texas, Henry had been at his side, and of course, Aunt Elizabeth had been busy packing. Amy had had no one to talk to, and her imagination was working overtime. She asked herself over and over, was Henry the reason Matt insisted he marry her. Forgotten were the long pleasurable hours she had spent in Matt's arms. She knew little about this man who was to become her husband. There had been a time when she had been sure that he would betray her. She wondered now if there had been any grounds to her suspicion. She even played back the conversation she had overheard between Matt and Phillip when Matt had mentioned prison.

In her bed, her mind was still clogged with doubts. She tried to remember what Matt had said about Texas, but she couldn't think past her fears. Texas was at the end of the earth for her. It was a wild place, and there were Indians there. Most of the white people there were Southerners. And she was leaving family and friends to travel across the country with a man she knew very little about. Over and over the thought that she didn't know Matt Treadwell at all kept repeating in her head. She felt her throat tighten. She couldn't go through with it. She couldn't marry Matt Treadwell.

Dawn was spreading a pink tint to her room when sleep finally came. It was late when she awoke. After her breakfast in bed, Aunt Elizabeth arrived to help her dress. With one look at Amy's dark eyes and pale face, she sank into a small chair and gazed into Amy's troubled face.

"Amy, you don't have to go through with this if you don't want to. We can call the whole thing off, if you think you are making a mistake."

Unshed tears glistened in Amy's eyes. "Oh, I don't know." Her voice shook. "I guess I'm just scared."

Aunt Elizabeth peered into Amy's wet, frightened eyes. She asked quietly, "How do you feel about Matt? I could have sworn, from what I've seen in the last several weeks, that there was a special feeling between you two. I'm sure Matt loves you, and I thought, well, it seemed that you loved him too."

Amy couldn't hide her startled look from Aunt Elizabeth. The woman smiled.

"I know I'm right. Matt loves you. He hasn't said anything to me personally, but I've watched that boy grow up and I know him. I'm sure he loves you very much."

Amy sighed. "I love him, I know what I feel but . . . well . . . he hasn't said . . . well, you know . . ." Her voice trailed off.

Aunt Elizabeth breathed a deep sigh of relief. Amy was suffering from bridal jitters.

"Amy" — she smiled at the nervous girl — "you've been through so much in the last year. It's no wonder you're doubting everything and everyone. But, you'll see, it will be all right." She put her arms around the slender form and kissed her gently on the forehead. "This doubting is normal for all brides, and in your case I'm sure you have reason to doubt three or four times as much. Amy, Matt does love you, I know it. I just know it." She rose to leave. "Now, you get dressed. You'll see. Everything will be fine."

While Amy was dressing, her confidence restored a bit, she heard Aunt Elizabeth urging Matt out of the house. Even if she had finished dressing before Matt left for the church, she was certain that Aunt Elizabeth would have kept them apart. Aunt Elizabeth believed in tradition. Amy sobered a bit. Did the older woman know her nephew as well as she had said she did? She lost a little of her confidence.

Downstairs, Henry was waiting for her. "Mother would have been so proud of you," he told her, his eyes misting as he helped her into the carriage.

When they arrived at the church, Amy was surprised by the number of well-wishers. As she came down the aisle on Henry's arm, she tried to smile at them. She caught sight of Matt standing so tall, waiting for her in front of the candle-bedecked altar. For a fraction of a second she tensed, and she fought the urge to pick up her skirts and run.

She tried to make her mind a blank as Henry handed her to Matt. They exchanged their vows before the stern-faced minister, who was mopping a flood of perspiration from his ample face, and then Matt placed a thin gold ring on her finger. At the minister's instruction, Matt planted a timid kiss on her lips, and as his eyes met hers for a brief second, she was stunned. She recognized the same worried expression in his eyes that she felt. Why, he's as frightened as I am, Amy thought, a lump forming in her throat. As they started back down the aisle as man and wife, Amy really smiled for the first time that day. He must love her, to go through with the ceremony as worried as he was. Aunt Elizabeth was right. He did love her.

Supper was a gay affair with friends and family offering many sincere and flowery toasts. Matt's family and friends really liked the young man, Amy decided. The fact that the war was still raging at the moment didn't daunt the wedding guests' spirits with Matt providing good wine and Aunt Elizabeth good food. Everyone was having a marvelous time.

Long before the guests had started to depart, Matt cornered Amy in the drawing room and whispered in her ear, "We can slip away any time you're ready."

Amy froze. She turned wild eyes on Matt and managed to mumble, "They'll know!"

"So what." Matt grinned at her. "We're married."

"Not—not yet," she pleaded.

Matt stared at her, startled by the embarrassment he read in her eyes. He hadn't counted on this. "Soon," he muttered.

Matt watched Amy and from time to time glanced at his watch. He caught her looking at him and then quickly away. After he had waited impatiently for almost an hour and Amy had seemed even more reluctant to leave the party, he went looking for Aunt Elizabeth. He found her in the kitchen, directing the preparation of trays of food and pulled her into the pantry away from the servants.

Matt hesitated and then ventured to say, "Amy's too embarrassed to leave the party."

She gazed up at her nephew and then looked at him more closely. "I'm not surprised. Perhaps you should wait a bit." At Matt's frown, Aunt Elizabeth patted his arm, untied her apron, and went in search of Amy. She successfully pried the girl away from a group of older friends and herded her upstairs to Matt's room. "You need to rest," was all she said, as she gently pushed her into the room and softly closed the door.

The door opened quietly and then closed so softly that she wasn't sure if someone had come into the room or not. She turned around slowly. Leaning against the door, his hand still on the knob, Matt stood staring at her.

For the first time in his life, Matt was unsure of himself. The rest of their lives depended on his actions in the next few hours. True, he had made love to the gorgeous woman in front of him, but tonight was his — and her — wedding night. He moved to her side and placed his hands on her shoulders. She was trembling. She was unsure of him as he was himself. Tonight was special, it had to be just right. He lowered his head to hers.

As Matt's warm lips touched hers, the nerves in

her body began to tingle. He kept kissing her, and as she started to relax in his arms, he pressed her body against his. His lips brushed her cheeks, her eyelids, her temples and then moved to kiss her ears, nibbling lightly on first one earlobe and then the other. He kissed her throat, sending streaks of fire through her before he claimed her lips again. This time the kiss was filled with more passion, and Amy's legs turned to soft butter. Suddenly, Matt's strong arms were supporting her full weight.

With his lips still covering hers, he moved one hand to the front of her gown and started to release the small buttons of her bodice. She tensed and started to draw away. Leaving his task unfinished, he concentrated once more on his kisses. He tried to stroke her soft curls, but she was still wearing her veil. Gently, he pulled away from her and, in a hoarse voice, murmured, "Let's do this right." Carefully, he unpinned the veil and laid it on a chair. Then, trying not to look at her, he unbuttoned her bodice, helped her from the pale pink creation, which he tossed on the same chair. Placing his arms under her knees and around her shoulder, he carried her to the bed. When he felt the soft touch of the mattress, he slipped his arms from under her and let his gaze move back to her wide, blue-gray eyes. He tried to smile. "This time we'll try making love on the bed."

Standing, he kept his eyes locked on hers, removed his coat, and threw it on the other chair in the room. His cravat and shirt followed. Then he lay down next to her so he could cradle her in his arms and kiss her at the same time.

He touched her lips gently. Without conscious thought, his tongue glided past her parting lips, and he slowly drank the sweetness of her mouth. As he touched her tongue, he sent little shivers through her body as well as his own. With infinite care he trailed one hand from her waist, where it had been resting, to the chemise-covered breast that heaved as she tried to control her breathing. Instantly, the peak responded to his touch, and he teased the invisible nipple that pushed up through the soft fabric. Her arms moved up to his neck, as he pushed the transparent fabric from his goal, and Amy pulled his head even closer to her breast.

Matt took the tiny nub in his mouth and sucked gently. Softly, she moaned under the impact of his searing mouth and arched her body so that he could reach her more easily. She tingled all over, and she could sense the taut nipples expanding, growing until she thought they would burst. There was a tight ache between her thighs, but she wanted to prolong this special night. All she wanted was for Matt to continue.

He caressed her breast, first with his hand and again with his tongue, his teeth, his lips, as he reached to untie her petticoats. With a sigh, he stood up to finish disrobing her and remove the rest of his own clothing. As he stood, Amy lay still, allowing herself to float in a sea of sensation. When he joined her once more, the soft golden glow from the fireplace softly kissed the naked bodies lying together on the bed.

Matt's mouth lingered at the tips of her breasts, and she could hear her heart beating frantically. She wondered if Matt could hear it, too. Suddenly, she realized that his fingers were teasing at the curls between her legs. Aware in some dark corner of his mind that he didn't want to rush her, he concentrated on bestowing a wealth of kisses on her breasts. Once more she enjoyed the warm sensations of his hot mouth as he caressed her.

Matt moved back to her lips and covered her mouth as gently as a brush of spring rain. But that wasn't enough, and as he kissed her deeply, he let his fingers work their way up her legs, then, between the curls and finally to the source of her womanhood. She was burning now with a desire so intense she could hardly breathe, and she began to wander between reality and pleasure. The feeling spread and expanded until she begged for release. Her whole body trembled, and she made soft moaning sounds as she climbed up, up, and ever upward.

Matt moved carefully over her and felt a surge of passion so great he prayed for control. He nudged her knees apart and slid between her thighs. With hesitation he eased himself into her. He lay still for several minutes, joined in the ageless union, and delayed any movement even though his own body was screaming in agony. Deliberately, sensing her need, he began to move as slowly and tenderly as he could, but she matched him stroke for stroke. As she reached the peak, she tried to make him move faster, urged him on, pleading for an end to her torment. He abandoned his timidity and thrust into her with a spreading heat that sent tendrils of flames brushing across his skin.

A part of her brain registered alarm. Her whole body was out of control. Her heart was pounding so hard she was afraid it would burst, and she could feel his heart beating against his chest. Her breath was coming in jagged gasps, and then for one second, her whole world stopped. In that next instant, she was plummeted into a spiraling vortex of joy so intense that she cried out.

Matt exerted every bit of control he had, and when she began to tremble and cry out, he felt his release as well. He fell forward, aware that his whole weight pressed against her frail form, but he could not move, not even if his life depended on it. Never before had he experienced such completeness. When he could breath again, he rolled to one side and held her gently. Smiling down at her, he kissed her tenderly.

Amy slowly resurfaced and felt his lean muscular body poised at her side. His warm lips evoked a welter of emotions, and she looked up at the man who had just given her a taste of ecstasy. Gazing into his eyes, she saw there a tenderness that spoke of love, even if his lips did not. She sighed. "I didn't think the vows would have that much of an effect. I never . . ."

"And we have years and years of loving ahead of us," he murmured as he pulled her slight frame closer to his heart. Tenderly, he kissed her once more, as he cradled her in his arms, still playing with the soft warm flesh of her breast.

She cuddled up next to him and felt contented. She smiled. How marvelous to be loved so completely even if he didn't know he loved her. Cradled in Matt's strong arms, she drifted off to sleep.

Matt was stunned with his own feelings, more complete and satisfied than ever before in his life. He closed his eyes and gave in to the pleasant sensations of total fulfillment. He too slept.

Sometime in the middle of the night, Amy stirred. She could feel eyes staring down at her even though the room was lit only by the soft moonlight of the quarter moon shining through the lace-curtained windows. She could make out Matt's head as he leaned over her. When he pulled her to him, covering her lips with his, she responded without hesitation. As his hands traced her body all over again, she melted into his embrace. She gathered her courage. This time she wanted to touch him, and she stroked his shoulders, his stomach, his thighs. She trailed her hands over the broad shoulders that towered above her and ran her hands through his ruffled hair.

She had been aware of how different their bodies were, but now she gloried in that difference. Where she was soft, he was hard; where her skin was smooth, his was covered with a light furring of hair. As he cupped her breasts, she trailed her fingers across his chest and brushed his tiny nipples. He gasped in pleasure. Delighted, she stroked them until they hardened as hers had done. When he ran his fingers over her legs, she copied his movements and thrilled to the soft covering that hid the firm muscles that tensed with her touch.

She felt his maleness pulsing against her thigh, and she wiggled under him to let him know that she wanted him, desired him, was willing to beg for him. And as he entered her, she grabbed at his shoulders, feeling the ridges of his muscles, hard and firm, under her fingers.

She followed his lead, but her movements were awkward until he whispered instructions in her ear. Suddenly, she was flying, above the bed, above the room, out into the celestial ether, and once more she found ecstasy. Slowly she drifted back to reality and smiled up at her new husband. She was so full of the thrill of love she was speechless. Closing her eyes, she again slept.

It was very late in the morning when they awoke. As Matt lay in bed and watched Amy dress, he was struck with how beautiful she was. She glanced over at him, and he watched the blush travel over her face as she struggled with her pantalettes, chemise, and petticoats. Matt bounded from the bed, naked, and grabbed her tightly. "You are so beautiful," he whispered. He sighed as she struggled playfully to free herself from his hold.

When Matt bent his head and kissed her hard, her bruised lips spread into a beatific smile as she looked up at him. Without thinking, she said, "If you keep that up, I may want to go back to bed." She gasped and blushed. She could not believe she had said that.

"Let's go," came Matt's quick response.

"B-b-but we have to see Aunt Elizabeth and Henry off," she stuttered.

Matt chuckled. "Then we'll go back to bed afterward."

They came down the stairs together, arm in arm, smiling happily. Henry was waiting for them. He had spent a sleepless night, worrying that he had pushed his sister into an unhappy union. When he saw her face as she descended the stairs, he was delighted beyond words. She was glowing, and Matt didn't look the least bit frustrated. Henry smiled to himself. They were every bit as much in love as Aunt Elizabeth had said, and they appeared to be well suited. Amy would have a happy life.

"Where's Aunt Elizabeth?" Matt asked as he looked around the hall. The house seemed very quiet.

Henry grinned. "All the guests have gone. Aunt Elizabeth left with them. Your Uncle Charles took her with him. He's going to Atlanta for business and welcomed her company. She left you a note." Henry handed Matt a folded piece of paper.

"You stayed?"

"Well, I had to give you her note, and I wanted to see Amy before I left."

Over coffee Henry and Amy said a tearful good-bye. They promised to write, and Matt reissued his invitation to Henry to visit their Texas ranch. In the frosty afternoon Matt and Amy huddled on the porch and waved good-bye to Henry's retreating back. Matt squeezed her hand tightly.

"He'll come to Texas to see us as soon as we're settled. Texas isn't the end of the world."

Grinning down at Amy, he put his arms around her waist, as she looked up at him shyly. The house was theirs alone, with only the servants to witness their displays of emotion. Aunt Elizabeth had ordered them all to stay out of sight unless needed. "Is there anything you'd like to do?" he asked softly.

"No!" she answered quickly. She glanced up at him and blushed. He seemed to be able to read her mind.

"What about the servants?" she said, hesitatingly.

"Do you see any servants?" came his reply.

She looked around. No, there were no servants to be seen, so she let him lead her up the stairs to his room. He swung her up into his arms and deposited her on the freshly made bed. Before she could draw a breath, he started to remove the clothing she had just recently donned.

As he lifted a petticoat from her waist, he murmured, "You are just too beautiful to wear all of this." He walked to the armoire in the corner. Pulling a large box and a small velvet package from the dark recesses of the closet, he moved to stand in front of her. Grinning, he handed her the large box.

She looked up in surprise. More gifts? Carefully, she raised the lid of the box and extracted a vision of silk and lace in the most delicate shade of cream she had ever seen. It was the color of the new moon in October, just as it rose above the sleepy earth. The gown had a low neckline and was of such sheer silk that Amy blushed at what it would not cover. The skirt fell in yards of silk, covered with matching bands of lace. The robe was of the same fabric and tied under her breasts.

"This was for last night, but I forgot," Matt mumbled in apology, then breathed in excitement. "Put it on."

She stepped out of her remaining clothes and slipped the gown over her head. Then she added the robe. She stood before him, waiting for his approval. It came in the form of a fiery kiss that left them both fighting for air. The new robe and soon the gown were discarded as they again shared the newness of their unpledged love. Holding each other tightly, they drifted off to sleep.

Matt shook Amy awake gently. "Woman," he growled, "I'm getting very hungry. Let's go see what's for dinner. All this work is giving me a man-sized appetite."

Amy stretched and grinned up at him. "Work? I thought you were enjoying yourself," she teased. She glanced at the open window and marveled as the setting sun paraded its vermilion and bronze for them to view.

"Matt," she asked, suddenly very serious, "may I do the cooking?" When he turned his startled gaze in her direction, she smiled. "I'm a very good cook, and I would really like to prepare something to eat for you."

"I don't want you to do anything. When we get to Texas, you'll have to cook all the meals," he said softly.

"But I want to cook for you now."

Matt rolled off the bed, and grabbed for his pants. "So, feed me," he teased. The small velvet box he had taken from the closet along with the robe and gown lay on the chair next to the bed. When he had fastened his waistband, he reached for it.

"This is for you, too."

Amy took the velvet box and looked up at Matt. "This is overwhelming." Opening the small box, she saw another golden rose, much like the rose of the pendant. This was a cameo-shaped brooch, but instead of a woman's head, a golden rose was molded above a bed of porcelain, the same blue-gray as her eyes. She held it in her hands, staring down at it. It obviously had been made especially for her. A lump formed in her throat. For Matt to take the time and go to the expense of such a gift meant he must care for her very much. She approached her new husband shyly.

"You're spoiling me. Thank you." She threw her arms around his neck and pulled his head down so that she could express her appreciation in a way she knew he would enjoy. She kissed him deeply.

When they surfaced for air, Matt said in a shaking voice, "That is the second time you have kissed me. I must remember that you come to me when I give you jewelry."

Amy stepped out of his embrace and blushed furiously. She quickly dressed and then pinned on the brooch. Then she started for the kitchen, Matt following her, and tucking his shirttail into his pants as he went.

In Aunt Elizabeth's large kitchen, Matt told the slaves to retire, that they would see to their own needs. Amy took utensils down from their hooks and soon had prepared a platter of ham and eggs, coffee, and fresh biscuits.

As they ate, they discussed the wedding, and once more Matt commented about Alex's absence. Then, they made plans for the next several weeks. Matt insisted that they had a great deal of shopping to do for their new home, and Amy talked him into showing her the sketches he had made for the foreman.

"You have to act surprised. I told everybody it was a secret," he whispered as she nodded with satisfaction.

"Oh, Matt. It's perfect," she proclaimed as she studied the detailed sketches of courtyard and living area. It was very late when they finally crawled back into bed.

Chapter Nineteen

While Amy had happily made plans for her wedding, Phillip had been busy with plans of his own. On the fifteenth of January, he thanked his commanding officer for the leave and started north from Atlanta. Instead of heading for South Carolina, he traveled into Tennessee. Along the way, he changed from his Confederate uniform into his own clothing so that he would appear to be nothing more than a gentleman farmer. In Nashville, he met Harvey Paxton, and the two men traveled west. When they arrived at the inn Phillip had arranged for, they spent an hour going over the information their investigator had accumulated. Alex Sanderson of Anderson, Indiana, was now a lieutenant assigned to General Don Carlos Buell. And he was being sent less than fifty miles away in southern Kentucky. Phillip beamed with his good fortune.

Harvey Paxton informed his boss, to Phillip's delight, that he had already made contact with the Union Army intelligence unit and a meeting with a

Pinkerton man was arranged for the next afternoon. Phillip was surprised, and he smiled, wondering what the South would give for the information that Pinkerton had men in the central country as well as the east.

More than satisfied with what the investigator had accomplished in such a short time, Phillip sent him back to South Carolina. Someone had to attend the wedding in Anderson. If any of the officers in Georgia should ask about the wedding, Phillip would need to have all the details correctly.

The next afternoon, Phillip was at the assigned meeting place early. It didn't take him much more than twenty minutes to arrange an invitation to visit the Union Army only a few miles away when he hinted that he had information about a dangerous Confederate spy—his brother, Matthew Treadwell.

Just after dawn the following morning, the Pinkerton man arrived to take him to the army camp. Phillip learned that he was to meet a Colonel Brown, who wanted all the information Phillip had about the Confederate spy.

It took hours to get to the camp, and Phillip spent the time mentally going over each detail. He had to be careful to give them only enough information to hold Matt, not sentence him to death.

When he met Colonel Brown, who seemed friendly enough but reserved, Phillip came right to the point.

"All this war activity is going to ruin the cotton market. Why, already with the blockade, we're having trouble shipping our goods. And personally, sir, I don't give a damn who wins this war!"

Phillip wondered if he had gone too far when he saw the colonel, who was about his own age, bristle in indignation. Phillip took a deep breath and told himself to tone his story down. Amy's story, at least his version of it, would be more productive.

He continued softly. "However, the reason I'm here is not because of the cotton, but because of a beautiful young woman from the North." He fought to suppress a self-satisfied grin as the colonel and his young aide, a lieutenant, exchanged glances.

"Her name is Amy Sanderson, and she has a brother in the Union Army. She is loyal to the cause and helped with the underground railroad for several years. She ended up in my brother's less-than-honorable hands when she was captured by some slave agents my brother had hired to track down a group of escaping slaves.

"My brother has convinced the girl that he loves her, and they are to be married in a week. I've tried everything I could to stop the wedding, but Amy won't believe a word I say. I'm positive that Matt, my brother, is marrying her to use her brother Alex, the man in the Union Army." Phillip paused to wring his hands and assume a distraught look.

"I would never turn my brother in, if it weren't for the fact that this girl is going to be badly hurt if her husband spies on her brother. Of course, my brother is helping in other ways, too. With men like Matt stirring up trouble, this war could go on for years. The North will win in the end. I just want to see it over sooner."

Phillip took a deep breath and tried to keep his expression blank. His last sentence had almost

284

choked him. He wasn't sure the colonel was buying his story, and in an impassioned plea, he tried for more sympathy for Amy, since they had seemed interested in her.

"I can't stand by and let my brother ruin this poor girl's life and destroy her brother's career," he said in a husky voice. "Oh, we had our disagreements, but for Matt to use this sweet little girl for his own gain, it isn't gentlemanly. I sincerely hope you can understand why I can't let this happen. He's coming here on the pretext of meeting her brother, but I know what his true assignment is—to check on your strengths and try to locate all of Buell's regiments. He can't be allowed to take that information back with him."

Phillip sat back and tried to appear grim, but he had a devil of a time containing his amusement. It appeared that the colonel had accepted the whole story. The interrogation Phillip had prepared for began. He mixed enough truth with his lies to make Matt a suspicious character. Phillip felt comfortable with the knowledge that Matt's activities would be checked carefully and that the army could pin nothing on him. His brother would come to no harm but would be held and probably denied any outside communication until the investigation was complete. At least Paxton had assured him that was what would happen. By the time all the facts could be checked, Amy would be back in Indiana, hating her new husband with a passion. Also there was always the outside chance that Matt, while held in a Northern prison, would blame his dear wife for turning him in as a spy.

Phillip left the Union camp early the next morning and traveled leisurely back to Georgia, inordinately pleased with himself. It wouldn't hurt Matt a bit to be kept in a cell some place until he was cleared. The war might even be over by then. But Amy Sanderson would be gone, back to Indiana where she belonged. All Phillip had to do was wait.

Colonel Brown, for his part, didn't like spies, and he didn't like brothers who turned in their relatives either, but Phillip Treadwell's story had to be checked out. He sent word that he wanted to talk to Alex Sanderson as soon as possible.

Alex arrived and admitted to the colonel that Amy Sanderson was indeed his sister, that she had been kidnapped and seduced and had ended up marrying the scoundrel. He was shocked when the colonel hinted that Matt was coming for a visit. "I didn't invite him," Alex exclaimed, losing his temper just a bit.

"Well, don't!" the colonel snapped back. "We have reason to believe that he is not what he seems. We've been given information that he is planning to use you to gather some information for the Confederacy."

Alex shook his head, wondering if Henry and Amy had been charmed by a traitor. He agreed that he would send no correspondence to either his sister or her new husband unless it was cleared first with Colonel Brown.

Colonel Brown then gave instructions to his aide. The facts had to be checked when the fighting slowed, and if the information was correct, Matt Treadwell would be tried and shot as a spy.

* * *

The months following the wedding were busy ones for Matt and Amy. They went into town and ordered supplies for their trip to Texas. Furnishings for their new home were selected, and they spent hours over the rough sketches Matt made of the placement of the rooms.

When spring arrived, Matt and Amy spent long afternoons at the lake where Matt had proposed, planning their future life and home in Texas. And each day began with a romp in bed. One special morning stood out in Amy's mind. They had been very busy for over a week with shopping for the ranch house, and she was exhausted. She fell instantly asleep the moment her head touched her pillow. Something tugged at her dreams, and Amy drifted between the golden touch of sunrise and the velvet midnight of unconsciousness.

She felt warm, and shreds of pleasure nibbled at the corners of her mind. Gradually, the pleasure grew in intensity, and she knew that Matt was touching, caressing her, bringing her back from her dreams. Her buttocks were pressed into his groin, her back against his chest, and her breast was cupped by his hand. He was running his wet tongue across the tendons of her neck. She sighed in contentment and started to roll over. He whispered in her ear, "Stay the way you are."

She stayed, anticipation tracing tendrils of excitement down her limbs. What was he doing? She could touch his bare flank, but other than that, she was at his mercy. His warm breath tickling her neck and the sensations of his fingers tugging at her nipple made her breathing shaky and hesitant. She could feel his firm flesh pressing against her thigh, and she wondered what would come next. Surely, he would roll her over, but he continued his onslaught, nipping at her shoulders, running his free hand over her quivering stomach, down through her moist curls. She had reached the point where she was ready to beg, when she felt his pulsing manhood probing for its home, and she pushed against him. Beads of bliss gathered between her legs as she felt him expand, forcing himself up, up, until she was full of him.

He whispered against her ear, his voice husky with his own daring. "Do you like that?" Unable to respond, she could only nod her head. He trailed his hand to the dark curls between her long graceful legs and sought out that small kernel of desire. As he moved within her, he stroked and kneaded until she screamed her pleasure. Then it came, as before, the feeling that she was leaving her body to waltz among the stars. Vaguely, she knew that he, too, had joined her in that special place known only to lovers. She pushed back against him and sighed in perfect peace. For him to give her such pleasure, he must love her. He would tell her in time.

After that glorious morning, Amy often initiated the morning's loving, waking Matt from a sound sleep. Other mornings Matt would wake her and find her arms gliding up around his neck before she was completely awake. Each night ended as the day began, with the young couple falling asleep in each other's arms. Matt did not mention his love for her, nor had Amy admitted her own feelings for him, but to anyone who viewed the young couple, it was clear that they were deeply in love with each other.

The only dark cloud in their bright future was the war news. Kentucky and Tennessee were becoming a battleground in the conflict between the states. The war moved south and into Georgia, and Aunt Elizabeth became involved in the relief effort. She wrote that she was needed in Atlanta, and she would stay with her relative until the end of August. She assured both Matt and Amy that she would arrive home long before they left for Texas.

As the conflict heated up in Kentucky and Tennessee, Matt and Amy discussed the necessity of moving Emma and Jacob from Tucker's Inn to a safer locale. Their original plan had been to travel to Tucker's Crossroads and continue on to St. Louis with Emma and Jacob. Matt had already sent orders to his cattle broker that he wanted the stock to arrive in St. Louis by the middle of October. He sent word to his foreman that his ranch hands should arrive in St. Louis about the same time. Then Amy and Matt, Emma and Jacob, the men from the ranch, and his one hundred head of cattle would travel to Texas.

When Matt insisted that their travel route be changed, Amy was inclined to send Emma and Jacob by train from Nashville to St. Louis, but when the Union Army started blowing up the Confederate rail system, they had to abandon that idea. Finally, Matt decided that there was no other way. He had to travel to Tucker's Inn and bring Emma and Jacob back to South Carolina before they went west. Amy agreed that the slaves could be hidden for several days until they began their trip west, but she tried every argument she could think of when Matt told her he would travel north alone.

"There's still too much that has to be done here, and you'll have to do it while I'm getting Emma and Jacob. Then, you'll have a week to gossip with Aunt Elizabeth before we leave."

Matt decided to leave on Wednesday, even though the last letter from Aunt Elizabeth indicated she wouldn't return to Elton Estate until Friday.

"I can't wait any longer. There are too many skirmishes between here and there. I don't want to be caught in a crossfire, and I don't want any monumental delays. I have to leave Wednesday."

Tuesday, Amy helped Matt pack his clothes, and she ordered a lunch prepared for his dawn departure the next day. Tuesday evening they shared a quiet dinner and retired early.

Even after Amy had playfully dressed in the gown Matt had given her the night after their wedding, Matt sat on the edge of the bed, still fully dressed, his face dark and brooding.

Finally, he turned to her and said quietly, "Maybe I should take you with me."

Amy glanced at him. The sudden lump in her throat made speech impossible. She felt like crying, and fought to hold back her tears. She didn't want him to remember her with streaks running down her cheeks.

"I'll miss you terribly, but it's a little late for me to go too. You'll travel much faster without me, and if there's trouble, you'll be able to handle it much easier if I'm not along. You know how much I want to go, but I do think it would be better if I wait here. You'll only be gone for two weeks," she said softly.

Matt stood to remove his clothing. "I have an uneasy feeling about leaving you here. I guess I just don't want to leave."

"I'll be waiting right here for you, so you'll have to hurry and come back," she whispered as she put her arms around his muscular frame.

Matt wriggled out of his clothes while she clung to his waist. Putting his arm around her, he drew her even closer. He murmured against her lips, "You'd better be here."

He picked her up and pressed her into the bed as he kissed her thoroughly. She returned his kisses, letting her lips speak for her silently, without benefit of words.

Soon, the gown was discarded, and soft moans and gentle whispers floated into the night. Matt teased and played with her, aware that she felt the same desolation over the coming separation that he did.

Once more, he cupped her full breasts and nibbled at the tiny peaks that blossomed with his touch. Trailing his hands over her twisting form, he teased and caressed every inch. As his fingers trailed over her trembling frame, the anticipation of their mutual pleasure blocked out all thought.

Amy, now no longer timid in the expression of her feelings, stroked and caressed Matt's broad, muscular frame with enthusiasm. She ran her fingertips across his shoulders, learning the knobs of his spine once more, down his back to knead his buttocks in her firm grip. As Matt continued his play, she felt her world slipping from control, and when she could take no more, she begged him, "Now. Oh, Matt, now!" He shifted his large body above her smaller one and slowly glided home.

Savoring their near-perfect union, he lay still for several minutes, holding her tightly. Sensing his need for tenderness, she touched his forehead and caressed his cheeks, substituting her lips for her fingertips. Slowly, he began to move, and she moved against him, matching his rhythm but trying to draw him deeper and deeper into her very soul.

Suddenly, she realized that he had ceased all movement, and she opened her eyes and gazed up into his searching eyes. It seemed as if he was memorizing her every feature, and a chill passed through her. Tears filled her eyes, and she couldn't explain why. Was he afraid that he wasn't coming back to her? She pulled him tighter, clasping his warm body tightly to hers, as if his warmth could block the fear that suddenly threatened to overcome her. Then he began to move, and they were both lost to the world, as she surged forward to meet his thrusts.

Together, they climbed into a place where thought was impossible and the atmosphere prevented a deep breath. Suddenly, pleasure beyond comprehension flooded them, and Amy cried out her deep satisfaction as Matt groaned in an agony of joy. Slowly, they returned to the bed and the room that had seen so many exchanges of love.

Still joined, they lay quietly for a long time, each silent, thinking of the days ahead. As if he had read her mind, he muttered against her hair, "I'll be back, I'll come back," and pulled her closer.

Amy clung to him just as tightly, and they drifted off to sleep. Twice during the night, they shared their love, once slowly, savoring each second, and then, almost violently. Amy wondered if Matt was trying to force her very spirit into his body. At last, shortly before dawn they both slept.

With the new sun peeking above the tree branches, Matt kissed his wife soundly and left her waving from the porch, tears sliding down her face.

That afternoon, Aunt Elizabeth's overseer was looking for Amy. He had brought two letters from town. The first letter was from Aunt Elizabeth. Amy recognized the script. The message was blunt. Matt's second cousin, the son of the people she was visiting, had been killed in a battle along the Mississippi. She was needed in Georgia until after the funeral. She would be home in three weeks, in plenty of time to see them off to Texas.

The other letter was addressed to Matt and looked official. It had a Union Army stamp on the envelope. Amy laid the letter aside and went about her tasks. As she worked, she wondered who in the army might be sending Matt a letter. The thought troubled her. The only person she knew in the Union Army was Alex. Had something happened, and they were trying to notify her through Matt? No, Henry would have let her know.

She became worried. She couldn't understand why the Union Army would send something to Matt. Surely he wasn't being asked to enlist. Convincing herself that it must be very important and she would have to get a message to Matt, she tore the envelope open. She stared at the official invitation from her brother Alex and read the message carefully several times. Alex was requesting that Matt come north to meet him before they left for Texas. Alex hadn't even mentioned her. Weren't women allowed to visit an army camp?

She was more than a little upset, but she gritted her teeth, and remembering Matt's anger that Alex hadn't come to the wedding, she sat down and wrote her husband a note, explaining why she had opened the letter and what it said. In her letter she mentioned that Aunt Elizabeth was not returning for another three weeks, but she didn't tell Matt why. Sitting at the desk, she wondered how she should close the letter. She decided to keep it light and happy and teasingly wrote that he should not spend too much time with Alex. She was waiting for him.

The next day she traveled into Anderson to post her letter. Part of her hoped that it would not reach Crossroads until Matt had left for home. Feeling guilty, she told herself that Matt might not have another chance to meet Alex, at least not for many years. She sent the message on its way.

While Amy awaited some word from Matt, she finished the packing and worked on some of the sewing and mending that required her attention. During the day there was more than enough to keep her busy, but at night she was desolate. She crawled into the big, lonely bed and wondered how one person could become so important to another person in so short a time. Feeling so alone, she tossed and turned. Sleep came slowly each night.

* * *

The day before Matt planned to leave with Emma and Jacob, Amy's letter arrived. He considered ignoring the invitation Amy told him about and going ahead with his plans, but he knew she would ask when he got her letter, and he couldn't lie to her. Also, he had made such a fuss over Alex not coming to the wedding that he wondered if perhaps Henry had stopped to see his brother on the way home and suggested that Alex send an invitation. Henry might even have insisted. At any rate, Matt mumbled to himself, if he didn't meet big brother, Amy would be more than a little disappointed with him.

For an hour he vacillated between going home and going to meet Alex. It disturbed him that Aunt Elizabeth was still in Atlanta. He didn't like Amy being at the plantation alone, with only the slaves for company. He made some quick calculations and decided that a visit to Alex would add six days to his travel plans. Meeting his wife's brother was important. Whether he wanted to accept the invitation or not, he knew he really had little choice. But, damn, he didn't want to go.

With no other course open to him, he went in search of Emma and Jacob. Then he met with Ben.

"Amy wrote that I've received an invitation from her brother. He's stationed north in Kentucky, and she wants me to meet him. I'll pay you what I owe when I return. I should be gone only about six or seven days."

He secluded himself in his room to write a return letter to his wife. After several attempts to tell Amy how much he missed her and that he was only going to see Alex because she had asked him to, he tore the papers up in disgust. There was no way he could put on paper what he felt. He ended by writing only four lines. He had received her note, he would travel to Kentucky to meet her brother, Emma and Jacob were ready to go, and he would be home in two weeks instead of the seven days he had originally planned.

After an early breakfast, he gave the letter to Molly to post, told Ben and Molly good-bye, and assured Emma and Jacob that they should be ready to travel in one week. The sun was peeking over the horizon as he headed west toward Nashville.

Another South Carolina guest had arrived at the inn shortly after Matt. Harvey Paxton had followed Matt in a state of near panic. The letter inviting Matt to meet Alex hadn't had time to arrive when Matt had headed north. Harvey cursed his bad luck. Phillip would be furious. He wondered if he should let Phillip know about this hitch in their plans, or wait to see what Matt's next move was. He decided on the latter.

He made it his business to stay as close to Matt as he could without drawing suspicion. And when Amy's letter came, Paxton drew a deep sigh of relief. Obviously, the girl had opened the letter addressed to her husband, and the forgery had fooled her. Matt was going to meet Alex Sanderson.

Harvey left the inn before dinner. He had enough information to contact the Pinkerton man that Matt

Treadwell was about to descend on the camp. There was the message to Phillip Treadwell to be sent, to let him know the trap was closing over Matt and he would be in the hands of the Union Army in three days. He returned to the inn and packed his bag. The job had not been too difficult, and he grinned, thinking of the fee Phillip Treadwell had agreed to as full payment. It would be waiting in the bank in Charleston by the time he returned.

As Matt headed west from Crossroads to Nashville, he wondered about the logistics of fighting such a war. It seemed amazing that the soldiers could move around at will. Alex was meeting him at an army camp north of Nashville, and he distinctly remembered Amy telling him that her brother was with Buell in Missouri. He remembered seeing several friends in Anderson at various times in the last months. "Some war," he mumbled as he rode.

He let his thoughts drift to his beautiful young wife. God, how he loved her. She had been delighted over the rough sketches he had shown her of the house in Texas, and he made a mental note to check on the progress of the house he requested for Emma and Jacob. Before sunset he was west of Nashville, and he stopped at an inn, ate a good meal, and retired early. Just before he drifted off to sleep, he counted the days until he would be back at Elton Estate and Amy would be back in his arms.

Matt was up before daybreak and on his way. Before he left the inn, he had calculated his arrival at the army camp for late that morning. The road he traveled was in excellent condition, and he made record time. Since he arrived more than an hour before the time Amy had mentioned in her letter, he guessed that was the reason why the young sentry acted so surprised. As Matt watched the lad holding the old musket tightly in his arms, he wondered why the young man seemed so afraid of him.

In an attempt to relieve the boy's fear, Matt explained as carefully as he could that his brother-in-law, Alex Sanderson, was expecting him. In seconds, another young soldier arrived and insisted that Matt follow him to an empty tent, not far from the posted sentry. "Wait," was all the young soldier said.

In minutes an officer of about his own age walked into the tent and stood at attention, gazing directly above Matt's head. Matt asked in a friendly voice, "Alex Sanderson?"

"No sir!" came the crisp reply.

Matt watched the man with some amusement; evidently Amy's brother was an important man now. Perhaps he had been promoted to a much higher rank.

An older man, balding, with a fringe of dark brown and gray hair around his head and beady gray eyes, strolled into the tent. Matt whirled around in his direction. Surely this wasn't Amy's brother.

The older man spoke, his voice emphatic, almost cold. "Matt Treadwell?"

"Yes sir. You aren't Alex Sanderson?" Matt managed, his voice registering surprise.

"I'll ask the questions here," the man stated briskly. "Are you Matt Treadwell, formerly of Anderson, South Carolina?"

"Yes," Matt responded, confusion evident in his voice. What was going on here? Where was Amy's brother? Had something happened to him? Had he been injured in a battle? Was Alex Sanderson a casualty of war?

The officer snapped to attention. "I'm Colonel Brown of the United States Army, and you, Mr. Treadwell, are under arrest."

Chapter Twenty

Matt's mouth dropped open, and he stared at
Colonel Brown, then blurted out, "Under arrest?
What for? I was invited here by Alex Sanderson, of
your army, to meet him before I take his sister to
Texas. I have a ranch in Texas." His voice was husky,
surprised.

The colonel continued as if Matt hadn't spoken.
"You will be held until a lawyer can be appointed.
You will talk to no one, send no messages, and can
have no visitors. When we have the time, you will be
tried as a spy." He turned on his heel and strode
from the tent. Matt, dumbfounded, stood very still
as the man left.

He looked at the officer who had arrived just
before the colonel. The man was still standing at
attention.

"There's a mistake," Matt muttered. "I came here
to meet my brother-in-law."

The young officer stared straight ahead.

The colonel's words registered in Matt's mind.
This was ridiculous, he was no spy. He took a step
toward the entrance of the tent. Immediately, the

flaps were pushed aside to admit four bluecoats, all carrying rifles pointed at him. Matt looked around. Surely, this was a joke. He had done nothing to warrant arrest on such a serious charge. But no one was smiling.

"Please, sir, follow me," the young officer said curtly. The soldiers raised their guns in unison, convincing Matt that he had better do as the officer requested, at least for the moment. Matt followed in a daze. There had to be a simple explanation for this. A simple mistake. They thought he was someone else. That was the only thing that made any sense.

Matt glanced at the officer and asked to see the colonel again. For a minute the young officer hesitated, then he replied, "Later, sir."

They all left the tent, the officer leading the way, a soldier on either side of Matt, and the remaining two walking behind him. With their guns trained on him, they were certainly taking no chances, Matt decided, and he immediately discounted the idea of escape. They would shoot, Matt was sure, even though their information was false. He was no spy, but an attempted escape at this moment would end his life as effectively as the hangman's noose.

As they walked, he wondered how long it would take to correct this nasty situation. He wanted to leave for Tucker's Inn tomorrow, but his instincts told him this might take some time. Obviously, they had been expecting a spy, and he had arrived at the wrong time. The important thing was to leave this camp with his name cleared. If he attempted escape, he would have trouble traveling west for he was sure that if they thought him a spy, they would seek him out. No, the army had to admit that they made a terrible mistake, and that might take some time.

The officer was speaking as they stopped before an old barn, but Matt, deep in his own thoughts, had to ask him to repeat what he had said.

The officer stated, "This is where you will be held, sir, at least for the present. You will receive three meals a day, and you will have exercise twice a day. You will have a guard with you at all times. The men have been instructed to shoot if you do anything that might be construed as an attempt to escape."

Matt shrugged helplessly, and once more, he asked, "May I please talk to the colonel? There is a mistake here. I must talk to him immed—as soon as is possible." Matt looked at the man, his helplessness clouding his eyes.

"I'll tell the colonel that you would like to talk to him, but I doubt that he'll see you." The officer held the barn door open and beckoned Matt into the dark interior.

As Matt's eyes became accustomed to the dark, he could make out a cot with a straw mattress, a chair, and a small table with a candle on it. The officer motioned to one of the soldiers to light the candle, and Matt was given a better opportunity to survey his surroundings. It wasn't a barn at all but some sort of fruit or grain cellar. They evidently didn't take many prisoners because the place didn't appear to have been occupied for some time.

The officer ordered a change of the guard and left Matt standing in the middle of the enclosure, staring at the first of the men assigned to guard him. Matt, without thought, started for the door to tell the officer to remember to send the colonel as soon as possible. The click of the gun reminded Matt of the guard who stood at attention at the door. He raised his rifle and stepped in front of Matt. Matt glared at the man as he indicated that Matt was to move away from the door.

Matt sank down in the lone chair in the room and considered his plight. If he was being held for spying . . . But that was ridiculous. The only person to whom he had ever indicated his feelings about the war was Henry Sanderson. Henry knew how he felt. They had talked about the reasons for the war, about states' rights, and about slavery for days as they had returned to South Carolina. If Matt had spied for anyone, it would have been for the Union. No, someone had lied to get him into trouble. But why? He immediately thought of Phillip. No, Phillip was in the Confederate Army and would have been captured himself if he had tried to talk to anyone in the North. Could it be Henry? No, Henry was his friend, and there was no way that Henry could have dreamed up anything to make the Union Army hold him.

Matt stood and started to pace the floor, his hands gripped behind his back. He had never met Alex Sanderson, and the man knew nothing about him except what Henry had told him, so he doubted that Alex was the culprit. That left only one person. He stopped his pacing and stood still, almost afraid of where his thoughts were leading him. No, Amy loved him; she couldn't be the one.

He sank back into the chair. Surely, her feelings for him and her expressions of those feelings were not false? He knew what he had read in her eyes, and disgust or suspicion was not there, had never been there. But she was the one who had sent the message that Alex wanted to meet him. Still, the day of the wedding Aunt Elizabeth had assured him that Amy loved him. She had told Aunt Elizabeth that she was in love with him. Could she have fooled Aunt Elizabeth as well? No, there was no way Amy could have betrayed him. It was a case of mistaken identity. The army had him confused with someone else.

Matt sat quietly for over an hour. Mentally, he made a list of all the questions he wanted to ask the colonel. Then he started to pace again. Sometime during the afternoon the guard was changed, and Matt stepped up to the new guard.

"I'd like to talk to the colonel. Can you get a request to him?"

Nothing. Matt tried a different tack. "What kind of day is it? It was cool this morning." The soldier said nothing. "When am I going to be fed? I'm getting hungry." Still nothing. It was obvious that the soldier had been told not to talk to the prisoner. Was he to have no communication with anyone? He might have trouble beyond what he expected if he couldn't convince someone to talk to him.

As he paced, he tried to remember the exact wording of Amy's note. Suddenly, he wondered why she hadn't sent the original letter to him. For an instant he wondered if there was a note. Trying to dismiss his suspicion he concentrated on what answers he wanted from Colonel Brown. As time passed and nothing happened, he surrendered to his anger and banged his fists against the table in frustration.

With the changing of the next guard, Matt was given a plate of beans, bacon, and a piece of dry bread. Again, he requested to be allowed to see the colonel. At the end of his meal, the officer came to check on him.

"The colonel has given orders that you are not to bother the guards. If he has time, he'll talk to you in several days, perhaps by the end of the week. He's too busy to see you now."

Matt was stunned. That they had made a mistake was one thing, but to take their own sweet time trying to straighten it out was something else again. He watched the soldier lift the rifle into a ready position, in case Matt tried to flee.

Through clenched teeth, Matt pleaded. "Could I send a message to my wife? At least let me tell her that I won't be home in a week."

"No, sir."

"If I give you the address, could you let her know that I am detained?"

"No, sir."

Matt lost his temper. He banged on the table as he roared about the inconsiderateness of people in general and the colonel in particular. He demanded to know what he was accused of and who had accused him. The more he yelled the angrier he got. When he glanced at the door, he was surprised to see that the guard had raised the gun to his shoulder. The officer glared at Matt.

"Sit down and calm yourself or I'll order chains!"

Matt slumped onto the bed wondering who had decided to turn his world upside down. His thoughts again turned to all the people he had suspected when he first entered the makeshift prison. Phillip still seemed the most likely candidate, although Matt couldn't figure out how he could have managed it. And the colonel wouldn't talk to him until the end of the week. Between then and now, what was he to do? It would be better to be pressed into some kind of physical labor than to sit there and think. Perhaps he could ask for a book or two, so that he at least could keep his mind on other things.

The rest of the day dragged by, and Matt finally decided that it was late enough to try to sleep. When he walked to the table and started to blow out the candle, his present guard stepped forward and in a husky drawl muttered, "Nope, candle gotta stay lit." Matt threw himself back down onto the mattress. He was not even to be allowed darkness in which to sleep. He wanted to curse the federal army into oblivion. The colonel had better see him soon, or he might lose his sanity.

Phillip waited impatiently for the summer months to pass, knowing that the next step in his plans would not take place until the middle of September. There were several limited engagements in Kentucky and Tennessee, but Phillip stayed in Atlanta with the bulk of the troops. Once Amy was in Indiana, he would be much more interested in the battles that were occurring.

Phillip's one fear was that Aunt Elizabeth would

306

return to Elton Estate before the next step in his plan. In an effort to stay apprised of her actions, an investigator was assigned to watch Aunt Elizabeth. He was not unhappy to learn that she had decided to stay in Atlanta. He hadn't expected to hear from Harvey Paxton about Matt until the end of September so the message that arrived the fourth day of September was upsetting. When he finally had the time to read the communication in private, he was livid. How dare Matt take off before the forged invitation arrived. He had thrown all of Phillip's carefully laid plans awry. In spite of his attempts to the contrary, his work for General Bragg and his staff suffered for several days.

He spent long hours trying to salvage his plans, but he couldn't think of another way to get Matt away from Amy. There was no help for it, he was going to have to ask for a couple of weeks of leave to see what he could arrange.

He approached his commanding officer and was surprised at how swiftly his request for leave was granted. He was ready to leave when Harvey's next communication arrived. Trying to hide his delight, he pleaded for additional time, telling his commandant that he had serious problems at home.

He drove his horse unmercifully and covered the distance to Anderson in just two days. Allowing himself a nap of several hours, he then freshened up and went to Aunt Elizabeth's estate. One of the household slaves showed him to the study, where he sat waiting for Amy to appear, trying hard to compose himself. Despite his delight with his plans, he knew he had to look sufficiently tragic when he gave

Amy the news about her dear husband.

When Amy entered the study, a grave and somber Phillip greeted her. Her breath caught in her throat as Phillip said very quietly, "Amy, I have some very bad news about Matt."

Fingering the golden rose with its small letter *A* hanging around her neck, she sank into a nearby chair. As she stared at her tall, thin brother-in-law, the color faded from her face. Matt couldn't be hurt, he couldn't be . . . She asked Phillip in a voice that was barely above a whisper, "Is he . . ." She couldn't put her fears into words.

Phillip realized instantly where her mind was leading her and that he didn't want. He said quickly, "He's not dead, but I almost wish for your sake he were."

She looked at him in confusion. What could be worse than death? Something terrible had happened, of that she was sure. Had Matt been wounded in a skirmish, wounded so seriously that he would never lead a normal life?

Phillip enjoyed her confusion, but he knew he must explain quickly or else lose any chance of driving her away. "He's been arrested by the Union Army. They have charged him with spying. The message came across my commanding officer's desk two days ago."

Amy laughed. Matt a spy? No, that was silly, ridiculous. Matt was not a spy. When she looked at Phillip's face, his grim countenance, his solemn eyes, she paused. Phillip was serious. He thought Matt a spy, and she became frightened.

"No, he's not a spy. It's a mistake. He's not a spy.

308

I would have known." She sagged back into the chair and in a strangled voice added, "They shoot spies." Her slender frame started to shake as terrible sobs escaped her.

As Phillip approached her and placed his arm tenderly around her shoulder, he tried not to smile. It was going even better than he had hoped. He could smell success. "He used you, Amy. He married you just to get to your brother, the one in the army. He should be shot!" He waited for this piece of information to sink in, then he continued. "He told me what he was doing when he came back into the house the day you came to tell me about the engagement. I didn't believe him at first, but . . ." His voice trailed off.

Amy stared up at him in disbelief, tears streaming down her face. "No . . . no," she whispered. "He went to meet my brother. The invitation — Alex sent an invitation."

"An invitation? When did it arrive?"

"The day Matt left."

"Amy, I wouldn't be surprised if Matt had it sent himself, especially if it arrived just after he left. He probably wanted you to think — "

"He's not a spy." She rose from the chair, her expressive eyes glaring with fire. "Get out! Now!" she breathed in a husky voice. "I don't believe you. It makes no sense. I would know. Get out!" she screamed and pointed to the door.

Phillip started to walk toward the door, more than a little surprised at her reaction. "Amy, come back to Willows until I can arrange to send you home."

"Get out," she said quietly.

Phillip turned to her once more. "I'll be back in a couple of days to check on you. Perhaps you'll change your mind."

"Get out!" Amy screamed.

When the front door slammed shut, Amy ran to her room and threw herself on her bed. She brushed at the tears streaming down her face. Could Phillip be right? Did Matt marry her because she had a brother in the Union Army? Had he been arrested, as Phillip had said? No, Phillip was lying. He hated Matt. But what would he gain? Amy drew herself up into a tight ball. Why, oh, why wasn't Aunt Elizabeth here? She needed desperately to talk to the woman who knew Matt better than anyone.

For over an hour she lay on the bed, sobbing her heart out. Eventually she drifted into a haunted sleep. She could see Matt standing proudly in front of a firing squad and smiling a smile that looked suspiciously like Phillip's half-smile. Then his form faded, and Phillip was standing in Matt's place. He kept repeating, "He's a spy. He married you to get to your brother. He should die."

When she awoke, she was trembling and the tears were still streaming down her face. Her pillow was soaked. She left the bedroom, drying her tears, and went down to the kitchen for a strong cup of coffee. As she sank into a chair beside the worktable, she tried to reason the thing out. Henry came to mind, and somehow she knew that her brother could not have been deceived.

She took a deep breath. Henry could tell her what to do, he could advise her. A letter! She had to write to Henry immediately and ask him what she should do.

She dashed for the study where she grabbed pen and paper. In her haste she spilled some of the ink onto the paper she prepared for her letter. After cleaning up the spill, she sat chewing the tip of her pen, trying to put her thoughts in order. Bending over the desk, she began scratching out her concerns and ended her many pages of questions with a request for an immediate reply. She addressed the envelope and sent one of the younger boys off to Anderson to post the epistle with friends who would smuggle the letter north. Hours later the boy returned. Yes, her message was on its way, and he handed her a letter from Matt.

She rushed to the study and devoured Matt's one page of information. Thinking about what Phillip had told her only hours before, she frowned. The invitation had arrived from Alex, and she herself had sent the information on to Matt. The letter in her hand confirmed that Matt was only seeing Alex because she had insisted that he go. She smiled to herself. Matt went to see Alex for her, not for himself. Phillip was mistaken. Matt was not a spy and had never been one. In a day or two he would come home, and they would travel to Texas together. She felt guilty about troubling Henry with her silly concerns. Now he would think she was an addlebrained ninny. And, she told herself angrily, Phillip would never be allowed in the house again.

Phillip forced himself to wait for two days. When he could wait no longer, he saddled his horse and rode to Elton Estate. He came, he told the slave who answered his knock, to check on Amy.

"Missus Treadwell don't want to see you. She says her husband ain't no spy, and that you'll see," the black woman told him softly. He left word with her that he would be available for another two weeks if Amy needed him. Almost choking on his words, he added that she was to consider Willows her home. He left Elton Estate angry, furious in fact. What if she decided to stay at Elton Estate until Matt was released? The little bitch had too much faith in his brother. There had to be something he could do. He would have to think of something that would shake her opinion to its very foundation.

After a day of pacing, he had had an idea and poured himself a brandy, smiling broadly. He sent word to Harvey Paxton that he would require the use of one of the investigator's men. Paxton's men were better than some of the Northern spies. He requested someone who had the look of a Southern gentleman and a Confederate officer's uniform.

Three days later, a short, wiry man, with hair as black as midnight, came to see Phillip. He informed Phillip that he was from Harvey Paxton and his captain's uniform in correct gray was pressed and waiting. Phillip gave him a packet of papers and a sack of gold coins with instructions to give both to his brother's wife at Elton Estate. "First, ask for Matt Treadwell, then deliver the packet and the sack to his young wife reluctantly. It's important that she think it's a communication from the Confederate Army. Insist that she give it to her husband immediately, as soon as he returns. And, above all, don't answer any of her questions."

Phillip gave him directions to the plantation and asked the man to meet him in Anderson in about five hours for payment and a report. Phillip watched the man, attired in the gray uniform, leave Willows, and he smiled happily. The loss of the gold, if it ended Amy's residence, would be well spent. Surely this would shake her confidence in her husband, and she would head for home.

Amy was startled and a bit frightened when one of the slaves announced the Confederate officer who waited for her in the parlor. She went to the parlor and asked what he wanted.

"I need to see Mr. Matt Treadwell, ma'am," he drawled.

"My husband has not yet returned from his trip to Tennessee, but I'm expecting him at any time."

The officer handed her the packet and the sack of coins. "Would you see these reach his hands when he returns? It is imperative that he get them immediately."

Amy nodded and wanted to ask him whom they were from, but the officer merely turned on his heel and left her.

She found herself shaking violently. Fingering the sack hesitantly, she looked at the packet of papers, trying to understand just what they both meant. Could Phillip have been correct, and Matt was indeed in the employ of the Confederate Army? She took the packet and the sack up to the room she shared with Matt and laid them carefully on top of the dressing table.

For over a week, since that fateful day Phillip had tried to tell her that Matt was a spy, Amy had been throwing herself into the cleaning of Aunt Elizabeth's home. She had cleaned and scrubbed harder than any of the slaves. Now, walking out of her room, she tried to ignore the implications of the packet and the sack and went back to the task she had set for herself, preparing fruits and vegetables for the long winter months ahead. As hard as she tried, she could not forget that the papers and the pouch, obviously full of money, were upstairs on her dressing table.

She threw herself into her work, hoping against hope that by the time the sun dipped over the horizon, she would be too tired to think. When she crawled into bed, she was exhausted, and soon sleep, blessed sleep, came to block out any thought.

The next day was a repeat of the day before as far as Amy was concerned, but that night, despite her exhaustion, sleep would not come. She tossed and turned and tried not to look in the direction of the dressing table upon which the packet and the sack rested.

Early the next morning, as dawn was creeping through the windows of her room, she gave up and slid from her bed. Reaching for the packet and the sack, she sank into a chair. It was still too dark to read the name on the packet, but as she sat holding both items in her hands, she finally decided to open the pouch, which she was sure held money.

Carefully she released the ties and shook the contents into her hand. She stared down at ten gold pieces. As she placed the gold back in the sack, her mind was in a whirl. Something was very wrong here, but she was just too tired to try to figure out what it was. Certainly, she couldn't allow the money and the papers to fall into the wrong hands, not until she had time to consider what must be done.

Glancing around the room, she ruled out each hiding place until she came to Matt's armoire. His clothes were still there. She opened the side door and worked the packet and the pouch into the inside pocket of one of Matt's jackets. It would be safe there for a while, at least until she could decide her next course of action.

In agony she crept back to bed, refusing to speculate on what the items might mean. Stretching out on the bed, she tried hard not to think at all. Sleep finally came, and she was too tired even to dream.

Each day dragged by until one week, then two, then the end of the month came. Matt never came, and there were no messages, not from Matt, Aunt Elizabeth, or Henry. When she was sure she was about to become a raving idiot, a note arrived from Henry, smuggled through the underground. As she read the one-page letter, her eyes filled with tears. Henry was no help at all. He informed her that there was nothing to do but wait, and he assured her that Matt wouldn't be involved in anything as underhanded as spying. Phillip was not to be believed. His advice was to dismiss the whole thing from her mind. There were countless encounters in both Tennessee and Kentucky. Henry was certain that Matt would wait until things quieted down and he could move Emma and Jacob through safely. That was the reason Matt was not home yet.

Amy sat in the study, more confused than ever. If Phillip was so wrong, then why had the Confederate officer arrived with the things for Matt? Was her husband being framed for something he hadn't done? What could be gained and who could benefit? Amy had no answers, and she had no one to talk to. She couldn't talk to the slaves. Aunt Elizabeth wasn't there. There was no word from her, and Amy refused to consider what that might mean. She tried to shake the feeling that she was the last person on the earth. Once more she threw herself into cleaning the house.

This time she was not successful. She did not feel well, and she was afraid she had overworked. She was having trouble keeping down food. Even the smell of coffee made her nauseated. As soon as she received some word from Matt, she told herself, her stomach problems would disappear. And she was more than a little grateful that Phillip avoided the plantation. Certain that he had already returned to Atlanta, she breathed a sigh of relief. She simply could not face him again.

Chapter Twenty-one

The days dragged by just as slowly for Matt. On the third day, he found a lump of charcoal in the small stove, and prying a loose board from the wall of the shed in which he was confined, he constructed a daily calender on the rough wood. He tried continually to talk to his guards about the weather, the Tennessee countryside, his farm in Texas, but with the exception of an occasional grunt or groan, they would not respond.

On the fifth day, the soldiers woke him before dawn, and he was escorted to a makeshift stable. He was forced onto a horse, his hands tied in front of him, and one of the guards took the reins. They rode west all day, not stopping until after dark. That night he slept in a tent with three guards instead of the usual one.

He was confined to the tent for twenty-four hours, then without any explanation, the whole procedure was repeated, and he was taken back to his shed in northern Tennessee. Even though he asked numerous questions of his guards, he was not told why the move had been necessary.

He was still convinced that the only course open to him was to wait until the army corrected the whole affair. His name had to be cleared before he left the area. If not, the Union soldiers might follow him to Texas and shoot before asking any questions.

He kept his calendar and established a routine of exercise for himself. He asked for and was given three books, and he set aside a specific time to read each day. Once he was back in the fruit cellar, he was allowed outside each day for some fresh air, but always with at least two guards in attendance with their rifles in firing position. Once outdoors, he made a systematic study of the camp itself.

Whoever had selected the shed for a prison had some experience in such matters, because the small building was ideally located to keep the prisoners in view at all times. The field soldiers' tents were to his right, and the officers were billeted to his left. A large vacant field lay in back of the shed, and in the distance Matt thought he could make out a lake. He couldn't see the corral for the horses. Escape would be difficult, perhaps impossible.

Each morning and again in the evening, Matt asked to speak to the colonel. Each time he was given the same excuse. "Not today. The colonel is too busy to talk to you." Matt gritted his teeth and began to give serious consideration to escape.

He was shocked when he counted the days on his calender and realized that October was ten days old. If he didn't get out of the camp and back to Amy, his cattle and his men would be confined to the stockyards of St. Louis for who knew how many days. Travel with a herd of restless cattle would be dangerous, and that was what he would have if he couldn't get underway before the end of November.

By the thirty-first day Matt was nearly frantic, and he decided that the only way out of his prison was to get as far away, as quickly as he could. He continued to ask to speak to the colonel but told himself that the bastard was probably never going to speak to him until he was put on trial, if he ever had a trial. The army would never admit making a mistake. Escape was his only chance.

He made up his mind that he was going to leave the hospitality of the North by the middle of the next week. He had seven days to perfect an escape plan that would take him far from Tennessee. His first concern, he decided, was the routine of the camp. Groups of soldiers came and went continually, but there was always a small contingent that remained. He discovered that during the evening meal, most of the officers gathered with whatever soldiers were in camp and shared the campfire for their meal. That was the time, the only time he had a chance, when the camp was more relaxed and fewer men were roaming about.

Since his confinement, he had been allowed to use the privy. That small building was closer to the horses than any other spot in camp. The only possible chance he had to reach any of the horses was while he was making use of the privy. An idea sent him into chuckles. He would pretend a stomach ailment that required frequent visits to that convenience. Long stays might lull the guards into complacency. It was worth a try.

If he convinced his guards that he was really sick and had a disease that they might contract, they might stay far enough from him to permit a lengthy lead after he escaped. It was growing dark earlier each day, and he reasoned that he might be able to get enough of a headstart so that they could not track him until morning. If he could use the darkness, then he had an even better chance. For three days he watched the evening sky. By Wednesday the moon would be a slender sliver.

Monday night, he began his playacting, complaining about feeling feverish and aching. The next morning, he lay on his mattress, holding his head and groaning. He had already been accompanied to the privy twice by a frowning guard named Joe. Things were going well. Joe stayed as far away from him as he could and acted as though that was not far enough. Matt tried to suppress the grin he knew would give him away.

Shortly after his breakfast was delivered, the young officer that had been present that first day arrived with another tall, lean man wearing the blue of the Union. He made the introductions. "This is Captain Joshua Eller. He is a lawyer, and the army has asked him to plead your case at your trial."

Matt sat up quickly, his playacting forgotten. His trial? Had it gone that far? He got to his feet quickly and shook the hand of the older man. Turning to the young officer, Matt asked quietly, "May I be permitted to speak to my lawyer alone?"

The lieutenant nodded and signaled the guard to leave. Then he turned and walked briskly out the door, closing it behind him.

Matt groaned. Why now, when he was fairly certain that he could make good his escape on his own? He mentally assessed the man before him. He was tall and thin, perhaps forty, with gray eyes. He had the look of some schooling about him. If he seemed incompetent, Matt decided, he would go ahead with his plan. Somehow, he would get free and to Texas if it was the last thing he did.

The lawyer sat down at the table and asked Matt to sit on the bed. Taking a stack of papers from his satchel, he glanced over at Matt. "There is much I need to know." Matt spent the next thirty minutes answering questions about his activities before the war, then about his relationship with his wife and his brother. He answered all the questions and glanced over at the lawyer. "I have some questions, myself."

Captain Eller smiled slightly. "It's my job to ask questions. But I'll see if I can answer a couple."

Matt took a deep breath. "Would you please tell me what I am supposed to have done to be arrested in the first place?"

The lawyer looked surprised. "Didn't they tell you the reason for your arrest?"

"Hell, no. They wouldn't tell me a thing. I've asked to speak to the colonel every single day, but the man claims that he is too busy to see me. I also want to know who gave the army my name and accused me of whatever it is I'm supposed to have done."

"As to the first question, you have been charged with trying to solicit information from an officer of the Union Army," the lawyer said quietly.

"Who? I don't even know anyone in the Union Army."

"The union officer named was Lieutenant Sanderson, sir."

Matt stared at him in disbelief. "I don't know the man. He's my wife's brother, but I've never met him. In fact, I thought I came here at his request. I received a letter from my wife, and she told me that she had an invitation for me from her brother, Alex Sanderson. I came here to meet him."

The lawyer looked a little dubious and gazed at the pad of paper on which he had written notes while questioning Matt.

Matt stood and started to pace back and forth in front of the bed. "Who put me here? My brother or my wife?"

The lawyer frowned. "I'd rather not answer that question yet. I want to check out some of this information. It's at variance with what I have. And I want to communicate with Henry Sanderson. I'm going to ask you to wait for four or five days, then I'll answer your questions. When did you say your brother joined the Confederate Army?"

"A year ago. Sir, I have been here for thirty-five days. If my wife had nothing to do with this, and I don't think she did, then she has no idea where I am or what has happened. I have friends at Tucker's Crossroads that I was supposed to meet weeks ago, and my cattle is due in St. Louis in days. Is there some way you can get word to these people? I don't want my wife to worry. We've only been married for a little while." His voice was husky and shook slightly.

The lawyer gave Matt a long stare of concern. "Give me several days, and if what you have told me checks out, I personally will notify your wife and your friends." The lawyer stuffed the papers into his case and walked toward the door. "Don't try anything foolish," he said.

Matt nodded, his expression grim. He could wait for several days. If the lawyer reached Henry, his troubles would be over, Matt thought as he sank down on the bed. And if not, then there was no other way, he would feign the stomach ailment again and leave before the moon was bright enough to give him away.

The next afternoon, Matt's reading time was disturbed by a knock on his door. Captain Eller stood in the doorway. "I need some additional facts."

After Matt answered his questions, the two men discussed raising cattle. When the lawyer left, Matt chuckled. The lawyer wasn't going to let him attempt anything. The next afternoon, when the lawyer arrived again, this time with coffee, Matt asked him, "Are you concerned that I might attempt to take things in my own hands?"

Captain Eller chuckled. "The thought occurred to me. Son, you don't want to do anything to jeopardize your future." And the next afternoon, when Captain Eller asked for names and addresses, Matt was overjoyed.

"I told the colonel—by the way Colonel Brown has been replaced—that you were arrested on very flimsy grounds. He agreed that your family and friends should be notified. I'll send the telegrams tomorrow morning and explain the delay."

"Is there any way I can send a letter? I want to write to my wife."

Captain Eller frowned and stroked his beard. "It would be better if I made the request after we have some testimony to present."

Matt gritted his teeth and gathered his courage. "Can you tell me when that might be and how soon I'll be out of this godforsaken place?"

The lawyer chuckled. "One thing at a time. But if Henry Sanderson arrives on time, then we'll have you out of here by the middle of the month."

Damn, Matt thought and glanced at his calendar. That was three weeks away. At least the lawyer did say that he would be released and Amy would be notified. At the moment, he supposed, it would have to do.

On the eighteenth of October, a lone rider approached Elton Estate on a skittish mule. Amy met him on the veranda.

"I brung a telegram for Mrs. Matt Treadwell."

Amy grabbed the folded paper and sent the boy to the study. It was from Matt, it had to be from Matt. Gathering her courage, she pored over the message.

Matt Treadwell detained by U.S. Army — Will advise throughout investigation.

It was signed by a Captain Joshua Eller, U.S.A. She reread the message at least a dozen times. Investigation? Detained? Was Phillip right? Had Matt been arrested? Her heart breaking, she made her way to her room. Matt was no spy. He couldn't have married her only to have access to Alex; it just wasn't possible. She couldn't have fallen in love with someone so devious. And she did love him. Suddenly, she remembered the packet of papers that had arrived with the pouch of money. She would not see him shot either. She dashed for the jacket, and taking the unopened packet from its hiding place, she crept to the fireplace. Striking a match, she carefully held it to the bottom of the papers. Slowly, the flame caught, and the official stack of papers was devoured by the licking flames.

For how long she sat, gazing at the bits of black ash that remained on the grate, she did not know. Sighing, she forced herself up onto her feet. At least, now, if anyone came to search, whatever evidence there had been was destroyed. She took the fabric pouch of coins and tucked it into her own garments. Who could say that her husband had not left a stash of coins with her, in case she needed money? Satisfied, she returned to the study.

She glanced around the room, aware that Matt might have left other papers in the house that could add fuel to whatever investigation the army was conducting. Would the North send someone to search Aunt Elizabeth's home? It made no sense, but to be on the safe side she spent the next hour, hunting through all the papers, prepared to burn anything that hinted at any of Matt's activities, anything the least bit suspicious. That done, she breathed a sigh of relief and went to the kitchen. She had found nothing.

As she fixed a cup of tea, she struggled with nausea. Just the smell of food made her sick. Once more, she returned to her bedroom, and this time, she fell across the bed.

What was she going to do? She couldn't very well write to Aunt Elizabeth and tell her that the nephew she loved was being investigated by the Union Army. No, that kind of thing must be told face to face. But there had been no communication from Aunt Elizabeth for over five weeks. Was the mail in the South that affected by the war? Perhaps the woman was on her way home at the moment. Amy closed her eyes and offered a silent, heartfelt prayer.

As she frequently did when she was troubled, her fingers drifted over the golden letter Matt had given her for her betrothal. For some reason, today, touching that token of love didn't make her feel any better, as it usually did. There were other considerations. Some men, she thought, would do anything for love of money or country. Did Matt fit into one of those categories? Even though she had been married to him for almost nine months, she still didn't know that much about him. But one thing she did know, she sat up, a determined look on her face, Matt Treadwell was not a spy. Phillip yes, but Matt no! The army had made a mistake.

But would the army admit its mistake? Stuck here in the South, with no friends or family, she could do nothing. If she went home, at least Henry could counsel her and Alex could help, too, if they could get a message through to him. Grim determination lined her face. As soon as Aunt Elizabeth returned from Atlanta, Amy would go home herself.

With thoughts of returning home swirling around

in her tired head, she crawled into bed that night. Just as soon as Aunt Elizabeth returned, she would pack. The money from the Southern army would see her home. Aunt Elizabeth just had to send word or arrive soon; she had been gone too long as it was.

Bright sunshine streamed through the window the next morning, as Amy was startled awake by her maid gently shaking her shoulder. Bewildered, she tried to rub the sleep from her eyes and concentrate on what the maid was saying. She obviously had slept half the morning away, and someone had arrived to see her.

For a second the words made no sense, then when she finally understood what the girl was telling her, Amy gave a cry and leaped out of her bed. She threw on her robe and ran from the room. Aunt Elizabeth was home. Pulling the robe closed, she started for the stairs. Halfway down the steps, she realized she heard a low masculine voice. For one tiny instant her heart tricked her. Matt, she breathed. No, the voice was not as deep as Matt's, and it sounded older. Her lower lip trembled as she glided slowly into the foyer.

"Mrs. Treadwell? Mrs. Matt Treadwell?" A gray-haired gentleman stood just inside the door. His voice registered surprise.

Amy nodded. "I'm Mrs. Matt Treadwell. May I help you?"

"If I could speak to Mr. Treadwell, Mr. Matt Treadwell?"

Amy's heart sank, not another Southerner to see Matt. "I'm sorry, but my husband has not yet returned from the North. He has been—detained. I'm not sure when he will be returning."

"Oh, no. This is terrible. This is awful. This places me in a most peculiar position. I am at a most terrible disadvantage." His voice rose in alarm, and he stood shaking his head back and forth.

Amy turned to one of the slaves. "Miranda, if you will get the gentleman some coffee, I'll dress, and then we can discuss your problem, sir. I'll be but a few minutes." Not waiting for his reply, she hurried up the stairs. The man was obviously distressed about something. What news did he have? He seemed most upset that she was still in the house and that Matt was not at home. Donning one of her better cotton dresses, then brushing her hair, she quickly tied it back and descended the stairs.

As she rushed through the dining room door, she extended her hand. "Mr. — ? I'm sorry, I don't believe you told me your name."

The gray-haired gentleman, only a little taller than Amy, rose from his chair. He still looked very upset, but he took her offered hand. "I'm Charles Elton, a second cousin to Elizabeth Elton."

Amy looked into his gray somber eyes, her heart sinking still lower. Something was wrong with Aunt Elizabeth. "Mr. Elton, why are you here?" she blurted out.

"I've come to close the house, but, with you here, I . . ." His voice trailed off as he watched Amy sink into one of the dining room chairs.

"Aunt Elizabeth?" Amy whispered.

"Oh, my dear child. Of course, you don't know. Elizabeth was taken ill several weeks ago. We are afraid it's serious. The family decided that I should come and close the house for several months. If Elizabeth recovers, it will be months before she can return. We were told that you and Matthew were leaving for Texas in September. I have letters asking friends to care for her slaves. I don't know what to do, I just don't know." He looked extremely uncomfortable. Noticing the letter he clutched in his hand, he held it up for her inspection.

Amy fought a storm of tears. She wanted to cry, to scream; instead she took the note and read the request for care of Aunt Elizabeth's slaves and authorization to close the house. Her heart sank. Now she had no choice. She would have to go to Willows, at least until she could make arrangements. There was no place to go but back to Indiana. Attempting to calm herself, she murmured in a strained voice, "You may close the house tomorrow. I can leave today."

"Oh, you don't need to leave today," he replied, his voice heavy with relief. "I don't need to close the house until I have taken care of the slaves. It will be several days before I have everything ready."

Amy could only stare ahead, seeing nothing. She was heartsick. Aunt Elizabeth might be dying, Matt was detained by the North on charges of spying, and she had to go crawling back to Willows, if Phillip would have her. Would he be willing to take her in? She almost cried aloud, "Oh, Matt. What is happening to us?"

She sent one of the older slaves to Willows to tell Mr. Phillip that she would have to accept his hospitality until she could make arrangements to return to Indiana. Would he please send a carriage for her and some of her things? With her eyes brimming with tears, Amy trudged up the stairs to her room to pack.

She folded her day dresses, her underthings, and the blue-gray dress Matt had given her so long ago and stored them in the trunk. She wrapped her jewelry and the ten gold coins and added them to her things. Touching her wedding dress and the gown she had worn the night of her engagement party, she gave in to the flood of tears that threatened to wash her away. Why? Dear God, why? She turned her back on the wardrobe, leaving her wedding gown and ball gown and all of the dresses the dressmaker had readied for her life in Texas. She couldn't bear to take them too, not until she knew what was going to happen to Matt. Once things were normal again, she would send for them. The tears flowed even harder. There might not be anyone at Elton Estate to fill her request. It was another hour before she could continue.

By early afternoon, she had finished her packing and had just started to say good-bye to the slaves when another young man, in the official gray of the Confederate Army appeared at the front door, asking if he could speak to her in private for a few minutes. Confused, not thinking clearly, Amy stood in indecision. "What do you want of me?"

"Ma'am," he said quietly, "I would like to speak to you in private. Could you grant me a few minutes of your time? This won't take long."

She led him out to the garden. "We can speak here."

Twisting his cap in his hands and looking at her

shyly, he cleared his throat. "Ma'am, the army is aware of your situation. Measures have been taken to rescue your husband, but until he's freed, his commanding officer thought you might need this." He pressed a small purse into her hands, mumbled his sympathy, and strode from the garden.

Amy watched him go, frozen in place. What on earth was that all about? Was someone trying to convince her that Matt was a member of the Confederate Army? Matt had no commanding officer. Why was the Confederate Army trying to free him? What kind of a nightmare was she living through? Tears streamed down her face, and she sat down on one of the benches in the garden, clutching the purse in her hands.

In the distance she heard a carriage rumbling up the drive and a horse's hooves crunch over the stones, but she could not bring herself to rise from the bench in the garden. She could not concern herself with this latest visitor. No! In a second or two she would wake up, and Matt would be beside her, and the whole month and a half just past would be a bad dream. Please, only a dream.

Chapter Twenty-two

Amy sat on the small stone bench, holding the purse and staring off into space, her eyes dry. She had to get hold of herself, she decided and shook herself out of her despair. She was startled when she looked up into Phillip's eyes, which seemed to be sympathetic. "You came," she said a little too breathlessly, she thought.

"I came as soon as Isaac told me you changed your mind. I brought the carriage. If we hurry, we can make it back to Willows before nightfall." Phillip noticed the small purse that he had given the young investigator Paxton had sent. It seemed to have done the job. Now, if he could get her back to Willows without laughing in her face, he could proceed with his plans.

Amy watched Phillip's face carefully. He was being too nice. There was even a hint of humor in his eyes, and suddenly she realized that she didn't trust Phillip Treadwell, she didn't trust him a bit. Still, he did look concerned.

"I'm all packed. As soon as the trunk is loaded, we can leave," she said quietly.

Phillip looked a little surprised but decided this was not the time for comment. He had to make certain that she saw him as the concerned older brother. Trying for a compassionate expression, he stepped forward and awkwardly patted her shoulder.

"Amy, go home. Forget about Matt. Try and make a new life for yourself. He isn't worth this. I'm so sorry I ever brought you here. This is all my fault."

Amy looked up at the man offering her what seemed like sincere sympathy. But why would a man be so willing to condemn his own brother? Well, she had enough of this Treadwell, and she jerked away from him.

"I am going home, just as soon as I can arrange it."

Phillip moved away from her just as quickly.

"It's for the best. I'll do whatever I can to help you, before I have to back to Atlanta." He moved toward the house, then turned and looked at her solemnly. "What made you decide?"

Amy ignored his question and stared at the house. Should she tell him about the telegram that had come only yesterday? Or confess that Aunt Elizabeth was ill and she had no other place to go? No, she wouldn't tell him a thing. And she would find her own way back to Indiana. She didn't need his help. She wouldn't accept his help. She would do it on her own.

While Amy finished saying her good-byes, Phillip loaded her things into his carriage. Then there was nothing left to do but allow him to help her into the vehicle. Phillip jumped into the carriage, signaling the driver, and they started down the drive. Amy refused to look at him or look back. As the carriage pulled into the road, Amy remembered that this was the first time since Matt had left that she had ventured from the estate. Despite her attempt to keep her emotions under control, a little sob escaped.

Phillip pretended not to notice and asked in a quiet tone, "You never answered my question. What made you decide to go home?"

Amy glanced over at Matt's brother and then back out the window. "There is nothing for me here," she whispered. Closing her eyes, she rested her head against the cushion. Phillip looked out the opposite window, trying hard to control his features. It had worked. Somehow, he had forced the Northern beauty to abandon her Southern husband. Willows was safe.

The temptation to say something more was too great for Phillip, and after they had been on the road for the better part of an hour, he leaned forward. "Amy, I'll help in any way I can. We'll get you home as fast as we can." Amy made no comment, and Phillip wasn't even sure she heard him. He grinned to himself. It was obvious that she was angry and hurt. The sooner she was in Indiana the better for everyone involved. Then he would have to see about getting Matt released. But not too soon. And, of course, with the battles raging in Kentucky and Tennessee, it would be a long time before Matt could reach Indiana, if he even tried.

The sun had already set when the carriage pulled into the drive lined with willow trees. Amy stirred from her nap, and as the slaves crowded around the carriage, Amy swiped at some of the tears gathering in her eyes. It had been so long since she had seen them.

Jenny took her in hand and led her up to the room she had originally occupied at Willows. Jenny and, in fact, all the slaves seemed pleased to see her, but no one dared to ask why she had returned. They appeared to be afraid.

She ambled down to the kitchen at Jenny's insistence and helped herself to some cold chicken that was there. After she had made her self some tea, she went back to her room, physically and emotionally exhausted and still not feeling well. Jenny followed her and helped her prepare for bed. Amy gave her a half-smile and crawled into bed. At least she had a place to sleep. She drifted off, grateful for that small favor.

Shortly after the sun rose, Amy woke and dressed. She had a great many things to accomplish that day. Somehow, she had to send a message to Henry. Just thinking about her brother made her feel guilty. She hadn't tried to sneak a message north to Henry since she had asked for his advice, and so much had changed since then. When she told him about her two visitors from the army, would he still defend Matt so diligently?

She stole down to the kitchen, trying to avoid Phillip. Jenny greeted her with an enormous smile.

"Massa Phillip left you a message. He be gone, left before sun up."

Amy read the short note Jenny handed her and smiled to herself. Phillip had written that he had much to do and would probably not be back until late that night. He would see her in the morning. She had her work cut out for her. Somehow, she had to convince Phillip that she didn't need nor did she want his help. She would go back to Indiana on her own.

She tried to eat a little breakfast, but her stomach was churning. Giving up on food, she went to the study. She had a great deal to tell Henry, and the sooner she started the better. The words flowed easily as Amy explained about the information the Confederate officer had brought, Phillip's insisting that Matt was a spy, the telegram, and why she had had to leave Elton Estate. When she came to the part about returning to Indiana, she stopped. She knew she was going back, but not how. Before she could finish her note to Henry, she had some decisions to make.

She dressed quickly and arranged for the carriage. First, she decided, she needed to locate a carriage and a team of horses. No way was she going to accept Phillip's offer. She would make all her own arrangements. And a driver. She would need a driver, someone she could trust. Amy frowned, remembering that Matt had said the only man he trusted was the banker in Anderson. The man handled all of Matt's drafts for the supplies they had purchased, and Amy had met the man on two different occasions. She would ask the banker for help.

On the trip into town, Amy thought through what she wanted to tell the banker. He knew Matt and Phillip both and was sure to ask questions, questions Amy had no intention of answering. She would stick as close to the truth as possible, she decided, telling him that Matt was in Tennessee and that she had to go home to see her brother. And that was all she would tell him.

Her meeting with the banker went much better

than she had thought possible. The man had asked only if there was trouble at home. Her reply was close to the truth, if not all of it. "I have to go home to see my brother."

When she was assured that the banker knew of several trustworthy drivers to escort her to Indiana, she thanked him and made her way to the stables in back of the carriage shop. She talked to the little old man, who was also a friend of the Treadwells. Quickly, she explained that she wanted two carriage horses, suitable for a long trip. The bent old man, who smelled of sweat and horses, cocked his head and grinned up at her. "Ain't them boys got enough horses?" Then his grin spread even wider. "Gift for the husband?" A deep blush stained Amy's cheeks, and he chuckled. "Missy, I can keep a secret," he croaked. "I'll find you two beauties, war or no war."

"Not too expensive," Amy pleaded.

The old codger nodded. "Leave it to me. Should have 'em in a week or two."

Amy took a deep breath. In two weeks, perhaps even sooner, she would be on her way home. She hurried to the carriage shop. Amy scowled when the clerk told her a carriage, even a used one, was impossible. "With the war . . ." She would have to accept Phillip's help at least with a carriage. Amy frowned, there was no help for it.

A half-smile played across her lips. Now, she could tell Henry of her plans and send her message. The only difficulty she had left was getting the message on its way. With no mail moving between the North and the South, that was going to be a real problem.

The next morning, Phillip solved one of her problems in a grand manner. She explained about the carriage, and Phillip magnanimously insisted that she use one of his. Watching her carefully, he added, "You must let your brother know that you are coming home. If you'll write him a note, I'll see that it's on its way." He smiled at her, pretending a sincerity that Amy never saw through.

She's so gullible, Phillip thought. There was no way Phillip wanted Henry to know that she was coming until she arrived, and with the trouble in Tennessee and Kentucky that could take months. If the charges against Matt were dropped before Phillip was ready to have him released, he certainly didn't want Matt contacting Henry and finding out that Amy was on her way home. Phillip could pay off the banker and the old man in the stables, and a threat or two would keep his slaves quiet. Amy's trail had to stop at Willows. Then, when Matt started asking questions, there would be no answers.

Later that morning, Amy took her letter to Phillip. He accepted the envelope with a frown. "Amy, I have some unfortunate news. I will not be here to see you off. I have been called back to my unit. I must leave tomorrow morning." Phillip pointed to an official-looking envelope on his desk. "I'll need to go into town today and finish my business, and tomorrow at dawn, I'll have to leave."

Amy smiled herself. "I don't need you here to see me off. Your banker assured me that I'd have a driver in a week or two, and the horses have been promised about the same time. I should be on my way by the middle of the month, by November fifteenth at the latest.

"Use whatever you need, and use my name for any supplies you have to buy. When I'm in town today, I'll check with the bank and the stables and make sure everything will be ready for you."

"That's not necessary," Amy protested.

Phillip waved his hand. "I insist. I'll see you tonight, in case you think of anything else you need."

Before Amy could assure him that she needed nothing, he was out the door. "At least," she muttered as she made her way back to her room, "Henry will know I'm coming home."

Phillip was several miles from Willows, before he stopped his horse. He reached into his pocket and withdrew the letter Amy had given him, and a smile lit his face. From all the gossip he had heard, Matt and Henry were good friends. If Matt secured his release before Phillip was ready, he had no doubt that Matt would contact Henry as soon as he found Amy gone. It was truly a shame, he thought, smirking, that Henry didn't know anything, wouldn't know anything. Phillip tore the letter into small shreds and scattered the pieces to the wind. He laughed out loud as he whipped his horse into a trot. No, Matt would find nothing out from Henry. And, with the direction the war was taking, it would be months before Amy reached Indiana.

The next morning, shortly after dawn, Amy saw Phillip off. She wished him luck, and he wished her happiness, adding that he hoped she had no difficulty getting home safely. As she watched him ride away from the plantation without a backward glance, she prayed that if Matt was ever released from the army, he and Phillip would get along better. "At least, I won't be here to cause more trouble between them," she sighed as tears slid down her face.

Suddenly feeling violently ill, Amy dragged herself to her room. She tried to shake the sensation of nausea that threatened to render her immobile. This would not do at all. She could not start for home, unless she was certain that she would not be ill along the way. There was no alternative. She had to see the doctor in Anderson. She sent word to the stables that she would need a carriage that afternoon for a quick trip into Anderson.

By early afternoon, when the carriage had been prepared, Amy felt foolish. Her malaise had passed once more, and she felt fine. But there had to be a reason for her bouts of discomfort, she decided. She was not stupid enough to attempt the trip North without first getting a clean bill of health from the doctor who had been so kind to her well over a year ago. No, she had to see the man, if only to assure herself that nothing was wrong. Resignedly, she started for Anderson.

As long as she was in Anderson, she decided that she would do a little shopping and check on the progress of her horses. She stepped from the carriage, intent on visiting the stooped little man at the stables when her eyes were drawn to two familiar shapes standing in front of the general store. She stared in horror. No, it couldn't be! But it was. Standing in the shade of one of the oak trees, passing the time of day, Norman Barber and Clarence Glanzman stood talking to each other. Amy swung back up into the carriage and quickly tried to hide her face with her hand and her bonnet. Had they seen her?

What were they doing here? Had Phillip sent for them? No, she reasoned. Phillip had fired them months ago and had never hinted that he wanted them involved in any of his affairs again.

Her voice hardly above a whisper, she ordered the driver to turn the carriage around and head back to Willows. Forgotten was her need to see a doctor. The threat Norman had shouted so long ago came reverberating back through her head. They were there to get even with Phillip, but Phillip wasn't there. Suddenly, she was frightened. Would they make good on their vow?

She tried to reason away her fears. Rumors were rampant. President Lincoln had already said he would free the slaves, and daily more and more plantation owners were pursuing runaways. Both men were slave agents. They were no doubt involved in tracking down some Southerner's property. They didn't know she was there. How could they know? And they would find out, soon enough, that Phillip Treadwell was away serving the Confederacy. Still, she would have to be on her guard. She settled back in the carriage, trying to calm her beating heart.

Amy considered whether she should borrow Phillip's horses, take one of Phillip's slaves as a driver, and make a run for the North. No, she had made her plans, Henry had been notified. She would see the thing through as she had planned. She would just have to keep her eyes open and her ears tuned for any gossip, and the sooner she was on her way the better for everyone.

* * *

As Amy was climbing into the carriage, the objects of her concern stood talking quietly. Norman's dirty face framed an unpleasant smile. "See, I told you. It was her. Now, we'll find out what she's a-doin' here, and take care of the little bitch."

Clarence whimpered, "Why can't we just grab her like we did afore? I never did get to try her."

Norman glared at the man beside him. "On account of her, I lost me my business. I had a good business, but that little lady done ruined it. No, grabbin' her ain't bad enough. She's gonna pay for what she did. Yes, sir. Come on, let's go find out what she's still doin' here." Clarence followed him back toward the stable.

Late that afternoon, Amy roused from a nap when Jenny shook her gently. "There a boy downstairs. He's a mite anxious, and he's sayin' he gotta talk now."

Slipping back into her day dress and smoothing her hair, she told Jenny to see to the lad's comfort. She would be down directly. When she stood in the foyer, she gazed at a tall, gangly lad of fourteen or fifteen. He held a small scrap of paper in his tightly clenched hand. Wary, she stepped up to him.

"I'm Mrs. Treadwell."

The boy turned his confused face in her direction, "Mrs. Matt Treadwell? You weren't at the other place. The man sez you be here."

"I'm Mrs. Matt Treadwell," Amy assured the boy.

He hesitated another minute, then handed her the scrap of paper. "I been told to give this to you and only to you."

Amy opened the crumpled telegram. Her eyes misted with tears as she read the words.

Matt Treadwell detained. Deliver Emma and Jacob to Elton Estate. Into care of Mrs. Matt Treadwell — only.

It was signed by Captain Joshua Eller, U.S.A. It bore the same date as her telegram of a week ago.

Amy brushed at the moisture gathering in her eyes. "Where are they?" she whispered.

The boy glanced at her, and his relieved expression made her want to laugh. "I'll get 'em," he almost shouted. Thank the good Lord, Phillip has already left for camp, Amy thought as she lifted her arms to welcome the only friends she thought she had left.

She threw her arms around a happy and well-fed Emma, who was followed closely by a concerned and obviously very frightened Jacob. "Phillip's in Georgia," Amy told them as she pushed them toward the study. Closing the door on her friends, she ordered the boy into the kitchen for something to eat, then rushed back into the study. With tears streaming down her face, she hugged first Emma and then Jacob and then Emma once more.

Finally, wiping the tears from her eyes, she disentangled herself from her friends and sank into one of the chairs. "I have so many questions and so much to tell you."

Two hours later, Amy cautiously opened the study door and scurried to the kitchen. Jacob and Amy both felt that the fewer slaves who knew they were back the better. Amy smiled to herself as she remembered Jacob's belligerent defense of Matt. "No way dat boy could spy. No, suh! I don't care what Massa Phillip sez he done. He ain't done it. No, if Massa Matt's with the army, then that Massa Phillip's doin'. Massa Matt ain't no spy!"

"Jenny," Amy called out. Not even Jenny could know that Emma and Jacob were back. When Jenny stuck her head out of the pantry, Amy gave her order. "I want you to go out to old Maude's cabin. The overseer says she's ailing. Take her some of the broth you made for dinner and bring me a full report."

Old Maude would love the attention and the broth. The old woman would also be amazed that the overseer had noticed that she was not up to her usual self, Amy thought, almost giggling. That would keep Jenny busy for an hour, which was enough time for Amy to feed and hide Emma and Jacob.

She took Emma and Jacob up to Matt's old room. No one would even consider looking there, she was sure. She fixed enough food to feed three of them and carried it upstairs. While they ate, Amy told them her plans.

"I want you to come with me. Henry will take you on to Canada when we get home. And this time"— she pulled out the small purse and the pouch filled with gold coins—"we'll travel in style." Just before she left the room, she turned back to Jacob. "Can you drive a carriage?" When Jacob grinned and nodded, Amy laughed. "All we need now are the horses. Then, we'll be on our way."

For the first time in days, Amy felt hopeful. She

congratulated herself on conquering her anxiety. Even though Matt had been gone for almost two months, Amy felt that her future was no longer filled with despair. Now, at least, she had someone to talk to, and she didn't feel so alone. Emma and Jacob would help her get to Indiana, and Henry would aid in freeing Matt. If Emma and Jacob didn't want to go to Canada, they could all head west, as they had planned.

The next afternoon, Amy sent two notes, one to the banker, telling him that she had obtained a driver herself, and one to the little man at the stable. She needed the horses in two days, and she would take whatever he could find. After the messages had been sent, Jenny confronted Amy.

"I knows Emma and Jacob are back. I won't tell, but Emma is my friend. I wants to see her."

That evening, Emma, Jacob, Jenny, and Amy ate together in the kitchen. Jenny was sworn to secrecy, and she volunteered to help get things ready for the trip. Amy scowled inwardly as she thought of the little lie she told Jenny. It was better that Jenny not know that they were heading north. Amy told her instead that Emma and Jacob were taking her to Aunt Elizabeth in Atlanta.

Amy spent the next day with Emma and Jenny, packing the trunks and basket they would take. She also spent an hour closeted with Jacob discussing the war. Tennessee and Kentucky had seen numerous battles, and Jacob pleaded with Amy to consider traveling to Tucker's Crossroads before they tried to move through Union lines.

Amy smiled up at the thin, serious black man.

345

"You'll be driving." She went back to help finish the packing. As soon as the horses were delivered, they could leave.

When Jenny came running from the kitchen before dinner, Amy felt her heart quicken. "They's here, they's here." Jenny met Amy on the stairs. Amy followed her down the stairs, with orders to find the overseer. Amy looked the horses over, and she was pleased with what she saw. Two of the slaves led the animals to the barn, and the overseer met her there. He too congratulated her on the fine horseflesh she had obtained. She thanked the man and hurried back to the house. They could leave tomorrow.

After a hasty dinner, Amy hid Emma and Jacob in Opal Mae's old room. They had to leave before the first light of dawn if they were to get away from the knowing eyes that could report the appearance of Emma and Jacob to Phillip. The overseer brought several of the field hands to the house to help with the loading of the carriage. Finally, long after dark, Amy discarded her brown day dress and let Jenny pull one of her nightgowns on over her head. Her clothes were ready, the carriage was packed, and Emma and Jacob were safely hidden downstairs. They would begin their trip to Indiana long before any of the hands at Willows were up and about.

Amy crawled into bed that night, tired but satisfied. Tomorrow she would start home. In a matter of weeks she would have Henry's help. Somehow, together they would find out what had happened to Matt and why the army had detained him. Then, with the help Henry could obtain from teachers and friends, they would see Matt released. She sighed her contentment and snuggled down into the quilt to sleep.

She found that, despite her fatigue, she was too excited to sleep. And something more, she finally admitted. She was apprehensive as well. Long after the household had retired for the night, she was still prowling around Anna Treadwell's room. She finally made her way through the dark to the kitchen and warmed up enough milk to induce sleep, she hoped. Back in bed, she lay worrying about the coins and the jewelry she had packed in the trunk.

She glanced at the dark shadows of her blue-gray dress hanging in the armoire. The cameo of a rose that Matt had given her the night after their wedding was pinned to the collar, and around her neck she wore the golden letter *A*, but the rest of her things were in the trunk in the carriage. Anyone could get to it.

Quickly, she donned her robe and slipped from the house. It wouldn't hurt to check the barn just one more time. Then, if everything was as it should be, she would go back to bed, and this time she would sleep. She picked up a lantern and headed for the barn.

She lit a lantern and glanced at the carriage. Everything was as she had left it, and her two horses were nodding in sleep. As she started for the door, something startled her, and she stopped to listen. In the distance she heard the sounds of horses coming across the field, or perhaps she felt the approach of horses. She lowered the flame of the lantern and stared into the dark night toward the direction of the noise she had heard.

At first, all she saw were torches, and as they moved closer, she could distinguish the masculine forms on horseback. Were they being invaded? Had Phillip returned? As they moved closer, Amy saw seven men on horses, torches held high. She was frightened, something wasn't right. Why were they coming at a breakneck speed and late at night? She extinguished the lantern and pressed her thin figure against the doorjamb of the barn. She waited to see who was coming so late at night.

They were about one hundred yards from the house when they stopped. The men moved in a circle around the two men who seemed to be the leaders. They were not wearing any kind of uniform, so she ruled out soldiers. More torches were lit. With the torches held high, Amy could make out the faces of the leaders. A small gasp left her trembling lips. The torches lit the grim faces of Norman and Clarence. Amy knew, as she stood frozen in the barn door, that they were intent on at least mischief and perhaps murder.

Chapter Twenty-three

As the riders disappeared around the front of the house, Amy was spurred into action. She dashed for the kitchen and yanked the door open. Even before the glass started to break in front of the house, Amy could smell the smoke. There was no doubt in her mind. Norman and Clarence were going to burn everything on the plantation.

She ran for the small bedroom and threw the door open. Jacob was already dressing, and Amy started throwing things at Emma. She grabbed at Jacob's hand before he had his shirt buttoned. "We have to go," she screamed. They could hear the crackling flames, and great plumes of smoke were billowing into the kitchen. Amy led the way out the door.

Outside, total panic had erupted. Slaves were running in every direction. Amy heard the yells of the overseer as he tried to start a bucket brigade. Above the din, sounds of frantic animals could be heard coming from one of the barns, which was already in flames.

Amy pushed Jacob and Emma in the direction of the barn that held their carriage and horses. In the distance she saw the night riders torching the small huts that housed the slaves, and Amy knew they had only minutes to spare before the men on horseback would get to the other two barns.

Somehow, Jacob and another slave dragged the frightened animals from the barn, and while Amy held Emma close, the carriage emerged from the structure. Suddenly, three more bodies appeared to hitch up the carriage. As slaves led the many horses that comprised Phillip's prize stables past them, Jacob climbed into the driver's seat. He picked his way through the mayhem surrounding the burning structures.

Amy and Emma sat stiffly in the carriage as Jacob worked his way toward the road. As they rounded the front of the house, Amy heard the ringing of the big bell that signaled to the neighbors of an emergency. In the distance, moving toward Anderson, she saw the men responsible for the flames. She offered a silent prayer of thanks that she and her friends have been spared, they had escaped with their lives.

As they moved down the road, Amy turned back to view the disaster illuminated by the darting flames. She had, by some miracle, been downstairs and had managed to escape. With Emma crying softly next to her, they traveled into the night. She could imagine the grim look on Jacob's usually somber face. As it was, she could barely make out his straight back and his thin shoulders that radiated tension. For a long time they said nothing, and finally Amy dozed off, huddled beneath the carriage robe she and Emma shared.

Amy came awake with a start and realized it was long past dawn, the sun was well up in the sky. She took a deep breath, and the smell of burning wood filled her nostrils. The horror that they witnessed the night before came back vividly. She glanced over at Emma, still sound asleep and snuggled up in the carriage robe. On the driver's seat, Jacob's nodding head told her that he too was dozing as the horses slowly picked their way along the road.

She straightened up and stretched. Glancing down at herself, she was first embarrassed and then mortified. Here she was, in the middle of the morning, in a carriage traveling north in her robe and gown. They had to stop so that she could change.

Her thoughts turned to the blue-gray dress hanging in the wardrobe at Willows, and she remembered the cameo brooch on the collar. Tears sparkled in her eyes as she thought of the day Matt had presented the brooch to her. They had been so happy then. Once more she fingered the delicate golden *A* on its shining rose as she thought of the other things Matt had given her tucked away in her trunk. At least she had those. Tears rolled down her cheeks because the cameo had been so special. Was there anything left of Willows, she wondered.

She roused Jacob and then woke Emma. Explaining her dilemma, she asked Jacob to stop when they got close to a grove of trees. He soon spotted a place, and while Amy changed clothes, Emma took the basket of food and arranged their breakfast. After resting the horses for a while, they were on their way again.

In just a matter of minutes, Amy grabbed at Jacob and pleaded for him to stop. Her nausea was back, and this time she lost her breakfast. Emma wet a handkerchief and with the cool liquid smoothed Amy's burning face. Then, without a word she loosened the collar of Amy's dress and soothed her neck with more of the refreshing water.

When they were on their way again, Emma turned to her and asked softly, "How far along are ya, honey?"

Amy stared at the woman in confusion. "Emma, what are you talking about?"

"Ya's havin' a wee one, ain't ya?" At Amy's puzzled expression, Emma demonstrated by holding her arms out, grabbing each forearm and moving her arms in a rocking motion. "A babe?"

Amy was stunned. The queasy stomach, the exhaustion—was that what was wrong? She thought back. When was her last monthly flow? So much had happened, she couldn't remember. Tears clouded her eyes, and she turned to face her friend. "I guess I am."

"It's not somethin' to cry 'bout." Emma patted her arm in an attempt to comfort her.

Amy turned her head away from Emma's smiling face and sobbed. "I don't want a baby—not now," she said softly. Emma put her arms around Amy and held her close.

For miles Amy sat huddled in the corner of the carriage, her mind in turmoil. Occasionally, her hand drifted to her stomach. What would Matt say, she wondered. Her tears started again; Matt might never know. He was accused of being a spy and both armies shot or hanged spies. He could already be dead. In desperation she tried to block thoughts of Matt from her mind and concentrated on home and Henry. Henry! Somehow Amy didn't think he would be too happy about a child.

As the days passed, Amy thought more and more about the child she was sure she carried. Matt's child. A father arrested as a spy, an uncle who would be very unhappy with its appearance, and a mother who declared she didn't want a baby. Another sob clutched at her tight throat. It might be a boy, an exact copy of his father . . . Emma held Amy close as she sobbed, somehow knowing Amy's thoughts.

As they traveled slowly through the hills of North Carolina, Amy accepted the idea of a child. She still wasn't sure she wanted a baby right now, with her whole life in fragments. Perhaps, if she knew Matt was all right . . .

Everywhere they traveled they were greeted with columns of men in the gray coats of the Confederacy. Twice their movements were restricted for several days until Amy was able to convince them that she was traveling home. Phillip's name proved to be her salvation on two different occasions. After one wait of three days, Amy muttered to Jacob, "The babe will be here before we get home." Jacob stared at her, his face contorted in horror at the idea.

By the end of November, they were a day's journey from Tucker's Crossroads. For two days they had seen no gray uniforms, and Amy asked Jacob if they were possibly moving into a pitched battle between the North and the South. Jacob smiled grimly. "It's possible."

Amy wilted. They didn't stand a chance of getting through both battlelines without getting hurt. They had no choice. If Ben and Molly Tucker were still at the inn, they would stay with them until the area was more secure. And Ben seemed to be something of a leader in his community. He would know what was going on in the vicinity of the inn. He had to know.

Late afternoon of the next day, the three travelers arrived at Tucker's Inn. Ben and Molly were indeed at the inn and greeted them as long-lost relatives. After Emma told the Tuckers about Amy's condition, Amy was given a large room at the top of the stairs. Emma and Jacob insisted that they be allowed to stay in the barn where they had spent such a pleasant summer together.

Even before they sat down for supper, Ben wanted to know everything she knew about Matt. When she explained about the visits she had from the Confederacy, Ben stared at her in disbelief.

"Matt Treadwell is no spy. The army's made a big mistake."

Dinner was a solemn affair, and there was little conversation. After dinner, Ben pulled Amy aside. "Tomorrow, I'm taking a horse and going into Nashville. I intend to talk to the Union Army. They've established an office of sorts in Nashville. I'm getting to the bottom of this."

Amy frowned. "Ben, my brother Henry is studying to be a lawyer. We have friends who knew my father and who are also lawyers. If you can't learn something, Henry may be able to do something."

"It can't hurt, if I made a few inquiries now. After all, as his wife, you should be told something."

Amy changed the subject. "Right now, we need to know what's happening around here. We passed so many Confederates on our way that Jacob and I both are afraid we'll get into the middle of a major battle. What can you find out about that?"

Ben smiled down at her. "I'll find out about that as well."

Later that evening, as they sat around the large fireplace, Ben and Molly told Amy about the property they had purchased in Cairo, Illinois. "It's on the Mississippi," Ben said, his enthusiasm bubbling into excitement. "It'll be a big city some day, and I intend to be part of it."

Molly introduced a cousin who had arrived late in September to take over the Tennessee inn. "We wanted to leave for Cairo in early October, but the army's made that impossible. The best we can hope for now is the first of the year."

Amy looked over at the big lion of a man and thought to herself, "He's like a little boy with a new toy." To Ben she asked, "What are you going to call the new inn?"

Ben looked at her sheepishly and grinned. "Tucker's Inn, of course."

Amy laughed for the first time in weeks, amazed at how good it felt. Chuckling, she said, "I can see a whole string of inns from here to the west, all called Tucker's Inn."

Ben laughed, too, "We'll run out of cousins before we get through Kansas."

At length, Amy excused herself and went to her

room. She was so very tired. The carriage trip over the rutted roads had been uncomfortable, and she was stiff and sore. Maybe she should consider staying at the inn for a few days before starting north again. And just maybe, the news that Ben would gather about troop movements might make leaving the inn impossible for the moment anyway. She would have to try to get another note to Henry, she thought as she stretched out on her bed. With her hand cradling her small rounding belly, she drifted off to sleep.

Ben was gone! He had left at dawn, Emma told her. The Union army at Nashville was going to answer a few of his questions, he had informed Jacob before he charged down the Nashville road at sunrise. And Amy waited. She waited all day and into the next. At three o'clock, when Ben finally returned, Amy was frightened, alarmed, and a little angry. He had left without a word to her.

Ben pulled Amy over to the fire and gently pushed her into one of the plush chairs next to the warmth. "They never heard of Matt Treadwell, or so they say."

Amy looked up at him in shock, "But they must know. I got a telegram from Joshua Eller. You got a telegram from Joshua Eller, too. They must know something."

"Well, they ain't saying then," he grumbled, and at once he was sorry he had said anything. Her eyes filled with tears, and she made no attempt to brush them away. Realizing his mistake, he tried to reassure her. "The army has a lot of men and they move around a lot. It's possible that he's being held by another regiment, or that he's been moved someplace else, or—"

"Or they've shot him already," came Amy's raspy reply.

"They would have sent word if he had been executed." Amy shook her head in disagreement. Ben didn't argue with her because he wasn't certain himself. That night Amy cried herself to sleep.

It took Ben another week before he had anything he considered substantial to tell his guests.

"There's a large force moving south under General Rosecrans. The South has a unit moving north with Bragg. A big battle is shaping up, probably around Nashville. Molly and me think you had better stay put for a while."

Amy looked around the room, her eyes resting on the warm fireplace with the cozy fire eating away at the ash logs Ben had arranged. She nodded her head. Yes, she would stay for a while. At least until the troops moved on. Ben looked relieved.

That afternoon, she sat down to write her brother a long overdue letter. First she told him that she was with Ben and Molly at Tucker's Crossroads. She apologized for changing her plans, but insisted that she was safer with Ben and Molly than traveling around the countryside. She explained about the fire, adding that Phillip had probably lost everything. For some reason she didn't want to mention the baby, not yet anyway. After she addressed the envelope and sat staring at it, she felt a weird sensation in her belly. Almost like butterfly wings, it pulsed. She sat very still, willing it to happen again. There, there it was. With her hand on her stomach, she smiled. Her child had started to move.

The initial testimony taken from Alex Sanderson on October twentieth had given Captain Eller more than enough fuel to sway the present commanding officer. Matt was given permission to send the messages he wanted. The first letter was to Amy. As Matt waited anxiously for a reply, Henry arrived to give his own testimony to the lawyer. Henry was even granted permission to spend several days with Matt after the interrogation. As the two men talked, Henry told Matt about Amy's letter full of doubts and fears.

Henry reassured Matt that Amy was safe in Anderson and waiting impatiently for his return. He did mention that Amy wrote that Aunt Elizabeth stayed on in Atlanta to help with the funeral of a cousin. "But, I'm sure she's back now," Henry added with enthusiasm. Neither man was concerned that Henry had received no other letters from Amy, for what mail came from the South had to be smuggled through.

Henry and Matt both pleaded with Captain Eller for the date of Matt's release. "In another week or two, all the paperwork will be finished, and you can go home," Captain Eller promised.

Promising to visit in Texas come spring, Henry took off for home, and Matt waited for some word from his wife. Several uneventful days passed, and Matt resigned himself to wait for only a couple more. Then he would start back to Anderson and Amy.

One chilly morning, one of the guards came bringing an envelope for Matt. He beamed as the man approached, Amy had written. His insides twisted and terror surged through his body as he stared at his own letter, marked Address Unknown, Not Deliverable. Reacting violently, he attacked the guard and raced for one of the officer's tents. When the guards had subdued him, they sent for his lawyer. Matt showed the letter to Captain Eller, tears streaming down his cheeks. "I have to go home now. I can't wait."

Captain Eller saw Matt back to the shed and took the letter, the testimony from the Sanderson brothers, and marched to the commanding officer's tent. In a matter of minutes, Matt Treadwell was judged not guilty and released from captivity.

"Matt, it's already after one o'clock. If you'll wait until dawn, your horse and all your things will be ready. You can start fresh," Captain Eller said quietly. Matt agreed and the two men walked freely through the camp that night.

Sometime during the evening Matt approached the lawyer about the charges. "Now will you tell me who accused me of spying? I can't believe it was my wife." Matt frowned, her disappearance did make her look guilty.

"The person who presented the original charge to Colonel Brown was a man claiming to be Phillip Treadwell," Captain Eller said.

"Damn," Matt muttered. Could Phillip hate him and Amy so much that he would put them both through something like this? If he could jeopardize his own brother's life, what else might he be capable of? He couldn't, he didn't want to answer his own question.

At dawn Matt was on his way. The army had taken good care of his horse and all the things they had confiscated when he was arrested had been returned. He stopped along the trail only when the horse demanded it. Making good time, he reached Elton Estate in five days.

He groaned when he found the windows and the doors boarded up, and no sign of Amy or Aunt Elizabeth. All but one of her slaves were gone as well, and that old man told Matt that a relative had come. "Ah don't know nothing about your missus. Master Philip came, and she went with 'im. I can't tell you no more." Matt cursed Phillip as he traveled to one of Aunt Elizabeth's neighbors. Perhaps someone there could tell him what had happened.

Luck was with him, for he found three of the house slaves at the plantation. They explained as much as they knew, Phillip's visits, Amy's refusal to see him after the first visit. Matt listened, his distress growing as they described Amy's labors and her obvious despair. They couldn't explain why Amy went to Willows, but Phillip had come for her. The owner of the plantation filled in some of the questions Matt had when he showed Matt a copy of the letter he had received, asking him to care of Elizabeth Elton's slaves while she was ill.

As Matt dashed for Willows, he prayed that Amy was there, waiting for him. Phillip had maneuvered the whole scheme with some goal in mind, Matt was

360

sure of it. Had he wanted Amy for his own? Matt knew, before he got to the circular drive at Willows that something Phillip hadn't planned had occurred. He could smell the charred wood from the main road. As he surveyed the devastation Matt was numb. If Amy had been in the house . . .

One barn was still standing and as Matt walked his horse toward it, the overseer left the barn and hailed him. Matt spurred his horse forward in a brutal charge. "Where is she?" he shouted.

The overseer stood on one foot and then the other. "We think she got out."

"You think! What do you mean, you think!" Matt roared

"Her carriage and the horses she bought were not in the barn when we checked the wreckage. Some of the slaves thought they saw her leaving when the house was aflame," came the hesitant reply.

Matt turned back to the pile of black timbers, not yet ready to face his fears. "Who did this?"

"Oh, we caught most of 'em. They were led by those two agents Mr. Phillip hired to bring back that last bunch of slaves that escaped. Guess they didn't like the way Mr. Phillip fired them from bringing the white girl—" The man stopped speaking abruptly. The murderous expression on Matt's face made further comment a possible death warrant.

Matt looked around at the burned slaves' quarters and asked in anguish, "Where are the slaves?"

"Some of 'em ran off during the fire, but we have several families in the barn with us," the overseer said quietly. Matt pointed toward the barn and moved ahead of the overseer. He would talk to the slaves that were there.

The information the slaves gave Matt was encouraging, but he had more questions as they talked. Jenny who stayed close to old Maude assured Matt that Amy had escaped and Emma and Jacob had been with her. In fact they had been at Willows for a couple of days before the fire. "Funny thing, though, Massa Matt. Massa Phillip tol' us, all the house slaves, leastways, that Missus Amy was a-goin' to your place. But Emma and Jacob sez they was headin' north. Missus Amy tol' me herself that she was a-goin' to Atlanta, that Emma and Jacob was a-takin' her to be with Aunt Elizabeth."

Was it possible that she was going to Texas? Surely Amy wouldn't have tried to go to Texas without him. It was too long a trip, and with both armies on the move, attempting to get to Texas was dangerous, too dangerous for a lone woman and two slaves. Amy was too smart to try that. It made a great deal more sense to travel to Aunt Elizabeth in Atlanta. Certainly, she would have tried to see Aunt Elizabeth before going home. From there, she could have headed north. Perhaps, he could find the answers to some of his questions in town.

He raced into Anderson, but there were no answers there, only more questions. Hurriedly, he composed a letter to Henry, even though he knew it would take days for the message to find its way to Indiana. He wrote that Henry should contact him in Atlanta. Amy had to be with Aunt Elizabeth, and Matt wanted to get there as soon as possible. He hired a local boy to see the message far enough north so that it could be mailed.

He stopped at the bank and quickly scanned the account and the drafts he had left for Amy's use. Even though he had been gone for a much longer time than they had figured, very little of the money he had left for her had been used. There were several small drafts for supplies, but nothing that would cover a journey of any kind. The more Matt thought about the situation the more frustrated and angry he became. She just couldn't vanish. The sooner he got to Atlanta the better.

He stopped at the jail to talk to the sheriff about the fire at Willows. "There's no question, we got the leaders. It was those two agents that Phillip fired, Norman Glanzman and Clarence Barber. Do you want to press charges?"

Matt looked over at the bulky man with the dull gray eyes. "I certainly do! And, I want to know if those two know anything about my wife."

Matt stood at the edge of the tiny office while the sheriff talked to the two men. He got a good look at both from his position in the shadows, and he watched as the sheriff asked them about Amy.

Clarence said nothing, but Norman had a lot to say. "You tell that Matt Treadwell, he ain't never gonna see his wife again. If it weren't for her, we wouldna been here. I hope she got caught in the fire, but if she didn't, we'll get her."

The sheriff interrupted him. "No one was seriously injured in that fire, or you two would have swung by now. But you're not gonna do Mrs. Treadwell any harm. You're gonna be here for a long time."

Norman laughed out loud. "Ain't been a jail yet

363

that could hold us." He started yelling, "That white girl done ruined my business. If she'd didn't burn, then she ain't paid for it yet, but she's gonna. Do you hear me, Mr. Treadwell? She's gonna."

Matt was visibly shaken. "Don't let them out. I have to find my wife. How long can you keep them?" He jerked his head toward the door the sheriff had just closed, separating the small office from the rest of the jail.

"Well, you've pressed charges, there'll be a trial, and then they'll go to prison for a nice long visit. I don't think you have anything to worry about."

Matt headed for the only door. "I'm going to Atlanta. I'm sure that Amy went to see Aunt Elizabeth. If you don't need me here . . ." His voice trailed off.

"Nope," the sheriff said firmly. "We have witnesses, you've signed the papers, I have all I need."

Within ten minutes, Matt had gathered his things and was on the road to Atlanta.

He sat in the parlor waiting for Aunt Elizabeth who was now much better. "Why, Matt," Aunt Elizabeth said. "What are you doing here, and where's Amy."

It took two hours to sort through everything that had happened and Aunt Elizabeth was more than upset when Matt asked, his voice breaking, "She hasn't contacted you? I was praying that she was here with you."

Aunt Elizabeth only shook her head. Matt agreed to stay for another day, commenting, "She had to go to Indiana. She has too much sense to travel to

Texas. I'm sure Phillip knows where she is. Now, if I can find Phillip."

Aunt Elizabeth nodded and murmured, "Phillip is with Bragg. I understand that they are headed toward Tennessee. But, Matt, if you plan on seeing Phillip, you have to promise me something." Once again she made him promise not to ruin his life by doing something violent to Phillip. "Willows meant everything to the man. Its loss will be enough punishment. Matt, he lived for that farm. Now, he has nothing."

Matt gave her a disgusted look. "That farm is only land. I lost my wife!"

"You don't know that. Right now, you have a missing wife. I can't believe that something has happened to Amy. I just feel that Henry's letter, when it arrives, will say that Amy's with him. Just wait and see."

Matt waited another day. But the next morning, he faced Aunt Elizabeth. "If I don't hear from Henry tomorrow, I'm starting north. If nothing else, I'll find Phillip and make him tell me where she is."

Aunt Elizabeth frowned but said nothing. He had promised not to do anything foolish.

Early the next morning, the lad Matt had hired to carry his note north to Henry arrived at the house. "I couldn't get through. I was stopped a half-dozen times and they wouldn't let me through." Matt didn't bother asking who had stopped the boy.

Calling his aunt into the parlor, he explained what had happened. "I'm heading north. If I find Phillip along the way, then perhaps I can get some answers. I should be in Indiana in another four or five weeks."

She tried to hide her concern. "It's time I went home as well. Now, you must promise me that you'll send word now and again. In fact, I brought Ned's youngest boy with me. You take him with you. He rides well. He can bring your messages to me himself, and you won't have to worry about hiring someone to see to it."

Arrangements were made, and Ned's boy, Ira, packed his things. Matt was pleased with the young man. He was thin, about fifteen, a quiet slave, and he seemed to appreciate Aunt Elizabeth's faith in him. Matt packed and together they started north. Without a word, master and slave followed the trail of soldiers. As they traveled, Matt tried to think of all possibilities. Still, nothing he had learned made much sense. He had to find Phillip and discover if Amy had really tried to travel to Texas. Then, his brother had a lot of explaining to do, starting with the accusations he had made about Matt to the Union Army, but, Matt clenched his teeth, he better be able to tell him where Amy was.

Chapter Twenty-four

Matt followed Bragg's army north through Georgia and into Tennessee. Twice, he sent Ira back to Elton Estate with a message for Aunt Elizabeth. On the return trips, Ira found him with very little difficulty, and the word from Aunt Elizabeth was always the same. She had heard nothing.

The third week of December, Ira returned with a message from Aunt Elizabeth. She had finally received a message from Henry, but the news wasn't good. Henry hadn't heard from Amy since the letter he had told Matt about. If she was planning to come home, he knew nothing of it. Henry wanted to know if he should contact Alex. Perhaps someone in the Union Army had seen the girl and her companions.

By the fourth week of December, Matt finally caught up to Bragg's army. They were camped outside a small town called Murfreesboro. Matt joined a small group of families who had traveled north to be with sons or husbands for Christmas. The staff officers and General Bragg had a small office at the edge of town, and he found the place easily.

Matt marched into the building, a little surprised that no one ordered him out. The officers standing around didn't even ask who he was. He glared at the men. Did he and Phillip look that much alike? He was ushered into a small office in the back of the building. And Phillip was there, seated at a makeshift desk. Matt lunged at him and grabbed his brother by his uniform. "I want some answers."

The look on Phillip's face told Matt a great deal more than Phillip intended to divulge. When Matt jerked Phillip into a standing position, the expression on Phillip's face turned from surprise to horror. As Matt looked around, still holding his brother by the collar, the other officers quietly left the office, one by one.

Matt let go of his brother's collar and dropped his hands to his side. He clenched his fists and whispered in a voice of deadly calm, "Why, Phillip? I want to know why? And where is my wife?"

Phillip tried not to look at Matt. "She should be in Indiana. I left her at Willows months ago, preparing to go home."

"She isn't there." Matt choked out the words.

Phillip appeared genuinely stunned. "Matt, I didn't do anything to her. I just sent her home. I didn't want to hurt her."

"You left all the slaves with the impression that she had gone to Texas. That was expressly to keep me away from her. I know it and you know it. You let her travel through the area of heaviest fighting, and you didn't want to hurt her! You sent her into God knows what, and you didn't want to hurt her!

You're insane. How was she supposed to travel? The money I left for her was never touched. She had no guard, no letters of authority. Just how was she supposed to achieve this journey? How did you get her to go home, anyway? She promised to wait for me. What did you tell her?"

Phillip bristled. "I saw that she had funds. And I talked to the banker. He was going to send someone with her who was handy with a gun. She should have been perfectly safe."

"Is that why you had me arrested, so she would be safe? I'm sure she's gone through hell, and all because of you. The army lawyer sent her a telegram telling her I'd been detained. Did you tell her I was a spy? Did you even think about what you did to me? All that false information you fed the Union colonel—the army might have shot first and asked questions later, you know. Then what would you have done? You'd have been responsible for the murder of your own brother. It would have been murder because you lied to them. If Aunt Elizabeth hadn't dragged a promise out of me . . ." His voice faded into a whisper.

Phillip let out a slow breath as he looked at the white knuckles of Matt's clenched fists.

Matt glared at his brother with disgust. "I want to know why. And, I want to know now! You are going to tell me all of it."

Phillip stood up straight and squared his shoulders. He threw his head back, and his face took on a look of arrogance. "Why? I'll tell you why! I didn't want her or her kin controlling Willows. When you marched into Willows and announced that you were

369

going to marry a piece of trash from the North, I decided that you would not. It took a while, but I figured that in time Amy would be glad to go back to Indiana, and without a husband that would spy on his own brother-in-law. It took some convincing, but she finally saw you as the scoundrel I wanted her to see. She left for Indiana several days after I went back to Atlanta."

"She is my wife!" Matt roared. "We are married and we will stay married. I want to know about the money. Where did she get the funds for that kind of a trip?"

Phillip grinned at Matt a little sheepishly, "That was the easy part. I had my investigator send a couple of men who posed as Confederate officers. They paid you well for your work, brother dear. She had money in gold." Phillip shoved Matt's hand from his uniform and sat back down. "And by now, she'll want nothing to do with you. My plantation will never fall into the hands of Northerners or their heirs. Go to Texas. Forget the girl! Find yourself a nice Southern girl."

Matt laughed then, a cold harsh laugh. "Amy is my wife. I will not forget. And if this whole sham was to prevent someone from the North from inheriting your stinking land, then brother, you don't have a thing to worry about. Willows was burned to the ground. All you have left is one slightly scorched barn. The rest is gone, Phillip! Gone!"

Phillip's face lost all its color, and he sank back into a chair. Matt was still laughing mirthlessly. "If all your efforts were to prevent Amy from inheriting your rotten plantation, you have no concerns. You have no plantation."

Phillip stared at Matt for several minutes and then stuttered, "W-w-when? H-h-how?"

Matt turned, his eyes glazed with contempt. "I'm worried sick about the woman who has become the most important thing in my life, the woman you wanted to force out of my life. I don't know whether she's alive or safe or . . . And you sit there in shock over the loss of a pile of wood, black, charred wood! I consider that place a symbol of your greed and your hatred. You're a sorry excuse for a human being, even if you are my brother." Matt strode out the door. He had to get a breath of clean air, and he needed to calm down before he let Phillip suffer the full force of his anger. He was angry enough at the moment to kill his brother.

Matt stood outside the door of the building for a long time. His head hung down almost to his chest. Phillip didn't know where she was. He had sent her to Indiana, and she hadn't made it. She could be anywhere, perhaps sick, being held by some army unit. Perhaps she had met with foul play. He felt close to being beaten. Where could she be? Where could he look? What happened to her?

Phillip was the last person to see her. Slowly, he turned around. And Phillip would help him find her! He would help if Matt had to beat him to a pulp. Matt charged back into the office and stood in front of the desk. Phillip was sitting just as he had left him, dejected and forlorn. Damn him! Matt wanted to scream. Instead, he slammed his fist into the wood-paneled wall. His knuckles throbbed, but the pain felt good.

For three hours, Matt tried hard to keep his temper in check, remembering his promise to Aunt Elizabeth, as he attempted to dig information out of Phillip. When Matt quit arguing and cajoling Phillip, he was more dejected than ever. Phillip didn't know much more than Matt did.

Finally Phillip leaned forward. "I didn't realize that you were so taken with the girl. I meant the girl no harm. I didn't do this so that she would be hurt. You should have told me you felt so strongly about her." Matt walked out on Phillip once more. It was hard to accept that the stupid man hunched over the desk was his own flesh and blood.

Some time later, when Matt had cooled down somewhat, he and Phillip went to the mess tent. After the evening meal, Phillip pulled Matt away from the other officers and apologized.

"I'm sorry. I didn't know she meant so much to you."

Matt couldn't quite accept Phillip's words. He turned to find his bedroll.

Phillip said softly, "Would you tell me about Willows?"

Matt turned back and looked at his brother, his face grim. He owed Phillip that, at least. After Matt had told him everything he knew about the interrogation of Norman and Clarence, Phillip asked, "Why don't you stay here for a day or two? I'll check with some of my men and perhaps we can find out at least which direction Amy traveled."

Matt stared into the dark, cloudy night. If Amy hadn't made it back to Indiana, as Henry had written Aunt Elizabeth, then he didn't have any place to go. He nodded and left Phillip standing in the cold December night.

Matt spent a restless night, rolled up tightly in his bedroll, and stared at the cloudy sky as dark as his soul. He had reached Phillip, but Henry's letter had devastated him. Where was his wife? Could she have decided at the last minute to try for Texas? No, Amy was too intelligent to try something that stupid. She was someplace between North Carolina and Indiana. Please, God, he prayed, don't let anything happen to her. When he thought back over Phillip's offer to help by talking to his fellow officers, a spark of hope burst into his brain. It died almost as quickly as it surged forward. A beautiful woman, with two slaves, traveling alone would be easy prey for any number of animals, both the two-legged kind and the four-legged kind. He remembered Phillip's words. Would she have made enough of an impression on the soldiers for someone to remember her? It was very late when Matt finally drifted off into sleep.

The next morning, Matt sent Ira back to Elton Estate. He told Aunt Elizabeth that he found Phillip and what Phillip had described as his reasons for what he had done. Assuring his aunt that he had kept his promise, that he hadn't once touched Phillip in violence, although sorely tempted, he insisted that she keep Ira with her. Matt had no idea where he was going. If he learned anything, he would hire someone to carry a message to her.

He saw Ira off and then sought Phillip out once more. He was surprised that Phillip already had a sizable investigation under way. Before noon, word reached the men that several of the different regiments traveling through North Carolina and into southern Tennessee remembered seeing a girl who fitted Amy's description. She was traveling in a carriage, and she had a black maid with her. Her driver was a tall, thin black man.

Early the next day, a junior officer approached Phillip to tell him that he had detained a girl that fit the description Phillip had passed around. The girl insisted that she was related to Phillip Treadwell of the Confederate forces. Matt listened anxiously as the young man explained that he had let her go and she had continued on to the north. The officer reported that he thought he stopped them in southern Tennessee. "About the end of November," he told Phillip, "if I remember rightly."

Matt took a deep breath. She was alive and well, at least in November. He wondered if the war was the only reason that she was traveling so slowly. The thought occurred to him that Emma might have been hurt in the fire or Jacob injured. By now, she had to be with Henry. Matt told Phillip what he thought and added, "Tomorrow, I'll go into Nashville and see if I can get a message through to Henry. I'll wait there until I hear from him."

Phillip countered, "Not tomorrow! Tomorrow is Christmas Day. You'll have to wait until day after tomorrow. You'll not find anyone to send a message tomorrow."

Matt's shoulders slumped. Phillip was right; he would have to wait for at least another day.

The day after Christmas, Matt was off at the crack of dawn. He stopped at an inn on the north

374

side of Nashville, after he had worked his way around the Union forces. He hired a soldier on leave and bought two horses that would have been rejects in any war. They would have to do, he told himself. He gave instructions to the soldier and a promise of several gold pieces if he got to Henry and back inside a week. Making himself as comfortable as he could, he waited for an answer to the message he sent to Henry.

As he waited, he considered all the places Amy had been seen according to Phillip's men, and the thought struck him that she might have stopped at Tucker's Inn. She certainly was in for a surprise, if she thought to see Ben and Molly. He smiled as he remembered the long evening he spent with Ben in September. Ben had enthusiastically described the inn he had just acquired, and they had discussed all of the Tuckers' plans. Matt had even suggested that Ben train a relative to operate the Tennessee inn, while he and Molly set up the inn in Cairo. Matt smiled slightly. He wondered if Ben had taken his advice and kept the title to Tucker's Inn in Tennessee. Then, again, the man had wanted to sell the place before they traveled west. Perhaps, when he found Amy, he would take the time to search out the Tuckers.

On the first day of the new year, very late in the afternoon, the soldier returned with a short message from Henry. Matt held the envelope in his hands for a long time before he opened it. After he read the words, his heart fell and he stopped breathing. Amy was not in Indiana, she had never gotten to Indiana. Henry still had not heard a word. Matt sank down into the chair before the fireplace in the common room. He stared into the fire, but he saw nothing. He didn't feel the tears slip down his cheeks. Would he never find his wife, the joy of his whole world, his reason to live? Why, why, why, he screamed at the dancing flames.

Later, Matt packed up his things, paid his bill, and started back to Murfreesboro. He would say good-bye to Phillip and travel to Tucker's Inn. Perhaps the new owner — or if Ben had placed the business in the care of a relative, then the relative — would remember a young girl with expressive deep-blue-gray eyes.

Matt could hear the rifle reports and the screams and yells even before he got back to camp. He had taken the long way around, arriving late in the morning. He found his way through the wounded who had been carried to the rear and arrived at the office building, when a young aide rushed forward with messages. Matt stood off to one side as the soldier delivered his news. He paid little attention until Captain Treadwell was mentioned. As the boy moved off, Matt grabbed him by the collar. "What about Captain Treadwell, son?"

When the boy hesitated, looking at Matt's dark-blue suit, Matt said in disgust, "I'm Captain Treadwell's brother, from South Carolina."

The boy started to move away. "He was leading the charge. One of those blue-bellies got a lucky shot. He was knocked off his horse. I think he's pretty bad."

"Where?" Matt yelled.

The boy pointed toward a stand of trees in the

distance, by the river, and Matt grabbed his horse and took off in the direction the lad had indicated. As he neared the woods, he noticed gray-clothed bodies strewn over the ground, and he wondered how he would find Phillip. Suddenly, he saw the gold stripes and the sash, now covered with blood.

Phillip heard the horse, and despite the burning, tearing pain in his gut, he lifted his head. He saw the horse and the blue-garbed figure approaching, but something told him it was not a Yankee. He raised himself up on his elbow and through clouded eyes, he saw Matt and realized that Matt had seen him. Even through his dim vision, he saw Matt stop the horse, dismount, then run toward him. A movement to the left drew his attention. Before he could gather the strength to warn his brother, he heard the crack of the rifle and watched as if in slow motion as Matt grabbed his bloody head, then sank to the ground, motionless.

Through the last two weeks of December, the discussions at Tucker's Inn were long and intense. Amy wanted to go home. The more she pleaded and insisted, the more adamant Ben and Jacob became. A battle was brewing, and both men pleaded and finally insisted loudly that she delay her plans. "I ain't driving," Jacob told her quietly. Ben pointed out that if she waited to start her travels until the forces, both sides, had cleared out of the area, she would be safe.

Surprisingly, Molly tried to come to Amy's aid by telling Ben, "The good citizens of Tucker's Crossroads are all heading away from the village."

"But," Ben said quietly, "they're all heading northeast. Amy means to go west and then north."

The argument lost, Amy stood at the front windows of the inn and watched as wagons and carriages moved through the village, many to spend several weeks with friends or family.

Christmas came and went, and still word was that the battle had yet to begin. It would probably be south of Nashville, Ben told her after a night with his friends. Rosecrans' forces were massed along Stones River, and Bragg was coming up from the south. There was a large contingent of Confederate military in the area already. Amy started packing, and Molly and Emma both made her unpack. "Not yet, chile. Wait until it's over," Emma scolded. To make matters worse, Amy had to receive an answer to the letter she had sent to Henry.

Finally, four days into the new year, a young soldier approached the inn. "I have a message from Henry Sanderson to his sister. Is she here?"

Amy dashed forward. "I'm Amy Sanderson, Henry's sister. When did you get this?"

"Ma'am, it's nigh on to impossible to get mail through. I was home on leave, and when your brother asked if I'd deliver this before I report to my regiment, I agreed. He told me it was a matter of life or death."

"It is," Amy whispered and grabbed the letter from his hands. She sat down by the fire to devour the first of several pages, and her hand flew to her throat. Her screams brought her friends to her side.

"It's from Henry. Matt's been released. It was all a

378

mistake. Matt's in Nashville. He's been here for two weeks. He came to find Phillip. He's been looking for me. Two days before my letter came, Henry sent him a message. Henry told him I wasn't in Indiana, and he didn't know where I was." She laid the letter aside and stood up. "Ben, I have to go to Nashville. We have to go, now. Today! I don't care how many armies are in the way, I'm going to Nashville."

"Does Henry say where Matt is? Nashville is a big place," Ben asked, afraid of Amy's reply.

"He wrote the name of the inn, see, here it is." Amy picked up the letter and pushed the paper in Ben's face. "I'll be ready to go in fifteen minutes."

Jacob spoke softly. "No, Amy. Y' must not go. If there's trouble, y' be in the way. Ben'll go. If Matt be there, he'll bring 'im back."

"Amy, Jacob's right," Ben spoke just as softly. "Jacob and I both will go. If Matt's there, we'll bring him back."

"Oh, he'll be there. He's waiting for Henry's answer. But you'll not go without me. He's my husband. I'll go too." The tears started to slide down her cheeks. "I have to go, I have to."

"Jacob and Ben are right, Amy, you must stay here. And the longer you argue with them, the longer it will take to get them on the road," Molly pleaded. "Come on, let's get some food packed so they can be on their way."

Amy glanced at her friends. She sighed. They were not going to let her travel to Nashville, and Molly did have a point. The sooner they had things ready, the sooner Ben and Jacob could leave.

The whole next day, Amy waited impatiently, and

by the afternoon of the second day she was beside herself. Surely, Matt would come. He had to come. But where was he?

Late that evening, Ben and Jacob returned, and Amy knew before they said a word that the news was not good. "Where is he?' she asked bluntly.

"He left the inn five days ago, late in the afternoon. He was going to say good-bye to his brother at Murfreesboro. That was where the fighting was, Amy. At Murfreesboro." Ben tried to keep the fear out of his voice, but he was unsuccessful, he realized as he watched Jacob grab for the girl as Amy melted onto the floor.

Amy was unconscious for a very short time, and when she regained her upright position, she started ordering the men and Emma and Molly as if she was born to command. She, Ben, and Jacob were going to Murfreesboro. "The battle is over, I believe," Ben answered hesitantly when she insisted he tell her.

"We'll go by carriage, at first light. And if you two don't want to go, I'll go by myself." She left Ben and Jacob standing with their mouths open.

It took most of the day to travel to Murfreesboro, and when they arrived, Ben made arrangements for them to stay with a friend of his. His friends informed the travelers that the Southern soldiers had left five days before, taking the less severely wounded with them. The rest of the wounded and the doctors were at the courthouse.

Amy was heartsick. There was no one there that she could talk to. Once more Matt had disappeared. "Perhaps, one of the doctors or some of the wounded know something about Matt or even Phillip," she suggested, fighting her tears. Ben assured her that he and Jacob would check the next morning.

Amy didn't wait long the next morning. Ben and Jacob were back inside an hour, and Ben pulled her into the family's parlor. "Amy, we found Phillip. He's been wounded, and the doctor says he won't live much longer. He's been asking for you. But you don't have to see him if you don't want to. In your condition, maybe you shouldn't see him," Ben mumbled almost to himself.

At first, she agreed with Ben. No, she wouldn't see Phillip; he would only tell her more lies. Jacob stood quietly off to one side listening as Amy rationalized. Finally, he stepped forward. "I ain't agreeing with Ben, nor am I disagreein'. But I thinks that Massa Phillip wants to say he's sorry. And I thinks he probably knows where Matt is. I thinks y' ought to see 'im."

They traveled in silence as they made their way through town. Her heart beating frantically, Amy struggled with her decision. Part of her wanted to run, run and hide, as far away from this place as she could possibly find. She didn't want to see Phillip. The letter Henry had written, the part that she had taken the time to read, had said that Matt had been arrested because of information supplied by Phillip, and he could have easily been shot before the information had been investigated. A second sense told her that Jacob was correct. Phillip knew where Matt was. Still she fought with herself. Phillip had tried to ruin them and she never wanted to see him again. But a larger part of her had to know, needed to know, where Matt was, with a desire so strong that the thought of meeting her betrayer seemed dim in comparison. She would see him, and she would make him tell her where Matt was.

None of what Ben or Jacob had said had prepared Amy for the carnage that greeted her at the makeshift hospital. Cots, many with dirty linens, were lined one next to another, and the loud moans and bitter curses of wounded men were a constant din in the big rooms. An impatient doctor told Ben that all of the seriously wounded officers had been moved and were now in the small rooms around the official chamber. Phillip was there, but they would have to find him themselves.

As Ben and Jacob led her to each small alcove, Amy grew paler. The smell of death was everywhere. Grimly she clenched her teeth and mumbled, "Let's get this over as quickly as we can."

Jacob finally found Phillip in a bed behind a small screened enclosure. Phillip lay there, his face white and pasty looking, and he was burning up with fever. It took Ben several minutes to rouse Phillip out of his delirium enough so that the man could be told that Amy had come.

When Phillip's cloudy eyes cleared a bit, Amy stepped forward and stood at the edge of his bed. Phillip looked into her eyes, and it took him several minutes before he found his voice. With tears sliding down his graying face, he pleaded, "Forgive me, Amy. Forgive me."

As gently as she could, she took his hand, and forgotten were her feelings of distrust and dislike. The skin of his hand was so hot to the touch that

Amy knew he was burning up with fever. She smiled through her own tears. "I forgive you, Phillip."

As Phillip faded in and out of consciousness, she sat quietly at his bedside. Each time he became aware of her, he pleaded in a shaky voice for her forgiveness. Each time, she reassured the dying man that she forgave him. She also asked, as softly as she could, "Phillip, where is Matt?" At the mention of Matt, Phillip groaned and faded back into the nether world of delirium.

For what seemed like hours, Amy sat with him, bathing his face with cool water that Ben kept replenishing for her. Ben and Jacob both begged Amy to leave, but she wouldn't go. Phillip was dying, and he needed someone with him. As the day stretched out into late afternoon, a doctor stopped to ask how he was. Ben shooed him away. There was nothing the doctors could do for Phillip now.

As the dullness of the day was replaced by the darkness of the night, Phillip seemed to improve. He spoke with a stronger voice, seemed more alert than he had been all day, and even held Amy's hand with some strength. Once more, he begged for Amy's forgiveness, and when she nodded, tears in her eyes, he added, "He did love you, Amy, very much. He was building a place for you in Texas." Phillip turned his head away so Amy couldn't see the tears coursing down his cheeks.

Amy missed the past tense of his statements and asked again, "Where is Matt, Phillip?"

"Matt is . . ." His voice was so low that Amy had to bend over him to hear his words. Again, he started, "I was hit . . . I . . . saw Matt . . . he got

383

off . . . his horse, he was hit . . . he fell . . . his head was . . . bloody." Phillip's voice trained off.

Amy stared at his glazed eyes in disbelief. She whimpered, "Oh, no!" Then she seemed to float from the chair on which she had been sitting toward Ben and Jacob. As she took a step or two toward the men, her face as white and ashen as new snow, her eyes stared straight ahead, as if she was no longer a part of the real world. Ben rushed to her side as she lost consciousness. From the bed he heard the distinct rattle of death. Phillip had become one of the casualties of the battle of Stones River.

Chapter Twenty-five

Ben lifted Amy up into his strong arms and carried her motionless form from the room while Jacob went to find the doctor and tell him that Phillip Treadwell had passed on. Once they were in the carriage, Amy regained consciousness, but she was in shock. Neither Ben nor Jacob had heard what Phillip told her in those seconds before he died, and they could only guess. It was not good news, both men were sure.

As quickly as they could, they drove back to Ben's friends. The wife undressed Amy and put her to bed. For several hours, her condition did not improve, and she seemed unaware of what was going on around her. Meals were brought, but she wouldn't eat. When Ben or Jacob tried to talk to her, she looked straight through them. Ben wanted to send for a doctor, but there were no doctors, his friend informed him. They were all busy at the makeshift hospital. In the gloom of the rainy day, Ben and Jacob decided that the best thing to do was to get Amy back to Emma and Molly. Perhaps they would know what to do for the girl.

They started back to Tucker's Inn immediately. Each man took a turn at driving the carriage while the other one sat holding Amy close and talking quietly to her. Neither man could have explained to the other, or to anyone else who might have asked, just what he said to her, but they both felt the need to try to rouse her.

As they made their way through the mud back to Tucker's Crossroads, there was no change in the ashen-faced, pregnant young woman. She continued to say nothing and to stare ahead with unseeing eyes.

By the time they reached the inn, the men were nearly frantic. Both were worried about Amy and concerned about the babe she carried. Molly and Emma were waiting anxiously because they had expected their return the day before. Taking one look at Amy, Emma started to berate Jacob. Molly gave Ben a scathing look as he tried to explain what had happened. But neither he nor Jacob could tell what Phillip had said that had caused Amy's condition.

Emma flashed a glance at Jacob that plainly said, "How could you?" and took charge. Wrapping Amy in warm blankets, she led her upstairs and tucked her into bed. She sent for some hot broth and coaxed Amy to take some. Then Emma and Molly took turns sitting with her.

Very slowly, the care of the two women started to break through Amy's icy shell, and by evening of the next day, Amy looked at Emma with recognition. All at once the dam burst, and Amy started to sob. She cried uncontrollably for a long time while Emma or Molly tried to quiet her. Emma kept telling her that she would hurt the baby by crying so hard. The softly spoken words gradually made an impact on Amy, and her tears slowed and her small frame relaxed. As Emma and Molly listened solemnly, Amy told them what had happened and what Phillip had told her. "Matt's gone," she whispered, the tears streaming down her face once again.

For several days Amy staggered around as if without the will to live. It was only after Emma sat with her long into the night listening to her grief that the black woman took matters into her own hands. She grabbed Amy by

386

the shoulders and shook her hard. "You listen to me, girl. You carry that man's chile. You gonna harm that babe, and then you'll have nothin' of that man left. You wanna kill your baby, you wanna kill Matt's chile?"

Amy's tears slowed and the sobs stopped. She looked at Emma, dazed but aware of what she had said. Putting her hand to her belly she felt the unborn child move strongly, as if to remind her of its presence. At least, she had her child, Amy thought to herself. No, not her child, but Matt's child, a miniature of his father, a boy. In that instant she decided her future. She would take the child to Texas where he would grow up on the ranch his father had planned for them. Her son would become the cattleman that his father had wanted to be.

The next morning, she left her room alert and feeling better than she had in days. Now she had a purpose. First, she must regain her strength, and then she must make plans for herself and Matt's son. At breakfast, she thanked Emma for making her realize what she had been doing to herself. Then she asked Emma and Jacob if they would honor their agreement with Matt and go west with her.

From her end of the table, Molly asked dryly, "Before or after the baby comes?"

Ignoring Molly, Amy turned to Ben. "I want to go with you to Cairo. After the baby's born, I'll go to St. Louis, get the cattle Matt wanted, and then, if Emma and Jacob will come with us, the baby and I will go to Texas."

Ben stared at her in astonishment. "You plan to go to Texas? Amy, that ain't no life for a widow lady with a small child. No, you'd be much better off in Indiana."

Molly joined in the argument. "The trip to Cairo is not

387

going to be a picnic. We're not even sure we can get through. At least stay in Tennessee until after the baby's born."

Amy raised her chin and glanced at her friends around the table. Her lips trembled slightly, but Emma recognized the stubborn tilt of her head. Amy snapped at Molly, "I still have three months to go before the baby arrives. If we get started for Cairo soon, I'll have no problem. And, it would be infinitely better for me to be busy, helping you with the new inn, rather than sitting here and feeling sorry for myself. At least in Cairo, I would feel as though I had started my journey west."

While Ben tried to change Amy's mind, Emma gathered together her and Jacob's clothes and packed Amy's trunk. She knew Amy would not change her mind. When she finished, she went back downstairs and found the arguments were still in progress. Ben, and even Molly, had not changed Amy's mind in the slightest. Emma smiled. They would learn that when Amy made her mind up, nothing anyone could say would sway her.

Ben tried a final argument. "Don't you think you ought to go home, at least until the baby is born?"

Amy shook her head. "I'm not going home. Henry will offer all kinds of resistance to my plans for Texas. I have no intention of even letting him know where I am or what I'm planning to do until the baby has arrived and I'm in Texas. I'll send a letter and tell him I'm all right, and that's enough."

"Henry won't like it," Emma said quietly, "not with the baby coming."

Amy grinned at her friend. "Oh, Henry doesn't know about the babe, yet, and no one's going to tell him either. He'll find out when I'm in Texas."

The Tuckers gave up the argument, and within the week, everything was packed and made ready for the trip west. The cousin was given detailed instructions, and arrangements were made so that the cousin could send any messages to Ben in Cairo. With three wagons of kitchen equipment and linens, they started for Cairo.

As they traveled, Amy listened to Ben and Molly discuss their plans for the new inn that Ben was sure would line their pockets with gold. Most of the nights, Ben arranged for their small band of travelers to stay at an inn run by a friend or acquaintance of his. Once, they had to stay in a barn, but the whole trip was filled with laughter and companionship. Amy almost enjoyed herself.

She wasn't uncomfortable, and, with frequent rest stops, the trip went smoothly. Amy suffered more from twinges of guilt than anything else. Emma constantly muttered about Henry finding out, but Amy squared her shoulders and stuck out her chin. It was her life, hers and the child she carried. For Matt's sake, she would provide a decent home for the child. After the child was born and she was at the ranch, then she would make Henry understand why she had gone off to Texas, alone.

When they finally arrived in Cairo after traveling three weeks, there was a frantic message waiting for Ben. Tucker's Inn was no more. One of the guests had been smoking in bed—which was prohibited—and the hot ashes from his pipe had started a fire that destroyed the wooden structure. Everyone had gotten out safely, but the main building and the big barn were completely destroyed. The cousin wrote that he was going back to his Ohio farm.

Ben took the news stoically. "Well, so much for my string of inns from Tennessee to Kansas." He tried to comfort Molly, who was much more upset. "At least no one was injured. And we had already decided that we wanted to stay in Illinois. Perhaps, it's a blessing in disguise. There was really no way that we could have managed both places, and we wouldn't want our name associated with something not well run."

Amy smiled at Molly. "Now aren't you glad you let me come with you? One fire was enough for me."

Ben took possession of the new Tucker's Inn. It was smaller than the one in Tennessee, but Ben was already looking for ways to increase the size of the place. His reputation had already spread into the area, so within two weeks all the rooms at the inn were taken. Emma, Jacob, and even Amy were busy with the operation of the establishment.

The only source of argument was the amount of work that Amy should do. Amy insisted that she do her share, and Jacob and Ben wanted her to sit and sew. Emma assured them that as long as she didn't overdo, the work would keep her mind busy, and that was good for her. Life settled into a pleasant routine at the new Tucker's Inn.

While Matt was being transported to the hospital for his head wound, he regained consciousness. After the Yankee doctor cleaned his wound, he sent Matt on to one of the inns that were caring for the less seriously wounded of the Northern army. The officials at the hospital weren't too sure who he was, or why he wore plain dark-blue clothes and not the uniform of the North. They speculated that he might be a special agent. Matt was no help to any of them. He couldn't remember who

390

he was, where he was from, or why he was at the site of a battle between the North and the South. The only thing he could remember was that he was trying to do something important, very important.

Matt's head wound healed quickly, but inside, there were no answers for the hundreds of questions that surfaced through his waking hours. He might have gone without a name for months, but one of the wounded prisoners saw him walking the halls. The prisoner told the doctors that he knew about the brother of Captain Phillip Treadwell of the Confederate Army.

One of the doctors did a little research and found that Matt had an aunt in Anderson, South Carolina, and arrangements were made for Matt to return home. One of the prisoners who had survived the loss of his right arm was being released to travel south to his own home, and the doctors persuaded him to take a detour and accompany Matt to Anderson. Letters of instruction were composed for Matt's care, and four weeks after that fateful day in January, the two men started for South Carolina.

Matt still had no idea who he was, except that the hospital staff had told him his name was Matt Treadwell of Anderson, South Carolina, and that sounded right. Before he left the makeshift hospital, the doctor told him that they knew very little about what happened to people who had memory lapses. He might remember bits and pieces, and then his whole life might come flooding back to him, or he might never remember a thing. How long it would take before his memory returned, if it returned, the doctor couldn't or wouldn't say. It was better for him, the doctor commented, if Matt were around familiar people and things. He might remember more easily at home.

As the soldier and Matt traveled south, Matt felt sure he had been on the route before. He continued to feel that there was something he needed to do, something very important, but he couldn't say what. The closer they got to Anderson, the more agitated Matt became. Something told him he should be moving in the other direction.

The young soldier taking him south knew nothing except that Matt was going to his aunt. He couldn't explain why Matt was on the south side of the river, or what he was doing with a brother in the Confederate Army. Was he in the Confederate Army as well? Or was he a spy? Matt asked himself if people with no memory ever went mad trying to figure out who they were. He smiled grimly, he should have asked the doctor if his sanity was in jeopardy. He clenched his fists in his frustration.

When the two young men arrived at Elton Estate, Aunt Elizabeth was nearly beside herself. She hugged Matt and kissed his cheeks before she realized that something was terribly wrong. His softly spoken words alerted her. "Do I know you?"

She backed away from him, astonished. "Matt, I'm your aunt, your mother's sister. Don't you know me?" Matt said nothing but shook his head. He couldn't remember.

Aunt Elizabeth arranged for a lunch and left the men while she took the letters the young soldier carried to the study. While the men ate, she read the communication and the instructions from the doctor. She folded the letters and stared into space, remembering the weeks that had just passed.

She had been notified of Phillip's death, and she had been sure that Matt was dead too. Ira returned with the information that Matt was in Nashville, and he told her then that Matt was going back to see Phillip and tell him good-bye. But that had been five weeks ago, and in all that time she had heard nothing. Somehow, she had felt that Matt had been injured or killed when he went back to see Phillip, especially when the information about Phillip had come. Thank God, she hadn't shared her suspicions with anyone. Now, here Matt was, but he couldn't remember a thing. And, to make matters worse, Henry had managed to get one message through. Henry told her that Amy had written from Tucker's Inn the end of December and that she was all right, but she had never arrived in Indiana.

After lunch Matt's traveling companion said good-bye and left for his home. Aunt Elizabeth tried to talk to Matt, but he said, frowning, "I don't believe I've ever seen you before. And although I feel comfortable here, I know this place is not my home."

Aunt Elizabeth was patient. "No, this is not your home, but you have stayed here often. Don't worry, I'm sure you'll remember in time. Just don't give up."

She paced the parlor and the study floors for two days. Matt had no idea who he was or where he came from, and he didn't seem at all happy with her or her home. She was worried sick about what she would do when he did remember. There was nothing she could tell him about Amy, and the sheriff from Anderson had been to call.

He had come the week before Matt came home. "Missus Elton, I have to find Matt Treadwell."

She had patted the tears from her eyes. "I'm afraid Matt may have been injured, or worse." Her voice had broken. "Phillip died from wounds he suffered at Stones

River. We have reason to believe that Matt was with him.

"Is there any way we can find out? I have to know.

"No." She had shaken her head. "But is there anythin I can help with."

He had refused to explain. Now he came back agair She tried to explain. "Matt was injured during the battle He doesn't know who he is. There is nothing anyone ca do until he recovers. We must wait."

"I have to talk to him. Maybe, if I could see him, h would remember."

But Matt hadn't, and the sheriff went back to Ander son. Aunt Elizabeth promised that just as soon as Ma remembered, she would send him into town.

For the next week, Matt wandered about the pleasar estate, but he remembered very little. Occasionally, h would have a fleeting glimmer of a slim chestnut-haire girl in a cream-colored ball gown, and then tall moun tains and cattle. But the visions, if that's what they wer never stayed long. He still had no idea who he was, where he came from.

One rainy afternoon, he ambled restlessly from roor to room in the large house. Aimlessly, he strolle through the now-familiar lower floor and then went u the stairs to the bedrooms. He roamed around in three the bedrooms and then wandered into a room he ha never been in before. For an instant, he knew he had bee in the room, and there were very pleasant memories con nected to the room. Damn, if he could just remember

Giving in to his frustrations, he hit the wall with hi fist. The door to the armoire popped open, and h walked over to close it, slightly ashamed of himself. In stead of closing the door he pulled it open and stared a several dresses hanging in the cabinet. He pulled a sof pale-pink satin gown from the armoire and sat down in one of the chairs in the room, holding the dress in his big hands.

Aunt Elizabeth found him there, almost an hour later. Tears were streaming down his face, and the front of his vest was soaked. Matt stared up at the woman who claimed to be his aunt. In a soft husky voice, he asked, "This belonged to my wife, didn't it?"

Aunt Elizabeth tried desperately to hide her shock, "Yes, it did."

Matt looked at her through his tears and asked in the same low voice, "Is she dead?"

Aunt Elizabeth was stunned and she hesitated. How much she should tell him? He was remembering bits and pieces, and if she told him too much, would the shock send him back into his vacant past? She had to answer his questions, but how much information could he take? The Northern doctor had written that they knew little about Matt's trouble. He had scant advice to give. She decided to give him only the facts for which he asked.

She said quietly, "We don't know if she's dead." While she waited for another question, Matt took out his handkerchief and wiped his eyes. He asked her no more questions.

Later that evening, Matt asked, "Where did I live, before I lived with you?"

Aunt Elizabeth tensed. What would happen when he saw the burned shell of his former home? Suddenly she doubted the wisdom of the Northern doctors. There had been such tragedy here, for Matt. Seeing the results before he could remember could not be good.

In almost a whisper she answered, "Your home was Willows."

"I want to see it."

Aunt Elizabeth took a deep breath, "It burned down several months ago. There's very little left."

"I want to see it."

She sighed. "If you want to go, then we'll go."

"When?"

"If the weather stays decent, perhaps we can go later in the week.

Matt stood up and started pacing on the floor. "Can we go tomorrow?" He stopped and glanced at the attractive matron. "I'd like to put my life back together as soon as I can. Surely, you can understand."

"Yes, I can understand. We'll go tomorrow."

Matt was up before dawn, and Aunt Elizabeth was immediately concerned. He seemed agitated and much more anxious than he had been all week. She suggested "Perhaps, we should postpone the trip for several days. I don't want to upset you more."

"No, we have to go today," Matt insisted.

It was clear and cold, and by the time they had breakfast, the carriage had been brought around, and a lunch packed, it was late in the morning. They left Elton Estate.

When they finally arrived at the charred ruins that once was his home, Matt stood in front of the building, confused and worried. Aunt Elizabeth watched him carefully as he stared at the shell of the house. Picking his way through the debris, he kicked at the blackened timbers and the ashes around his feet. He bent over once or twice to pick at something. As he started to leave, a small object reflected the sun in the ashes, and he stopped and picked it up.

As he walked back to the carriage, he pulled his handkerchief from his pocket and cleaned as much of the soot from the piece as he could. It was a small brooch, much like a cameo, but an indistinct blob of gold rested on the cracked porcelain base. Still holding the pin in his hands, he ambled down the curved driveway for several hundred feet. Turning around, he started back toward the house. When he was almost even with the carriage, a look of intense pain crossed his face and he turned the brooch over in his hands to stare at it again.

He looked up at his aunt, recognition clearly visible in his troubled eyes, and in a breaking voice, he sobbed, "I don't have anywhere else to look." Still holding the brooch, he stumbled toward the carriage, tears streaming down his face. He struggled up into the seat of the carriage. Aunt Elizabeth followed him and put her arms around him. There was no question, he remembered everything.

"Do you remember Henry?" She waited for a sign from Matt, and when he glanced up at her to say yes, she continued, "Henry heard from her in December. She was fine and she was at Tucker's Inn, in Tennessee."

Matt looked at her blankly for a second, then frowned, and commented as if to himself, "Ben and Molly should be in Cairo. Why did she stop there?" He looked over at her, his excitement a tangible thing. "Where is she?"

"Matt, I haven't heard from Henry for weeks. Mail is nonexistent. Henry sent one message through with a friend of his that was traveling south, but I haven't been able to get word to him." Aunt Elizabeth watched as his eyes grew cloudy with grief.

As the slaves turned the carriage around and started back to Elton Estate, Matt sat frowning, trying to put the pieces in their proper place. Once he turned to his Aunt.

"And Phillip?"

"Phillip is dead, Matt," she said gently.

"I thought so. He tried to help at the end," Matt stated dryly.

They rode on in silence for some time, but the closer they got to the estate the more alert Matt became. "I have a lot to do," he stated emphatically.

"You can't overdo, not yet!"

"I have to find her."

"I know," Aunt Elizabeth said sadly. "Matt, there is one other thing." After a time, she continued, "The sheriff has come three times now to talk to you. I promised that you would see him as soon as you remembered. I think you better see him first, when you do go to Anderson."

They were back at Elton Estate less than an hour before Matt insisted that they go through the things Amy had left behind. "Why didn't she take her clothes? I can understand her reluctance to take the wedding dress and the ball gown, but she left all of the things . . ." His voice trailed off.

"You'll have to ask her, when you find her." Aunt Elizabeth smiled gently. "There is one thing that has bothered me since I got Henry's message. Why didn't you go to Tucker's Inn? You were so close."

Matt glanced at her in surprise. "I only met the cousin once, and with Ben and Molly in Illinois, why would I go to Tucker's Inn? I wanted to talk to Phillip before I went north. I never dreamed Amy would stop at the inn." Nervously, he ran his fingers through his sandy hair.

"The Tuckers were still at the inn when Amy got there. She mentioned them in her letter to Henry."

"Do you suppose they came back?" Matt asked.

Aunt Elizabeth couldn't give him an answer. They left the room Matt and Amy shared after the wedding and as they descended the stairs, Matt listed the things he planned to do the next day.

"I'll have to try to get a message to Henry. I can't imagine what I'll find when I reach Texas. I don't suppose I can send any messages to my foreman. I won't be a bit surprised if the man with my herd hasn't already sold them. While I'm in town, I'll have to do something about Willows, and my banker." He smiled sadly. "And, I'll stop in and see the sheriff."

"Matt," Aunt Elizabeth scolded softly, "a little bit at a time, please. You've been ill." She might as well have saved her breath, she realized as she saw Matt off at dawn the next morning.

Late that night Matt arrived back at Elton Estate, and Aunt Elizabeth was waiting for him. "I've made arrangements to sell Willows," he told her. "I found a job for Phillip's overseer, and I gave all the slaves, the ones that were left, their papers. Phillip wouldn't have liked it, but they're all free now."

"Mr. Lincoln beat you to it." She smiled up at him. "Did you talk to the sheriff? The man would never tell me what he wanted you for."

"He wasn't there. Out of town on official business. He's coming back tomorrow. I'll see him then."

He stared at the window, out over the brown expanse of lawn, drab in February, and poured himself a brandy. "I'm going to Tucker's Inn."

Chapter Twenty-six

"They what?" Matt screamed as he stood looking at the sheriff of Anderson, South Carolina. He had been at the office of the jail since shortly after dawn, waiting for the man so that he could leave for Tucker's Crossroads. In fact, he had even considered ignoring the sheriff's command that he see him as he paced the planks of the boardwalk for almost an hour. "How did it happen?" Matt asked, his face pale and grim.

"I'm not too sure yet. George is still unconscious. I don't know if he's going to make it. They beat him up pretty bad. He managed to hang on until I finally came to relive him. Thank God he did, or they might have gotten away scot-free. Norman emptied the other cell and let several rather dismal characters loose while Clarence was beating George. I might have thought that it was the other way around, if George hadn't told me. But that's not why I wanted to talk to you. You do know where you wife is?" he asked hesitantly.

"I'm not sure. I think she went home to Indiana."

The sheriff took a deep breath. "I sure hope so. George managed to tell me that those two are hell bent on revenge. They swear that they're going to find Amy Treadwell and if they do half of what they said they would do, she'll not live out a day."

Matt felt icy chills prickle his skin. What if they found her first? No, he couldn't think that, he wouldn't let himself think that. She was home with Henry, she had to be. It took Matt less than fifteen minutes to finish with the sheriff, get the money he needed from the banker, and send a note to Aunt Elizabeth. Please, he prayed, as he raced north out of town, let her be with Henry. Henry could protect her.

Henry paced the floor of the parlor in agitation. Seven weeks had passed since the last message from Amy. She had told him about Phillip and his death and the awful news Phillip had given her. Somehow, Matt was still alive. Henry couldn't believe that he had died. Amy must have been devastated when she heard the news. But where was she? In truth, he had assumed she would continue her trip home but she hadn't come. There had been more than enough time for her to cover the distance. March was two weeks away. The weather hadn't been that bad, and the fighting in Tennessee had slowed for the moment. No, there was no reason why Amy was not already there. Something must have happened to her.

For the last three days, he thought of nothing else. After long agonizing hours, he decided on his course of action. He knew he had no choice. It was time to send for Alex, in spite of the inherent problems and the agony he would cause.

In less than a week, Alex Sanderson strode into the farmhouse. "What's this all about? I thought Amy was on her way home. What's happened?"

Henry glanced at the broad shoulders of his older

brother and grimaced. The war had changed Alex. He was a captain now, and the responsibility weighed heavily on him, Henry could tell. The laughter was gone from his dark-blue eyes. "She isn't here yet. I'm afraid something has happened to her."

Alex took a deep breath and looked right through Henry. "I have only three days' leave now. In three weeks or so, I can put in for more days, but if I have to search for her, it must wait until then."

Henry nodded and fixed his brother a drink. Together they poured over the messages that Henry had received. "She's hiding something," Alex whispered. "She's not telling us everything."

Henry frowned. He had hesitated to tell his brother that was his suspicion when the last communiqué had arrived. Well, Alex had more opportunity to travel, could talk to more people, and had at his command an unlimited number of investigators. Still, there was one thing that Henry felt he had to mention. "You don't suppose that she would go to Texas alone, do you?"

Alex shook his head. "With Amy, you never know. If I can spare a man, I'll send someone to Tucker's Inn in Tennessee. Perhaps she's still there. If not, it will have to wait until the end of the month."

Unable to do more, Henry and Alex enjoyed a day of camaraderie before Alex headed back to his unit.

On parting, Alex said, "If I can get free for a couple of weeks, I'll see you at the end of March."

Henry sighed in relief. Perhaps Alex could do what he had not been able to do—find their missing sister.

"Damn, it's cold for February. It is February, ain't it?"

Clarence asked as he slapped his hands against his arms in an attempt to warm them.

"Yah, it's February." Norman glared at his companion. All Clarence had done for the last two weeks was complain. In fact, all he had done since they had been captured was complain, and Norman was getting tired of it. "It'll be March in two days, maybe three. Quit your bellyaching."

"Well, if I'd a knowed we had to walk, and fix our own grub, I mighta not let ya talk me into this."

Norman's lips curled in disgust. Clarence wanted out of the jail as much as Norman.

"We ain't in that jail no more. And, with the war on, they'll never get us back for trial. If you can't do anything but complain, shut your mouth."

Norman was as cold and as hungry as Clarence, but he didn't talk about it. If he figured right, they ought to be a day, maybe two, from Tucker's Crossroads. He thought back over his plans, certain once more that he had planned well. Tucker's Crossroads was a known slave stop. It was the only place Amy Sanderson could have gone with the slaves that were with her, where she would be safe. If she wasn't there, he would be able to find out where she had gone. He and Clarence had been to Indiana several times. If he had to follow her there, well, then, he would.

Norman huddled closer to the small fire they had risked against the spring chill. The escape from the small jail had gone without a hitch, if Clarence's beating the guard near to death could be considered no problem. Damn fool. One of these days, Clarence would get them in real trouble. Norman sipped at the hot coffee, cupping the tin mug in his hands. Tomorrow, or at least the next day, he would get his hands on the little bitch that had caused all this trouble. He would kidnap her just like before, only this time, he had things planned for her. He would have his revenge, and then he and Clarence could sell her to the Rebs, if she were still in once piece. He smiled at his thoughts. Yes, he would have his revenge.

Matt stood in the cold March rain, rage and anguish twisting his insides. He stared at the burned timbers of Tucker's Inn. Was this some more of Clarence and Norman's handiwork? Could she have survived two fires? His heart was heavy as he thought about the last ten days. He had dashed away from Anderson, and twice he had been sure that Norman and Clarence were only a few hours ahead of him. Somehow, though, they had managed to elude him.

He went in search of someone who could answer his questions. One of the neighbors was almost too help-ful. "Everyone got out and they didn't even lose any stock. No, I don't remember any tall slender girl with two slaves. And the Tuckers ain't here. They left a month or so afore the fire."

She tilted her head and looked up at him quizzically. "Strange ya should ask, though. Just three days ago, two men, and to my way a-thinkin' they wasn't no gentlemen, asked about the girl. I tol' 'em the same as I tol' you. The Tuckers left in January, and they was a-goin' on to a place they bought out west."

Matt tried to smile. "The inn in Cairo?"

"Ya, that's what I tol' 'em, they went to Cairo."

Matt spent the rest of the day in Tucker's Crossroads,

trying to find someone who remembered seeing Amy. He discovered quickly that most of the townspeople paid little attention to the wagons and carriages that passed through town. One old man explained, "What with all them soldiers and people runnin' for their lives, there was too much traffic. Surely, you understand?"

Matt noded and headed west. Once more he traveled through the night, walking his horse and praying that he could get to Amy before Norman and Clarence reached her. He paused for a brief rest before dawn, but at sunrise he again mounted, urging his tired horse forward once more. When he could go no further, he stopped on the outskirts of a large Tennessee town at a small inn that was still filled with the wounded from a local skirmish.

After a warm bath and a filling meal, he considered his options. There was a good chance that Amy had left Tucker's Inn for Anderson, Indiana. If she traveled north and he went west, he might miss her completely. Norman and Clarence might trail her north, and she would have no protection from them. If he went north and she went west with Ben and Molly—although he thought that a remote possibility—he might never find her. If he could only be sure which way Clarence and Norman had gone. He shook his head, trying to make the correct decision. No, he knew he had no choice. Ben and Molly Tucker had seen Amy last. They were his only chance. If they had no idea where she was, he would then go to Indiana. Perhaps with Henry's help, they could find his missing wife.

He started west. Twice the Union troop movements slowed him down, and once he was certain that several of the soldiers had seen Clarence. Some of the chickens

405

the army had confiscated for their own use had disappeared, and the soldiers' description of the man they saw stealing away from camp sounded like Clarence. It had been dark, and the more Matt thought about their information, the more he was afraid they had not seen Norman.

He had almost given up hope when he came to a tavern forty miles from Cairo. He had traveled for more than forty-eight hours, stopping only to rest the horses. He could go no further without rest. Dusting off his pants, he entered the tavern. A warm meal and a few hours' sleep, and he could be back on the road. Late the next day, he would be in Cairo.

He approached the owner in the main room and instantly was aware of the man's hostility. Matt asked about a room and a meal, and the man glared at him. Embarrassed, Matt reached into his pants and pulled out several coins. "I can pay," he said, thinking the owner had probably suffered a monetary loss from some of the military in the area.

The man glanced at the coins and back at Matt and slurred, "We don't cotton much to strangers, not since yesterday."

Matt's curiosity was touched. "Trouble with the soldiers?"

"Nope." The man looked Matt over again. "These two gents showed up about suppertime. I fed 'em, and while I was out back, they slipped out without paying. That ain't bad, I know, but what they did to Sam Brusserd's young'un is what boils my blood."

Matt was more than a little interested when he mentioned two men. "What did they do?"

"Young Sam was out front with their horses. Samuel

stopped for a brew before he went home. Those two musta heard him tell the boy to wait, because before Sam finished his tankard, they sneaked out, grabbed the boy and the horses and took 'em south a couple of hundred yards. One of the men beat that boy up something fierce. He hurt that boy real bad."

Matt was bristling. "What did they look like, these men?"

"Well, one was thin and 'bout normal height, and the other was shorter, but broader. Neither one of them was what I'd call clean."

Matt was no longer tired. "How long ago were they here?"

The tavern owner looked over at Matt suspiciously. "You know these two?"

"If they are the men I'm looking for, they are after my wife. I've been trailing them from South Carolina."

The man was genuinely concerned. "Well, I didn't talk much to them, but Jenkins, over there . . ." He pointed to a gray-haired wiry man of undeterminable age. "Hey, Jenkins, come over here. This here man needs to talk to you."

Jenkins joined them, and they talked for several minutes before Matt said quietly, "I think I know who your assailants are, but better yet, I'm fairly sure I know where they're going."

"I'll be damned," the tavern owner muttered. "You stay right here, and I'll go get the sheriff. He's agonna want to hear this." He hurried through the door. In a few minutes, he returned trailing a tall man, hunched over a homemade pair of crutches. "This here is our sheriff, Paul Bates. He lost his horse and damn near lost his leg chasing those two."

Matt shook the man's hand and explained again why he thought the men in question were the two he sought. Paul Bates agreed.

"You're headed for Cairo, then?"

Matt nodded. Paul Bates continued, not waiting for any further answer. "I'll deputize you, and you can carry a warrant to Cairo. I know the man there, and he'll see we get those two back."

"What will you do when you get them?" Matt asked, certain that if the punishment was not severe enough, he would see to his own revenge.

"They'll face swinging. Young Sam ain't out of the woods yet, and as far as I figure, that's attempted murder. And that, my friend, is a hanging offense in this town."

Matt was satisfied and agreed to carry the warrant. He retired to a small but clean room for a couple of hours' sleep, while the sheriff wrote up the warrant and the tavern owner fixed a meal for him. Feeling better than he had in days, Matt left the tavern before the sun was up, the warrant and a letter explaining what was needed from the sheriff in Cairo tucked in his jacket pocket. Now, Matt thought, if he could just get to Cairo before Norman and Clarence did something to Amy.

Ten miles to the south, Norman was screaming at Clarence, "How many times have I tol' ya that I'll tell ya when I want somebody eliminated. The young boy had friends, ya dummy! Now, we'll have the law from Illinois on our trail, and if that boy dies, like as not, we'll face a hanging. From now on, ya do exactly like I tell ya, or you and me are done traveling together. Is that clear?"

Clarence stood beside the stolen horse, mute and troubled. If Norman left him, what would he do? They were wanted men. They even had the army after them. He thought back over some of the antics he had pulled in the last six weeks and scowled. Norman had a right to be angry. He had done fool thing when he beat up that boy. Well, it was done and he would do as Norman said from now on.

Norman's mind was following the same path as Clarence. In six weeks' time, Clarence had done many offenses. He had beaten near to death that deputy in Anderson and the boy the night before. After complaining about their diet, he had grabbed those chickens from that widow in Tennessee. Norman had found him minutes after he had raped the scrawny witch. If she hadn't been so angry that her shot was wide, Clarence would be sporting a butt full of buckshot.

Of course, stealing the chickens and the hay from the Yankees was the dumbest thing Clarence had done. Those soldiers had chased them for two days, but Norman had held the young farmer and his wife hostage at the farm where they had hidden until the soldiers had left. By golly, he meant it. If Clarence didn't follow orders, he was going to leave him.

He glanced at the source of his disgust. They were just a day from Cairo, now that they had the horses. After he had that bitch in his hands, he was going to walk away from Clarence. Of course, until he had Amy Treadwell in his clutches, he needed Clarence, but then . . .

* * *

That same week, Alex arrived at the farmhouse outside Anderson, a worried frown etching his brow. He had been granted three weeks' leave to find his sister. When word came back with the sergeant he sent to Tucker's Crossroads, Alex went to the general. He couldn't believe that Amy had perished in the fire at the inn. And there was the comment by the woman who had talked to the sergeant. There were other men, one a tall blond man who had been asking about a brown-haired, blue-gray-eyed woman of unusual height. Who else was looking for his sister?

He and Henry had discussed the latest turn of events as Alex told him about the inn in Cairo, "The woman told Sergeant Buckmor that the Tuckers left in early January, several weeks before the fire. They bought this place in Cairo last fall, and she was positive they went there. But we can't be sure. It seems the woman wasn't in town, but visiting relatives until the area was secure."

"You don't suppose Amy went with them, do you?" Henry asked.

Alex ran his hands through his dark curly locks. "I just don't know what to think. She could have sent us a dozen messages, and we have not gotten a one, or she could have had trouble. We won't know until we find her."

"You're going to Cairo then." It was more of a statement than a question.

"I don't have much choice, do I?"

Chapter Twenty-seven

Business was excellent at Tucker's Inn. February had been a busy month, and March gave every indication of being even better. There had been much work to be done. Repairs to the barn and outbuildings had been completed. Molly and Emma had cleaned, painted, and decorated all the rooms. And Ben had planned an extension to the kitchen. For several days, Ben talked to builders in the area. His greatest problem was obtaining finished wood to complete the project. And nails were also at a premium.

March was just a week old when Ben announced, "There's no help for it. If I'm going to get the wood I need while Jacob's here to assist with the building, I'll have to go to the mills. I'll take one of the wagons and go for the lumber I need. I figure I'll be gone about ten days, and I want to be back long before the babe arrives." He squeezed Amy's hand.

The five of them had become a family, and the plans were discussed in detail. Several problems needed solving before Ben could leave. Since they had opened their doors for business, Ben and Molly had gone to the docks on the Mississippi and invited travelers to stay at the inn. Many of their guests preferred the comfortable inn rather than the cramped paddlewheelers. And word was spreading. Ben had discovered, only a few days before, that travelers had already heard of the inn and wanted to stop at Cairo, be picked up by the carriage from Tucker's Inn, and enjoy a comfortable night with excellent food. Ben wanted the practice continued, in his absence.

Amy was a problem too. She refused to take it easy, often doing more that she should. "You'll not wait on guests," Ben told her when she objected to any curtailment of her duties.

While Molly was off with Jacob at the docks, Emma couldn't serve the guests as hostess because former slaves could not be innkeepers. As Emma nodded her understanding, Ben explained that they could not jeopardize their trade. This was not the time to force their opinion of the evils of slavery on their patrons.

Always practical, Molly came up with the perfect solution. One of the merchants down the street had two daughters. "The older one is very friendly. Her pa says she's a willing worker, but he doesn't have enough to keep both girls busy. I think he'd like to have one of them out earning her keep. I think the older girl would do nicely."

Ben contacted the merchant, and the girl came to visit. She was everything Molly had said she was, friendly, considerate, a willing worker, and she could do sums. Emma and Jacob liked her as well. When she told Amy that she shouldn't be doing the washing, it was too hard on her, that settled it. Ben hired her on the spot.

Molly pointed out to the group that afternoon over lunch that soon Amy would be delivering, and after her confinement, unless she changed her mind, she and Emma and Jacob would be leaving. If the girl worked out between now and then, Ben could keep her, and it would solve the problem of what to do after Amy left. Ben agreed that it was all very sensible, and he made his plans. Celia, the new girl, moved in and took her place on the staff. At first light on the second day of the third week of March, Ben left the inn and headed for the forests north of town.

Unknown to Ben, Norman was watching from the corner of the dry goods store. He and Clarence had arrived in Cairo late the night before and quickly located Tucker's Inn. Clarence had taken the first watch, and Norman had been at his post for over three hours when the activity at the inn alerted him that someone was leaving very early. Guests usually stayed on for breakfast at the Tucker's Inn, so this was probably no guest.

Working his way toward the stable, Norman arrived in time to see Jacob, the lantern held high, conferring with a big man preparing to mount his horse. Norman listened intently to their conversation. The big man was leaving, and he mentioned the duties of each of the inn's permanent residents. He must be the owner, Norman decided. Amy's name was mentioned, and Norman wanted to shout his pleasure. He had found the girl.

The smile that played at his lips spread across his face. The owner would be gone for several days, it seemed. Not only that, but the black man and someone named Molly, probably a servant, were being directed to go to the docks each day to pick up arriving guests. Norman couldn't believe his luck. He would have a clear shot at the girl, and there would be no one to interfere.

He crept back across the dusty street and swung himself onto the back of his horse. Minutes later he was back at the camp he and Clarence had made outside town. In only a few hours, Amy Treadwell would be his captive. She would be at his mercy. He ached with the need to shout his joy at the waning moon. He kicked Clarence awake.

"We got plans to make. Get up!"

Norman outlined his plan. They would wait until the black and the servant named Molly had left for the boat. Then they would enter the inn by the back door. Clarence would keep anybody they saw at the inn occupied, while Norman would find Amy and drag her out of the inn.

"She'll probably yell the house down. How ya gonna get her outa there without a hundred people coming to see what the commotion is?" Clarence asked.

Norman grinned an evil smile. "I'll knock her out. Then she can't make no noise. Besides, who's gonna stop a man rescuing his sister."

"But she ain't no kin of yers."

Norman gave him a disgusted glance. Nobody could be that dumb. He started for his horse.

"Come on! I need me something to drink afore we start this here kidnapping."

Matt had ridden hard, but he didn't reach Cairo until several hours after midnight. The sheriff had long since retired. After rousing the deputy, Matt paced the dusty street in front of the jail. How long would it take the deputy to go to the man's house, wake him, and bring him to the jail? He wondered how far behind Norman and Clarence he was. They couldn't have gotten there before him, please God, he murmured as he waited.

Finally, just as the eastern sky was hinting of the bright day to come, a tall, thin man strode up to him. "I'm the sheriff. Now what is so damn important that I couldn't finish my night's sleep?"

Matt glared at the man. At that very moment his wife might be fighting for her life, and all the sheriff could worry about was his sleep. Matt swallowed his anger and explained why he was in Cairo. Handing the sheriff the warrant, he told what he knew about the trouble forty miles east.

The sheriff unlocked the door to the jail and ushered Matt into the office. After lighting the lamp, the sheriff introduced himself and read the warrant. Matt gathered his courage and asked about Tucker's Inn. The sheriff glanced at him sadly. "You mean Ben Tucker's new place? If you came all this way expecting your wife to be there, I'm sure sorry. Only the Tuckers and their two blacks are there. They hired on a local girl to help them. Ain't nobody else there. No, there ain't no Amy Treadwell there."

Matt felt sick. Why didn't he agree with the man? He had been so sure after he had heard that Clarence and Norman were headed in this direction that Amy would be with the Tuckers. He raised his head. At least they had two blacks there. They might be Emma and Jacob. And, if nothing else, Ben would know when Amy had started for home. He wasn't ready to consider any other possibilities. What he needed was something to eat, maybe even a glass of ale, something, anything to take away some of the pain. He left the sheriff's office and headed for the tavern he had passed on the outskirts of town.

He ordered a meal and made himself comfortable in

a dark corner, his mind in turmoil. If he could be certain that Norman and Clarence hadn't found his wife yet, he could relax, at least a little.

The thin, blond serving girl brought his plate and he began to eat. He almost finished when his attention was drawn to the front door of the tavern. He had seen Norman Barber and Clarence Glanzman only once before, but he was positive that they were the two men now swaggering into the dimly lit room. He glanced toward the back of the room. In the shadows was a door. If it didn't lead to the outside itself, he hoped there would be another door that would. Keeping his back to the two agents, he slipped through the door. He had to get the sheriff.

The next two and a half hours couldn't move quickly enough for Matt. He had found the sheriff, told him where the men were, and then sworn volumes when the sheriff had ordered him to stay behind.

"If they recognize you, it's all over. Now you stay put, or I'll put you in one of them cells until I get back." Matt frowned as he wrestled with a promise he didn't want to make. "You better stay, or we may never find out about yer woman," the sheriff muttered. That did it. Matt agreed to wait.

The sheriff and the deputy were gone less than an hour, but to Matt it seemed like a lifetime. Matt heard Norman's loud curses before he saw the man. The sheriff dragged Norman, and the deputy brought a subdued Clarence along behind.

The sheriff said quietly, "They ain't found yer wife yet. That one told us plenty." He pointed in Clarence's general direction. "You'll have to excuse us, but we're taking these two back to Paul Bates. Then I'm staying

416

for the hanging. This one"—he slammed Norman into a wall—"deserves everything he's gonna get."

Matt tried to relax as he walked away from the jail. It must be about noon he decided as he glanced at the sun. It was long past time to talk to Ben and Molly.

It was almost noon when Jacob and Molly made their usual trip to the docks for passengers, and Emma went upstairs to prepare the bedrooms for their evening guests. Amy was still allowed to do some of the kitchen work, and she was busy with preparations for the evening meal. Celia was in the front room to take care of any guests that arrived before Molly returned.

Matt found the inn easily and arrived shortly after lunch began. He was greeted by a young stout girl with mousy-brown hair and a lilting smile. "May I help you, sir?" she asked softly.

"I'm here to seen Ben Tucker," Matt replied. "May I speak to him?"

"He ain't here, sir," she said, her expression puzzled.

Matt's heart sank. Maybe Ben didn't own this inn. Maybe there was a Tucker's Inn in Cairo when Ben arrived, and he and Molly called their establishment by a different name. And if that were the case, how would he find them.

In desperation, Matt tried again. "Does Ben Tucker own this inn?" Matt waited.

"Oh, yes, sir. But he went to get wood, and he won't be back for a week or two."

Matt felt something tug at his heart. He was faced with yet another delay. But perhaps he could find out more. "Did his sister, Molly, go with him?"

The girl laughed nervously. "No, but she ain't here either. She went down to the docks to pick up guests.

She'll be back in maybe an hour."

Through most of the conversation Matt stood with his back to the kitchen door, so he didn't see the kitchen door open up a crack.

Amy had heard the voices and was concerned that Celia was having trouble with a guest. Smoothing her hair, in case she had to intervene, she raised her hand to straighten the golden trophy of love with its golden letter resting on its delicate rose. Her fingers frequently found the small token from her dead husband.

Amy thought the man sounded annoyed, and she pulled the door back a little bit further to determine if Celia needed her help or not. What she saw was a tall man who reminded her of Matt. Amy knew it wasn't possible — Phillip had seen him fall — but for a fraction of a second her heart leaped in her breast. To add to her confusion, when she heard him tell Celia that he would be back, his voice sounded so familiar to her. She fought against a sudden lump in her throat, and she blinked the tears from her eyes.

As he took his leave, he turned around, and Amy stared at a ghost. With her hand still clinging to the golden letter, she slumped against the door, unconscious. Her fingers caught in the chain, and the pendant fell to the floor.

Both Celia and Matt were startled by the thud and started toward the noise. Celia tried to push the door open, but it would not give. Matt offered to help, but Celia thought he seemed a bit reluctant. "I can handle Mr. Tucker's wife, sir. You come back, in say an hour or two, and Miss Molly'll be here then." She pushed Matt out the front door.

Matt had a touch of a smile playing across his lips as

he let the girl push him out the door. So Ben had taken a wife. He chuckled. He would surely have to return, just to meet Ben's wife. He mounted his horse and started toward a tavern he had spotted earlier that morning. A jug of ale and something to eat was what he wanted at the moment. In an hour or two, he hoped beyond believing, Molly would tell him where Amy was.

As Matt walked out the door, Celia charged up the stairs to fetch Emma. On the way back down the stairs, Celia told Emma the young Mrs. Tucker had fainted dead away. "She's against the door, and I can't get it open."

Emma went out the front door and around the building and entered through the back door. Amy was still lying in a heap in front of the inner door just as Celia had said. Emma knelt in front of Amy and slapped her cheek.

"Amy, Amy, chile. What's wrong? What you doing on the floor? Wake up, girl!"

Amy's eyelids fluttered, and she looked up at Emma's concerned face. As Emma helped her to stand and guided her to her bedroom, Amy refused to answer Emma's questions. In reality, she heard little of Emma's quiz. Her mind was awhirl. Was Matt alive? Or now that the baby was close, was she fantasizing? Did pregnant women see things they wanted to see? Matt couldn't be alive, Phillip had seen him fall. She was only setting herself up for more pain. Shaking her head, she tried to banish Matt's face, but the picture would not leave her mind's eyes.

Emma was much more worried than she let on. Amy was not responding to her at all. Something mighty strange had happened, and Emma wondered if the babe

419

was all right. She had heard tell of women's minds going while they carried a babe. Was that what was happening to Amy? She tucked Amy in bed and rushed downstairs to wait for Jacob and Molly.

Molly and Jacob soon arrived. They had brought no passengers with them, for the paddlewheeler due at noon had had trouble and would not be arriving for several days, if at all. Emma pulled Jacob and Molly out to the kitchen to explain what had happened and whispered her fears.

Twisting her hands together, Molly groaned. "Oh, this is terrible. Ben would know what to do." Then she shouted, "Why did he have to go, now of all times?" Molly paced the kitchen. "Amy is three, maybe four, weeks from her time. This can only mean trouble, serious trouble." She glanced up to see Emma and Jacob nodding in agreement. "We have no other choice, I have to go get Ben. Jacob, you get the doctor, and Emma, you pack me a valise. I'll saddle my horse and I'll track Ben. His first stop was about fifteen miles north of here. If I can catch him there, we'll be back before morning."

Jacob started for the door and then paused. "Miss Molly, it won't do at all for ya to go riding through the countryside by yerself. I will have to go with ya. Ben would have my hide if'n I let ya travel by yerself."

Emma nodded emphatically. "Jacob's right. Ya can't go off like that by yerself. Anything could happen. If'n ya think we need Ben, then Jacob can go with ya. I'll go for the doctor. He's only a couple of blocks down the street. Celia can handle things until I get back."

Molly looked at Jacob and then at Emma. She tossed her bright red hair. "I guess you're right. Jacob, get two horses ready, and Emma, send Celia here. You pack a bag for Jacob and one for me." Emma was gone before Molly stopped speaking.

In a few minutes Celia asked from the doorway, "Miss Molly, you want me?"

"There aren't going to be many guests tonight. Emma will help you, but I want the meals very simple. Serve stew. Jacob and I are going for Ben. Don't worry about the steamboats, and be as sweet and gracious as you can be. We'll be back late tonight or early tomorrow. You do what Emma tells you to do, you understand?"

Celia nodded, and as she started toward the front room of the inn, Emma came through the door. "Here's a satchel for you and one for Jacob. I'll get some food together, and then you can leave."

In minutes, Molly joined Jacob in the barn. Their two best horses were saddled, their change of clothes stored in the valises Emma had packed and thrown over the saddlehorn and the foodstuffs packed in the saddlebags.

"Don't worry, I'll get the doctor here right away. I'm sure she'll be all right, I hope," Emma said softly, anxious as Jacob and Molly started from the stables.

Emma was back in less than twenty minutes with the doctor in tow, and the two of them went up to Amy's bedroom. Celia went to the kitchen to finish the evening meal.

Matt was surprised that even the mousy-haired girl was not in the front room of the inn. His voice husky, he asked, "Anybody here?" He heard noises from the kitchen and started toward the door. As he reached to

421

push the door in, he spotted something bright on the floor and stooped to see what it was. Picking up the small object, he turned it over in his hand. For a second, he couldn't breathe. He was sure his heart had stopped. In his hand he held a small golden letter, the letter *A*, resting on an ornate golden rose. With his wife's name on his lips, he reached for the door. Then he froze.

The scene of just an hour before replayed through his mind. "I can handle Mr. Tucker's wife, sir." Mr. Tucker's wife? No, it wasn't possible. There was no way his Amy could have married Ben. Once more he reached for the door, and once again he stopped. How could she have married again, when he was very much alive? It couldn't be Amy, it wasn't possible. Matt put the tiny charm in his pocket and left the inn. He shuffled slowly through the streets of the river town with no destination in mind.

"I can handle Mr. Tucker's wife," kept repeating over and over in his mind as he walked. The word "handle" bothered Matt. Was it Amy? Was something wrong with her? Of course there was, or she wouldn't have fainted. And the serving girl had not panicked. Mr. Tucker's wife obviously fainted frequently. Stunned, he wondered if Amy had been hurt in the fire at Willows. Was Ben caring for her, thinking Matt dead? Or maybe she had been hurt traveling to the inn? Any number of things could have happened to her.

As Matt reviewed what little he knew, he was fairly certain now that Ben Tucker's wife was his own wife, his Amy. There was nothing he could do until he had had a chance to talk to Ben. His mind in a turmoil, Matt continued to walk the streets. As the chill evening winds swept across the river, Matt found himself back where he had started, standing in front of Tucker's Inn. He had to know, he admitted to himself. He would wait for Ben and at least get his questions answered. And, no matter what the situation, there was no way he was going to give Amy up without a fight.

Matt yanked the saddlebags from his horse, tied the animal securely to the post in front of the inn, and went inside. He would need a room for the night, and he would find out just when Ben Tucker would return. The same girl was in the main room.

"Oh, yes, sir," she answered his question. "We have plenty of rooms for the night. I'm sorry, but you'll have to see to yer own horse tonight."

Matt looked at her a bit surprised. "Mr. Tucker has not returned?"

"No, sir. But he should be back late tonight or early tomorrow. Miss Molly went to get him, on account of Mr. Tucker's wife. You remember, don't ya, sir?"

Matt nodded his head and scowled. Yes, he remembered, he remembered all too well. He signed the guest book and took his key, then went out the front door. Leading his horse, he found the barn, unsaddled the stallion, fed and watered the animal, and went back inside. The news that Molly had gone to fetch Ben could only mean that Amy, if it was Amy, was ill. The possibility that it might be Amy made him physically sick.

Matt followed the girl up the stairs to his room. "I'll rest awhile, then I think I'll wait for Mr. Tucker downstairs," Matt said, frowning.

"Would you like something to eat?"

Matt certainly didn't feel like eating. "No, I'm not hungry." He paused, "Perhaps after I rest, I will have an ale, but I'll have that downstairs."

Still deep in thought, he entered his room, threw his saddlebags in a corner, and sat down on the edge of the bed. Maybe Amy wasn't even here. If Ben married a girl whose name began with *A* . . . Sighing deeply, he gritted his teeth. Who was he trying to fool? Ben couldn't afford to copy Amy's pendant. It was Amy's pendant. Matt knew he had to wait until Ben came back. He stretched out on the bed and tried to sleep.

It was dark when Matt awoke, and he pulled his pocket watch from his vest, raised himself up from the bed, and read the numbers in the embers of the dying fire. It was after ten. Surely, Ben had returned. He rolled out of the bed and moved to the washstand. Throwing some water onto his face, he straightened his coat jacket and left his room. The girl must have heard him coming, Matt thought, as she met him at the bottom of the stairs.

"Mr. Tucker ain't come yet, sir," Celia told him quietly. And, as if she could read his mind, she added, "I'll get your ale now?"

Matt glanced around the room. In front of the fireplace, where a fire was blazing were two large comfortable chairs. The backs were so tall that once seated only a man's shoes could be seen. There was a small table beside each chair.

"Over there." Matt pointed to the chairs. When she had brought a pitcher and a glass, she stood waiting as if she felt Matt might require something more.

"That will be all," he said dismissing her. He poured his ale and sat staring into the fireplace. Occasionally, Matt's hand drifted into his jacket pocket, and his fingers touched the delicate token of love. Finally, he withdrew the object from its resting place and stared at for a long time. The glow from the fireplace caught the petals of the rose and the tiny sparkling rays made it appear to be opening in his hand. Just like a blooming rose, he thought and tried to swallow the lump in his throat.

All the memories that Matt had suppressed these past several months, and even the shadows that had tormented him while he himself had been lost, came flooding back in a torrent. Once more Amy was as he had first seen her, standing proudly before him in her slave dress with her bare feet, defying him, demanding that he be allowed to leave. Tears gathered in his eyes as he remembered the regal woman descending the curved staircase at Willows in the gown of rich creamy silk. He could almost feel her swaying with him to the lilting strains of the waltz to which they had danced. Her soft rose fragrance haunted him now. Tears slid down his face as he gazed into the glowing embers, and he could almost feel her snuggling next to him under the sun as he had by the lake on the day he had asked her to marry him.

His heart ached with love as he remembered the way he had expressed her pleasure when he had presented her with the blue-gray brooch. How he missed her smile, the feel of the soft silken flesh as she melted into his arms, and the taste of her lips as she surrendered to his caresses. He hung his head, the tears flowing freely. Would he never again be able to hold her in his arms or kiss her sweet lips? The ale was abandoned, and through his tears he stared into the fire.

Chapter Twenty-eight

Something jarred Matt from his reverie. He swiped his tears and started to reach for his glass of ale, but dim light coming down the stairwell stopped his movement. He watched as a woman came through the entrance. The light from her single candle illuminated her face, and the flickering light played through the long dark hair that he knew captured the reds and golds of sunrise. He knew that face so well, he had dreamed about it for months.

But this beauty was not the slim figure he remembered. The gown she wore did nothing to hide her enormous stomach. She was pregnant, and apparently ready to deliver at any time. Stunned, Matt sat frozen in his chair. This was more than he could comprehend.

Gingerly, Amy placed the candle on the small table that stood by the stairway to hold an evening light for late guests. She maneuvered her large form to her knees near the kitchen door and began searching for something. Feeling with her fingers, she ran her hands over the floor where the light didn't reach. Totally engrossed in her search, she was unaware of the dark figure watching her intently from his chair.

Matt mentally shook himself. Had he dreamed the vision or was she real? As he watched, a smile played

426

.cross his lips. There was no doubt in his mind that she was hunting for her pendant. With his heart in his throat, he rose from his chair and approached without a sound. Dangling the small gold letter in front of her, he asked in a trembling voice, so husky that he didn't even recognize it himself, "Are you looking for this?"

Amy gazed at the pendant, and a small sigh escaped. She said, "Oh, you found my necklace! My husband gave it to me. I thought I had lost it. He was killed . . ." She glanced at the man bending down to her. The hand that had been reaching for the letter, flew to her mouth as her heavy form sank to the floor.

In the pale candlelight Matt saw the color fading from her face as she stared up at him. Matt was stricken. Would she faint again? For a fraction of a second, he berated himself. Seeing her condition, he should have waited. Stooping down, he gently pulled her to her feet. As his hand touched hers, the tears started falling from her eyes.

"It was you," she whispered. "You are real. You aren't dead. Phillip said . . . You're alive . . . You are . . ."

Matt held her gently, and she clung to him, patting his cheeks, touching his mouth, his ears, his hair. Tears were streaming down his cheeks.

Tenderly, Matt tried to bring her closer, but her swollen figure prevented that. Gently, holding her away from himself, he gazed down into her wet, sparkling eyes. Then he drew her back to him and kissed her brow and her cheeks, salty with her tears. He kissed her eyelids and her tangled curls. Without releasing his hold, he pulled back and asked hesitantly, "Mine?" as he glanced at her protruding stomach.

Amy's eyes met his, and they were full of her unmi[s]takable love. "Ours!" she whispered tenderly, and sh[e] reached up to wipe the tears from his cheeks.

Holding her carefully, Matt asked in a shaky voic[e] "The young girl who works here seems to think you a[re] Ben's wife. Are you?"

Amy glanced up into her husband's worried fac[e] raised her arms to encircle his neck, and drew his lip[s] down to hers. Matt kissed her gently, then pulled awa[y] from her slightly and stared down into her mischievou[s] eyes. Amy giggled.

"She assumed it," she whispered. "No one bothere[d] to tell her whose wife I am." Her radiant smile almost l[it] the room.

"Then you are still Mrs. Matt Treadwell?" Matt['s] husky voice trembled.

Amy patted her large form and grinned. "Very muc[h] so!"

Matt sighed in relief. Then he kissed her with all o[f] the love that he had been hoarding for the months the[y] had been separated. When he finally released her, sh[e] was breathless and swayed against him. He led her t[o] one of the straight-backed chairs, seated himself, an[d] then lifted her down onto his lap. "When did you se[e] Phillip?"

Her eyes were suddenly filled with tears, and sh[e] rested her head on his shoulder. "I was with him whe[n] he died." Then she told him about Phillip, his apology and the news he had given her just before he died. "[I] forgave him," she whispered, her voice breaking.

Matt held her close and kissed away her tears, offer[r]ing his comfort. "He tried to help at the end."

When Amy's tears were done, she looked at Matt i[n]

confusion. "Where were you? Phillip said the Union Army had you, and I got a telegram, then nothing."

Matt explained about his head injury and how he had not remembered who he was and what he was trying to do. When she started to describe the fire at Willows, she was so tired that she yawned.

Matt stood her on her feet, got up from the chair, and swung her into his arms. As he started for the stairs, he asked, "Your room or mine?"

She smiled up at him. "I have a big, soft bed, just meant for two people. Do you?" she asked quietly.

Matt grinned. "Yours!" He started for the stairs, pausing so that she could pick up the candle. He stared down into her brilliant eyes, kissed her once more, and started up the stairs.

After he had placed her on her bed, he stared at her, concern wrinkling his brow. "Are you all right? I know you fainted. Did the doctor come?"

Amy smiled. "The doctor came after you left. I'm fine, even though you scared me to death. I thought I saw a ghost. Remember, I thought you were dead." She shuddered slightly.

"After I saw Willows, and then Tucker's Inn, I was sure I'd lost you," Matt replied through clenched teeth. She reached up to touch his cheek, but Matt grabbed her hand before she could and brought her fingers to his mouth for a soft kiss. Putting his arms around her shoulders, he gazed into her eyes. "I died a thousand deaths when I saw Willows. Then, when I got to Tennessee . . ." He stopped and scowled at nothing. "You are the most important thing in my life. I didn't realize how important until then. I'm never going to let you out of my sight. I love you so much, it hurts."

"Oh, Matt!" Amy sighed. "I love you, too. I wante to die when I thought you were dead. The only thin that kept me going was the baby." Her eyes clouded wit her tears as she tried to smile up into his beaming fac

Once more, he kissed her slowly and deeply befor pulling away from her to undress. He glanced at her. " you're fine, when does this little one plan on arriving? can't be too long."

"The doctor says in two or three weeks," came th sleepy reply. Matt grinned. He could wait.

Matt blew out the candle and slid into bed, wrappin his arms about his wife's rounded figure. He pulled he close and kissed her once more. Amy yawned again and tried to snuggle closer, but again her extended bell prevented that. For several minutes, Matt lay quietl next to Amy, his heart nearly bursting with joy. Sud denly, he jerked and sat up straight. "What was that? he said, his voice registering alarm.

Amy giggled. "The baby is moving. See!" She place his hand on her large stomach.

Matt's voice was a husky whisper. "I'll be damned! Keeping his hand on Amy's stomach, he returned to hi prone position. As he drifted off to sleep, he smiled t himself, a baby! Well, why not?

Early the next morning, Emma tapped on the bed room door, but neither a contented Amy nor Matt, wh was sleeping soundly for the first time in months, hear her knock. Emma pushed the door open and entere the room with a breakfast tray in her hands. Amy wa snuggled up to the side of a shirtless form. It wa obviously a man, and the blanket covered only th lower half of his body. His arm and part of the pillow covered most of his head. Emma started screaming an dropped the tray with a crash.

Jerking into a sitting position, Matt looked around wild-eyed and tried to remember where he was. Amy raised up on her elbow and smiled broadly. "Emma, Emma, shh— It's all right. It's Matt."

Emma stared first at Amy and then at Matt, who was obviously still confused. "Oh! Massa Matt! We—we thought ya was d-d-dead!"

Celia had heard Emma's scream, and now she stood at the door, trembling. "Are you all right?" she asked hesitantly, her eyes wide as she spotted Matt. All occupants of the bedroom answered at once, Matt a bit gruffly, Amy between giggles, and Emma between sobs.

Emma glanced at Matt rather dubiously, then stooped to clean up the mess she had made. As she stood up to leave, her black face broke into an enormous grin. "Breakfast for two. Yes suh, breakfast for two." Softly, she closed the door behind her.

Matt turned to Amy, who hadn't moved from her half-raised position, and planted a wet kiss on her forehead. "Good morning." His eyes absorbed the glowing face turned up to his, and he didn't bother to hide his desire. He bent over and kissed her long and hard.

When Emma returned, still grinning from ear to ear, Matt was up and completely dressed. In the center of the bed, Amy rested against both bed pillows, her face beaming. Emma set the tray down on a table by the bed and shook her head. "You is a sight for these eyes, Massa Matt."

"You look good to my eyes, too," Matt responded. "I know where Ben and Molly are, but where is Jacob?"

"They ain't back yet," she answered quickly. "When your little girl fainted, Molly and Jacob went after Massa Ben. He's looking for to buy wood to make this place bigger," she said, indicating the size by spreading her arms wide.

After Emma left, Matt said quietly, "I have a lot of things I have to do. The first thing is to try and get messengers through to two very anxious relatives and let them know that we found each other and that you're all right." He gave her a critical glance.

Amy's eyes filled with tears. She offered, "They both would have stopped me from going to Texas with you, son."

Carefully, he helped her from the bed. Something she said registered, and he frowned. "What makes you think you'll have a boy?"

Amy just shrugged her shoulders. Grinning down at her, Matt put his arms around her large frame and whispered, "A little girl, who looks just like her mother, would be nice."

After breakfast, Amy dressed while Matt continued his account from the night before. Amy tried to tell him about all the things that had happened to her, but Matt kept kissing her, and she forgot her place in her narrative. Arm in arm, they left the room, talking and laughing together. In the kitchen Matt talked quietly to Emma, and before he left, he gave instructions to both women. "Now, I don't want Amy doing anything. She can sit and . . . and sew."

Shortly before noon, Matt returned after sending his messages to Aunt Elizabeth and Henry. When he walked into the kitchen, the first thing he saw was Amy on a stool, busy chopping vegetables for dinner. H

432

started to object, but Amy smiled up at him. "I'm fine, Matt, really. And I've got to keep busy now."

Matt watched her for a moment, then asked Emma to show him the barn. Turning, he met his young wife's surprised expression. "I've got to keep busy, too." He winked at her, and as Matt followed Emma out the door, Amy laughed and blushed a pretty pink.

Late that afternoon, Matt sat in the main room with Amy on his lap. He was tired but contented, and he grinned down at his wife before he kissed her. A noise from the kitchen interrupted his kiss and alerted him to visitors. He had just enough time to lift Amy from his lap before Ben came striding into the room. Behind him trailed Molly, who looked exhausted, and Jacob brought up the rear, looking just as tired.

Ben nearly crushed Matt in a bear hug, Molly started crying, and Emma joined Jacob who stood off to one side, suspiciously blinking his eyes rapidly. There was confusion as everyone tried to talk at once. After Matt explained a little of what had happened to him, Ben insisted that he and Matt go to the barn. "To check on the horses," he said, grinning.

Emma and Amy finished preparing the meal while Molly changed. Molly went out to the barn to announce dinner, and she came back frowning. In disgust, she commented, "They've been into the cider."

The next ten days were filled with planning, Ben and Matt planned the addition to the inn, and Molly helped Emma with plans for their home in Texas. Matt insisted that Emma and Jacob go over the plans he had made for their house in Texas, and Amy talked Jacob into a shopping trip with Emma for furniture for their new home. The three couples agreed that by the middle of

June, Matt, Amy, Emma, Jacob and the new baby could start for Texas.

Over lingering dinners, they spent many happy hours talking over their plans. "The only thing that really concerns me," Matt said quietly after dinner one evening, "is the attitude of some of the people in Texas."

Amy looked at him in surprise. "I thought you liked Texas?"

"Yes, I like Texas, but it's in the South, and a lot of the citizens are for the South. I don't think we'll have any problems, but we'll have to stay pretty much to ourselves until after this war." He grinned at Amy. "Anyway we'll be too busy starting our ranch and family."

Jacob picked up his coffee cup, glanced over at Amy, and said without a smile, " 'Pears to me that the family done been started."

Celia stayed on when Matt insisted that Amy could do no more kitchen work. By the end of March, Amy was complaining that she would forever carry her large stomach in front of her. When she needed to stand up, Matt had to help her from her chair. He started carrying her up the stairs to bed, even though she mumbled sadly, "I'm too heavy, just a big fat lump."

Matt tilted her chin up and gazed into her eyes. He whispered softly, "You're a beautiful lump, and you're not heavy at all." She tried to hug him, but even that was difficult.

Each afternoon, Matt took Amy upstairs for her afternoon nap, which she needed since her sleep at night was frequently interrupted by the activity of the child. On the afternoon of the second day of April, Matt had carried her up and tucked her in as usual. Emma and Jacob had taken the day off to accompany Molly to a household sale for things for their new home. Ben was smiling with some of the local merchants, and Matt had the main room of the inn to himself.

He poured himself a glass of ale and sank into one of the chairs before the fire to reflect on his good fortune and his greatest joy, his sleeping wife. Celia came bustling out of the kitchen to greet an arriving guest. Matt paid little attention until the deep masculine voice asked if Ben or Molly Tucker were there. He turned in his chair to catch a glimpse of this visitor.

Matt stared at the tall Union officer in his rumpled captain's uniform. The man had broad shoulders, brown wavy hair, and dark expressive eyes, but there was a striking resemblance to Henry Sanderson. Matt jumped out of his chair, a grin spreading across his face. There was no question in his mind. He started toward the man.

"Alex Sanderson?" he asked.

The man looked up in surprise. "Yes?" he said hesitantly.

"I'm Matt Treadwell."

"Matt Treadwell is dead," the man said firmly.

"No, I'm very much alive. A bullet grazed my head, and Phillip told Amy—"

"My sister? Is she here?" the man interrupted him.

"Yes! She's napping, and if you don't mind, I'd like to let her rest for a little longer before I tell her you are here." Matt smiled at his brother-in-law. "Come, sit down. Celia, bring the officer a glass of ale."

435

Matt and Alex, for indeed it was Alex, spent the next hour discussing the events in the life of the woman upstairs in bed. Matt mentioned nothing about Amy's condition, certain that her big brother would be more than a little angry when he found out that she had traveled west with the Tuckers instead of going home in her condition. Alex filled Matt in on some of the particulars of his initial interview with Colonel Brown when Matt had been first arrested. Matt grinned.

"It was a shame you couldn't come to the wedding. Phillip would never have gotten away with what he did if you had come."

Alex frowned. "That's the strangest thing. I requested leave and it was granted. I planned on arriving the day before the wedding to surprise Amy. But I received a special summons from two Pinkerton agents about three days before I had planned to start south, and my leave was canceled. I had to hurry to a town in southern Ohio. When I got there, a message was waiting. Both men had been called back to the eastern front. I never was told what they had wanted of me. You don't suppose that your brother . . ."

"With Phillip, almost anything was possible." Matt glanced at his watch. "I'll go wake Amy. You wait here."

Fifteen minutes later, Matt returned with Amy in his arms. She was barely on her feet when she ran for her older brother. "Alex!"

Alex stared at her, disbelief, wonder, anger flitting across his face as Amy threw her arms around him. "You didn't tell us," he accused her.

"Henry would have said no to Texas," Amy replied, wiping at the flood of tears that streamed down her face.

436

"And so he should," Alex mumbled as he finally drew her into his arms.

Alex stayed for two days, and Matt decided that the Sanderson family were a special group of people. As Alex prepared to leave, Amy hung on his arm.

"Now, Sister, I've already told Matt that if I manage to get through this war, I'll be in Texas two weeks after I'm discharged."

"You must take care of yourself," she said through her tears. He nodded, his own eyes suspiciously bright.

"Take care of her," he directed Matt as he swung into his saddle.

"I will. I love her," Matt said quietly and he shook Alex's hand. "I'll be waiting for you and for Henry when this is over."

"I'm so sorry I never had the chance to meet your parents," Matt told Amy over coffee that night. "They must have been truly marvelous." Amy nodded her head, and wiped the sudden wetness from her eyes.

By the twelfth of April, Amy announced that the baby was never going to come. All day long she squirmed in her seat and asked Matt frequently to help her from one chair to another. After her fifteenth or twentieth request, Matt asked in a voice trembling with concern, "Are you all right? You're not ill?"

Amy gave him a disgusted look. "My back aches," she snapped.

Amy missed the look that passed between Molly and Emma, but Matt didn't. After he helped Amy to a large chair in the main room, he followed Molly and Emma into the kitchen.

"All right. I want to know what's wrong. What's going on?"

Molly and Emma exchanged glances again, and Emma, all smiles, answered, "Why, she's going to have a baby, Massa Matt."

In total disgust, Matt barked, "I know that!"

Molly, laughing now, said, "Today, Matt, or maybe tonight!"

At dinner, Amy only nibbled, and Matt had trouble hiding his concern. Repeatedly, he asked her if she was all right. Trying to smile, she told him, "I'm just tired." Before the meal was finished, she asked to be excused. "I think I better retire. I'm very tired."

Matt carried her up the stairs, and before he tucked her into bed, he asked again, "Are you sure you're all right?" She nodded and yawned. He returned to the dining room, but before the coffee was served, Emma slipped upstairs to check. Matt grinned and said to himself, "I'm not the only one concerned." Emma returned quickly and announced happily that Amy was sleeping soundly.

Much later, Matt sought their bed, but Amy was still sleeping peacefully. Emma and Molly really didn't know anything about having babies, he told himself. After all, they hadn't had any, yet. He climbed into bed and instinctively, she snuggled up next to him. Grinning, he put his arm around her and tried to hold her close and drifted off to sleep.

It was still very dark when Amy woke Matt. He stared at her for a full minute before he realized what she was telling him to do. When reality dawned, he grabbed at his pants as he charged to the door.

"Emma!" he yelled as he took the stairs two at a time.

He found her in the kitchen, calmly having coffee with the midwife the doctor had recommended. Dumbfounded, he stood in the doorway with his mouth open.

"How did she get here?"

Emma just grinned at him as the two women started for Amy's room. Matt followed them up and sat holding Amy's hand, as the midwife and Emma prepared the room with linens and blankets and banked the fire. With each pain, Matt turned a little paler. Quietly, he pulled Emma over to a corner. "Isn't there something for the pain?"

Emma looked up at him and asked, "For you or her?"

Matt went back to the bed in disgust. As Amy's pains lengthened, Matt turned even more ashen. Finally, Emma pulled him up from his vigil and pushed him toward the door, Matt protesting loudly all the while. "You go talk to Ben," she said.

Ben was ready and waiting for him at the bottom of the stairs and led him to the barn. "Time to check the horses."

The horses could get along fine by themselves this night, Matt thought to himself, but Ben insisted. Jacob joined them, and the three men sat in the hay, drinking the sharp cider from the jug Ben had brought. They watched the shadows move back and forth in Amy's room, and Ben and Jacob watched Matt. Whenever Matt made a move to return to the house, either Ben or Jacob grabbed his arm and insisted that he have just another little one.

The pink and gold sunrise was heralding a new day when Ben leaned over to Jacob and whispered solemnly, "She better hurry up, or we'll be stinkin' drunk."

Already feeling the effects of the aged brew, Jacob

whispered back, "But he don't look drunk." Matt indeed was not too affected by the heady juice.

A short time later, Molly came running toward the barn. "Matt, come quick. It's a boy." Matt dropped his glass and ran after the girl, leaving his two friends to stagger to the house by themselves. Taking the stairs two at a time, Matt reached the bedroom door before Molly had even started up the steps. Gingerly, he opened the door. His beautiful wife was resting against the pillows, looking tired but happy. Next to her lay a bundle of blankets. He sighed in relief. It was over.

As Amy motioned Matt over to the bed to view his child, his eyes never left her face. Finally Emma reached down and picked up the baby and introduced Matt to his son. Matt glanced at the small wrinkled red face as Amy sighed, "Isn't he beautiful?"

Praying fervently that he was not required to answer, he turned his gaze back to the radiant face of his wife. As he took her hand, he asked in a husky voice, "How do you feel?"

"I'm very tired, but I feel wonderful." She smiled up at him, then laid her head back on the pillows, and her eyes drifted shut. Matt sat there for a long time, holding her hand.

Emma placed the infant in the cradle that Ben had made and moved back to the side of the bed. She patted Matt's shoulder. "Ya go across the hall. Molly's got a bed ready for ya. Ya need some sleep." Matt didn't move, but sat holding his sleeping wife's hand. "Matt, yer wife is fine," she reassured him.

Slowly, Matt released Amy's hand and stood. His face covered with a ridiculous grin, Matt announced, "I have a son!"

Emma grinned back at him. "Yes suh, yes suh, ya has a fine son." She steered him toward the door and sleep.

Matt slept late into the day, and when he finally awoke he was hungry but completely rested. After he splashed water onto his face and combed his hair, he started for the stairs. He couldn't remember when he had ever felt better and began to whistle.

In the main room, Ben sat in one of the big chairs, holding his head. Glancing up at Matt who was still whistling, he groaned loudly. Matt stopped whistling and wondered if Ben was ill. He headed for the kitchen. If Emma was around, perhaps she would fix his breakfast. He was hungry enough to eat a cow.

Emma was in the kitchen, and as Matt started to describe what he wanted for breakfast, he noticed Jacob at the kitchen table, his head bent forward. As Matt went into detail, explaining how he wanted his eggs, Jacob left the table and ran for the kitchen door. Matt stared after him in surprise. "What's wrong with him?" he asked Emma.

Emma chuckled. "He worked hard last night, having your son."

After breakfast, Matt headed for the stairs to check on Amy. He had just started up when a loud cry sounded. Dashing for her room, he reached the door when the crying stopped, and he cautiously opened the door.

Amy sat in the middle of the bed, holding the baby to her breast. From where he stood, Matt could hear the suckling noises, and he walked over to the bed. Amy glanced up at him and then away quickly, a blush staining her cheeks. Sitting down on the edge of the bed, Matt watched the tiny fingers of one small hand

clutch and knead the breast from which he was sucking
Matt chuckled, "Well, I can see that he's his father'
son."

Amy turned crimson and glanced at Emma, who ha
been standing to one side. Emma laughed and quietl
left the room.

Matt took the tiny hand in his, and the baby wrappe
his fingers around one of Matt's much larger ones
Matt grinned in surprise. "He likes me!" He gazed int
the tranquil blue-gray eyes of his smiling wife. Leanin
over, he kissed her tenderly. "He's a beautiful baby
Thank you. If you don't mind, I'd like to call hin
Phillip."

Amy nodded and said quietly, "Phillip Matthew."

Matt looked down at the baby solemnly. "With ou
love, he'll grow into a fine man." He glanced up at Amy
Tears were streaming down her cheeks. "What's this
Tears?" He reached to brush them away.

"Just tears of happiness," she said softly.

Gently, Matt kissed her again, and then smiling dow
at her, he whispered, "From now on — no — forever, m
perfect rose, only tears of happiness."

Epilogue

"Jacob just rode in. They're comin'," Emma crowed in delight. "They be about an hour away."

Amy shifted the baby, Elizabeth, to her shoulder and closed her bodice. The three-month-old child wailed her disappointment as Amy patted her back. "Did Jacob see much? Is Matt alone?" Her voice was full of dread, anxiety that her husband had returned alone.

Emma grinned. "Jacob sez there's enough dust to equal a wagon train."

Amy sighed in relief. "Well, let's get things finished." She laid the baby in her crib and started for the kitchen. Amy smiled at Emma as she started the coffee and set water on for tea.

Emma headed out the back door. "I'll go see to little Jacob. I'll be here to help in about half an hour."

Amy nodded as she reached for the tray of pies she had waiting. There had been so many guests that summer that she had a routine established. In June, Henry and Alex had come as they had promised. She giggled when she thought of their arrival. Six hours after they had ridden up, Elizabeth made her appearance. Matt

443

had told her the next day that neither Henry nor Ale
were in any condition to visit with her. The corn whiske
Jacob had made the year before had been consumed i
quantity while they all waited for Elizabeth.

Amy went in to check on her sleeping daughter an
Phillip, who was taking his afternoon nap. She smile
at her son. Even at two and a half, he looked so muc
like his father. She went back to the master bedroo
and prepared to change her clothes, a frown crossir
her face and her eyes registering pain. Matt had left wit
Henry and Alex the end of June. The news they ha
brought of the devastation of the South had nearly tor
Matt apart. They had made their plans and Matt ha
ridden away with her brothers.

Matt had been gone for three weeks when anothe
group of visitors descended on the prospering ranc
Molly had fallen off the wagon seat into Amy's waitin
arms, and the two women had laughed and cried to
gether like two long-lost sisters. Ben had climbed dow
from the wagon, and under his dark skin Amy had bee
sure she saw a blush. "I think you remember Celia
She's Missus Tucker now." Ben rested his arm aroun
the beaming girl.

They couldn't wait for Matt, Ben had told her quietly
"We have two more inns in Illinois. I figured we coul
only be gone fer about six weeks." His face turne
scarlet as he leaned toward Amy. "Sides, I want to ge
Celia back. I'll be a father come February."

Amy had proudly shown them the house Matt ha
built for her, and Emma had insisted that meals b
served at her house, what with Elizabeth being onl
seven weeks old. Jacob had shown Ben the ranch an
the cattle that Matt was raising, and the two men had

pent quiet afternoons playing with young Jacob, who was a year and a half. Amy had watched the men and miled at Celia. "Your husband is going to make a good ather." Celia, her round face beaming, had nodded. Amy had turned to Molly, a question in her eyes.

Molly had laughed, knowing the question before Amy even posed it. "I doubt I'll ever find anyone that uits me. I really think I much prefer being an aunt than being a mother."

Amy shook herself from her reverie and buttoned her dress. Matt was going to be disappointed that he had missed Molly and Ben. She hurried into the guest room and then made her way into the kitchen. Everything was ready.

Emma came bustling into the house. "Everything eady?" Amy nodded, and the two women made their way to the veranda to wait for their latest guest.

From the north, Amy saw the dust, and her excitement grew. Then, it faded as she recognized a single horse racing for the house. She pointed out the lone rider to Emma, her panic rising. "Oh, is that Matt? Something must have gone wrong." She grabbed at Emma's arm.

In minutes, Hank Wilson, Matt's overseer was riding into the yard. "Matt sent me ahead. Everythin's allright! He knew you'd be worried."

Fifteen minutes later, Amy was flying toward the approaching wagons. They were still a hundred yards from the house, but Amy didn't care. Matt pulled the horses to a stop and jumped down from the wagon. He met his wife on the run and swung her into a rib-crushing embrace. "I got her," he whispered into Amy's ear. "And she's here to stay." Matt released his wife and lifted his hand up to the older woman still seated in the wagon.

"Welcome to Texas, Aunt Elizabeth," Amy shouted she embraced Matt's aunt.

Later that night, in their bedroom, after Matt had spent time getting acquainted with his daughter, he held Amy in his arms. She smiled up at him contentedly, her arms holding his naked body close to hers. They had just spent a delightful hour getting reacquainted themselves. "God, how I missed you!" Matt leaned over her and his kiss consumed her.

When she could breathe again, she asked hesitantly, "Was it bad?"

Matt shook his head, his expression grim. "There's not much left. People are hungry, and so much has been destroyed. The South will never be as it was."

She ran her hands over the tense muscles of his back, wanting somehow to erase the hurt on his face. "Matt," she whispered, "somehow the people will survive. The country is whole again. We're, all of us, together again. In time, the scars will heal." She traced a hand over his frowning face. "And, while we wait . . ." She drew his head down so that she could touch his lips. "Love me," she whispered against his mouth.

As his lips grazed the golden rose that hung around her neck, a pledge of their love, he murmured against her throat, "I do."

GIVE YOUR HEART
TO ZEBRA'S HEARTFIRE!

COMANCHE CARESS (2268, $3.7
by Cheryl Black
With her father missing, her train held up by bandits and h
money stolen, Ciara Davenport wondered what else could po
sibly go wrong. Until a powerful savage rescued her from
band of ruffians in the Rocky Mountains and Ciara realiz
the very worst had come to pass: she had fallen desperately
love with a wild, handsome half-breed she could never hope
tame!

IVORY ROSE (2269, $3.7
by Kathleen McCall
Standing in for her long-lost twin sister, innocent Sabrina B
chanan was tricked into marrying the virile estate owner Ga
rison McBride. Furious with her sibling, Sabrina was eve
angrier with herself — for she could not deny her intense year
ing to become a woman at the masterful hands of the han
some stranger!

STARLIT SURRENDER (2270, $3.7
by Judy Cuevas
From the moment she first set eyes on the handsome swas
buckler Adrien Hunt, lovely Christina Bower was determine
to fend off the practiced advances of the rich, hot-blood
womanizer. But even as her sweet lips protested each cares
her womanly curves eagerly welcomed his arousing embrace!

RECKLESS DESIRE (2271, $3.7
by Thea Devine
Kalida Ryland had always despised her neighbor Deu
Cavender, so she was shocked by his brazen proposal of ma
riage. The arrogant lady's man would never get his hands o
her ranch! And even if Kalida had occasionally wondered ho
those same rough, powerful hands would feel caressing h
skin, she'd die before she let him know it!

Available wherever paperbacks are sold, or order direct from t
Publisher. Send cover price plus 50¢ per copy for mailing an
handling to Zebra Books, Dept. 2368, 475 Park Avenue Sout
New York, N.Y. 10016. Residents of New York, New Jersey an
Pennsylvania must include sales tax. DO NOT SEND CASH.